IT'S IN HIS KISS . . .

Rick pressed their joined hands to his lips. "Feel that?"

She jerked.

"I'm as real as you are." He curled their hands to his chest. "Let me show you. Open your eyes for me, Angel Liz."

He made it sound easy, as if what she'd endured since July had been nothing but a nap.

"Come on, you know how. Think of all the other times you woke up with me."

Yes, but those were dreams, she thought. They were different. She had been someone else in those dreams.

"Lizzie?" There was a catch in his voice. His hands tightened around hers. He trembled with an urgency that she felt outside as well as in.

She gritted her teeth, summoned every shred of energy she could gather, and concentrated on lifting her eyelids. They felt sealed shut, as if her lashes were glued together.

"Please," he whispered. "I don't want to be alone."

Neither did she. *Rick, help me!*

His lips touched hers.

The kiss was brief, no more than a fleeting contact at the side of her mouth, but the force of it continued to rumble through her mind after he pulled back. She grabbed his energy to add to her own. A crack appeared in the void . . .

DREAM SHADOWS

INGRID WEAVER

BERKLEY SENSATION, NEW YORK

THE BERKLEY PUBLISHING GROUP
Published by the Penguin Group
Penguin Group (USA) Inc.
375 Hudson Street, New York, New York 10014, USA
Penguin Group (Canada), 90 Eglinton Avenue East, Suite 700, Toronto, Ontario M4P 2Y3, Canada
(a division of Pearson Penguin Canada Inc.)
Penguin Books Ltd., 80 Strand, London WC2R 0RL, England
Penguin Group Ireland, 25 St. Stephen's Green, Dublin 2, Ireland (a division of Penguin Books Ltd.)
Penguin Group (Australia), 250 Camberwell Road, Camberwell, Victoria 3124, Australia
(a division of Pearson Australia Group Pty. Ltd.)
Penguin Books India Pvt. Ltd., 11 Community Centre, Panchsheel Park, New Delhi—110 017, India
Penguin Group (NZ), 67 Apollo Drive, Rosedale, Auckland 0632, New Zealand
(a division of Pearson New Zealand Ltd.)
Penguin Books (South Africa) (Pty.) Ltd., 24 Sturdee Avenue, Rosebank, Johannesburg 2196,
South Africa

Penguin Books Ltd., Registered Offices: 80 Strand, London WC2R 0RL, England

This is a work of fiction. Names, characters, places, and incidents either are the product of the author's imagination or are used fictitiously, and any resemblance to actual persons, living or dead, business establishments, events, or locales is entirely coincidental. The publisher does not have any control over and does not assume any responsibility for author or third-party websites or their content.

DREAM SHADOWS

A Berkley Sensation Book / published by arrangement with the author

PUBLISHING HISTORY
Berkley Sensation mass-market edition / February 2012

Copyright © 2012 by Ingrid Caris.
Cover photo © by Andy & Michelle Kerry / Trevillion Images.
Cover design by George Long.
Interior text design by Tiffany Estreicher.

ISBN: 978-0-425-24612-2

BERKLEY SENSATION®
Berkley Sensation Books are published by The Berkley Publishing Group,
a division of Penguin Group (USA) Inc.,
375 Hudson Street, New York, New York 10014.
BERKLEY SENSATION® is a registered trademark of Penguin Group (USA) Inc.
The "B" design is a trademark of Penguin Group (USA) Inc.

PRINTED IN THE UNITED STATES OF AMERICA

10 9 8 7 6 5 4 3 2 1

This book is dedicated to the late Wesley Scott,
the most outstanding English teacher ever to grace
the classrooms of Kenner Collegiate.
You opened my teenage mind to the power of words
and the symphony of language,
thereby giving me the tools that shaped my life.
Though more than forty years have passed
since I had the privilege of being your pupil,
I still hear your voice in my memory.
I only wish that you could hear mine as I say
thank you, thank you, Mr. Scott!

PROLOGUE

THE PATIENT WAS IMPRISONED IN FOG. IT SHACKLED HER senses. It shrouded her mind. She had no will, no body, no self. Beyond the void, women were talking, but their words cracked into meaningless fragments that failed to penetrate the patient's bonds. Her reality remained a blank slate . . .

"How long has she been here, Beryl?"

"Let's see. They brought her in the weekend of my daughter's wedding. That was the second to last Saturday in July, so that makes it fifteen weeks."

"That long!"

"You sound surprised. You must have gone through several books by now, Norma."

"That's true. I already finished my favorites and borrowed this one from my cousin. I wish I knew whether any of what I read is getting through to her."

"According to the doctors, she still has brain activity, so it's possible."

"Then why hasn't she regained consciousness?"

"The damage was extensive."

"I know, Beryl, but she's been breathing on her own for ages. She looks as if she should be waking up any minute."

"It's my guess her brain needs more time to rewire itself."

"From what I heard, she had some brain."

"True enough. She was a very successful woman."

"And with millions in the bank and that hunky fiancé, she has lots of incentive to wake up."

"You're not getting discouraged, are you?"

"Not really. I can't help feeling sorry for her, though. It seems like she had it all."

"She's young, and was in good health before the head trauma, so it's still possible . . . Norma, what in the world did you put on? That's not one of her CDs."

"I know. I was getting tired of Mozart and Beethoven all the time."

"Mrs. Harrison specifically requested that we play the music she provided."

"She didn't say not to play other stuff."

"Really, Norma. I don't believe a woman like Elizabeth Graye would care to listen to country music."

"She probably wouldn't care for my romance novels, either, but don't ask me to read the *Wall Street Journal* to her or it would put *me* into a coma. Besides, the whole idea is to provide mental stimulation, right?"

"That's true."

"And who knows? A change in the way her brain's wired might do her some good."

ONE

IT WAS THE MUSIC THAT FINALLY REACHED HER. DISTANT and sad, it teased her toward consciousness. At first she could only drift where the melody led her, as helpless as a leaf in a lazy current. She was content merely to exist as her senses awakened.

A man was singing. She couldn't grasp the words, he was too far away, yet she swayed, rapt, as his voice stroked her mind. It was deep. Rich. Like velvet wreathed in smoke. He strummed a series of chords, and her bones rang with each shift of harmony. Her blood pulsed to the rhythm of his song, carrying sparks of life to her groggy brain.

And slowly, Elizabeth surfaced.

How long had she been asleep? She was stiff. Her shoulder and hip were numb with cold. Whatever pillowed her head reeked with dankness. Her eyelids were heavy, as if she'd been out for days. Opening her eyes took more effort than she could have dreamed.

The room wavered before it came into focus. The floor was stone. She had a close-up view because she was lying on it. The walls appeared to be made of stone, too. Dust motes drifted through a shaft of sunlight that slanted from a high, narrow window.

That's where the music was coming from. It was fading now. She could barely hear it over the babble of voices and squawking chickens . . .

Chickens?

She pushed herself up on one elbow. Her hands refused to function. Pain sliced through her skull, sending her back to the floor. Sleep beckoned, tempting her to escape the suffering. It would be so easy to give in.

Yet since when had Elizabeth Graye chosen the easy path? She clung to the music as desperately as she hung on to consciousness.

Something creaked open behind her. Footsteps gritted against stone. "The king will not be swayed, Lady Elspeth."

Her throat was too dry for her to respond immediately. Her tongue felt as heavy as her eyelids had, as if she hadn't used it in weeks. Months? She swallowed, giving herself time to gather her strength. The music had completely disappeared.

Four sets of boots moved into her range of vision. Strange, low-heeled boots in coarse leather. They belonged to four men who wore leggings and knee-length tunics, complete with swords hanging from their belts.

Swords?

She attempted the sit-up again, steeling herself against another blast of pain. She got as far as her knees when she discovered her legs were tangled in layers of fabric. Fine, purple wool covered her arms. Wide cuffs that had been intricately embroidered with what appeared to be gold fell over her wrists, nearly concealing the metal bracelets . . .

They weren't bracelets, they were manacles. That's why her hands wouldn't work. Wide, iron bands weighed down her wrists. A short length of chain hung between them.

What was going on? Could these medieval handcuffs be someone's idea of a practical joke? If it was, she saw no humor in it. There was nothing funny about being shackled and drugged. That's what must have happened, because she had no memory of being brought here. Or being stripped and re-dressed in some kind of period costume. She braced her knuckles on the floor. The chain clinked against the stone. She waited until her head no longer felt in danger of coming off—no doubt a side effect of whatever drug had knocked her out—and finally managed to get to her feet,

The men stood between her and the room's only door. It was thick, unpainted wood. Beyond it was a dim hallway of more stone. If she didn't know better, she might think she was in a castle.

It had to be a stage set. An authentically detailed one, right down to the sound effects outside the window, but still phony. Except for the floor. There was no way the stone could have been faked.

Who would do this? Not her friends. They knew she wouldn't appreciate being the butt of a prank, regardless of how imaginative it was. She had no shortage of people who might be considered her enemies, but what could they hope to gain? Whoever had staged this scenario had gone to considerable trouble to make it appear real, yet it made no sense. Elizabeth grasped the chain to ease the weight on her wrists and focused on the man who had been speaking. "I demand to know what's going on here. Where am I?"

He had a thick beard and overgrown, shaggy eyebrows. What skin she could see appeared to have been weathered to the toughness of his boots. "My lady?"

"Whoever did your makeup was masterful. Same with the costumes, but the joke's over. I have no intention of playing along."

He placed one hand on the hilt of his sword and glanced at his companions.

Elizabeth moved around him. "This has gone far enough. Tell whoever hired you that you did your best but I have appointments to keep and—"

Two of the men seized her by the arms, halting her before she could take another step. A third unsheathed his sword and held the tip to her throat. "We cannot let you pass, my lady."

Her temper rose but she didn't struggle. Not only would it have been undignified, it would have been useless. For actors, the men had surprisingly strong grips. "I don't know what you were told about me or what compensation you've been promised," she said. "However, if you don't unlock these manacles and release me this instant, I intend to file kidnapping and forcible confinement charges against each and every one of you."

The sword tip touched her skin. Warm liquid trickled down her neck.

She was too incredulous to be alarmed immediately. The sword must be a stage prop that had been rigged to squirt fake blood on contact. It was the only logical explanation. This troupe of actors was big on realism. Not only did they look the part of medieval soldiers, they even smelled the part. The oniony aroma of dried sweat that radiated from the swordsman made her eyes water. She jerked back her head.

More liquid drizzled down her neck and dampened the fabric of her dress.

"Lower your weapon," the man with the beard said. He appeared to be the leader. "Be mindful of your duty. She thinks to provoke us in a bid to cheat the hangman."

The sword hissed into its sheath. The men who held her arms released her and stepped back.

The chain between her wrists clinked as Elizabeth raised her shackled hands to her throat. There was a narrow scratch above her collar. It stung.

Fear finally stirred. The blood that beaded against her fingertips wasn't fake. The man's weapon was no prop. It was so razor-sharp she hadn't felt the steel pierce her skin.

If this was a joke, it was a dangerous one. No one seemed disturbed by the fact they'd wounded her and had thus added "assault causing bodily harm" to the list of potential charges they were accumulating. These men were too thoroughly into their roles to be ordinary actors.

Then what were they? Kidnappers with a shared delusion? Why had they mentioned a hangman?

What the *hell* was going on?

She moved her hands to her head. The more she tried to think, the worse the ache in her skull became. Her eyelids felt heavy. It must be more aftereffects of the drug that had been used on her. "I wish to speak with the person in charge before this farce goes any further."

"It is too late, Lady Elspeth."

"Why do you keep calling me that? My name is Elizabeth, not Elspeth. Elizabeth Baylor Graye, as whoever organized this charade must surely have told you. Give me your cell."

He regarded her blankly. "I am not a prisoner. I have no cell."

She held out her palm. "Your phone. We can cut this short with a simple call. If you have demands, I'm sure we can negotiate an agreement. What's your price?"

The men scowled and muttered what sounded like curses, as if she had somehow offended them. The bearded one ordered them into the corridor with a gesture of his hand. "Do not seek to corrupt me or my men. I am sworn to obey my liege."

"Yes, yes, and you're doing a fine job of remaining in character, but that's no reason to bury yourself deeper. The 'I was only following orders' defense hasn't worked since Nuremberg. Your smartest move would be to let me go now."

He backed toward the door. "I cannot."

"Perhaps you're not fully aware of with whom you are dealing. I have powerful connections. My absence would be noted. People would already be searching for me, so there is a finite amount of time left if you're contemplating striking a deal."

"Your friends cannot change your fate. It has been decreed."

"Decreed? By whom? Who's giving the orders? I demand to see someone in authority."

"Do you wish to speak with a priest, my lady?"

"A priest? Is that who's in charge?"

"Nay, but he may ease your conscience before your execution."

Irrational or not, a chill slid down her spine. "There has obviously been some kind of misunderstanding here," she said. "The more promptly you correct it, the better it will go for you in court."

He paused at the threshold. "Your mind is muddled. The trial is over."

"I'll testify you cooperated," she continued. "But you do

need to take some initiative and set me free. It's your wisest move."

"We will return at dawn to carry out your sentence. May you go to your death with dignity, Lady Elspeth." He dipped his chin in a curt bow and swung the door closed. There was a jingle of keys, then a dull thud, as if a bar had been dropped into place.

She waited until the guards' footsteps faded, then tested the door herself. It was shut solidly and it didn't even wiggle in its frame. She pounded it with the sides of her fists. Her head spun from the exertion of lifting the extra weight of her manacles. She leaned over, braced her hands on her knees and breathed deeply, waiting for the dizziness to pass.

How much longer would it take for the drugs to work their way out of her system? Had her kidnappers given her an overdose? Whoever had done this evidently wasn't concerned with her physical welfare. She returned her fingertips to the scratch on her neck. If those men's personal hygiene habits extended to their weapons, there could be entire colonies of germs already multiplying in the wound. She should have demanded a doctor instead of a phone, but they likely wouldn't have agreed to that, either. What would be the point, since she would be executed at dawn?

"No," she muttered. "I'm not going to die. This has to be a sick joke. Either that, or somebody's attempting to make me question my sanity."

The thought made her straighten. Was that it? Plenty of people opposed the way she had tried to assume control of Grayecorp after her father's death. Her own stepmother had spread rumors that had attacked her mental competency. Could someone have decided to go further? Could they be hoping to trigger a mental breakdown?

The explanation seemed too far-fetched, yet she couldn't for the life of her think of another way to make sense of this nightmare . . .

Nightmare. Of course. She must be dreaming. Any second now she would wake up to her alarm and the aroma from the coffeemaker that she'd programmed to switch on at five thirty. Fifteen minutes on the Bowflex, a quick shower, then into a power suit and her pearls, like every other morning. She certainly wasn't going to *die*.

She closed her eyes, fisted her hands, and willed herself awake. She pictured her bedroom, the Egyptian cotton sheets, the blue and white wallpaper, the French provincial armoire she'd found at an auction last month. Or had it been last winter? Her sense of time was gone. What day was it? What season?

Who cared? She was dreaming. Nothing made sense in dreams. That's why she needed to wake up. She pressed her nails into her palms hard enough to prick and opened her eyes.

Nothing had changed. She was still manacled, dressed in a purple gown, and trapped in the stone room. If it was a dream, it was a peculiarly persistent one. Vivid, too. Damn, this was unbelievable.

She pushed away from the door and set about methodically exploring her prison, trying in vain to find a way out. Nothing budged. The stone that formed the walls seemed as genuine as the floor. Aside from a three-legged stool, an empty wooden bucket in one corner, and a bundle of rags that had served as her pillow, the room was bare. She turned her attention to the window. It was little more than a slit set high into the wall. In had no glass or screen, which was consistent with the era depicted by the rest of the props. She moved the stool beneath it, hitched up her skirt to climb on top, and stretched on her toes to see past the sill.

A cobblestone courtyard spread at least three stories below her. It was filled with wagons and wheelbarrows that brimmed with everything from cabbages to wooden crates of chickens. Men and women dressed in clothes of plain brown homespun haggled over the piles of goods, while scruffy-looking children raced among them. Horses neighed from within a thatch-roofed building that was likely a stable. Beyond that, men with what appeared to be crossbows patrolled the top of a crenulated stone wall.

The scope of the charade was incredible. So was the

attention to detail. She moved her gaze to the center of the courtyard where a platform rose above the crowd. A scaffold fashioned of squared-off timbers had been erected over it. From the middle beam dangled a thick rope that had been knotted into a loop.

No, that was more than a loop, that was a noose. They had built a gallows.

Another chill, deeper than the last, shuddered through her body, despite the yards of wool that clothed her. Either the creator of this stage set had been given an unlimited budget, or . . .

Or Elizabeth had somehow been transported back in time and was being held prisoner in a real medieval castle. Complete with gallows. Where she would be executed at dawn.

No. It would be madness to even consider it. *Time travel?* Ridiculous. That couldn't happen. It was impossible.

The sunlight that came over the parapet cast slanting shadows. It was late afternoon. How long would it be before the sun set? How many hours before it rose again?

It didn't matter. None of this was real. Any minute she would see a plane cross the sky or she would detect the whir of a hidden camera or hear the ring of a cell phone from one of the extras who milled around the set below her. She clawed at the window sill until she could wedge her head into the opening. "Hello!" she yelled. "Can anyone hear me?"

A boy eating an apple was the first to spot her. He tugged at a woman's skirt and pointed. Several faces turned toward her window.

Elizabeth raised her voice. "Help!" she cried. "I've been locked in here! Someone call nine-one-one."

No one appeared surprised. If anything, they seemed amused. A few nudged each other and laughed. Others shrugged and went back to their haggling. The boy hurled his apple at her but it struck the wall well below the window. He snatched another from a nearby cart and was about to try again when a man in a hooded cloak plucked the apple from his hand. The boy looked around quickly. He seemed puzzled, as if he couldn't see who had taken the potential missile from him, then scurried toward the cabbage wagon. The man tucked the fruit under his cloak and turned in the opposite direction, revealing a strangely shaped object that he carried in his other hand. It appeared to be some kind of stringed instrument. A small, rounded guitar or a lute. He must be playing the part of a minstrel.

Elizabeth caught her breath. This was the singer, the man whose music had awakened her. She didn't question why she was so certain. He hadn't glanced up, and even if he had, she wouldn't have recognized his face because she didn't know what he looked like, yet some part of her recognized him instinctively. His body language, his presence, something in the air around him, whatever, she *knew* it had been his voice that she'd heard. "Help me!" she called.

He stepped around a stack of chicken crates and headed for the stables.

"No, wait! Please, don't leave. Come back. Get me out of here!"

He continued walking, his gait unchanged, as if he were unaware of her existence. The further away he got, the less alive she felt. Her strength was ebbing. She was beginning to drift . . .

She screamed. The noise was swallowed by the renewed babble in the courtyard. The next time she tried, no sound came from her throat. She was incapable of forming words. She couldn't draw in enough air to produce a moan. She couldn't even whisper. The sky dimmed. The sun seemed as if it was being pulled into a tunnel.

Elizabeth's knees gave out. She fell off the stool. Oddly, she felt no pain as she hit the floor. Cold seeped into her body from the stone. The numbness was returning. Keeping her eyes open took too much energy. One by one, her senses shut down until only her hearing remained.

The minstrel was singing again. It was the same distant, sad melody that had pulled her from the darkness before. She clung to it as long as she was able. *Please, stay. I want to live.*

The thought faded, along with the music. She drifted for

a minute, an hour, a year, she couldn't tell, until at last the song ended and she sank back into the void.

ALAN FLICKED THE SNOW FROM HIS OVERCOAT AS HE walked into Elizabeth's room. The weather would have provided a legitimate excuse to skip the duty visit. The drive up from New York had taken twice as long as it should have in this weather, but reinforcing his position took priority over his comfort. There was no point giving up now after he'd already invested months. She had been here since July. It was already mid-November. How much longer could this situation drag on?

A night-duty nurse was sitting in the straight-backed chair beside the bed, reading aloud from a thick paperback. She broke off when she noticed him. "Mr. Rashotte!"

"Hello, Norma. You sound surprised to see me."

"With the storm and all, I didn't expect you to make it this weekend."

He tugged off his gloves and gave her an appropriately subdued smile. "It would take more than a few snowflakes to keep me away from my fiancée. How is she today?"

She placed a marker in her book and set it facedown on the bedside table. The table was burled pecan, like the matching dresser and the coat-tree in the corner. The pair of armchairs that sat beneath the window were upholstered in rich topaz, like the curtains. A flat-screen TV had been installed on the wall opposite the bed above a state-of-the-art sound system. From certain angles, the room might have been mistaken for a high-end hotel suite . . . as long as you could ignore the hospital bed and the bank of equipment that monitored the patient's vital functions. "Miss Graye is the same as always," Norma said. "I'm sorry."

A guitar twanged softly, not quite drowning out the muted beeps from the monitors. Someone must have slipped on a country music CD, which was a change from the classical stuff they usually played. He suppressed a snicker. Elizabeth detested country music. He tipped his head toward

the book the nurse had set down. "I noticed you were reading to her when I came in. That's very thoughtful."

"Mrs. Harrison wants us to do at least two hours each
shift."

"If anyone can reach her, I'm sure it would be you. I
imagine it would be a pleasure to wake up to a voice as
beautiful as yours."

"Thank you, Mr. Rashotte. We all do what we can."

Alan let his smile warm. Norma was an attractive girl.
The clinic's modest, dull blue uniform didn't look so dull
when it was stretched across her breasts. If she worked anywhere else, he wouldn't mind taking her out sometime. He
usually got good mileage out of playing the sympathy card.
Most women were suckers for the noble, grieving but loyal
boyfriend. "I would be here every day if I could. You have
no idea how much it comforts me to know Elizabeth is in
such good hands."

"We keep hoping for the best. It's such a shame. She's so
young."

"We used to talk endlessly about our plans. We weren't
in any hurry because we thought we had the rest of our
lives." He averted his face, as if overcome by emotion. In a
way he was, but it wasn't grief.

"Since you're here, I'll take my break now," Norma said,
getting to her feet. "I'll be right down the hall. Buzz if you
need me."

He snuck a glance at her ass as she left. Though it wasn't
as interesting as the front view, it wasn't bad. Once her
footsteps had faded, he pulled the door closed and switched
off the music so he could turn on the television. He settled
comfortably into one of the armchairs to watch CNN, as he
usually did to pass the time during these visits. Only when
the hour ended did he finally turn his attention to the figure
on the bed.

Even in a coma, Elizabeth Graye had an air of command.
He didn't understand it. She looked nothing like the she-
shark who used to run Grayecorp. That Elizabeth had worn
her hair in an elegant French twist, not loose around her

shoulders. She had rarely appeared anywhere without makeup and her signature string of pearls. The white knitted shawl that was tucked over her hospital gown would have better suited someone's septuagenarian maiden aunt than the woman who had once been the heiress to a multibillion dollar fortune.

Yet she had a presence. Her father had been the same way. Stanford Graye had drawn attention wherever he'd gone. He'd been a complete bastard, but the women had loved him. Elizabeth had been on the path to becoming just like him, only in her own female, ball-busting way.

Alan had always been fascinated by her. He counted having her in his bed, even for a brief time, as a major, personal triumph. He'd been jubilant when he'd finessed her into this engagement. They had been the ultimate power couple, a perfect match. The mere promise of gaining access to her personal fortune had allowed him to put together a private shopping mall deal off the Grayecorp books that made her last condominium project seem like a lemonade stand. His only mistake had been not pushing harder when he'd had the chance. Four months was a long time to put off his investors, so he'd been forced to borrow more money to keep them from pulling out. Getting involved with Jamal Hassan had compounded his problem, along with his debt. People who failed to pay that man tended to disappear.

His life would be so much simpler now if he'd had the foresight to have Elizabeth sign a power of attorney. He'd believed he would have plenty of time to persuade her to share the wealth. Who could have predicted she would end up like this?

There was no longer any trace of the black eye or the scratches and abrasions that she'd come in with. The gash on the back of her head that had taken sixteen stitches to close had healed long ago. The real damage wasn't visible. It had been to her brain.

The guy who had attacked her had targeted her by mistake. She'd been the proverbial innocent bystander. How was that for irony? There were plenty of people who would have liked to have given her a few whacks. She hadn't been known for her diplomacy. But she'd only been in the wrong place at the wrong time. Pure chance. Now his life and his career were shackled to a veritable vegetable. His creditors would get ugly if he cut her loose, so ending this engagement wasn't an option. His relationship to her helped secure his position at Grayecorp, another reason he couldn't voluntarily end it. Unfortunately, as long as she drew breath, he would be only the interim director, so his access to more company funds was limited. He couldn't touch Elizabeth's fortune. He couldn't move forward until his fiancée woke up.

Or died.

He rose from the chair and went to pick up her hand. Her fingers were cool and lifeless. He got no pleasure from touching her when she was in this condition, but it wouldn't hurt to keep up the act in case someone looked in. "I moved into your office yesterday," he said. "I'm very fond of that office. We had some good times on the desk, so I'll be keeping it, but your father's old chair has to go. I've also decided I can put those Picasso sketches to better use than you currently are. It was generous of you to promise them to me."

There was no response to his provocation. There never was. She wasn't capable of hearing what he said. She couldn't absorb the stories that were read to her or be aware of what music was being played any more than a turnip could. That was obvious. Otherwise, she would have woken up by now.

Was he the only one who recognized what a waste of time and effort this so-called therapy was? Her prissy, schoolteacher friend sure didn't. Her mouse of a stepmother didn't have much of a handle on reality, either. She was the one footing the bill for the private clinic and the extra nurses, which made no sense. Delaney Graye Harrison had plenty of reasons, a few billion of them, to want Elizabeth out of the picture.

Wind gusted past the window, driving a barrage of ice pellets against the glass. The trip back to the city was going to be messy. The roads might get dangerous. It was bad enough that he had been sacrificing every other Saturday for her, but now he could be jeopardizing his safety. The situation was becoming intolerable.

He let her forearm drop back to her side and regarded her feeding tube. It would be easy to tug it out and let nature take its course. She wouldn't be able to stop him. That would put an end to this incessant waiting. As her devoted fiancé, he would have a strong case to sue her estate for palimony. The problem was, taking action would probably set off the alarms on the monitors, so it would be difficult to claim innocence, unless . . .

Unless he could find someone else to do it.

"It might work," he muttered. "Any objections?"

Her face remained slack. Her expression was a complete blank.

"No? I didn't think so." Alan placed his mouth close to her ear. "So how about it, Elizabeth?" he murmured. "Why don't you do us all a favor and just die?"

TWO

ELIZABETH WOKE TO THE ROAR OF AN ENGINE. IT WAS SO close that the vibrations rattled her molars. Her head throbbed. Her skin itched. The air was foul with the metallic bite of exhaust fumes and humidity. She snapped her eyes open.

A canvas wall stretched in front of her. Rusty metal lay beneath her. To her left, pictures of dense, tropical foliage and vine-choked trees blurred past on a TV screen . . .

That was no screen, that was a real jungle. She was lying in the back of a moving vehicle. A pickup truck with canvas sides. It hit a bump and she was briefly airborne before she slammed down on her back. The impact was excruciating. Oblivion beckoned but she battled to remain conscious. She was certain her survival depended on it.

Where on earth was she? What was happening? How did she get here?

The memory of a castle crept through her mind. Stone walls, men with swords, a courtyard with a gallows that was meant for her . . .

Elizabeth rolled to her knees. The action was more difficult to accomplish than she could have imagined. Her wrists were still bound in front of her, not with iron manacles this time but with a plastic bundling tie. Her arms hung from her shoulders like dead weights. And the ache in her head was so intense it felt as if it were coming off. She doubled over so she could rest her forehead against the floor, but the movement of the truck made the pain worse. Her vision blurred. Her mind was groggy.

It was eerily familiar. Not the truck or the tunnel of greenery they were hurtling through but the sensations. Headache. Grogginess. She'd felt the same way in the castle. She'd concluded then that she must have been drugged. It was the only explanation for the blank spots in her memory. And for the fuzziness when she tried to think.

Why was this happening again? It couldn't be a dream. It was too vivid. At least she knew for certain no time travel had been involved this time. No one had trucks in the Middle Ages.

Gritting her teeth against the pain, she sat back on her heels. Circulation returned to her hands with a rush of tingling heat. She flexed her fingers, then lifted them to her throat. She couldn't find the scratch the swordsman inflicted. It must have healed. How long had she been kept unconscious? She wasn't wearing the purple wool dress anymore. Instead, someone had dressed her in baggy, cotton duck trousers and an oversized linen shirt. Her hair was loose, and judging by the jiggling she felt beneath her shirt at each bump in the road, so were her breasts. Her feet were bare. She tensed her thighs to brace herself against the truck's motion.

She was alone in the cargo bed. The canvas sides extended overhead to form a roof. Bark and wood splinters littered the floor. From what she could glimpse past the tailgate, the road they were traveling was nothing more than a rutted track that had been hacked through the trees. She could see no buildings, no utility lines, nothing to indicate they were anyplace near civilization.

Was this another elaborate stage set? If so, it must be even larger than the last one. She turned her head toward the front of the truck. There was a small window in the back of the cab. Though the glass was cracked and nearly obscured by dirt, she glimpsed what appeared to be the driver's silhouette. She inched forward until she was next to it.

Over the racket of the engine, she heard men's voices. They were speaking what sounded like Spanish. She lifted her bound hands, ready to pound against the glass to get their attention when she reconsidered. She was obviously still a prisoner. Complaining to her captors hadn't gotten her anywhere the last time. Whoever these people were, they didn't seem open to compromise or even to logic.

She worked her way back toward the rear of the truck, grasped the top of the tailgate and pulled herself to her feet. She had no idea how to jump from a moving vehicle without killing herself, but stunt men did it so there must be a way. She lifted one foot over the tailgate and lowered it to the bumper.

If she could slide off rather than jump, she might not hit the ground as hard. The vegetation that crowded the sides of the track should cushion her landing. Where she would go after that, alone and barefoot in the middle of a jungle, was another matter. She detested the outdoors. Even as a child, she wouldn't have been caught dead being a Girl Scout. But prepared or not, anything would be better than going meekly to meet her fate.

Before she could lift her other leg over the bumper, the truck stopped. Elizabeth fell backward to the cargo bed. She scrambled to her knees as the tailgate was wrenched open by men in dark green, camouflage uniforms. One of them seized her bound hands and hauled her outside. *"Vámonos!"*

Undignified or not, she struggled.

A second man jammed the muzzle of a rifle beneath her chin, brought his face to hers and shouted another order in Spanish.

Like the lead swordsman in the castle, most of his face was covered with a beard. Other than that, there was little resemblance. He was much shorter, his eyes were black and a gold cap gleamed from one of his incisors. He jerked his gun toward her left and repeated his order.

She didn't need a translator to grasp what he was trying to communicate. And she had no intention of testing whether the guns the men carried were stage props. She stopped resisting and walked where the men led her.

A path wound from the track into the jungle. After a few

minutes they emerged in a clearing. At first glance it appeared empty until she noticed it was in fact ringed by low, wooden buildings. Large nets laced with leafy branches canopied the roofs so they blended in with the surrounding trees. Other men, also in camouflage uniforms, watched from the shade as she passed. A few called out remarks that made her escort laugh. She was grateful she didn't understand the words because the tone was unmistakably lewd. How much could they see through her linen shirt? God, what she wouldn't give for a bra.

The possibility that she was in the middle of a practical joke seemed more remote by the second. The scope was too large. She'd been confined to only one room in the castle so its surroundings could have been faked, but this hidden encampment in the jungle had to be real. She'd seen similar setups in newspaper articles about Central American rebel groups. They frequently kidnapped foreigners to help finance their operations. It was also possible these men could belong to a drug gang. Didn't they often have secret camps for processing cocaine? Either way, she was in deep trouble.

A potbellied man emerged from the largest hut and waited in the doorway until she was brought to him. Her escort stepped back from her and saluted.

Judging by the salute and the extra stripes on his uniform, evidently this was their leader. Elizabeth straightened her shoulders, gathered every shred of authority her bare feet, peasant clothes, and lack of underwear allowed her to muster, and looked him in the eye. "I demand to know why I have been brought here."

He took a cigar from his breast pocket, drew it slowly across his lips to moisten it and stuck it in one corner of his mouth. "You know why, Isabella." His English was heavily accented, made almost unintelligible by the way he gripped the cigar between his teeth as he spoke. "Do not attempt to escape your fate again. You anger me."

"*I* anger *you*? There's been a mistake. My name is not Isabella, it's Elizabeth Graye. I'm an American citizen. You have no right to hold me prisoner."

He withdrew a gold lighter from another pocket and made a production out of lighting the cigar. He drew on it until the tip glowed, then exhaled a puff of smoke directly into her face. He grinned as she coughed. "Do not worry. You will not be my prisoner for long."

The men behind her snickered. They must understand more English than they'd let on. She kept her gaze on the leader. "Please explain."

"Your friends do not like you, Isabella. They refused to pay your ransom."

"Ransom? If this is only about money, I'm sure we can come to an agreement."

"It is about more than money. You dared to defy me. I cannot let the insult pass."

"How much do you want?" She extended her hands, turning her palms outward as much as the plastic tie around her wrists allowed. "Give me a phone and I'll have funds wired to your account by tomorrow."

"Tomorrow is too late. You will be shot at dawn. Your death must set an example."

Death? No, not again. She stepped forward. "Don't be ridiculous. You can't kill me. You'll never get away with it."

There was a chorus of clicks as at least a dozen men cocked their weapons. At the fat man's nod, the soldier who had escorted her earlier grasped her hands once again. The leader gave them an order in Spanish and pivoted to return to his hut.

The bearded man yanked her away. She twisted against his grip. "No! Wait! What's your price? We can negotiate."

Cigar man lifted his hand in a dismissive gesture without turning around.

"Stop!" she shouted. "You can't do this! Let me go!"

Her pleas had no effect. She was dragged to the other side of the clearing and tossed into a windowless hut. She couldn't bring up her arms in time to shield herself and fell on her face. The floor was packed dirt. Dust flew into her mouth and up her nose. She spat and sneezed to get rid of it as the door slammed behind her. Metal rattled, followed by what sounded like the snap of a padlock.

She blinked at a curtain of tears. This couldn't be happening. Maybe she was hallucinating. It could be another side effect of the drugs she'd been given. Perhaps all she needed to do was wait it out and the effects would fade. Perhaps if she went to sleep, everything would be back to normal when she woke up.

The thought of going to sleep brought on a spurt of panic. No. She had to stay awake. She had to remain in control.

Control? She had never had less control in her life. She had no idea where she was or who was holding her prisoner. Yet the where and the who hardly mattered if she didn't find a way out of here by dawn.

She thumped her fists against her forehead. Why dawn? Her hanging was supposed to have been at dawn, too. There was a pattern to this lunacy. She should be able to figure it out, but she'd spent all her energy on her show of defiance. Her headache was getting worse again. Reasoning was becoming difficult. Her mind was turning fuzzy. She needed to hang on. She needed to concentrate in order to solve this puzzle.

The last thing she remembered was waking up in the castle. Before that, she had been at home in Manhattan . . .

No, that wasn't right. She hadn't been in the city, she had traveled to Willowbank to meet her stepmother. She had taken a suite in the town's only decent hotel. *That's* where she had been. They had been in the process of discussing the lawsuit. Delaney wanted her to drop it and had offered her a portion of Stanford's estate. Elizabeth hadn't trusted the olive branch for a minute. Her stepmother had gone to great lengths to secure that wealth. She wouldn't have parted with even a fraction of it voluntarily.

Had Delaney done this to her? Had she hired someone to break into her hotel room and drug her, then kidnap her to get her out of the way? Elizabeth wouldn't have expected the woman to have the imagination or the nerve to orchestrate a plot on this scale. Still, there was no love lost between them. Delaney had been nothing but a trophy wife. Her professed devotion to her husband had been as shallow as her character.

She hadn't wasted any time latching on to a hunk of beef-cake after Stanford had died. Life was easy for her because she'd never had to think for herself. She'd never had to fight. Not like Elizabeth.

Your friends do not like you, Isabella. They refused to pay your ransom.

That couldn't have been true. She had many influential acquaintances. Her father had taught her early on the value of cultivating connections with the right people. Her reputation was impeccable. Everyone would have realized she would have reimbursed them for any expenditures they might have to make on her behalf. A clever accountant could probably find a way to make the ransom tax deductible. Whether or not she was liked on a personal level was immaterial when it came to business decisions. Her father had taught her that, too.

She tried picturing what Stanford would have done if he'd found himself in this situation. What would he have said? He'd been an expert at identifying and pushing the right buttons. In the first place, he wouldn't have wasted time contemplating a jump from a moving truck. He likely would have bribed the driver into taking him to the airport instead of this encampment. Or if that hadn't worked, he would have found a way to ingratiate himself with the cigar-smoking fat man. In all probability he would have ended up making a deal to develop this piece of the jungle into a tourist resort. Stanford always won.

Except for their last encounter. Elizabeth had triumphed then. She'd used everything he'd taught her. She'd kept her eye on the prize as she'd been trained and had reclaimed what should have been hers.

But then he had died and Delaney had gone into her martyr act and what should have been simple had become tangled in lies and hate and revenge and oh, God, her head was splitting.

Elizabeth curled into a ball on the floor as agony knifed through her skull. The daylight that seeped beneath the door was waning. Darkness spread over her, sucking away the air, bringing a creeping numbness that promised an end to the pain. Maybe death wouldn't be so bad . . .

The thought terrified her. She couldn't give up. She didn't want to die, she wanted to live. There must be a way out. She turned her face toward the breeze that stole beneath the door. One gulp at a time, she forced air into her lungs. Along with the smell of the jungle and the taint of engine exhaust came an odd, medicinal smell. Drugs? There was an electronic beep. No, it was more like a twang. It changed pitch, becoming the sound of a guitar.

A man was singing. She couldn't distinguish the words, but the voice was sad and haunting and . . .

And exactly the same as the one she'd heard at the castle.

Was the minstrel here, too? How was that possible?

On the other hand, how could *she* possibly be here?

Elizabeth raised her head from the dirt so she could listen.

He strummed an E minor arpeggio with aching slowness, waiting for each string to silence before he plucked the next. When it was done, he transitioned to the diminished seventh. She clung to the notes. His presence might not make sense, but the music did. It followed patterns that she'd first learned in childhood at the keyboard of her mother's Steinway grand. It transcended place and time and the instrument being used, evoking responses from a level that needed no logical explanation. And as it had done before, it gave her strength.

She dragged herself closer to the door with her elbows. "Help!"

The music halted abruptly, as if he'd clapped his palm over the guitar strings to silence them. Insects whirred in the sudden stillness. From the distance came the murmur of men's voices.

Elizabeth pitched her voice low, hoping only the musician would hear it. She couldn't afford to alert her captors. "Help me! Please!"

The insects continued undisturbed, as did the quiet conversations. Then she heard the scuff of a footstep on the ground. A shadow moved across the strip of light beneath the door.

Recognition sparked through her brain. The shadow belonged to the minstrel. The singer. The hooded man she had seen in the castle courtyard. Once again, she wasn't sure how she was so certain, she just was. She stretched her arms toward his presence. "Here! I'm locked inside. You have to help me. Unlock the door!"

There was no sound from the door or the padlock. He strummed another chord, as if he was oblivious to her plea.

But he must be able to hear her. He stood so close, she could hear the slide of his fingertips as he repositioned them on the strings. "You wanted to help me before," she said. "You stopped that boy from throwing fruit at me, remember?"

He played a series of chords.

"You were in the courtyard. You wore a cloak with a hood, and you carried a lute in your hand . . ." Her voice had become a croak. She stopped to swallow, but her throat was too raw for more speech. "I don't have much time," she whispered. "Please, get me out of here before they kill me."

He picked out a new melody on the bass strings. It was as sad as the first. He hummed along softly for a while, then moved away. The shadow beneath the door disappeared.

She stretched toward the remaining light. "No, don't go!"

The sound of the guitar grew fainter. His deep voice drifted through the dusk as he put words to the melody. She strained to make out the lyrics. He was singing of loss and pain and loneliness. His words resonated through her heart as easily as his music.

> *You taught me life, you taught me love,*
> *But how do I learn to go on without you . . .*

Wait! she called. *Take me with you!*

But try as she might, no sound came from her lips.

She laid her cheek back on the dirt floor, closed her eyes, and willed herself to follow the singer's voice. Time twisted and bent until it lost all meaning. For a glorious space she left her pain and her body behind and soared free . . .

But then the melody ended. Silence fell.

And Elizabeth's mind returned to its prison.

MONICA CHAMBERLAIN LOWERED THE NEWSPAPER. SHE hadn't been looking at the bed, she'd been concentrating on the article that she'd been reading aloud. The movement she'd glimpsed had been on the edge of her vision, only a blur, so it could have been the result of a stray eyelash or lamplight winking from the arm of her glasses.

Yet what if it wasn't? What if Elizabeth's lips had actually moved? What if *this* was the day?

She put the paper on the bedside table and rose to her feet. She told herself not to overreact. She couldn't begin to count the number of times she'd spotted what she'd taken for a sign of awareness. It had proven to be an involuntary muscle spasm or a trick of the light or wishful thinking. "Elizabeth?"

There was no response.

She turned down the music and moved next to the bed. "It's me. Monica. Can you hear me?"

Nothing. Her eyelids didn't twitch. Her lips remained motionless. No response other than the steady beat of the heart monitor.

There was a strong possibility she might not want to hear Monica's voice. They hadn't spoken to each other for almost a year. The wounds that had been inflicted from the last words they'd exchanged had gone too deep.

She lifted Elizabeth's hand from the blanket and cradled it between both of hers. Monica had never believed the rift would be permanent. There had been a time they had promised they would be best friends for life. What had happened to the two innocent girls they'd been in those days? "I know you're in there somewhere, kiddo. Aren't you tired of being alone? Don't you think this silent treatment has gone on long enough? There must be plenty you want to say."

Still nothing. To an impartial observer, Elizabeth would seem to be merely sleeping. She appeared so peaceful.

It was that very peacefulness that would alarm anyone who had known her before the attack last summer. Elizabeth Graye had rarely been at peace. She had seldom slept more than five hours a night, either, even when she'd been a child. She had viewed sleep as a waste of valuable time and maintained she wanted to get the maximum use of her days. The attitude had defined her life. When she decided on a goal, she pursued it with single-minded determination. The end justified the means.

Elizabeth had thrived on challenge. Any satisfaction she might have gained from closing a deal or completing a project had lasted only until she moved on to the next one. Her colleagues at Grayecorp often compared her to a bulldozer. Behind her back, of course. It was a predictable metaphor from people in the property development business. They were wrong. Though Elizabeth was adept at covering her feelings, she was far from mechanical. She was like a high-spirited thoroughbred. With blinders. Bred to compete, eager to get to the finish line, but unable to see what she might trample in the process.

Monica squeezed Elizabeth's fingers. "I compared you to a horse. You're not going to take that lying down, are you?"

Elizabeth's face remained impassive. Not a muscle moved, even when the window rattled as the snowplow did another pass down the driveway. Between the vibrations and the engine noise, it was loud enough to wake the dead.

But apparently not enough to wake the comatose.

The doctors hadn't been optimistic to begin with. Though Elizabeth's body was moved and her limbs flexed regularly to maintain as much muscle tone as possible, the longer the situation continued, the worse the prognosis got. Monica had done her own research on the subject, reading every book and article she could obtain about patients in long-term comas, yet she'd found no consistent explanation for why some awakened while others didn't. And of those who did regain consciousness, some made what seemed miraculous recoveries, as if they'd merely been sleeping, while others suffered varying degrees of permanent disabilities. Was she a fool to keep hoping Elizabeth would be one of the lucky ones?

The idea of providing mental stimulation had seemed like a good approach at first, since it paralleled the exercises for her body, yet it had been four months. All the music they played, the television programs that droned in the background, the books they read, and the one-sided conversations could be for nothing. If Elizabeth were capable of hearing on any level, she should have shown some sign by now. They might never reach her. She might never come back.

And what was there to return to? The job? She'd devoted most of her waking hours to Grayecorp, but with the feeding frenzy that had taken place after her father's death, her ascension to Stanford's corporate throne hadn't materialized the way she'd hoped. Her personal life hadn't been going any more smoothly. Her sole surviving relative was a stepmother she despised. She had lost her family home. She had alienated her best friend because she'd been obsessed by her quest for revenge. Was that why she had weakened and gone back to Alan? He could be charming when he put his mind to it, but Monica had never liked him. She would have done her best to talk Elizabeth out of the engagement, if only they'd been on speaking terms.

Maybe Elizabeth didn't *want* to wake up.

Monica lifted her glasses to rub her eyes, then sighed and returned to the chair. The Elizabeth she knew wouldn't give up. She'd been a fighter all her life. Her biggest problem had been allowing anyone to be on her side.

THREE

"THAT'S HER! KILL THE WITCH!"

"Hang her!"

"Long live the king!"

The shouts mixed with the sound of creaking wood and the clip-clop of hooves. The ground beneath Elizabeth swayed. The air reeked with the smell of horse manure and rotten vegetables. Her head was throbbing. She struggled to open her eyes.

Shadowed faces reeled past. Torchlight flickered over groups of men and women dressed in shabby brown costumes. Behind them was a low, wooden building with a thatched roof. Horses whinnied from a darkened archway. Gray stone walls topped by crenulated battlements were silhouetted against the sky. Only a handful of stars remained overhead. The eastern horizon was streaked with gold.

"The hour of dawn approaches, Lady Elspeth."

Her heart tripped. She recognized that voice. It belonged to the bearded guard from the castle.

But she'd left that scenario behind. How long ago? A month? A year? Her grasp on time was fuzzy. So was her mind. God, what was wrong with her?

Something splattered nearby, sending a spray of foul-smelling liquid across her cheek. Laughter followed.

Elizabeth pushed herself to her knees. The manacles were once more around her wrists. Pain bounced through her skull, sliding her body back toward the brink of sleep but she fisted her hands and refused to succumb. Her instincts screamed at her to remain conscious. She would be completely helpless otherwise. She breathed shallowly through her mouth until the pain receded, then lifted her head and took stock of her surroundings.

She was in the castle, all right. Not in the tower where she'd been held last time but in a small cart. Stout poles were lashed to the sides of it to form what was essentially a primitive cage. It was being pulled across the courtyard by a donkey. Two men with swords belted to their tunics walked on either side of the beast to clear a path through the crowd. Four more walked beside the large, wooden wheels. She wiped her cheek on her sleeve. It didn't surprise her to see that she had been put into the purple dress again. These people were nothing if not thorough.

What people? Why? Where were they taking her?

The answer to the last question was right in front of her. It was obvious where she was being taken. The cart was heading for the center of the courtyard and the gallows that she'd seen from the tower window. Torches had been placed in a circle around the base, eliminating the predawn shadows as effectively as a spotlight. Steps led to a stool in the middle of the scaffold. Above it hung the empty noose.

Regardless of how illogical the situation, and how primitive the apparatus, the threat of death it presented was far too real. If someone was trying to scare her, they had succeeded.

Elizabeth swallowed hard. As much as she wanted to, she would not scream. She was Elizabeth Graye. She never showed fear. She wouldn't allow herself to be intimidated. She was adept at facing down everyone from bankers to union bullies, and the number one rule of any negotiation was to display no weakness. She wouldn't give whoever had put her in this situation the satisfaction of knowing how close she was to breaking down.

But she *was* close, so very, very close. She stared at the noose. She could almost feel the prickle of the coarse fibers against her throat . . .

No. Absolutely not. She would not die like this. She grasped the side of the cart with both hands and pulled herself to her feet. She turned toward the guard who had spoken. "What's your name?"

"I am Ganulf."

"Gandolf? That's hardly original."

"Ganulf, my lady."

"What happened to the jungle, Ganulf?"

"Your words are strange. What is a jungle?"

"Still sticking to the period dialogue nonsense, are we? All right, did you use your magic and make it go poof?"

"I am no wizard!" he declared. "I am captain of the royal guard."

"That's right, I didn't see you with the jungle army. I suppose you and your friends prefer to parade around in tights and little tunics instead of camouflage uniforms."

He gripped the hilt of his sword. "If you have news of an approaching army you must speak."

"Better ask whoever brought me here. I doubt if they could have traveled this far from the jungle in your medieval excuse for a paddy wagon."

"Tell me of the army. Who rides at the head? Is it the baroness?"

"Why should I tell you anything? You're all in this together, aren't you? Have you made a deal to split the ransom?"

"Nay, there is no ransom. Methinks you create tales of other soldiers to delay the hour of your death. Your trickery is for naught. Your sentence must be carried out."

"What was my crime?"

"You defied the king."

"Fine, where is he? I'm not accustomed to negotiating with underlings."

"I am honored to serve my liege."

"At least the cigar guy met me in person. He understood the importance of hands-on management. What's wrong with this so-called king of yours? Does he have a speech impediment? Is he too cowardly to show his face?"

The people nearest to the cart must have been following their exchange. There was a general intake of breath at her insults to their monarch. They surged forward, blocking the path to the gallows. A lump of what could have once been a pumpkin hit one corner of the cage, spraying seeds and orange pulp over her skirt. A stone bounced off the bars and struck the corner of her eye. The impact sent her to her knees. She lifted her arms to shield her head.

As one, the guards drew their swords. Apparently, they were determined to see their prisoner hanged but not stoned. The crowd muttered angrily but eventually retreated enough to allow the cart to pass. No one appeared willing to test the authenticity of the steel the way Elizabeth had during her previous visit to this stage set. Or whatever it was. She lowered her arms tentatively. When no more missiles were sent her way, she touched her fingertips to her eye. The skin beneath her eyebrow was already swelling, but luckily it wasn't broken. She moved her hands to her collar.

There was a narrow ridge on her neck. It was crusty, like dried blood from a recent wound. The scratch from the sword tip hadn't healed. How could that be? Her skin had been smooth when she'd checked it in the truck. Could she have missed it? Or had the jungle scenario been a hallucination?

What the *hell* was going on?

The cart bumped to a stop at the foot of the gallows. One of the guards went to the rear and swung open the back of the cage. "Lady Elspeth, it is time."

"This has gone far enough. I have no intention of playing along with your preposterous charade."

"I beg you, my lady. Do not cause me to drag you from the tumbrel."

"Lay your hands on me and I'll have my lawyer slap you with a lawsuit that will set you back so far your grandchildren will still be paying off your debt."

A second guard stepped forward. "Lady Elspeth, the dawn is nigh. You cannot escape your fate."

She gathered handfuls of her skirt to draw the fabric aside and got back to her feet. She surveyed the crowd from the vantage point of the open door. "Are you all participants in this conspiracy? Isn't there anyone here who can think for themselves?"

There was a general muttering. There were a few cries of "witch" and "hang her," but no sign of anyone breaking ranks.

Elizabeth continued to scan the people around her. "There is no safety in numbers. Everyone who played a part in this outrage will face the full force of the law. Your only hope for leniency is to bail out now."

The only response was more catcalls.

"Use your heads, people. Whatever you've been promised isn't worth the consequences. This is the twenty-first century. There are laws. I have rights." She raised her voice. "I also have considerable resources. Anyone who helps me will be generously rewarded. Anyone," she repeated, focusing on each guard in turn.

"Pay no heed," Ganulf ordered his men. "She seeks once more to corrupt us."

The donkey in front of the cart brayed. It was answered by a high-pitched whinny near the back of the crowd. Elizabeth peered in the direction of the noise.

A man was leading a chestnut-colored horse from the thatch-roofed building. He was on the fringe of the crowd. The torches they bore didn't illuminate his face because a hood shadowed his features. One side of his cloak was flung back, revealing a lute that hung by a strap from his shoulder.

Hope uncurled. She steadied herself on the edge of the cage door and stretched on her toes to get a better look. She didn't need to see his face to know who that was. "Excuse me!"

The man kept walking.

"Hello! You in the hood!" She cupped her hands around her mouth. "Minstrel!"

He stroked the horse's neck.

"Call the police," she shouted. "You have to tell the authorities what's happening."

The horse tossed its head. The minstrel halted and reached beneath his cloak, but he didn't withdraw a phone, he withdrew an apple. He sang softly as he fed it to the animal. He seemed unaware he was the center of her attention.

Elizabeth couldn't understand how she was able to hear him so clearly over the distance that separated them. It could have something to do with the acoustics of the courtyard. Maybe the sound echoed from the surrounding stone walls. Whatever the reason, she recognized the tune he sang as surely as she had recognized him. His smokey-deep voice slipped into her mind with its accustomed ease. She knew it in her soul.

> *I feel your kiss in the wind,*
> *I hear your whisper in the falling snow,*
> *I see your smile in the sunrise,*
> *My love, my life, why did you go?*

He couldn't be one of the conspirators. His music was too beautiful. No one who could write songs like his would take part in something this cruel. "I'll pay you!" she said. "Name your price."

His song trailed off and he began humming a different one under his breath. He finished feeding his horse, gave it a pat, and grasped the bridle to lead it away. Music trailed behind him as the edge of his cloak brushed against the lute strings.

"No!" she called. "Don't go yet. These people are lunatics. They might really kill me." She jumped from the cart and lunged toward him. "Take me with you!"

Her sudden bid for freedom startled the guards. They reacted belatedly. She used the iron around her wrists like a battering ram to plow her way through the crowd and was almost to the minstrel before the king's men caught up to her. They grabbed her by the arms and lifted her from her feet. She twisted and kicked to no avail. Her feet quickly became tangled in yards of purple wool. Someone drew a sword. Only when she felt the tip against her side did she go still.

It wasn't soon enough. Cold steel pierced her dress and her skin. Blood trickled down her ribs.

Oh, God! These people were criminally insane.

Or else she was hallucinating.

Or she had traveled back in time and was caught in somebody else's life.

Or she had died and this was purgatory . . .

"No! I'm alive. Can't you see that?"

The minstrel was only yards away, but as had happened before, he acted as if he was unaware of her existence.

She moaned in frustration. She had to reach him. She might not get another chance. Already, she could feel her strength draining. What if she blacked out again? What hell would she wake up in next time? She inhaled as far as the sword allowed and put every ounce of her remaining energy into one last plea. "Hear me! Look at me!"

He pushed back his hood and cocked his head. Dark hair gleamed in the torchlight.

"Yes! That's it! I'm here. Right behind you. All you need to do is turn around."

He glanced over his shoulder. His face startled her. There was little gentleness in his features. His nose was large and his lips were thin. Beard stubble darkened his cheeks and bristled along the edges of his sharp jaw. He belonged in a cowboy movie, not a medieval stage set, because he had the lean, tough face of a desperado.

She had a moment's doubt. Could this truly be the man she had heard?

Then his gaze met hers. He *saw* her.

And the impact knocked her breathless.

Yes, this was him. His eyes were clear amber, as deep as his voice, as sweet as the chords she had heard him play, as haunting as the melodies of his songs. Though he didn't move toward her, she felt his presence in every nerve and bone. Her blood pulsed in rhythm with his. Their minds touched. Sparked. Fused.

Her strength returned, as if she were drawing on his. The connection wasn't physical, yet it suffused her with a sense of warmth and belonging and rightness. It was an embrace unlike anything she had experienced in her life. She clung to the sensation as desperately as she had clung to his music. "Please," she cried. "You have to help me. I want to live!"

He staggered sideways, clutching his head. The lute twanged sourly as he bumped into his horse. "What the hell . . . Who are you?"

The connection between them was no longer only in her mind. She didn't just sense his question, she heard it.

Judging by the number of people whose heads turned in his direction, others had heard him, too.

"Don't you remember?" she called. "I was in the hut in the jungle. You were there, too."

"I was?"

"Yes! You were playing your songs."

"Seize him!" Ganulf ordered. More guards swept past her. One caught the reins of the minstrel's horse while another brought the tip of his sword to the man's chest.

He tore his gaze from hers to focus on the weapon. He raised his hands. "What's the problem, officer?"

"Do not interfere with the king's decree."

"You got the wrong guy." His voice twanged with a Western drawl. "I didn't do anything."

"You conspire to aid the prisoner."

"Who? The blonde? I swear, I never saw her before in my life."

"From where do you hail, minstrel?" Ganulf demanded. "I have not seen you before this day."

"I'm just passing through. Why are you hassling me?"

One of the guards tore off the man's cloak and groped him roughly, as if searching for weapons. Another grabbed the lute, shook it, then looked inside the hole in the sound-board.

The minstrel lowered his hands to reach for the instrument. "Careful with that. I've got a gig tonight."

"Be still!" The guard who held the sword on him moved the tip from the man's chest to his throat.

"Whoa! Settle down. I'm not resisting."

"Don't hurt him!" Elizabeth cried. "He's done nothing."

"Yeah, what she said." The minstrel leaned as far back from the sword as he could. "How about if you boys put away those pig stickers before someone gets hurt?"

"Your speech is as strange as Lady Elspeth's," Ganulf said. "Methinks you share her guilt."

"Hey, wait a minute. I told you, I don't know her."

"What know you of the jungle? The army of which she spoke?"

"Not a damn thing. I'm nothing but a musician trying to earn an honest living."

"Mayhap you are a spy."

"Sure, and my horse is Goldfinger. Listen, whatever trouble's going on here doesn't involve me, so give me back my property and I'll be on my way."

Ganulf turned to regard Elizabeth, then nodded to the men who held her. "Return Lady Elspeth to the castle. We must bring this matter before the king. He will determine whether to question her further. Bring the minstrel as well."

THEY WEREN'T TAKEN TO THE TOWER ROOM WHERE SHE'D been imprisoned before. Instead, they were hustled through a maze of torch-lined corridors that sloped downward beneath the castle. They passed rooms filled with large wooden bins, others lined with casks or barrels along the walls. The deeper they went, the staler the air grew. No outside sounds penetrated here. All was silent save for the echoes of their footsteps, the rhythmic clink of the chain between her manacles, and an odd metallic rubbing that came from the guards' chain mail.

By the time they halted, Elizabeth had lost all sense of direction. They were in front of a floor-to-ceiling grate that consisted of crisscrossed metal bars. The guards swung open a door in the center of it, shoved her and the minstrel inside and locked the door behind them.

There was no window. The only light came from a torch in the corridor. The room—or to be more accurate, the cell—was furnished with two narrow, straw-lined pallets against the side walls and a bucket that was placed near the back wall. The pallets were likely meant to serve as beds. Elizabeth had a sinking suspicion of what the bucket was supposed to serve as. She fervently hoped they would find a way to escape before she needed to test her theory.

"Pardon me, ma'am, but would you mind telling me what's going on?"

She pressed her arm over the wound in her side. Now that the guards were no longer supporting her, she became aware of how weak her legs felt. The energy she'd gained from her initial contact with the minstrel hadn't lasted long. She wobbled toward the nearest sleeping pallet and sat. To her relief, the straw smelled fresh. She took a few steadying breaths, then regarded her companion.

The man stood with one shoulder against the grate. Torchlight flickered over half his face, leaving the rest in shadow. The guards hadn't returned his cloak. The tunic and leggings he wore displayed a long, lanky body in keeping with the cowboy cragginess of his facial features. He seemed taller than he had in the courtyard, perhaps because the ceiling was so low. "I have no idea what's going on," she replied. "I hoped you could tell me."

"Like I said to the cop, I'm just passing through. Whatever you're mixed up in—"

"Me? I don't know what I'm mixed up in. I don't know these people. I didn't choose to dress like this. I didn't voluntarily get myself locked in a tower or a dungeon or a *hut*. In case you missed seeing my shackles, I'm a prisoner."

"What did you do?"

"I don't know. They say I defied the king but I don't remember anything. It's all nonsense. They're either being paid off or they're sharing some kind of mass delusion or . . ." She winced as she repositioned her arm over her wound. "Whoever they are, you can't be one of them. You're not using the dialect."

He pushed away from the grate. "What's wrong with your side?"

"It's nothing. How did you get here?"

"My horse."

"Goldfinger."

"I said that to be smart because they accused me of being a spy. His real name's Chester."

"But you've obviously heard of James Bond, so you're not sharing the medieval times delusion. I ask you again, how did you get here?"

"Funny, I don't rightly remember." He started a circuit of the cell, inspecting the walls, poking the toe of his boot into the shadowed corners. "I suppose I was riding along and found the castle. I must have taken a wrong turn."

"You suppose? Where were you going?"

"I'm playing at the Cantina this month. That's my brother's bar."

"Where is his bar?"

"Tulsa."

"Tulsa? As in Oklahoma?"

"I didn't know there was another one." He stopped beside her pallet. "That looks like blood on your dress."

"It is. Those swords are sharper than they appear."

He leaned down, took her wrist and eased her arm away from her side, revealing the rip the sword had made in her dress. The wool around was completely saturated. It glistened. "That looks bad," he murmured.

The concern in his voice flustered her. So did his touch. She wasn't comfortable with casual contact and generally avoided it whenever possible. But this was hardly a caress. He was being practical. "It's not deep. The bleeding's almost stopped."

"Doesn't look that way to me. Those guys had no call to hurt you."

"It's the least of my worries. They were going to hang me if you hadn't distracted them."

"I can't take credit for the distraction." He grasped the bottom edge of his tunic and drew it over his head. "Getting me involved was your idea."

He wore a long-sleeved shirt beneath the tunic so he was still clothed. Technically, anyway. But the fabric of the shirt was worn thin and pulled tight across his shoulders and upper arms in a way that outlined every detail of his ropy muscles. The garment had no buttons. The cord that laced the neck together must have come unfastened during his brief struggle with the guards. The slit hung open to the center of his chest. She glimpsed a scattering of dark hair and an impressive set of pecs before she wrenched her gaze away.

This was hardly the time to notice his physique. Or to even think about him as a man. She lifted her chin. She wished she had the strength to stand so she didn't need to look up at him. It put her at a disadvantage. "What do you think you're doing?"

He used his teeth to start a rip in the bottom of his tunic, then tore off a wide strip and folded it into a thick pad. "You can use this for a compress. It seems clean."

"While I appreciate your show of chivalry, we don't have time for this. Our priority is getting out of here. Please, tell me you have a phone stashed somewhere in that costume."

"Costume?"

"That outfit. Whoever gave it to you must be a party to this insanity. Where did you get it?"

He frowned at the tunic he held. "Beats me."

"Why? Did they drug you, too?"

"Drug me?"

"Is your mind fuzzy?"

"No more than usual." He tore off a second strip from his tunic and went down on one knee beside her pallet. "Let me take a look at that slice."

She hesitated briefly, then lifted her arm.

The rip in her dress extended through a layer of fine cotton that was next to her skin. The undergarment appeared to be some kind of camisole. It might have started out white but was now red. He gently peeled back the edges.

She jerked as his knuckles brushed the underside of her breast. She pressed her back against the wall. "You don't need to do this."

"As I recall, you asked me to help you, right?"

"To escape these people. To get away from here."

"To live."

"Well, yes. I did say that, but—"

"Then you don't want to bleed to death before we get out of here." He widened the rip in the undergarment and slid the makeshift compress through to press it over the wound. "We don't have any disinfectant, so we have to hope the blood flushed out most of the germs. Hold this."

She pressed her arm against the folded rag. "I thought you were a musician."

"That's right, but I've done some doctoring."

"Then you studied medicine?"

"Nothing formal." He grasped her shoulder to lean her forward so he could loop the remaining strip of fabric around her ribs. "It was more what you'd call hands-on training."

"Excuse me?"

"Relax. I never lost a heifer."

"Heifer? As in *cow*?"

"Uh-huh. They're not as dumb as most people think, but from time to time one of them can get spooked into barbed wire or wander into some brambles." He eased her arm up and tied the rag in a firm knot over the compress. "But to tell the truth, their hide was a lot thicker than yours so I never had call to bandage them. Probably couldn't have stretched my shirt around one, anyway. Lucky thing for us you're not as big as a cow. How does that feel?"

Something pushed at her throat. It felt like a laugh, but it couldn't be. There was nothing funny about the situation. She scowled. "Better, thank you. I take it you work on a farm as well as play in your brother's bar."

"Not anymore. I grew up on a farm, and I used to work a few acres of my own outside Enid, but the bank owns it now." Still on his knees, he studied her face. His jaw went square, as if he'd clenched his teeth. He lifted one hand to the corner of her eye. "Who gave you the shiner? Did the cops do that, too?"

His touch was as gentle as his voice. Again, considering the situation, it would be ludicrous to enjoy either. She tipped her head to break the contact. "Someone threw a rock. It's nothing."

He stroked her hair.

There was no mistake this time, it was a caress, but she ignored it. He likely did the same thing to gentle the livestock he used to doctor. "You called those men cops," she said. "Why? Can't you see they're actors or madmen or anything but legitimate law enforcement?"

He sat back on his heels and braced his arms on his thighs. "Yeah, I suppose."

"You're only supposing again? Didn't their costumes and weapons strike you as odd?"

"Sure, now that you mention it. It's weird. Everything seems right until I think about it."

She hesitated. He seemed intelligent enough. The lack of cohesiveness in his reasoning process must be due to confusion rather than mental deficiency. At least, she hoped so. "You were probably drugged. I'm fairly sure I was. I can't remember how I got here, either. Do you have a headache?"

"No, do you?"

"Only when I move too fast or try to think. Which reminds me, you didn't answer my question earlier. Do you have a cell phone?"

He straightened from his crouch and redonned his shortened tunic. She couldn't help noticing it fell substantially above midthigh. "Nope."

"Are you sure? They didn't spend much time searching you. They might have missed it."

"I don't own a cell phone."

"But you do know what one is, don't you?"

"Sure, I just don't like them. Who wants to walk around wired like a Borg? You can't go anywhere these days without stumbling over people yelling conversations at people who aren't there. It's a plague."

"My BlackBerry is more than a phone, it's a vital tool. I should think someone in the entertainment business would understand the necessity of keeping in touch."

"Time's precious. I wouldn't waste it talking or texting into a gadget."

"I take it you wouldn't use computers, either."

"Not if I can help it. Me and computers don't get along."

"Great. I ask for help and I get a Luddite who can't remember who dressed him this morning."

"Hey, I was passing through, minding my own business. Getting tossed in a dungeon wasn't my idea. If you hadn't singled me out—" He broke off. "Sorry. I don't blame you. If I was in your fix, I'd want help, too."

"And I'm sorry if interrupting my execution has inconvenienced you. I'll be happy to compensate you for any income you might lose if you're late for your *gig* at your brother's bar on my account, but in order to do that, we'll need to get out of this dungeon. If you have any suggestions toward solving our dilemma, I would appreciate hearing them."

"I want to ask you something first."

"Go ahead."

"What's a Luddite?"

"Technically, it's a member of a group that originated in Britain during the industrial revolution who believed machines were evil. It's come to mean a person who shuns technology."

His mouth tilted in the ghost of a smile. "And here I thought you had insulted me."

She dropped her head back against the wall. "I don't mean to be rude. I'm . . . stressed."

"You're hanging in pretty good, considering. Most women would have been in hysterics over getting beaned with the rock. You don't even blink at getting skewered with a sword."

"I prefer to concentrate on my priorities, that's all. Gender has nothing to do with it. It's a male fantasy that women are prone to hysterics. We're not. Otherwise, the species would have died out the first time a spider showed up in the caves."

"I was giving you a compliment."

"Thank you. How tall are you?"

"Six three."

"Do you think you could reach that torch in the corridor?"

"Only one way to find out." He returned to the grate at the front of the cell and slipped his right arm through. "A torch might not do us much good against swords."

"We could use it as a club. It would be better than nothing, and we would have the element of surprise on our side."

He stretched, extending his fingers to the limit. Even from where she sat on the pallet she could see the bracket that held the torch was more than a foot out of reach. He shook his head, muttering a curse as he pulled his arm back inside. He inspected the door's hinges, then grasped the bars and gave them a hard shake. Aside from a trickle of dust that came down from the ceiling, nothing moved.

"It was worth a try."

"Yeah." He dropped his forehead against the bars. "By the way, I'm Rick."

She lifted her right hand as much as the chain allowed, then let it drop to her lap. "Elizabeth."

"They called you something else, didn't they?"

"Lady Elspeth. I assume it's a medieval variation of Elizabeth."

"I have a great aunt named Elizabeth, but everyone calls her Betsy."

"I loathe nicknames."

"What did your folks call you? No Beth or Liza?"

Her father was the only person who had gotten away with shortening her name. It was hard to believe that she'd once been naïve enough to assume he'd done it out of fondness. "Please, do I look like the kind of woman who would tolerate any of those?"

He turned his head to regard her. One corner of his mouth lifted in a half smile. "Actually, in that getup you kind of look like an Elspeth."

Half or not, his smile unsettled her almost as much as his accidental touch on her breast had. It was time to change the subject. "You mentioned a brother, parents, and a great aunt. Do you have a large family?"

He shrugged. "Depends on your point of view. We're hardly ever all in one place at the same time so it's tough to give you a head count. You?"

"No. I asked because the more relatives you have, the better. They should be looking for you when you go missing."

"My brother will. Not that many suckers willing to play for what he pays." He gave the grate another shake. "But I don't think he's going to look for me here."

"You said you were on your way to his bar in Tulsa. That means we must be somewhere nearby. Surely an installation this large wouldn't go unnoticed. These people have to live somewhere. They need to shop for food and go to the dentist. Someone's bound to get curious about a group of individuals who like to dress up in medieval costumes."

"Uh-huh. They'd be hard to miss, but I've never heard rumors about a castle cult in the area." He shoved away from the grate and went to sit on the cell's remaining pallet. It was lower to the floor than hers. His knees stuck up awkwardly. He ended up leaning his back against the wall and stretching his legs in front of him, which brought his feet almost to hers. "You said you saw me in a jungle. When?"

"I don't know exactly. Before this, I was at a camp full of guerrilla soldiers or cocaine smugglers, I'm not sure which."

"I don't remember it."

"They locked me inside a wooden hut. I heard your music. You played a guitar."

"Doesn't ring a bell."

"Their leader called me Isabella. I believe that's a Spanish form of Elizabeth, which makes sense, as much as anything about this madness could."

"Then the soldiers knew who you were, too."

"Apparently."

"And you saw me there?"

"I didn't actually see you. I recognized your voice and I . . ." She cleared her throat.

"What?"

"It seems silly to say now, but I, ah, seemed to sense your presence."

He shifted his foot so he could nudge her toe. "About what happened in the courtyard earlier, when you called to me."

"What about it?"

"That's what I'm asking. What was that? How did you get into my head?"

"So you felt it, too?"

"Yeah, whatever it was. For a few seconds there, it was like you were part of me."

"It was an . . . unusual experience."

"Have you ever done that before? Gone into someone's mind?"

"Certainly not. There's no such thing as telepathy. It had to have been some kind of fluke brought on by adrenaline."

"How do you figure that?"

What could she say? She wasn't about to confess that she had felt his music in her soul. It would sound even more ludicrous than admitting she had sensed his presence. "I was desperate to make you hear me. Combined with the aftereffects of whatever drugs that were used on us, it only seemed as if we, ah, met in our minds."

He crossed his arms. His nostrils flared, as if he were suppressing a yawn. "Yeah, that's probably what happened."

"Rick?"

"Uh-huh?"

"You're not sleepy, are you?"

"Sorry. It's the weirdest thing. All of a sudden I can hardly keep my eyes open."

"You have to stay awake!" She pushed off the wall to sit forward. "It's important."

"Mmm?"

"Don't go to sleep. You need to stay conscious. We both do."

"I can't see how we can break out of here. We'll have to wait for those guards to come back. Could get a chance then." He made no attempt to suppress the next yawn. It was wide enough to make his jaw crack. He swung his legs onto his pallet. "Might as well conserve our strength."

"No! You don't understand. This is how it always ends."

He stretched out on his back and closed his eyes.

"Rick!"

He didn't respond.

The fatigue that she'd managed to keep at bay suddenly engulfed her. Her eyelids were impossibly heavy. She strained to keep them open. "Wake up, Rick! Please!"

It was too late. His face was already lax with sleep.

She attempted to stand, but her legs wouldn't bear her weight. She dropped to her knees and crawled toward him. The room tilted. A familiar darkness descended over her vision, making it impossible to judge time or distance.

No! Not yet!

Her senses were shutting down. She couldn't hear her own voice. She couldn't even feel the stone floor under her hands and knees. Each inch she moved was a battle. It was hopeless. She would never reach him.

Rick!

A wisp of melody trailed into the darkness.

Elizabeth threw herself after it. For an instant, an hour, a year, she couldn't tell, she followed the trail of Rick's music.

Until finally, inevitably, oblivion dragged her back to the silent void.

FOUR

"MRS. HARRISON!" NORMA SPRANG FROM BEHIND THE counter at the nurses' station. "I'm glad you got here. They're still in her room."

Delaney Graye Harrison turned down the corridor without breaking stride. She seldom used the wealth she had inherited from her first husband, but purchasing the Gulfstream and arranging to have a private pilot on standby had been money well spent. She'd found it almost as useful as Max did. "How long have they been in there?"

"Almost an hour." Norma fell into step beside her. "I'm glad you were able to come so quickly. It's not really my place to interfere with a private consultation like this but when I heard who it was, I didn't know what else to do. We all know how much you care about Miss Graye."

"You were right to call me, Norma. No one will fault you for it."

"I hope not. It doesn't seem fair to think about giving up, especially now."

"Yes, we all had hoped Elizabeth would have been able to spend Thanksgiving at home."

"That's not what I meant. She's been . . . I don't know, different lately."

Delaney halted. "Different?"

"I think we're reaching her."

"How?"

"The last time I was changing her music, I thought I saw her move her lips. It wasn't a big motion, more like a twitch, but I definitely saw something."

"That's wonderful!"

"I didn't tell you right away because I didn't want to get your hopes up again and have you do the trip from Willowbank for nothing. We've had so many false alarms. This could have been one, too."

Delaney could understand her caution. How many times had she dropped everything to travel here on the strength of an excited phone call from one of the nurses? How often had she hoped against hope to see Elizabeth awake when she walked through the door? Each repeated disappointment took longer to fade. They reached the point when they had begun to accumulate, never entirely going away. It was becoming hard to see any possibility of change.

But if she'd learned one thing over the past year, it was that when it came to the power of the human mind, nothing was impossible. She kept reminding herself of that. Something had to reach Elizabeth eventually. They simply hadn't yet found out what it was.

Delaney continued down the corridor as Norma returned to the nurses' station. Though she tried to stay positive, the prospect of the impending confrontation was knotting her stomach. She hated arguments. She'd lived most of her life avoiding situations that bothered her. She'd come a long way in the past year, yet it was still a hard habit to break. She allowed herself to pause outside the door only long enough to poke a stray curl back beneath her hat, then lifted her chin and walked into Elizabeth's room.

For once, there was no music playing or TV program droning. Two men stood talking quietly beside Elizabeth's bed. One was Alan Rashotte. He had made it a practice to visit only on Saturdays, so Delaney hadn't run into him for a few months. His dark blond hair appeared freshly styled, as usual. His blue silk tie complemented the pale blue of his eyes, his charcoal gray suit was perfectly tailored and his shoes ruthlessly shined. An objective observer would describe him as handsome, as Alan was no doubt aware. She'd overheard more than one of the nurses commenting on his attractiveness.

To Delaney, he had all the appeal of a Ken doll. He tried too hard to polish away his imperfections, and as a result had lost some of his humanity. He hadn't been born into the circle of wealth and prestige that Elizabeth had. That could be one of the reasons he pursued both with an outsider's mixture of yearning and resentment. Though his business acumen had taken him to the top echelons of Grayecorp, Delaney suspected his methods might have bordered on unethical. She had been shocked to learn that Elizabeth had agreed to marry him. She'd believed their romance had ended more than a year ago. Still, since Stanford's death, her relationship with her stepdaughter had deteriorated to open hostility. She was the last person Elizabeth would have confided in about her love life.

To be fair, Alan had been one of the few regular visitors to the clinic. Plenty of people had sent flowers and cards when Elizabeth had first been hospitalized, but none besides Alan, Monica, and Elizabeth's lawyer had bothered to travel to Willowbank to see her. Delaney had hoped that would change when she'd had Elizabeth transferred here, since Seven Pines was close to the Graye estate in Bedford where her stepdaughter had grown up, and it was an easy trip from New York City, where her friends lived. Sadly, it hadn't worked out that way. Elizabeth might have had hundreds of business acquaintances, but in truth she'd lived a solitary life.

"Delaney," Alan exclaimed. His lips moved into a solemn smile that didn't reach his eyes. "I didn't know you were planning to come today. This is a pleasant surprise."

"Hello, Alan." She unbuttoned her coat and slipped it off. Not because she was too warm but because she was making clear she intended to stay. "How's Elizabeth doing?"

His smile faded. "The same."

"One of the nurses said she may have moved her lips."

"As much as we would all like to believe it, I don't think it's possible. Have you met Dr. Lidstone?"

She hung her coat on the coat-tree in the corner and turned her attention to the second man. She had run an Internet search on Lidstone while she'd been en route from Willowbank to verify what Norma had told her. He appeared much like the photo she'd seen in one of his articles. Instead of a suit coat, he wore a cabled navy cardigan over his shirt and tie. A neatly cropped black beard framed his mouth and extended from his chin, giving him the air of an intellectual. The effect was spoiled by his eyes. They were small and set close together, like a rodent's. "No, I don't believe I have."

"Edward, this is Delaney Harrison," Alan said. "The widow of my fiancée's late father."

She didn't offer her hand. "Dr. Lidstone."

"Ms. Harrison." He lifted one eyebrow. "Your last name is not the same as Miss Graye's?"

"Delaney remarried," Alan said. "She took her new husband's name."

"Ah, I see."

Delaney could find no fault in Alan's explanation. It was the tone he'd used, as if the fact that she'd already remarried was scandalous and something to be spoken of in hushed tones.

If he was trying to put her on the defensive, he'd chosen the wrong tactic. There were few things she was prouder of than being married to John Maxwell Harrison. He was quite literally the man of her dreams. Compared to what she and Max shared, the relationship she'd had with Stanford couldn't even be called a marriage. She controlled her irritation and got down to business. "I don't recall seeing your name on the clinic's roster of visiting physicians, Dr. Lidstone."

"Quite right, Ms. Harrison. I practice in Boston."

"In what field?"

"Edward is a neuropsychologist," Alan said.

"I specialize in the rehabilitation of patients with brain injuries."

Rehabilitation? Not according to what Delaney had read. "What brings you here?" she asked.

"I managed to persuade him to do a consultation," Alan interjected.

"You should have called me, Alan," she said. "I would have hated to miss hearing his opinion."

"I didn't think you would be able to come down from Willowbank on such short notice. I'm glad you're here, though."

"Yes, it should save time." She regarded Dr. Lidstone. "I've been closely involved in my stepdaughter's care since I had her placed at the Seven Pines Clinic. One of the stipulations the staff is fully aware of is that I need to be informed before there's any alteration to Elizabeth's treatment."

Lidstone arched his eyebrow again. He looked at Alan. "I understood that as her fiancé, you were her acting next of kin. Was I mistaken?"

"Neither Delaney nor I are related to Elizabeth by blood," Alan replied. "But I was far closer to her emotionally. We were engaged. I would understand her wishes better than anyone else."

"Blood or not, in the eyes of the law I am her family," Delaney said. "Her ongoing care is my responsibility, and I have the right to be kept informed."

"I've offended you," Alan said, dropping his voice. "I'm deeply sorry, Delaney. I'm so eager to help Elizabeth, I didn't even consider your feelings, but I wasn't trying to exclude you. We're the only hope she has. We have to work together."

"I couldn't agree more. Dr. Lidstone, have you formed an opinion concerning my stepdaughter?"

He glanced at Alan before he spoke. "Her condition is very grave."

"Please, explain," Delaney said.

"As you know, she is dependent on a feeding tube for sustenance. She would not be capable of surviving on her own."

"She is in a coma. That's to be expected."

He shook his head. "This has gone beyond a coma. She is in what is called a persistent vegetative state."

"You're wrong. She's been showing signs of regaining consciousness."

"A few involuntary muscle spasms, no more. The most recent tests demonstrate that her brain activity has stopped."

"Not according to the doctors on staff here."

"While I don't mean to question the competence of the individuals you have dealt with until now, interpreting scientific data correctly takes a much higher level of expertise than one could expect from physicians who practice in a long-term care facility. My conclusions are correct."

"I wouldn't put my faith in those tests," Delaney said. "There's no machine capable of measuring everything the mind can do."

"Ms. Harrison, I realize it's difficult for the family to accept, but in cases like these, the kindest option for everyone concerned would be to let nature take its course."

"That's what we've been doing. We're giving Elizabeth the chance to heal."

"Ms. Harrison—"

"This has gone far enough," Delaney said. "I know who you are, Dr. Lidstone. I've read the tripe that you publish. You may have a medical degree but you're no doctor. You're a self-serving executioner of those who can't speak for themselves and I want you to leave now."

"Delaney!" Alan stepped toward her but stopped when she crossed her arms. He turned to Lidstone. "I apologize. She's overwrought."

Lidstone showed no reaction to her comments. Neither denial nor defense. "I counsel nothing more than a humane solution to an inhumane dilemma, Ms. Harrison."

"I asked you to leave."

"I understand you were in a serious accident yourself recently. You underwent treatment for months and eventually did recover, but don't confuse your case with your stepdaughter's. Put aside your ego. This is about what's best for the patient."

"Exactly. Which is why I have to ask you once more to leave. You are not welcome here. You may have avoided prosecution until now, but if you go near any of Elizabeth's equipment I'll make sure that you're charged with attempted murder."

Lidstone reached for the overcoat that was draped on the bedside chair. "I'll be in touch, Mr. Rashotte." He passed Delaney without looking at her and went out the door.

Alan held out his hand. "Delaney, I'm sorry. I can see you're upset. I hope once you calm down and have a chance to think you'll be willing to hear him out at least."

She stepped back to avoid Alan's touch. "How dare you call in that quack?"

"Dr. Lidstone is a highly respected professional. We were fortunate he could fit this trip into his schedule."

"He's a murderer."

"He's an advocate of terminating unnecessary suffering. Surely you can see the difference." He turned to the bed and gripped the side rail. "You don't have any idea how hard it is for me to see her like this. I know Elizabeth. She would hate being so helpless."

"That's right, she would."

"She's the woman I love. We had planned to spend our lives together. No one wants her to recover more than I do."

"Then why did you call in that . . . death dealer?"

"I did it out of love."

"If you love her, you can't give up hope."

He bowed his head. His throat worked. "Delaney, may I speak frankly?"

"Please, do."

"While I admire the devotion you've shown to Elizabeth, you were never close to her the way I was. She didn't love you. She didn't even like you."

"Neither of us was to blame for that situation. Stanford manipulated both of us. He sabotaged any possibility of a relationship before it could start."

"Stanford was a brilliant man. He had his faults, as we all do. It was a terrible shock to Elizabeth when he died."

"Of course, it was. She was devastated. They were very close."

"She brought the wrongful death suit against you because she blamed you for causing the accident that killed him."

Was he trying to put her on the defensive again? Once more, he'd chosen an incorrect tactic. "Where are you going with this, Alan?"

"Dr. Lidstone was right. You need to put aside your ego." He looked at her. His eyes were moist. "Prolonging Elizabeth's life won't help you atone for her father's death."

"One has nothing to do with the other."

"I'm sorry if my bluntness hurts, but I'm trying to be honest for Elizabeth's sake. You don't love her the way I do. What you're feeling is guilt, not love, and it isn't benefiting her. Think about her needs, not yours. Think about what *she* would want us to do. Would she really expect us to keep her shell alive when everything that made her the woman she once was is gone?"

The electronic noises from the monitors seemed loud all of a sudden. Delaney regarded Elizabeth's slack face as she considered what he'd said. On the surface, her stepdaughter was indeed gone, and yet . . . "She's still in there, Alan."

"Not according to the tests."

"You mean according to how Lidstone interpreted the data. The doctors on staff here have a different opinion."

"The clinic's staff may not be objective. You're the one who placed Elizabeth in this facility, and I understand you're paying a substantial fee to keep her here. The opinions you've heard from clinic employees could be motivated more by profit than by compassion."

"If there's an error, I'd rather it be on the side of caution."

"Dr. Lidstone is an impartial observer. He's also an expert in the field of brain injuries. I don't understand why you refuse to listen to him."

If she told Alan the truth, he wouldn't believe her. No one would, unless they had experienced it themselves the way she had. "There's more to the mind than science can presently explain," she said. "During times of extreme trauma, certain instincts can be triggered that tap abilities we never knew we had."

"If you're referring to feats of physical strength from a temporary burst of adrenaline, those are well documented. I can't see how it applies to Elizabeth's case."

"I'm talking about mental strength, not physical. The mind is the source of our survival. It's where the essence of our life resides. Thoughts may seem too intangible to be measured, but they have substance. They have energy. They're what build our reality."

He swept his arm toward the machines. "*This* is reality. Elizabeth's existence depends on technology. It's inhumane, as Dr. Lidstone said. Don't dismiss the message because you don't like the messenger."

"We can't give up yet."

"This is going into its fifth month. It's time to let go."

"Not yet."

"Then when? How much longer will you put her through this torture?"

"Why are you in such a hurry to speed her death?"

He smacked the bed rail and dropped his arm to his side. Impatience flashed across his face, along with something darker. His Ken-doll-perfect features suddenly turned sinister.

Delaney recoiled. She bumped into one of the chairs beneath the window before she was able to steady herself. She wasn't going to back down. Not as long as there was any other choice. "Elizabeth deserves a fighting chance. I intend to give it to her."

He compressed his lips.

"Don't ask me to put a time limit on her life, Alan. And what she has *is* life, no matter how your so-called expert interprets the test data."

He shrugged into his overcoat and put on his gloves in silence. When he'd finished, his handsome mask had settled back into place. "We'll talk about this at some other time, Delaney. We're both too emotional to discuss it now."

She nodded. It was a gesture meant to acknowledge his comment, not to agree.

He leaned over to press a kiss against Elizabeth's cheek.

"I'm sorry, sweetheart," he murmured. "I love you. I'll see you again next Saturday."

Elizabeth lay as motionless as a mannequin.

Alan sighed, squeezed her fingers, then walked to the door.

Delaney waited until he was gone before she groped behind her for the chair and sat. Her hands were shaking. She truly hated confrontations, but this one had been necessary.

The worst part of it was, there had been more than a thread of truth in what Alan had said. The clinic's staff might not be completely objective when it came to Elizabeth. The profit motive could play a part in the doctors' willingness to continue the status quo. Many of the nurses had also become genuinely fond of their patient over the past several months, so they wouldn't provide an impartial assessment, either. In addition, guilt did contribute to Delaney's determination to give her stepdaughter every possible chance to recover.

Alan was off base about the source of her guilt, though. She didn't need to atone for Stanford's death because he'd brought it on himself. But she was partly to blame for the present situation: Elizabeth was in this coma because she had taken a beating that had been meant for Delaney.

It wasn't your fault she was hurt, Deedee.

Delaney closed her eyes as her husband's voice stole into her mind. *Oh, Max. I can't help feeling responsible. She had never wanted to harm me. If only I'd trusted my instincts about her sooner. We might have realized the extent of the danger we were all in. The attack on her might not have happened.*

No one can predict the actions of a madman.

I know, but I should have recognized the difference between someone being evil and someone who's simply striking out in pain.

You did. You had faith in Elizabeth, no matter how she treated you. You've got nothing to feel guilty about.

She sighed. *Thanks, Max.*

Alan was trying to play you. She was lucky to have you in her corner.

It sounds as if you heard everything.

Yeah. You were great.

I didn't realize you were with me.

He slipped her a mental caress. *I'm always with you, Deedee.*

It was true. Distance and time made little difference to the power of their connection. She returned Max's caress, then looked at the figure on the bed. *I wish I knew how to reach her.*

If she's meant to find a way back, she will.

Are you getting philosophical on me, Max?

Hell no. I'm lonely and thinking about you *finding your way back.* He brushed a phantom kiss across her mouth. *When are you coming home?*

Her lips tingled. She sent him a smile that became an embrace, then turned her thoughts to the other occupant of the room. Had Elizabeth absorbed anything from the conversation that had taken place here earlier? Though it might seem cruel, Delaney hoped she had. Hearing people discuss the possibility of terminating her life might have more effect on her than all the music and books in the world.

FIVE

"ELIZABETH?"

She opened her eyes. The world was a blur. Her body was a mass of aches. Pain throbbed through her skull. She wanted nothing more than to go back to sleep.

"Hey." A hand settled on her shoulder. "Are you okay?"

She knew that voice. She squinted until the blur fused into a face. Large nose. Beard stubble on a square jaw. Eyes of amber that reached as deep as his music.

The pain ebbed. "Rick?"

"Yeah." He loomed over her. No, *loom* was the wrong word. He was kneeling at her side, and there was nothing threatening about his size. Even in the dim light, the concern on his face was plain. He touched her temple. "Does your head hurt? You've been drifting in and out."

She blinked a few times, giving herself a chance to take stock. Yes, her head hurt. The agony was there, but it was retreating to the background. She flexed her limbs carefully. Her joints were stiff, her muscles sore, as if she'd overdone it on the Bowflex and had neglected to cool down.

But those memories were from *before*, when her life was normal. Reality was different now. She knew in her bones that she wasn't yet home. A chill seeped through her back from the floor where she lay. She moved her foot, expecting to feel the slide of stone.

Instead, she felt dirt. Her feet were bare. She looked past

Rick. The walls were made of wood. So was the door. A pale strip of light seeped beneath it. The air was muggy rather than damp, and it was ripe with the scent of vegetation. Insects whirred. An animal she couldn't identify screeched in the distance.

They weren't in the dungeon anymore. They were in the hut in the jungle.

She attempted to rise when she discovered her wrists were bound together with a plastic bundling tie. Again. Or had they never been in manacles? She groaned.

Rick slid his arm beneath her shoulders and helped her sit up. "Sorry I couldn't get that band off your wrists," he said, as if he guessed what she'd been thinking. "There's no slack in that plastic. It's locked tight."

"Did you see them?"

"Who?"

"The people who brought us here. Who were they? What did they do to us? How did they transport us?"

"I don't know."

"But you were awake. You must have seen something."

"I only woke up once we were here. I heard men outside, talking in Spanish. Couldn't make out much of what they said, but I did pick out your name. They called you Isabella. Is this the place you talked about before? The camp with the rebel soldiers?"

"It must be. The hut's the same."

"Not much to see except dirt and wood, but it seems built as solid as that cell in the castle basement."

"Then you tried to get out?"

He stroked her hair from her cheek. "To tell you the truth, I've been more concerned about you than about where we are. Something strange is going on."

"Something strange? *Strange?* And what would that be? The fact that we seem to have been magically transported from a castle to a jungle camp with no knowledge or memory of what happened?"

"Yeah, that, too, but I was talking about you."

"How so?"

"Your shiner's gone."

"My what?"

"The black eye you got from the rock." He touched the corner of her eye. "The swelling's gone down. There's no bruise."

She explored it herself as much as she was able with her wrists bound. He was right, the eye had healed. She touched her neck. The scratch had healed, too. Again.

"There's nothing left of that stab wound from the sword in your side, either," he said.

"We must have been kept drugged for months."

"By nothing, I mean nothing. Not even a scar."

She lifted her arms and twisted to see her side. She was once more wearing the baggy trousers and linen shirt. Dirt smeared the fabric, but there was no blood. She hooked her little fingers on the hem of the shirt, meaning to pull it up so she could inspect the wound herself, when she registered what he'd said. "How do you know there's no scar?"

"How else? I checked."

She jerked her chin up. Her vision swam at the sudden movement. She inhaled through her teeth. "You examined me while I was unconscious?"

"I was worried. I thought it might have gotten infected or something and that was why you wouldn't wake up. Glad you're okay."

"Thanks."

"Beats me why you are, though. I saw that wound, and it was deep."

She inched sideways until she could turn her back to him. She raised her shirt. Whoever had changed their costumes had been as thorough as the last time. She was once again braless. Which meant other people besides Rick would have seen her bare breasts.

The realization was more than upsetting, it was humiliating. She was no prude, but she decided to whom she showed her body. She would have no control over what was done to her while she was unconscious. People could strip her, examine her as intimately as they wanted or dress her in whatever they chose and she would have no more say than a rubber doll or a mannequin. They could cart her from place to place like a piece of meat. They could do with her as they pleased and she couldn't stop them. She was completely helpless.

Tears flooded her eyes. Why was this happening to her? What had she done to deserve this? Was Delaney really behind it? Was she retaliating for the lawsuit? Elizabeth still couldn't picture her stepmother organizing anything this vast. No, the only person who might consider going to such lengths to get even was dead.

You defied the king.

She shivered, dismissing the thought before she could follow it. Her father was gone, he had no power over her anymore, and even he wouldn't have stooped to such melodramatic methods. Not for this long. Not without crowing about his cleverness. It had been all about the win with Stanford.

"Elizabeth?"

She blotted her eyes on her sleeve and shoved back the self-pity. She couldn't afford to get emotional. She was awake now and planned to stay that way.

"You're in pain, aren't you?"

"Nothing I can't handle." She focused on her side. The wound appeared to be gone, but the light in the hut was too dim for her to be sure there was no scar.

It didn't make sense. Had they used steroids on her? Is that why she'd healed so quickly? Or had they done plastic surgery to eliminate the evidence so they wouldn't be charged with assault causing bodily harm? Why bother doing either when they planned to execute her?

"For the record, I was only looking at your stab wound. I didn't deliberately look at anything else. But I guess that does as much good as saying I didn't inhale."

"Don't worry about it. Modesty is the least of my concerns." She let her shirt fall back into place. "How long have you been awake?"

"Hard to tell. All I know is it was darker than it is now."

"Then it must be nearing dawn."

"I suppose."

"The other time I was here, they said I would be shot at dawn."

"I won't let that happen."

She blotted her eyes again. She had to stop feeling sorry for herself. She was no longer the only victim of this outrage. "I owe you an apology."

"Why?"

"I involved you in my problems by singling you out at the castle. They imprisoned you with me because I asked you for help."

"Yeah, well, I haven't been much help so far."

"That's not true. Just knowing I'm not alone . . ." Her voice broke. She wasn't sure what she was going to say anyway. Tell him that his presence gave her strength and made her feel alive? Confess her weakness to a man she hardly knew?

They had decided the mental connection they'd experienced initially had been a fluke. There was no hint of it now. She had made assumptions about his character because of his music, but music wouldn't break them out of a locked building. Appealing for help from a minstrel hadn't been logical. It would have been more logical to seek out the help of the castle blacksmith. "How long do you think it is until sunrise?"

"A while. I'm not sure. My sense of time is out of whack."

"Tell me about it. I don't even know what day this is, let alone what month."

"I'm pretty sure it's the end of November."

"November?" She slid around to face him. "Impossible. That would mean they've kept me prisoner since the summer. Someone should have found me by now."

"Sorry, but summer's long gone. My brother had just put up the Christmas lights in the bar last time I played there. He does that every year right after Thanksgiving."

"The last thing I remember was being in Willowbank. It was mid-July."

"Never heard of Willowbank. Where is it?"

"Upstate New York."

"Is that where you're from?"

"Lord, no. I have a condo in Manhattan. Willowbank is the town where my stepmother lives. We had scheduled a meeting."

"In my family, we don't schedule meetings." He shrugged. His shirt stretched tightly across his shoulders. "We just sort of show up."

"My stepmother and I had legal matters to discuss." Her attention was caught by what he was wearing. She hadn't taken note of it before, probably because the clothes were so ordinary. The medieval tunic and leggings costume had been replaced by a plaid shirt and blue jeans. His resemblance to a desperado was stronger than ever: a pair of scuffed cowboy boots covered his feet. "Are those your real clothes?"

He considered her question. "Probably. They feel like it."

"Wouldn't you recognize them?"

"That's something else strange. I never thought much about the Robin Hood outfit while I was wearing it, not until you pointed it out. It seemed right at the time." He pinched a fold of his shirt. "Like Chester."

"Chester?"

"My horse. I didn't think much about that before, either, because it seemed right at the time, too, but I don't ride a horse to work. That would be crazy. I drive an F150. When it works, anyway. She's getting temperamental in her old age."

She regarded him blankly.

"The F150. It's a Ford pickup."

"But you said . . ." She pressed the heels of her hands to her forehead. "Do you actually own a horse?"

"Uh-huh, and his name actually is Chester, but I keep him at my parents' farm."

"Then why was he at the castle?"

"Whoever snatched me must have taken him, too, but that seems even harder to believe than the rest of this."

"We must have been given hallucinogens."

"Seems like it." He tugged her hands away from her face. "Whatever drugs they used are seriously messing with our minds. Things that shouldn't make sense, do make sense, the same way they do in dreams."

"You think any of this makes *sense*?"

"Maybe not the whole picture, but the details do."

"I can't believe anyone is mad enough to assume they'll get away with this."

"They're doing a good job of it so far." He turned her hands to one side and then the other while he scrutinized the strip of plastic around her wrists. "Elizabeth, why would anyone want to lock you up?"

"I wish I knew."

"You've been mixed up in this longer than I have, and you're the only one they've bothered to bind. Both times. You must be at the center of the trouble."

"Don't you think if I knew I would tell you? Do you think I volunteered to be treated like this? In the real world, I have respect. I have power. I have manicures and wear pearls and heels and *underwear*. Nobody pushes me around. If they try, they find out fast that I push back."

"I'll bet."

"And as soon as we get out of here, I won't rest until every single person who had any role in this kidnapping is caught and convicted and has to serve the maximum sentence allowed by law, even if it means I have to build the damn jail myself."

He rubbed his thumbs over the plastic tie. "What do you do, back in the real world?"

"I run Grayecorp. It's a property development company."

"In Manhattan?"

"That's where we're based, but we have interests all over the continent."

"Sounds like you're a regular Donald Trump."

"I'm not in his league. Not yet, that is."

"But you're rich, right?"

Not a fraction as wealthy as she would have been if her

father had lived long enough to follow through on his promise. Instead, Delaney had inherited the fortune she'd had no right to claim. But thinking of the events surrounding Stanford's accident was enough to bring back the headache. Elizabeth sucked air through her teeth again. "The definition of rich is relative."

"Only rich people would say that. If you're poor, it's as plain as the holes in your pockets. So you're loaded, aren't you?"

"I have money, yes. Enough to pay a substantial ransom, but no one appears willing to negotiate. Whoever's doing this to us doesn't seem to be motivated by profit."

"Well, if it's a ransom they're after, I can't help you there. I pick up extra cash working construction, but those jobs are pretty scarce at this time of year anyway, and with the economy the way it is, there's even less. By the time I split what I take in from my bar gigs with the guys who play backup for me, I don't clear much more than my rent money. Maybe I should ride Chester to work after all. He'd probably be more reliable than the truck, and hay would be cheaper than gas. I could strap my gear to the saddle and—" He broke off suddenly. "Hell, I should have thought of it before."

"What?"

"My gear." He released her hands and twisted to reach for something in the shadows at the base of the wall. When he straightened to face her once more, he was holding a guitar.

She started. "Where did that come from?"

"It was here when I woke up." He shifted to sit cross-legged and laid the instrument flat across his lap. He ran his thumb lightly over the strings.

"Is it yours?"

He tapped the body. "Absolutely. See those scratches?"

Four short, parallel lines dulled the gleam of the varnish. "Vaguely."

"That's where Daisy landed on it back when she was a puppy. She was chasing a cricket."

"You have a dog as well as a horse?"

"Yep. A dog, a horse, and a truck. I'm livin' every American boy's dream."

"Is she with your parents, too?"

"No, I don't take her out there much. She's scared of the barn cats." He turned one of the tuning pegs. "Most days she hangs out with my landlady almost as much as she hangs with me. Probably lying on the couch eating bonbons by now. You like dogs?"

"As I've had no experience with them, I neither like nor dislike them."

"You never wanted one? Not even when you were a kid?"

"There were many things I wanted as a child but I grew out of them," she said. Or to be more accurate, she grew out of the desire to ask for them. She frowned as he continued to fiddle with his guitar. "Since they brought your instrument with you, then they really did plan for you to play the part of a minstrel. Or in our current circumstances, a musician."

"I suppose so."

"You had a different instrument in the castle. Wasn't that one a lute?"

"That wasn't a lute, it was a balalaika."

"Was that yours as well?"

"Uh-huh. It belonged to a friend of mine I used to jam with. He was Russian, but he was into country. It's got an interesting sound, like a mandolin only richer. I don't use it as often as the guitar."

"As much as I enjoyed your music, we should be concentrating on planning our escape. We don't know how long we'll have before dawn—" She stopped when he chuckled. "This isn't funny, Rick."

"Sure, it is. You assumed I was fixing on serenading you instead of helping you."

"I wouldn't have put it like that."

"And you're figuring a guitar won't do us much good." He gave the tuning peg another twist. "Whoever left it here must have figured the same thing."

She realized he wasn't tightening the string, he was loosening it. As soon as there was enough slack to unhook it, he pulled it free, set the guitar aside, and yanked off his boots. When he pulled off his socks, her curiosity peaked. "What on earth are you doing?"

"The socks are for padding." He wrapped one sock over his knuckles and coiled one end of the guitar string around it. He repeated the procedure with his other hand, then shifted closer. "Hold out your arms."

"What? Why?"

"I'm going to saw off that plastic tie."

Realization dawned. The guitar string he had removed was one of the lower ones and was in fact a metal wire that had been wound with more metal. The tight ridges from the winding weren't sharp, but they would be much harder than plastic. She extended her arms immediately. "I'm sorry, Rick. I, ah, didn't know what to think."

"Uh-huh, you thought I was an idiot."

"Of course not. Quite the opposite. This is brilliant."

"Let's see if it works first. It may take a while." He angled one elbow between her arms, fitted the wire against the plastic, and drew it across. His arm bumped into her shoulder. "Could you turn sideways? I'll get better leverage."

She rotated so that her legs were perpendicular to his. After a few more bumps, she swung her legs across his thighs so that she could hold her wrists directly over his lap. "How's that?"

He uncoiled the wire from his right hand temporarily so that he could slip his arm beneath hers and bring it up between them. He did a few experimental strokes across the plastic, then settled into a firm, back-and-forth rhythm. As he'd warned, it did take a while—the ridged wire wore the plastic away rather than cut it—but eventually a groove did begin to form. "Okay," he said. "Looks like we're in business."

The progress was slow but steady. Elizabeth told herself to ignore the proximity of their bodies. It wasn't easy, because he was a large man. He smelled surprisingly good for someone who had been around a horse and had been tossed in a dungeon and a dirt-floored hut. As a matter of fact, he smelled as if they were in bed. She caught a whiff of cotton that reminded her of crisp, freshly laundered sheets. And his skin exuded a mellow, early-morning scent, reminiscent of a man still warm and relaxed from a night's sleep.

But the way he smelled was no more relevant than the way the muscles in his thighs flexed beneath hers, or the way his forearm came so close to her breasts on each down stroke that she could feel his body heat. Breasts that he'd seen naked. She glanced at his bent head. The hair at his nape had a slight curl to it and was long enough to fall partly over his collar. She didn't normally care for the look of long hair on a man, yet on Rick it seemed perfect. She could all too easily imagine how the curls would wrap around her fingertips . . .

"Does that hurt?"

"No. Why?"

"You moaned."

"Headache." She focused on the wire. It had begun to squeak as it moved across the plastic. The groove was deepening more quickly as it heated from the friction. The underside of her thighs were heating, too, from the contact with his legs. "This was creative thinking. I'm glad now that you're a Luddite."

"To be honest, I don't think all technology is evil. I've got nothing against power tools, only cell phones."

"And computers."

"Yeah, but I do love my TV remote."

"Apart from news broadcasts, I don't watch television."

"Say it ain't so. You don't watch TV? No *Jerry Springer*? No *Monday Night Football*?"

"I don't have time."

"Too busy talking on your BlackBerry with the rest of the Borg Collective?" His elbow rubbed along the upper crease of her thigh. "Oops. Sorry."

"I usually don't leave the office until after ten."

"Huh. Lots of nights that's when I start working."

"With your song-writing talent, I'm surprised you have to play in bars to make a living."

"Thanks, but my songs aren't exactly popular. Seems audiences like them better the drunker they get. A lot of the time I do covers of old standards so I don't get pelted with peanuts."

"Nonsense. Your songs are powerfully moving. Your melodies are haunting. You're also a very skillful musician. You should have an exceptional career."

He paused. "You know about music?"

"I studied piano in my youth." How simple a statement that was. It didn't begin to describe the long hours of daily practice or the years of devotion. Or how precious that dream had once been. Another example of a desire she grew out of.

"I used to wish I could play the piano when I was a kid, but this old guitar was all my folks could afford." He resumed sawing. "Just as well, because I wouldn't be able to take a piano with me when I went to gigs, 'specially if I start going green and use Chester instead of the truck. What kind of music did you play? Ten to one it was the stuffy stuff."

"I wouldn't put it like that. Many of the men we consider classic composers were the rock stars of their day, quite scandalous and cutting edge. Don't you like classical music?"

"Can't say as I ever listened to it much."

"Don't let the packaging drive you off. The passion comes through, whatever format is being used. Good music is universal. It has the ability to take you out of yourself."

"Take you out of yourself," he repeated. "That's a good way to put it. That's pretty well what mine does for me."

"I believe music does even more than that. It's a kind of sharing that crosses all boundaries, whether they're time or place or genre. I learned to play the classics, so that's what moves me the most easily. Any emotion you can name has been expressed by the masters, and they do it on a level beyond words. When it's right, it can slip straight past your conscious thoughts and . . ." She trailed off when she realized he had stopped sawing again. "What?"

"It's good to hear you talk about emotions. Most of the time you seem to avoid them."

"They have their place."

"Uh-huh?"

"They're an integral part of the best music. However, they're counterproductive in crisis situations."

"You ever get a melody in your head that you can't get out? Like, if you hear a song first thing in the morning, you're stuck with it for the rest of the day?"

"From time to time. Why?"

"It's as useless to ignore what you're feeling. Seems to me you might as well give in and hum along." He dropped the guitar string, fitted a hand around each of her wrists, and gave them a sharp tug.

The plastic bundling tie snapped and fell off.

Her hands were free.

Finally. Yes. Yes. *Yes!*

The relief that crashed through her was out of all proportion to the situation. Regaining the use of her hands wouldn't matter if she and Rick couldn't find a way out of their prison. They weren't yet out of danger. This wasn't over.

But he'd given her hope. That was more than she'd had an hour ago. From what she understood, it was more than she'd had in months. She wiggled her fingers, delighting in the simple ability to move as she wanted. She was no longer completely helpless. "Thank you, Rick."

He smiled. It was a full-face smile, not a one-sided quirk of his lips. The corners of his eyes crinkled. His cheeks lifted. And to the left of his mouth, a dimple appeared. "You're welcome, Lady Elspeth Isabella Elizabeth."

She flexed her fingers again, then touched his dimple. His beard stubble was softer than she would have expected. It rasped sensuously against her skin. She wondered what it would feel like against her lips.

Which was an incredibly inappropriate thought. As she'd told him, she shouldn't allow herself to get emotional. They were in a life-and-death situation, and even if they weren't, she certainly shouldn't consider kissing him, no matter how enjoyable it would be to, well, hum along as he put it. The more time they spent together, the more obvious it was that they had nothing whatsoever in common. In the real world, they probably would have never met.

His smile faded. "Do you hear that?"

All she could hear was her heartbeat. She dropped her hand. He couldn't have heard her thoughts, could he? "What?"

He tilted his head. "It sounds like a helicopter."

She held her breath so that she could listen. There was a distant throb. It was unmistakably mechanical, and it was growing louder fast. It wasn't long before the ground beneath her vibrated in time with the engine.

They weren't the only ones who had noticed the noise. Men's voices came from outside. Footsteps pounded past the hut. Someone shouted orders in Spanish. Within seconds, the entire camp was abuzz with activity.

Rick yanked on his socks and boots.

"What's going on?" she asked.

"From what I can make out of what they're saying, they think it's a raid."

"A raid? As in police?"

"Or the army." The noise of the helicopter increased rapidly. It seemed to be coming from directly above the camp. Rick raised his voice. "Either one's good news for us as long as we don't get caught in a—"

His words were drowned out by a rapid burst of gunfire from overhead.

"Cross fire!" he yelled. "Get down!"

Elizabeth didn't have the chance to absorb what he said before his body slammed into hers, knocking her on her back.

Bullets tore through the roof. Splinters flew from the walls. Rick dragged himself on top of her as dust and wood chips rained down on them.

Answering gunfire erupted from everywhere as the guerrillas or drug smugglers or whatever they were fought back. There was a high-pitched whistle that ended in an explosion.

The ground shook. Men screamed. More explosions followed as rapidly as the gunfire. Soon a new noise joined the din: the whooshing crackle of flames. Black smoke wafted into the hut through the bullet holes.

Elizabeth struggled for air. Her vision dimmed. Frantic to stay conscious, she pushed at Rick's shoulders. "Let me up!"

"It's not safe." He cupped his hand protectively over the top of her head. "We need to stay put until the firing stops."

"No! The smoke! I can't breathe!"

He couldn't have heard her. The battle that raged around them was too loud.

She fisted her hand to pound his back, but didn't have the strength to lift her arm. The energy she'd awakened with had dwindled. It wasn't the smoke that was sapping her strength. The darkness that spread over her was coming from within.

It was happening again. She was slipping away. She splayed her fingers, trying to stay with him. "Rick, please, don't let me go to sleep! I have to stay awake!"

Her plea went unanswered. He couldn't hear her. She couldn't even hear herself over the earsplitting noise. Another explosion shook the ground. The wall beside them burst inward. The bullet-riddled roof collapsed, burying them under a pile of burning debris.

Rick! Get up!

He didn't move. A roof beam lay across his shoulders. His body was a dead weight on hers.

The void opened. Elizabeth screamed her resistance. *No!* She couldn't give up now. Rescue was within reach. She knew it. She felt it. All she had to do was stay alive. Someone was bound to find them.

ALAN CHECKED HIS WATCH, THEN AIMED THE REMOTE AT the TV on the wall to switch off the news and pushed himself out of the chair. He needed to get moving if he was going to make the game. The Rangers were playing the Bruins tonight and Grayecorp had season tickets on the blue line. He wasn't much of a hockey fan himself, but Sherri Stock was Canadian so what else could he expect? She also happened to be the only daughter of a man who owned a very lucrative gold mine.

Alan considered himself quite accomplished in the art of seducing poor little rich girls, but being shackled to Elizabeth cramped his style. If he'd been free to pursue Sherri openly, he would have had her in his bed months ago, but playing the sympathy card was slow work. The main reason he'd managed to get as far with her as he had was because she was impressed by his devotion to his fiancée. She was also impressed by his choice of fiancée. Sherri's father had begun as a common prospector, wandering around the wilds of Northern Quebec, before he'd struck it rich. Her family had wealth, but no roots or pedigree like Elizabeth's. Sherri was intelligent enough, but she had no competitive streak; she was more like a guppy than a shark. He suspected she felt flattered by his attention, since any comparison between the two women wouldn't favor Sherri. She couldn't open the doors Elizabeth could, or provide access to the kind of power that controlling Grayecorp would give him.

But Alan was at the point where he couldn't afford the luxury of being choosy. His expenses were mounting. So were the threats from Jamal. He needed to hedge his bets. Unlike the turnip he was still engaged to, Sherri was fully capable of signing a check.

"Damn you, Elizabeth," he muttered, pulling on his coat. "I've given you more time than you deserve. You've got no right to do this to me."

He eyed the equipment that monitored her continuing life. The hums and beeps were getting on his nerves. They were as relentless as she used to be. Too bad Lidstone got scared off by Delaney—pulling the plugs would have been the perfect solution, particularly if someone else had done it. Even the fraction of Elizabeth's estate Alan would get through a palimony suit would have been better than nothing. He shifted his gaze to the bed. "Why can't you just die?"

She moved her hand.

Alan froze. He couldn't have seen what he'd thought he had. It must have been an optical illusion, or maybe a reflection of his own hand in the metal bed rail. He rubbed his face and looked again.

There was no mistake. Elizabeth was holding her right hand an inch above the mattress.

Alan glanced behind him to make sure the door of her room was shut, then stepped closer to the bed. He kept his arms at his sides. "Elizabeth?"

Her breathing became ragged. Her body stiffened with her efforts to keep her hand in the air.

The occasional twitches he'd witnessed during his previous visits were nothing compared to what he was seeing now. She had never moved her hand before. This didn't appear to be the result of an involuntary reflex. The gesture seemed deliberate. It was more life than she'd displayed since July.

Could Delaney be right? Was it possible for Elizabeth to wake up? Hell, if she did, there was little chance of Sherri taking out her checkbook. He'd assured her that his fiancée's death was imminent. He needed time to consider a fallback position. He also had better watch what he said around Elizabeth. "Can you hear me, darling?"

She spread her fingers, as if she were grasping for something. An alarm dinged from the direction of the monitors.

Alan glanced over his shoulder again, then grabbed her hand and pushed it back to the bed.

She put up no resistance. Whatever strength she'd managed to dredge up appeared to desert her. Her hand went limp. Her body relaxed.

So did his. By the time the door swung open behind him, the sounds from the monitors had reverted to their typical monotonous pattern. "Mr. Rashotte! What's going on?"

Alan blanked his expression before he looked at the nurse. It was Beryl tonight, one of the older ones. He didn't like her. She was too rigid. She reminded him of a traffic cop. "Hello, Beryl. I didn't see you when I came in. Is something wrong?"

"There was a sudden increase in Miss Graye's heart rate."

She went to the other side of the bed to take Elizabeth's pulse. "Didn't you hear the alarm?"

"An alarm? No, I don't think so. What's wrong with her heart?"

Beryl didn't reply immediately. She frowned at the monitors. "Nothing, now. Her pulse rate appears to be back to normal."

"That's odd."

"Yes, it is. Didn't you notice anything unusual a few minutes ago?"

He shook his head. "I'm afraid I didn't."

"Any agitation? Any movement?"

"She was the same, no change. Could those machines be malfunctioning?"

Her frown deepened. "I'll make a note to have the technician check the equipment in the morning."

"That's reassuring. Elizabeth's so dependent on them, I'd hate to think what could happen if they break down."

"Are you certain you didn't see any change in her?"

"Sorry, no. Not a thing."

SIX

"HEY, BUDDY, ANYONE HOME IN THERE?"

Rick Denning ducked to the side before Jethro's knuckles could connect with his head. Rapping on his skull as if it were a door had been funny when they'd been kids. Not so much now. He squinted at his brother. "What's up?"

Jethro rapped on the bar instead. "I've been talking to you for the past five minutes. You turning into a zombie or something?"

"Wouldn't surprise me."

"Rough day?"

"Yeah, I guess." Rick hadn't rolled out of bed until nearly four this afternoon, which meant he'd slept a full eight hours. In spite of that, he didn't feel rested. He'd had another dream about the woman, and this one had ended worse than the last one. It had been so vivid, he'd actually gone to the mirror over the bathroom sink to check himself for burns and bullet holes when he'd finally gotten up.

It was crazy. He'd understood it had only been a dream once he was awake, but while he'd been asleep, he'd been convinced it was real.

"You better get it together." Jethro picked up a towel to polish a glass. "You're on in fifteen."

"Sure, no problem." Rick hooked two fingers around the neck of his beer bottle and swiveled on his stool to survey the room.

Jethro didn't believe in wasting a lot of money on lighting so it was hard to do a head count, but there appeared to be a fair-sized crowd. The previous owner had dubbed the place the Cantina and had been responsible for decorating it with stucco walls and fake wood beams. Jethro had added the sound system and the raised platform that served as a stage. He claimed he liked to give local musicians a chance to showcase their talents. In fact, he featured no-names because they worked cheap.

He couldn't picture Elizabeth coming to a place like this. Not that there was anything wrong with the bar, it just wouldn't be her style. A woman like her would be hanging out at country clubs or concert halls. Probably would prefer champagne and caviar to beer and peanuts.

But she had no likes or dislikes, he reminded himself. No matter how detailed his recollection of her was, she was only a dream, a by-product of working on the new songs until dawn and dozing off in front of the TV. That was probably where his subconscious had snagged the background for his latest dream: the top news story for the past week had been the kidnapping of a group of farm workers by a Colombian drug gang. Tragically, the hostages hadn't survived the army's rescue attempt.

He didn't have a clue why he'd dreamed he'd been in a castle, though. That was just weird.

A tall, skinny figure wove through the tables toward the bar. Rick nodded a greeting as he drew closer. "Evening, Zeb."

At twenty-two, Zebadiah was Jethro's oldest kid. He had the unruly hair and unique gold brown eyes that marked most of the Denning males. He was still too young to have filled in to his height so he bore an unfortunate resemblance to a grasshopper. He hitched himself onto a stool and did his best to adopt the casual slouch it had taken years for Rick to perfect. "Hi, Uncle Rick. I've got some good news."

"I could use some."

"I got your website up and running."

"Uh, great. Thanks." He lifted his beer in a toast. The

website had been Zeb's idea. He'd started up a website design and computer repair business in his parents' garage. Rick didn't go near computers if he could help it. He didn't even use bank machines. Then again, he'd need to have money in a bank account to use an ATM. "Now what?"

"I set up a program so we can sell your CDs online."

"Sounds complicated."

"There's nothing to it. The program takes the orders. All we need to do is mail out the CDs once the payment goes through. That way Dad won't be able to skim off any more of your profits."

"Hey, wait a minute," Jethro broke in. "Charging a commission isn't skimming. It's a fair deal for letting him sell the CDs in my bar instead of out of the back of his truck."

"How much will the postage cost?" Rick asked Zeb.

"Less than half what Dad gouges you for. We won't need to pay any postage to sell digital downloads, but I haven't finished setting that up yet. I'll try to have it going by the end of the week."

"How can you trust those online deals anyway?" Jethro went on. "All those numbers flying around cyberspace. They're liable to end up in Timbuktu. Nothing's going to replace good, old-fashioned cash money."

"Don't be paranoid, Dad. You've got to move with the times."

"Yeah, Jethro," Rick said. "Don't be a Luddite."

"What's a Luddite?"

"Someone who doesn't like technology," he replied.

"Bet you made that up."

"It's what Elizabeth called me. Luddites go back to the industrial revolution."

"Who's Elizabeth?"

"He must mean Great Aunt Betsy. It sounds like something she would say."

"Not her. She's . . ." Rick stopped. He wasn't contemplating telling his brother about the dream woman, was he? If he did, he'd never hear the end of it. "Forget it."

"Elizabeth, huh? Sounds classy." Jethro reached across

the bar to punch Rick's arm. "So that's why you've been dragging your butt lately. You've found better things to do than sleep."

Zeb's foot slipped off the rung of his stool and thudded to the floor. "Have you got a *girlfriend*, Uncle Rick?"

Rick winced at their shock as much as from Jethro's blow. "No."

"Then who's Elizabeth?"

He shrugged. "Just someone I met."

"Hey, Zeb, how about checking the connection on the mike," Jethro said. "It was crackling yesterday. Could be you overloaded the circuit with those Christmas lights."

"Sounded fine to me, Dad."

Jethro tipped his head to the side a few times.

"Oh, sure." Zeb stood. "Now I remember."

Rick watched him go, then held up his palm before his brother could get started. "Don't."

"It's been four years, buddy."

No, it had been three years, seven months, and seventeen days. "Not yet."

"Who's Elizabeth?"

"You wouldn't know her."

"You dating her?"

"Trust me, that's not going to happen."

"Why not? You can't live in the past forever."

"You're one to talk. I don't see you asking Zeb to build you a website."

"That's not what I meant. If I found out it was a woman who was cutting into your zees I'd be the first one to congratulate you."

"Drop it, Jethro."

"You've got plenty of opportunity. Haven't you noticed the way some of the chicks in the audience watch you when you sing?"

"They're watching Dwayne. The guy twirls a mean drumstick."

"That's what I figured at first, too, but you're getting your own set of groupies."

"I'm not interested."

"They probably won't be, either, once they get a good look at you. The light in here isn't that great so they can't tell how ugly you really are. You should take advantage of it."

Rick set his beer down, reached across the bar and fisted one hand in the front of Jethro's shirt. "I told you to leave it alone."

"Hey, I'm trying to look out for you, little brother."

"You're being a pain in the ass, old man."

"Better let go of my shirt if you want to keep your fingers."

"Tough talk. My fingers are safe as long as you're making a profit off them."

"Would it kill you to go on a date?"

"Geez, Jethro." He released his grip. "Now you're sounding like Ma."

"Does she know about Elizabeth?"

"Dammit, even *I* don't know about her."

"What's that mean?"

"When I figure it out, I'll let you know. Why are you hassling me about this now, anyway? I've got a show to do."

"That's something else that would improve if you had a woman now and then."

"How's that?"

"Your songs are too damn depressing."

"They're country. They're supposed to be sad."

"Sure, but there's a difference between lost-my-dog sad and I'm-goin'-out-back-to-eat-my-Winchester sad."

Rick grunted. "No use practicing your bartender psychology on me, pal. I'm the first one to admit I've got space for rent upstairs."

"It's not your upstairs that's your problem, if you get my drift."

"Does Josie know you talk like that?"

"She loves it when I talk like that. How'd you think we got all these kids?"

"Is that right? Funny how none of them looks like you."

The statement was too blatantly false to get more than a snort out of Jethro. He and Josie had been together since they had met in the eighth grade. They'd gotten started on Zeb before they'd finished high school and had proceeded to add more branches to the Denning family tree ever since. The latest twig would have his first birthday in January. They were one big, happy, loving family. Christmas at their place was going to be bedlam.

Rick was glad for them. He really was. He retrieved his beer and chugged the remaining mouthful a little too fast. It backed up in his throat, providing as good an excuse as any for the moisture in his eyes.

"Hey, go easy, bud. You've got a show."

Right. He had a show. He had his music. That was enough. It was all he'd needed for the past three years, seven months, and seventeen days.

Elizabeth's image flashed into his mind. Wild, blonde hair. Fierce expression. Attitude up the wazoo and blue eyes full of pain.

You have to help me. I want to live!

The words he'd heard her say when he'd first seen her still echoed in his head. But they served to prove she was merely a figment of his imagination.

Rick Denning was the last person a real woman would ask for help.

"On your feet, minstrel."

Rick struggled toward consciousness. His head was fuzzy, as if he'd just gotten to sleep. Must have played one set too many last night. He opened his eyes blearily.

This wasn't his bedroom. It was too dark, and it smelled wrong. Like stone.

Someone's boot nudged him in the ribs. "Minstrel."

The room slowly came into focus. Stone walls, stone floor, a floor-to-ceiling iron grate at the front. He recognized this place. It was the cell beneath the castle, same as before, only the door stood open.

His mind lurched into gear. He wasn't home. He must have only dreamed that. The last thing he remembered, he'd been locked in a wooden hut while all hell had broken loose outside. He'd tried to protect Elizabeth but the roof had fallen in and . . .

Elizabeth. He jerked upright.

The bearded guard named Ganulf stood in front of him. Another held a torch above Elizabeth's pallet. She was lying on her back, her eyes closed, her hair a splash of gold in the torchlight. The rag that Rick had tied around her midriff to hold the makeshift bandage in place was still there. The bruise above her eye and the manacles that had bound her wrists were not. Her arms lay limp at her sides.

The second guard leaned over, grabbed Elizabeth's shoulder, and shook it hard enough to make her head thump against the straw that filled the pallet.

"Hey! Leave her alone," Rick said, springing upright.

Ganulf raised his sword to block his path. "Halt."

"Tell your man to lay off. He's got no cause to get rough."

"Theobold," Ganulf said over his shoulder. "We cannot tarry."

"Lady Elspeth will not awaken," the guard said.

"'Tis a ruse."

"Nay, she appears dead."

No! Without thinking, Rick ducked under Ganulf's sword blade and fell to his knees beside Elizabeth. He pressed his ear to her chest.

They were wrong. Her heart was still beating. He exhaled the breath he'd been holding and glared at the guard who had shaken her. "Theobold. Is that your name?"

The man nodded.

"Can't you see she's hurt?"

"It is not your concern," Ganulf said. "On your feet. The king awaits."

"The king? Great. Then maybe he'll clear up this mess."

"What of Lady Elspeth?" Theobold asked.

"Leave her," Ganulf ordered. "The baroness is almost upon us. We must make haste."

Rick stretched his arm across Elizabeth's body. "No way. I'm not going anywhere without her. She needs . . ." He was about to say *me*, and that stuck in his throat. "A doctor," he said. "She needs medical attention."

Ganulf gestured toward the door with his sword. "Do not try my patience. You will tell the king all you know of the baroness's army."

"And I'm telling you again, you've got the wrong guy. I don't know any baroness."

"Rick?"

He returned his gaze to Elizabeth in time to see her open her eyes.

Her gaze slid into his mind, reaching him on a level that bypassed his senses.

God, she was beautiful. Stupid time to think of it. Even dumber to be affected by her beauty in the first place. He was a thirty-one-year-old man, not some hormone-driven adolescent, yet wherever they were, *when*ever they were, he enjoyed looking at this woman. And there was something about the way she looked at him that made him want to smile inside. As if they shared a secret, like music that no one else could hear.

He stroked the hair from her forehead. The strands slid like silk beneath his callused fingertips. "Hey there. How're you feeling?"

"Fine, I think." She blinked a few times. "Rick? You're okay?"

"Sure, but—"

"Bring her."

At Ganulf's voice, Elizabeth's gaze sharpened. She looked past Rick.

He saw the exact moment when she realized where they were. Confusion flickered across her face, followed by despair. "The fire," she said. "The gunshots. The hut collapsed on top of us. How . . ."

"I don't understand how we got out, or how we got back here." He took her hand to help her sit up. "But at least we're alive. How's your side?"

She touched it briefly, then slid her hand to his shoulder. "It's all right. What about you? Your back. Were you burned?"

"No. I—" He was about to tell her that he'd checked in the mirror, but he couldn't have. There was no mirror in here. "I'm still in one piece."

There was no opportunity for more questions. The guards prodded them out of the dungeon and led them upward through the maze of hallways and storerooms. Elizabeth was wobbly on her feet at first, but steadied when he slid his arm around her waist. As they walked, she seemed to gain strength from his support. He was relieved to find that the blood on her dress had dried, and no new blood seeped through the bandage.

But the wound had been gone altogether when they'd been in the jungle hut, hadn't it?

His mind stumbled over the thought. A roof had fallen on top of him, he'd felt a burning beam strike him across the shoulders and tear through his shirt, yet he could detect nothing wrong with his back now. How could they have sustained the injuries they had and survive? It didn't seem possible . . . and yet the stone beneath his feet was indisputably solid. So were the walls he was walking past. So was the woman who walked at his side. Her warmth seeped into his flesh. Strands of her loose hair tickled his chin while the faint scent of spices teased his nose. What he felt when he was with her was genuine. It mattered. He couldn't question the validity of her presence any more than he could question his own.

The guards ushered them into a large hall. Rick squinted at the change in brightness. Sunlight poured inside from narrow windows near the ceiling. At the far end of the room, there was a dais with a long, wooden table. A massive chair, or maybe a throne, sat in the middle of the dais. It was empty. The rest of the room was filled with chaos. People scurried across the rushes that covered the floor. A few were likely servants, since they carried earthenware jugs and baskets of what could have been bread. The rest were soldiers carrying everything from crossbows to axes and barbed spears. The nasty-looking weapons could have come straight from the set of *Braveheart*.

A gray-haired man sporting a metal breastplate separated from the crowd and jogged toward Ganulf. "Captain, we need more men at the walls."

"Where is the scouting party?" Ganulf asked.

"They did not return. We fear the worst."

"And the king?"

The man nodded toward a staircase that rose along one wall. "He could wait for you no longer. He has retired to the keep."

A deep thud vibrated through the floor. The activity in the room suspended momentarily as people paused to listen. A second thud followed. It was accompanied by a screeching crack and the clang of metal on metal.

A blood-spattered soldier burst into the room. "To the gates!" he cried. "They have come through!"

Pandemonium broke out. The servants scattered. Half the soldiers raced outside while the other half pressed around Ganulf for orders.

Rick didn't wait to see more. This was beginning to seem too familiar, and he'd already had his fill of getting caught in a cross fire. Taking advantage of the guards' momentary distraction, he tightened his grip on Elizabeth and joined the stream of retreating servants.

"The prisoners!" Ganulf shouted. "Stop them!"

Rick leaned to the side, levering part of Elizabeth's weight on his hip, and continued their progress across the floor. Her body trembled against his as she attempted to match his increased pace, but it wasn't enough. Heavy footsteps pounded behind them.

Rick didn't waste time looking back. He scooped Elizabeth into his arms and ran for the nearest door.

The courtyard was a mass of moving bodies. The huge gates at the castle entrance hung in broken shreds. Beyond them stood a machine of wood and iron that appeared to be a cross between a battering ram and a catapult. Swords and axe blades glinted in the sunshine as soldiers fought to hold back the invading army. Everyone who wasn't fighting was running for cover. Rick wedged into the melee, counting on the crowd to hide them from their pursuers.

Elizabeth locked her arms around his neck. "Where are you going?"

"We need to take shelter."

"No! We should go to the other army. They'll take us out of here."

An arrow whizzed past his ear. He ducked his head. "They don't seem too friendly to me."

"It's our chance to get away. They'll take us home."

"They're using crossbows."

"Yes, but—"

"Not guns. They have the same weapons as Ganulf and his pals."

"Oh, God! That means they're part of this delusion!"

"That's what I figure. We can't count on anyone helping us. We need to—"

"Rick, watch out!"

A burning ball of pitch arced through the air. It landed on the platform that held the gallows, spattering flames and panic across the crowd. Another fireball hit the roof of the stable. The thatch went up like a torch. Billows of black smoke blocked the sun. The screams of people mixed with the screams of horses.

Rick changed direction, heading straight for the fire.

Elizabeth struggled in his grasp. "What are you doing?"

"Chester's in there. I can hear him." He set her on her feet beside an overturned cart. "Get under this. I'll be right back."

"Rick, no! Wait!"

He caught her face in his hands. "Trust me, Elizabeth. I'll take care of you, I promise."

"But—"

He stopped her protest with a kiss. It was swift and hard and over in a heartbeat. It was a stupid, reckless thing to do. So was the promise. He knew better than to give his word to any woman.

Yet there was nothing logical about his feelings for *this* woman. He hardly knew her, yet he wanted to taste her smile and watch her laugh and lay his head against her breast to listen to her heartbeat again. He wanted to press his nose to the crook of her neck to smell the spices on her skin, and push his hands into her hair and feel those golden strands slide through his fingers. He wanted to hold her presence in his mind and share her senses like they had for that one glorious moment when they'd met . . .

But first, he had to do what she'd asked him. He had to help her live.

Rick pushed Elizabeth beneath the shelter of the cart, yanked his tunic over his head to keep off the sparks, and plunged into the smoke.

SEVEN

A TWIG SCRATCHED ACROSS HER BARE SHIN. ELIZABETH started awake, her arms reflexively tightening around Rick's waist. The monotonous gait of the horse must have lulled her to sleep. Much to her relief, she had fallen into only a shallow doze this time, not the mind-numbing oblivion she'd come to dread. She hoped that meant her strength was returning.

She unlocked her hands long enough to tug a fold of her skirt over her leg, then resumed her grip on Rick's tunic.

"Sorry about that branch," he said. "The trail's been getting narrower."

She lifted her head from his back to survey their surroundings. In spite of their desire to put as much distance as possible between them and the castle, Rick had reduced their pace to a walk when they'd entered this forest. She assumed they were still in it, since large trees pressed close on either side of them, although she couldn't see past the trunks. Thick fog must have descended on them while she'd dozed. It shrouded everything further away than a few yards. It deadened sound, too. She couldn't hear any birds or animals or rustling leaves, only their own voices and the rhythmic thud of the horse's hooves on the earth.

It was eerie, as if the outside world had disappeared. Or hadn't yet formed. Reality consisted of only the space immediately around them, giving the illusion they were making it up as they went along. "How far do you think we've come?" she asked.

"We only got a few miles into the forest before we ran into the fog. Since then, it's hard to tell whether we're making any progress."

"Do you recognize anything?"

"Not yet."

"Any sign of a road or house?"

"Nope, although in this soup we could walk right past one and not see it."

"That's not good."

"Might not matter. I've been watching the trail pretty carefully, and I haven't noticed any candy wrappers or empty pop cans or shotgun shells. I'm guessing we're a long way from a town anyway."

"It sounds as if you're using litter to judge our position."

"More like the lack of litter. A trail this clean couldn't be near civilization."

"I see your point."

"On the positive side, I haven't heard anyone following us, so that's good news."

She twisted to look behind them, but the fog swallowed everything as soon as they went by. She wouldn't be able to retrace their steps if she wanted to. Not that she did. She'd had enough of being kept prisoner. She never wanted to experience that total helplessness again. She returned her cheek to Rick's back. His tunic smelled like smoke, and it bore a few charred holes on the shoulder, reminders of how narrow their escape from the castle had been.

There had been blood and death all around them. Brutal, nightmarish death. People were being struck by arrows or hacked by swords, or trampled underfoot during the panic as the fire spread. She hung on to him a little tighter.

"I'm figuring Ganulf and his boys were too busy to chase us," he went on. "They didn't seem to be doing that good when we left."

She agreed; it was unlikely any of the guards had bothered to follow them. The people who had held them captive had been losing the battle. The soldiers had been breaking ranks, their resistance crumbling under the force of the invaders. She would probably be dead now, if not for Rick sweeping her onto his horse and galloping to freedom like . . .

Like a knight in shining armor.

God, where had that thought come from? It was inappropriate on so many levels. Yes, his rescue had been dramatic, and yes, she'd asked him for help, and she was incredibly grateful he'd saved her life, but their alliance was one of necessity, that was all. There was nothing romantic about it.

And this chestnut-colored horse could never be mistaken for a knight's noble steed. In fact, Chester didn't belong to any breed she recognized. He had short, sturdy legs, a wide, squat body and oversized ears reminiscent of a mule's. She'd learned to ride before she'd reached her teens—the ability to handle a horse properly was a requisite skill at the private schools she'd attended—yet Chester was as different from the well-bred mounts she was familiar with as his master was from the men she was accustomed to seeing.

Her mind faltered at that thought, too. She wasn't *seeing* Rick, not in that sense. Nevertheless, she had grown to like him. His lazy drawl couldn't hide his quick mind. He was inventive and practical, and he had a dry sense of humor that she had to admit was enjoyable. Their current situation was bound to raise her physical awareness of him. Riding double without even a saddle between them forced their bodies into constant contact. The strain of holding herself apart from him had proved too much, and now her breasts bumped against his back and the inside of her thighs rubbed his hips with practically every step the horse took.

With anyone else, the prolonged proximity would be making her uncomfortable. With Rick, though, it was different. She didn't feel as if he was infringing on her personal space. How could she set physical boundaries when she'd already felt him join her in her mind?

But they'd decided that . . . episode when they'd first met had been a fluke. Nothing but adrenaline and the aftereffect of drugs. It hadn't happened since. She shouldn't spare it another thought.

"Are you okay?"

"Why do you ask?"

"It sounded like you moaned. Is the jarring making your headache worse?"

"If that's why you're going so slowly, don't. Not on my account."

"Can't go faster in this fog or I risk laming Chester. If your head's bothering you, you can try sitting in front of me for a while. I could keep you steadier if I hold you."

It was a logical suggestion. Considerate, too, which was the type of gesture she'd come to expect from Rick. But if she took him up on it, it would be purely out of pleasure, not need. His rangy muscles were deceptively strong. The mere idea of being held in his arms again was making her pulse accelerate. Almost as much as his kiss had.

No, she wasn't going to think about that kiss, either.

The list of things she needed *not* to think about was growing at a disturbing rate. Since when had she avoided facing problems head-on?

Yet the challenges she encountered and dealt with on a daily basis in the real world pertained to business, not to her personal relationships, and she took care to ensure one didn't interfere with the other. Eye on the prize, as her father used to say. She had neither the time nor the inclination to indulge in navel-gazing. Analyzing her feelings was as foreign to her as . . . well, as being dressed as a medieval damsel and escaping a pillaged castle with a cowboy minstrel.

"Elizabeth? Is the headache bad?"

"My head's fine," she replied automatically. With surprise she realized she had spoken the truth. The pain had been so persistent, she had learned to push it to the background a lot of the time. She hadn't noticed when it had actually disappeared. "It's really fine."

"Could be the fresh air. Being cooped up in a prison cell's not healthy."

"Yes, and maybe the drugs are finally wearing off."

"You still figure we were drugged, huh?"

"It's the only explanation."

"I guess."

"We didn't get the chance to discuss it before, but do you remember anything about how we got from the jungle camp to the castle?"

"No. I only woke up a few minutes before you did."

"And you didn't see anyone else? You didn't hear anything?"

He was silent as he guided Chester across a shallow stream. "I'm not sure," he said finally.

"What does that mean?"

"I seem to remember being home for a while and playing at the bar, but the memory's hazy. I probably only dreamt that. What about you? Do you remember anything before you woke up in the dungeon?"

She lifted her hand from his waist.

"Elizabeth?"

She extended her fingers, grasping for the empty air, then frowned and folded her hand into a fist. Why had she done that? "I'm not sure. I'm relieved they didn't put the manacles back on. I hated not being able to use my hands."

"Yeah. A guitar string wouldn't have worked on that iron. The castle guys sure were into the whole Middle Ages thing."

"Yes, they were very authentic. I've heard of method acting, but—"

"They weren't actors, Elizabeth."

"We don't know for sure."

"That battle wasn't staged by some special effects department. The arrows that were zipping past our heads were as real as we are. So were those gates and that battering ram. The people who got hit bled. They weren't pretending. Unless they got airlifted to a nearby ER, most of them aren't going to make it."

She shivered. "What do you think is happening? A mass delusion? Was that a medieval times cult's version of drinking the poisoned Kool-Aid?"

"I honestly don't know what to think. The only thing I'm sure of is that we're both damn lucky to be alive."

"Thanks to you."

"Chester's instincts deserve most of the credit. He's the one who navigated us clear of the castle." He patted the horse's neck. "All we did was go along for the ride."

"You went into a burning stable for him. He owes you for his life as much as I do."

"Nah, he's smart. That's one thing about Chester; he's a survivor. He would have found his way out."

"Why are you downplaying what you did?"

"I got lucky, that's all. Besides, if I took credit for the good luck, I'd have to take the blame for the bad."

"Nevertheless, you thought quickly and acted very courageously, both here and in the last . . . place, scenario, whatever-it-was, during the gunfire and explosions. Did I thank you for sheltering me with your body?"

"You don't have to."

"Of course, I do. Your courage and quick thinking saved my life then, too."

"Save your gratitude for when we're out of—Whoa!" he said, pulling Chester to a stop. "Where did that come from?"

She leaned to the side in order to see around him. A barrier of moss-covered rock rose in front of the horse. It appeared as if the trail they had been following had ended at the base of a cliff.

Rick took her hands away from his waist and swung his leg over Chester's neck to dismount. "Stay put. I'll check this out."

She wasn't sure whether he was speaking to the horse or to her. She slid forward to retrieve the reins. "Can we go around it?"

Rick stepped off the trail and was immediately engulfed by the fog. Twigs snapped. There was a dull thud.

Elizabeth tensed. "Rick?"

More wood cracked. He didn't reply.

She felt a thread of panic at being left alone. "Rick? Are you all right?"

He reappeared a few minutes later, rubbing his head. "The brush is too thick. I'm not taking Chester through that."

Her panic receded. He seemed annoyed rather than injured. "We don't have much choice," she said. "We can't go back."

"We could backtrack to the stream and try following it, but it's going to be dark soon. There's what looks like a spring near the trail where we can get water for us and Chester, so this is as good a place as any to stop for the night." He lifted his arms to her. "Lean over, I'll help you down."

She fully intended to get down on her own, but her dismount wasn't as smooth as Rick's. Her legs got tangled in her skirt, and she would have fallen if he hadn't caught her by the waist and eased her the rest of the way to the ground.

Her hands ended up flattened against his chest. Her palms tingled. Sexual awareness shot through her body.

Don't think of him as a man, she ordered herself. This isn't romantic.

Yet standing toe-to-toe with him like this, she was more conscious than ever of how tall he was, how broad his shoulders were, how his grasp was strong yet gentle, how easy it would be to stay right where she was. "Thanks."

"No problem."

"Rick, why did you kiss me?"

His eyebrows shot up.

Of all the things she could have said, why that? She made an erasing motion with one hand. "Forget it."

"You brought it up. It must be on your mind."

"It was a silly question. The kiss was undoubtedly due to adrenaline."

"Adrenaline?"

"We were in danger. It makes a person react without thinking."

His gaze dropped to her mouth.

She felt pressure, as if he'd touched her lips. Frowning, she pushed at his chest. "I'm quite steady on my feet now."

"Mmm?"

"Let go of me, Rick."

He released his grip on her waist immediately.

She told herself she was relieved. Emotions really had no place in survival situations. She needed to stick to her priorities. She stepped back and briskly shook the wrinkles from her skirt. "Perhaps it's for the best that we stopped riding. We'll have a better idea of where to go once the fog lifts."

"I don't know why I kissed you, Elizabeth. I felt as if . . ." He hesitated. "As if I had to."

"Well, it's quite irrelevant. As I said, we should forget it."

"Did I hurt you?"

"What?"

"When I kissed you? I'm not usually that rough."

It hadn't been rough. It had been firm and wonderful. Part possession, part protection. A taste of what was possible. A promise of the chance for more. Though it had lasted less than a second, it was the closest they'd come to recapturing that marvelous union of their minds. "I don't remember," she lied.

"Ouch."

"Let's put it behind us, all right? I'm no outdoorswoman, but I'm sure there are things we should be doing in the way of preparations if we intend on passing the night here."

"Are you married?"

"What? No, I'm not married."

"Engaged? Going steady? Dating someone?"

"What difference does that make?"

"I wouldn't want to poach on another man's territory."

She put her fists on her hips. "Territory?"

"Easy there, I only meant—"

"Our costumes may be from the Dark Ages, but that doesn't necessitate adopting ancient attitudes. Women aren't possessions to be bought and sold or traded around. We're not claims to stake or prey to chase or any of those outdated clichés."

"Uh-huh, so I'm guessing from that rant that you're un-attached?"

She was about to say yes when she suddenly remembered Alan. She turned away. She walked to the edge of the trail, no further, unwilling to venture into the woods. The fog was getting thicker—she could see only a matter of feet now rather than yards—and she didn't want to risk getting lost. She knew instinctively that she wouldn't survive long if she got separated from Rick.

He spoke softly to his horse. She heard the sound of equine slurps, so she assumed he'd led it to the spring he'd mentioned finding. Shortly afterward, she heard his footsteps behind her. He spoke from over her shoulder. "You didn't answer me. Does that mean you're not single?"

"Yes and no," she said, keeping her back to him. "It's complicated."

"How?"

Confiding details of her personal life, like touching, was something else she'd never been comfortable with. Yet this was different with Rick, too. He'd saved her life more than once. The least she could do was trust him with the truth. "A man I know helped me out a while ago. When he claimed we were engaged, I wasn't in a position to contradict him."

"You're going to have to explain that one to me. How can someone *claim* you're engaged?"

"As I said, it's complicated. Once I settle the lawsuit with my stepmother and she agrees to drop the charges against me, I'll be able to clear up the situation."

"What charges?"

"Remember that I told you I had gone to Willowbank to meet my stepmother before all this . . ." She gestured at the fog. "Whatever-it-is happened?"

"Sure. You said you were meeting her because of legal stuff."

"That's right. I'm suing her for the wrongful death of my father. She caused the accident that killed him after she discovered he was about to change his will in my favor."

He took her by the shoulders and turned her to face him. "I'm sorry. Losing your dad like that must have been tough."

Tough didn't come close to describing how her world had

changed over the space of one fateful night. She had been on the verge of reclaiming everything that should have been hers. Instead, she had lost her father, her family home, her birthright, even her best friend. She moved her gaze past him to what she could see of the nearest tree trunk. "The accident happened last winter. The trouble started afterward, when I initiated the lawsuit against my stepmother. She countered with a harassment suit. Then someone tried to run her down, and the description of the car matched mine. She and her lawyer pointed the authorities in my direction and accused me of attempting to murder her. The Willowbank police made me their prime suspect."

Rick whistled softly. "When you said complicated, you weren't kidding."

"I didn't do it, by the way."

"Do what?"

"The hit-and-run."

"I know that."

"You do? How?"

"From what I've seen of you, you fight with words. You use your brain." He tapped a finger against her forehead. "It's a heck of a weapon but I don't think it could be lethal."

Her lips twitched. Considering the conversation topic, she couldn't believe he'd almost made her smile.

"And besides," he said. "Underneath all that prickly attitude, you're a big softie."

"A *softie*? Why on earth would you say that? I'm no such thing."

"Uh-huh. You are. You figure you need to act like you've got a thick hide but—"

"Please, spare me any more analogies from your livestock-wrangling days."

"Okay, we'll say skin, not hide. You feel everything deep, but you don't let on because you're determined to prove you're strong."

"And you know this how?"

"The way you've been rolling with the punches. You've got a thing about not admitting weakness. Mostly, I know it because of the way you talked about music. That's something that doesn't come from here," he said, rubbing his knuckles along her temple. He lowered his hand to the slope of her breast. "It comes from the heart, and I think you've got plenty of that."

She held her breath. He was barely touching her, yet she was incapable of stepping back. "I believe we're getting off topic here. You wanted to know about my engagement."

The moment dragged on until he finally withdrew his hand. "Right," he muttered.

She exhaled slowly, once again telling herself she was relieved.

"I still don't understand what getting charged with attempted murder has to do with sort of being engaged," he said.

"Alan provided me with an alibi for the time of the hit-and-run to keep me from being arrested."

"Alan. That's the guy who claims you're engaged?"

"Yes. He told the police he was my fiancé. If I revealed he lied about that . . ."

"Then the police wouldn't believe the alibi, either."

"Exactly."

"Huh. What a sleazeball."

"He saw an opportunity to advance his career and took it. In all fairness, I can't blame him. It was neatly done."

"Wait a minute. This guy wants to marry you only for the sake of *money*?"

The fierceness in Rick's expression startled her. He was normally so easygoing. She had seen his jaw clench in that way once before. It had been when he'd noticed the black eye she'd received when she'd been on her way to the gallows. "We're talking about a lot of money, even without counting my inheritance. He also works for Grayecorp," she explained. "He had started a personal relationship with me to further his position a few years ago as well, when my father was still alive. My father saw through it and warned me off."

"I'm glad to hear someone was looking out for you."

"I assure you, he didn't act out of paternal concern. Stanford Graye's prime interest was himself. He didn't want me dividing my loyalties, or aligning myself with Alan against him, if our association developed into something permanent."

"How come he didn't fire him?"

"Because he was good for the company. He's ambitious and he was good for our bottom line. He was useful."

"Then you don't love this Alan guy?"

"My relationship with him was one of expedience. I don't believe either of us harbored any illusions that our emotions were involved."

"I take it that means no."

A memory taunted her, of Alan and her in her office last summer, entwined on her father's old desk. She had been the one to initiate that particular encounter, and she had used him as much as he'd used her. It seemed so long ago now, as if it belonged to another lifetime. She crossed her arms, wishing she could forget. "Love is a myth perpetuated by Hollywood and the publishers of romance fiction. Oh, and children's fairy tales."

"Don't you believe in love?"

"Which love would you be referring to? The sexual urges people like to dress up by calling it love? The manipulative ploys of a parent who dangles the promise of love in front of their child like a carrot on a stick? Or maybe the possessiveness of a husband who sees love as a convenient tool for controlling his wife because it doesn't have the nasty side effects of an actual lobotomy?"

"That's not love."

"Which proves my point. Love doesn't exist."

He tugged her arms apart from their fold so he could clasp her hands within both of his. "I'm sorry, Elizabeth. You must have been hurt bad to think like that."

"Not at all. It's the way I was raised, and I'm pleased that I learned the lesson early. Emotions put a person at a disadvantage. They can be used as tools against you unless you learn to control them."

"What about music?"

"Are we back to that again?"

"It's about the only thing we have in common, so yeah, we're back to that. You told me you can find every emotion there is in music."

"Well, yes, but—"

"Isn't love one of them?"

She dipped her chin, focusing on his hands. His fingers were long, his knuckles large. She'd felt the strength in them on numerous occasions. His fingers were also nimble enough to produce heartbreakingly beautiful sounds from his guitar. "I've heard you sing about love," she said. "That's why your songs are so sad."

He didn't respond.

She looked up. "Rick?"

There was evidence of pain in the tight pinching at the corners of his eyes, yet he kept his amber gaze steady on hers. "My music's sad because love can hurt."

"Wanting to believe love is real is what hurts. It makes a person hope for the impossible."

He moved his head from side to side in a slow negative. "Love is real, Elizabeth. It's what makes the difference between genuinely living and going through the motions of drawing breath."

Though he'd spoken quietly, his words resonated inside her, the same way the lyrics of his songs did. "What happened, Rick?"

"Mmm?"

"Who hurt you?"

He lifted one shoulder. "You're the one changing the subject this time. We were talking about why I kissed you."

She sighed. "I would say we already exhausted that topic."

"Did we?"

"It would be best to forget the kiss ever happened."

"Do you think you can?"

"Certainly."

He leaned closer. "Let's see if you can forget this one."

"Rick . . ."

He didn't kiss her mouth. Instead, he pressed his lips to the outer corner of her eye.

She drew back.

He stroked a lock of her hair from her cheek, tucked it behind her ear, and slid his hand to the back of her head to hold her steady as he repeated the kiss beside her other eye. He kissed her nose next, then the center of her chin.

"Rick, what are you doing?"

He slid his mouth along the edge of her jaw. "Dang, if you have to ask, I guess I'm not doing it right. I must be out of practice. Maybe you could give me some pointers."

This time, she did smile. She couldn't help it. "We shouldn't be wasting time with this. We have other priorities."

"Seems to me, we can't do much until we can see where we're going."

"Yes, but—"

"One more kiss, Elizabeth." He rubbed his nose against hers. "Then we'll make camp."

Oh, why not? She tilted her head the fraction of an inch that was needed to bring their mouths together.

She couldn't excuse the rush of her blood on adrenaline this time. They weren't in immediate danger. Nor could she blame it on drugs, because her head felt clearer than it had in days. Weeks. Maybe months. She accepted the fact that the pleasure zinging through her body from the contact of her lips with Rick's was due purely to this man.

She did indeed like him. She was also physically attracted to him. That wasn't love, though. She knew better than to yearn for what she couldn't have. As she'd told Rick, she'd learned that lesson early. From a mother who rebuffed her hugs because they would wrinkle her clothes, from governesses who had been hired for their strict adherence to the social gulf between employer and servant. And most of all, from a father she'd sacrificed her dreams to please.

But that didn't mean she couldn't enjoy the moment. She stepped closer, sliding her hands to his shoulders as he wrapped his arms around her back. The embrace felt . . . right. Natural. They fitted together perfectly, as if they'd done this countless times before.

Rick didn't need any pointers. He was an excellent kisser. He seemed to know precisely the right amount of pressure to exert, stimulating her senses without smothering them. He explored the contours of her lips while she did the same to him. To describe what she felt as pleasure was too simple. Their mouths fit as perfectly as their bodies. Every shift, every nuance, each teasing lick or nibble built on the one before, filling her with the urge to draw even closer.

Until she opened her mouth for his tongue.

And he slid into her mind.

EIGHT

THE MENTAL LINK HAPPENED EFFORTLESSLY, AS IF IT WERE a natural extension of their kiss. Elizabeth sensed Rick's presence on a level far beyond the physical. Delight sparked through her nerves. *Rick?*

He smiled. She felt it in his lips and in her own. She tasted him, and she discovered what she tasted like on his tongue. Her awareness of her own body expanded to include his. Their hearts beat in a shared rhythm, two parts of one melody, trembling in perfect harmony.

A chain of images flashed across her vision. A scratched guitar leaning against a wooden chair. Bare tree branches silhouetted by a streetlight beyond a dormer window. A black-and-white dog curled into a nose-to-tail bundle at the foot of a brass bed.

And she saw emptiness. It was there around the edges. She recognized its wavering draw, because it wove through the fabric of her own life, only she took care to ensure no one else noticed it.

She blinked and pulled her head back, breaking the contact. Rick's face was a blur in front of her. Beyond him, the fog had dimmed from white to gray. Night was falling. She could no longer see any trace of the forest.

There was no trace of the guitar or the window or the dog, either.

He moved his hands to her waist. "Did you feel that?" His voice was hoarse. "For a second . . ."

"We were . . ."

"Joined. In our heads."

"How? It's crazy. We couldn't have."

"Yeah, but we did."

"I don't understand it."

"Do we need to? Elizabeth—" He broke off and glanced over his shoulder.

She peered into the gloom but could see less than she had before. "What is it?"

"I thought I heard something."

"What?" she whispered.

"A man's voice. Someone's out there." He squeezed her waist briefly and turned away. "Wait here."

"No. Rick, don't go."

"I need to see who it is."

"He could be one of Ganulf's guards."

"Or he could be our ticket out of here."

She caught his sleeve. "Please, don't leave me."

"It's okay, I won't go far." He rubbed his thumb across her lower lip. "After that kiss, you've got to know I'll be back."

He moved out of her grasp before she could stop him. Within two strides, he was engulfed by the fog. A twig snapped nearby. Another crackled faintly a few seconds later.

Elizabeth told herself he'd been right to investigate. At least one of them was being practical. They had to know whether it was friend or foe out there.

Yet she hadn't heard any voice. And now she couldn't hear Rick's footsteps, either.

Panic unfurled. It was far more intense than the last time he'd disappeared, making it hard for her to breathe. She hugged her arms to her chest as the dampness around her penetrated her wool dress. She hadn't noticed the cold until now. Rick's presence had kept it at bay. He'd kept her weakness at bay, too, but now the strength drained from her legs. She stumbled sideways, bumping into a tree trunk.

She barely felt the impact. It made no noise, either. She braced her palm on the tree and pushed herself back toward the trail.

She struck another tree instead. She waved her arms in front of her, feeling her way blindly, only to find her path blocked by something flat and hard. It was stone. Like the walls in the tower room or the dungeon . . .

No! She wasn't back there. She couldn't be. Rick had helped her escape. This must be the cliff at the end of the trail.

Then where was Chester? They'd left him here. But she couldn't see him or hear him. She sniffed, but she couldn't smell even a whiff of the horse. Instead, the air smelled faintly medicinal. Like plastic or disinfectant or boiled sheets . . . like a hospital.

What was happening? Where was she? "Rick?" she called. *"Rick!"*

Her voice was swallowed by the fog as soon as the words left her throat. She turned her back to the wall and stretched her arms in front of her again. Her hands grasped empty air. Even the trees had disappeared. *Rick! Please, help me!*

Her plea was silent. Her senses were beginning to shut down. The familiar blackness opened in front of her.

No! She staggered aside, groping at nothing. She couldn't let herself fall asleep or she would be completely powerless again. She was not going back to that prison. She had to find Rick. She wanted to live.

"I realize it's not literature or anything, but I love knowing there'll be a happy ending."

Elizabeth caught her breath. It wasn't Rick's voice, it was a woman's. She couldn't tell what direction it was coming from. It seemed to be everywhere, like the fog.

"Books are books, Norma," a second woman said. "I tell my students that all the time. I can't abide literary snobs. There's no reason to apologize for reading what you enjoy."

"I do enjoy them. There's so much misery on the news these days, it's nice to have an escape."

"Amen to that."

"The only thing that embarrasses me are the clinch covers. I usually end up laying them facedown."

The second woman laughed. "Ah, the mysteries of marketing. Not for readers to understand. Is it a good story?"

"So far. It's a book I got from my cousin. She's really into historicals." There was a faint rustling sound. "This cover's not too bad, except I'd think they'd be worried about catching a chill."

There was another laugh. "Oh, my goodness. I see what you mean."

Who were these women? And why on earth were they talking about books? They couldn't be connected to the guards or the people in the castle because their manner of speech was pure twenty-first century. In addition, the conversation was casual and blessedly ordinary. The odds were good that wherever these women had come from, they weren't her enemies.

Elizabeth decided to risk calling out. She parted her lips but when she attempted to speak she couldn't seem to make a sound. She stretched her hands into the void, splaying her fingers to extend her reach.

Someone gasped. "Norma, quick! Look at her hands."

"Oh, my God! It's like she's trying to grab something. She's never done that before."

"Elizabeth." The voice grew nearer. "Can you hear me?"

Yes! I'm here, she tried to respond, yet she didn't have the strength to push the words out of her throat. She clenched her fists in frustration.

"She made a fist!"

Warm fingers settled over her knuckles. "You *can* hear me, can't you?"

Elizabeth started. She squinted into the fog, trying to see who touched her.

"Hang on, kiddo. You're going to make it."

She leaned back from the encroaching darkness, her mind buzzing with questions. The second woman had addressed her by her real name, not Lady Elspeth or Isabella. She had sounded concerned. What's more, she had sounded familiar. And there was only one person Elizabeth knew who called her kiddo.

Monica Chamberlain. The girl had been her best friend from the day her parents had moved into the property that adjoined the Graye estate. They had taken different paths as adults, and the last time she'd seen her they had parted in anger, yet Monica couldn't be an accomplice in this nightmare, could she? Elizabeth was unable to imagine her going to such lengths to punish her.

"Look at the monitors," the woman called Norma said. Her voice trembled with excitement. "They're going nuts."

"Beryl told me they acted up last weekend, too. Everyone assumed it was a glitch in the equipment but obviously it wasn't. Is Dr. Shouldice still here?"

"I'll page him."

Elizabeth became aware of other noises in the fog. Muted beeps. A clicking whoosh. The squeak of crepe soles on a tile floor. The sounds, like the smells she'd noticed earlier, reminded her of a hospital.

"Open your eyes, Elizabeth. It's me, Monica."

But her eyes were already open, weren't they?

"If you can hear me, squeeze my fingers."

She tried, but she couldn't. She looked at her hands. They were still curled into fists, yet it felt as if someone had laced their fingers with hers. She still saw no one, but the touch was indisputably real and more solid than the ground she was standing on. She was as certain of that as she was sure of her own name.

What the *hell* was going on?

More voices approached. More footsteps, these ones heavier. Her other hand was picked up. Fingertips pressed her wrist, as if someone was taking her pulse. She felt a thumb brush her eyelid to slide it open. Yet she still saw nothing except the fog.

She pulled away, frightened by the phantom touches. Was she losing her sanity? Was she dreaming?

"Is she coming out of it, Doctor?" Monica asked. "She seems to be really waking up this time."

"Miss Graye hasn't regained consciousness yet," a man said. "Her ability to move her extremities certainly is progress, though."

"Did you hear that, kiddo? You're going to be okay."

"We'll have to take it one step at a time. I need to caution you that once she does wake up, we'll still need to assess for possible brain damage. With a coma of this length, full recovery is never certain."

"You don't know Elizabeth the way I do," Monica said. "When she puts her mind to something, there's no stopping her."

But I am awake! Can't you see that? Why don't you show yourselves? Why are you talking about me as if I can't hear you, as if I don't count . . .

Brain damage.

A coma of this length.

A coma.

The words the unseen man had said finally penetrated. Their effect spread through her mind with the force of a strong wind, blowing away the confusion; as if someone had thrown open a window in her head.

She wasn't in a forest. She hadn't been in a castle tower or a jungle hut or a dungeon, either. That would have been impossible. Patients with brain damage would be kept in a hospital.

As soon as the thought formed, her awareness expanded. Sensations sparked through her nerves. She felt the contours of the mattress she was lying on and the weight of the light blanket that covered her legs. She heard the doctor as he continued to speak with Monica, and she heard a faint electronic beep that matched the rhythm of her pulse. There was a taste of plastic in her mouth. A tube in her throat.

She tried to spit the tube out, she tried to sit up, she tried to lift her eyelids but could do none of those things. Her muscles wouldn't obey her brain.

Brain damage.

Terror, deep and primal, shuddered through her mind. She was paralyzed. Unable to move, incapable of calling out. How long had she been like this? How much longer would it go on?

Was this to be her new reality? Completely helpless, trapped inside her body the way she'd been trapped inside the prisons in her dreams?

Because that's what they must have been. Dreams. Created by her damaged mind to explain its imprisonment in her body.

Details began to click: the scope of the illusions; the way she had no memory of going from one place to another; the wounds that magically healed; the actors that had appeared willing to die for their role. They hadn't made sense, but this did. It was the solution to the puzzle. She had been in this bed all along. Not one of those scenarios she remembered had been real.

That meant Rick wasn't real, either. Nor was the connection they had felt. Their incredible kiss, his humor, his courage, his beautiful music had no more substance than the random flicker of an electrical impulse between neurons.

Of course, she should have realized Rick couldn't be real. Neither were the feelings he had stirred in her. She knew how the world worked. She knew better than to yearn for what wasn't possible.

Still, she fought the darkness that tugged at her consciousness, hoping against all logic to catch one last glimpse of a tall, cowboy minstrel with amber eyes and hair that was a little too long and a presence that she knew would haunt her the rest of her life . . .

If this paralyzed limbo could be called living.

No! Please! Help me!

Someone dabbed the corner of her eye. "She's crying."

No, I never cry. Only fools and weaklings can't control their emotions. And why should I cry over a man who doesn't exist? That would be laughable. Pathetic. Completely out of character for Elizabeth Baylor Graye.

But no one heard Elizabeth's words. No one saw her wipe her face on the purple sleeve of her imaginary dress as she stumbled back into the fog of her mind.

RICK MOVED CAUTIOUSLY, TESTING HIS FOOTING AS HE went further into the fog. The ground was becoming spongy, and he didn't want to get too far from the trail, but for a second there, it had sounded as if a man had been calling his name.

The voice trailed off. In the silence, he heard a distant, rhythmic beeping. The beeping gradually turned into a thumping noise. If he didn't know better, he would think someone was rapping against a door.

A dog barked. The knocking got louder. Rick squinted into the murk that surrounded him, trying to figure out where the sounds were coming from.

"Uncle Rick?"

He spun, reversing direction. That had seemed to have come from right behind him. It had sounded exactly like . . . "Zeb?" he called.

Hearing his own voice was strange. It seemed odd, sort of loud and hollow, as if he were talking through a tunnel.

The barking tapered off to a whine. Something cool and moist nudged against his knuckles. He lifted his hand and encountered warm fur. His palm curved over the contours of a familiar, canine head. Daisy?

Rick opened his eyes. There was darkness, but no mist. He could see the rectangle of a dormer window. Yellow light spread across the sloped ceiling from the streetlamp on the corner. Brass curves gleamed from the shadows at the foot of his bed. He was no longer in the forest, he was in his apartment.

How did he get home? The transition had been so smooth, he hadn't noticed it happening. He sat up. The bed creaked. It seemed even louder than his voice had.

Daisy wriggled onto his lap and went into full haven't-seen-you-in-days greeting mode.

Rick gave her a distracted ear scratch as he took a few seconds to get his bearings. The bedroom was small enough that even in the dark, he could see that he was alone. Aside from the dog, that was. "Elizabeth?"

She wasn't here. Not only couldn't he see her, he couldn't *feel* her. Her absence hit him in the gut, a tangled mass of panic and grief, as if he'd lost a piece of himself. Where the hell had she gone? How could he have left her behind when he'd promised her he would be back? "Elizabeth!"

Daisy barked and scrambled off the bed.

The pounding resumed. It was coming from the apartment door. "Uncle Rick?"

Though the voice was muffled, it was definitely his nephew's. Rick rolled to his feet and immediately bumped his head on the sloped ceiling. He staggered out of the bedroom. The first few steps were the most difficult, as if his feet weren't completely hitting the floor, as if neither his mind nor his body were entirely there. The world began to steady as he entered the living room. He switched on a lamp. The light confirmed what he'd already felt. Elizabeth wasn't here.

Daisy twined around his feet to continue her wiggling, dancing hello.

The knob on the apartment door rattled. "Yo, Rick. It's Stella. You dead, or what?"

That was his landlady's voice. He stepped over his dog, unlocked the door, and swung it open.

Zeb stood on the small landing outside the door. Beside him was Stella Davidoff, poised with a key in her hand. At six feet even and two hundred sixty pounds, she effectively filled the doorway. The skin that wasn't covered by her sweater and flowing skirt presented a living canvas advertising her skill with a tattoo needle. She ran her business out of the ground floor of her house, lived on the second floor, and rented what used to be the attic to Rick. She appeared to be still wheezing from the climb up the stairs. She looked him up and down, then slid the keys into her skirt pocket. "Took you long enough."

"Did you see her?" Rick asked.

"Who? The mutt? She's right in front of you."

"Uncle Rick!" Zeb reached past Stella to grasp his arm. "Are you okay? Did you forget you were on tonight?"

"Never mind me. Where's Elizabeth?" He looked past them to the staircase. "Did you see her?"

Stella cocked her head to the side. "Who're you talking about?"

"Blonde woman, about so high," he said, shaking off his nephew's grasp so he could level one hand at the height of his nose. "Had on a long purple dress. She was with me until a minute ago."

"I didn't see anyone," Zeb said.

Rick squeezed between Stella and Zeb and started down the stairs. He had to find Elizabeth before the guards or whoever was holding her prisoner did. He had to help her.

"You go chasing after a woman like that and she's liable to run the other way," Stella shouted after him. "If you don't freeze your assets off first."

Rick absorbed her words at the same time he noticed the cool air on his legs and the cold wood beneath the soles of his feet. He paused at the first turn of the staircase and glanced down.

Except for a crumpled pair of striped boxers, he was naked.

Where were the tunic and the laced-up shirt, and those medieval track pants and ankle boots he'd been wearing?

And what about Chester? Elizabeth might have gotten out of the house unnoticed, but what had happened to the horse?

Questions whirled through his head, each one spawning two more that made less sense than the last. His vision blurred. He grabbed the banister for balance.

Zeb's voice drifted to him from the landing. "I think Elizabeth's his girlfriend," he said.

"Since when? He never brings anyone up here."

"He mentioned her a while ago."

"Yeah? Sure he wasn't talking about the mutt? Yes, my sweetie girl, look what Mamma brought you." Stella's voice went up an octave with the last sentence, a sure sign she was talking to Daisy. She was probably giving her a chunk of cheese. Daisy loved cheese.

Elizabeth didn't believe in love at all. She'd told him that just before he'd kissed her and their minds had done that incredible meshing thing. And then he'd heard Zeb's voice and had gone into the fog and . . .

And then he'd woken up.

Right.

It had been a dream. Nothing but a dream. Like the other dreams. Elizabeth wasn't real.

Neither was the castle or the invading army or the battle. Or the fog-bound forest.

Well, duh. Of course, it hadn't been real. He should have realized it was too crazy to be possible. It had all been in his head.

Yet he was on his way to the street in his underwear in December to search for a woman who didn't exist.

He sat down where he was and put his head in his hands. He was losing track of the number of times he'd dreamt about Lady Elspeth Isabella Elizabeth. He should be able to snap out of it faster by now, yet each time he surfaced it took his mind longer to let her go.

He must be an idiot. A total moron. Couldn't bring himself to spend time with a woman in real life, so his subconscious had made one up. Not an ordinary woman, either. A smart, beautiful one. Classy and rich, too. A woman who depended on him to rescue her. How pathetic was that? What was next? An inflatable doll?

Nails clattered on the steps behind him. A wet nose nudged into his armpit.

Rick slung his arm around Daisy and hugged her against his side. "Sorry, girl. I didn't forget you, I . . ." He stopped. He couldn't expect a dog to understand what was going on when he didn't understand it himself.

A fanfare of tinny trumpets sounded from the top of the

steps. Rick glanced up as Zeb pulled his cell phone from his jacket. "Hi, Dad. Yeah, he was at home."

Stella left Zeb to talk with his father and came down the stairs to Rick. "So, who's Elizabeth?"

"No one. I was . . . confused."

She sniffed. "You back on the booze?"

"No, just slept deep."

"All this time?" she asked.

"That's right."

"You sure?"

"Why? Did you hear something?"

"Didn't hear so much as a floorboard creak since you got in last night." She lowered her voice so Zeb wouldn't overhear, even though he was still busy on his phone. "When the kid came looking for you, I got worried you might've tried, well, you know. Checking out."

"I wouldn't stiff you for the rent, Stella."

"I meant the kind of checking out you tried before."

"Yeah, well, I'm not planning on going that route again anytime soon, either."

"You were acting kinda weird a few minutes ago."

"Told you, I slept deep. Took me a while to wake up but I'm okay."

"You better be, because I sure wouldn't want to get stuck with having to clean up the mess if you don't miss next time. The stink of a dead mouse is bad enough. And then I'd have a bitch of a time renting that apartment once word got out."

"Honest. I'm past that."

She searched his gaze for a minute, as if verifying for herself that he was telling the truth. "I thought you were past it, too, but it's only a few weeks to Christmas, and holidays are tough. This is the time of year I miss Radomir the most. As soon as I hear Christmas carols, I remember the way he used to murder the tunes on that old balalaika."

"Rad had a style all his own."

"That he did. Sometimes seven years seems like yesterday."

"Keeping busy helps," he said.

"It does. So does having company."

"Are the kids coming this year?"

"As long as Merika's twins don't come down with the flu again. You going to your brother's place for Christmas day?"

"That's the plan."

She squeezed his shoulder. "It's only going to be your fourth one without her. It'll get better. The whole trick is trying to look forward instead of back."

He nodded.

"But if you ever want to talk, you know where I am."

"Same goes for me, Stella. We both know I owe you more than rent."

The squeeze turned into a swat. "Don't go all mushy on me. I'm just looking out for number one."

Under the tats and the attitude, his landlady was a big softie, but she would do her best to deny it, like Elizabeth . . .

No. Elizabeth wasn't real.

He ruffled Daisy's fur and pushed to his feet. "Speaking of number one, I better let the dog outside before she busts her bladder."

"I'll take her," she said, turning sideways to maneuver past Rick. She snapped her fingers at Daisy and pointed down the stairs. Her voice changed pitch again. "Mommy's sweetums want to go peepees?"

Daisy yipped once and shot down the stairs in a blur of black and white.

Stella followed, already digging into her pocket for another chunk of cheese.

"Thanks," Rick called.

She waved the cheese in a dismissive gesture. "Go put some clothes on, boy," she said over her shoulder. "I can't stand the sight of all that blank skin with no ink. It's such a waste."

"Uncle Rick?" Zeb asked. "Dad wants to know if you're still coming in to the Cantina tonight."

Rick climbed back to his apartment. "Yeah, I'll be there."

His nephew put away the phone as he followed him inside. "He told me to give you a ride."

He sighed. "Tell your dad I'm not drunk."

"He never said—"

"I don't have a drop of liquor in here. The only time I drink is at the bar."

"Geez, Uncle Rick. I know that. Dad wanted to make sure you got there since your truck's been acting up. You weren't answering your phone."

"I turned the ringer off before I went to sleep. Didn't mean to worry anyone."

"Oh." He hesitated. "Uh, you are okay now, aren't you?"

"Just peachy." His stomach rumbled loudly, making him wonder how long it had been since he'd last eaten. There hadn't been time to think about food when they'd escaped from the castle. Elizabeth must have been hungry, too, but she'd never complained . . .

Hell.

Elizabeth. Wasn't. Real.

He went to the kitchen, tore open a bag of Doritos, and crammed a handful into his mouth. Could be low blood sugar that was causing his confusion. He passed the bag to Zeb. "Breakfast," he mumbled. "Want some?"

"Sure. Thanks." He palmed a handful the same way Rick had. "Good news, you made your first online sale today."

"That's great." Rick spooned instant coffee crystals into a mug and mixed it with hot water from the tap. "I'm glad you brought that up. We never settled on what I owe you for running the website. It was decent of you to volunteer, but I don't expect you to do it for free."

"Well, I'm looking at it as an investment. I was hoping I could be your manager."

"There's not much to manage now, but if you think you could get a few more bucks out of your dad, go for it."

"I meant when your career starts to take off. You'll need someone to handle things like bookings and PR. The website's only the start. I've been thinking you should get yourself on the social networking sites. It'll make you easier to find and let people know more about you. It's free publicity. We could post a video."

"Uh, thanks."

"Don't worry, Uncle Rick. Computers can't smell your fear."

"Could have fooled me."

"I can give you a deal on one I'm fixing up. You can pay it off through what we make on your online sales. It'll be a good tax deduction, and once you're hooked up, you can check your website for orders and e-mail by yourself."

"Maybe we could put bamboo shoots under my finger-nails instead."

"Anyone who can work a TV remote can work a computer. I'll show you how to use it on the weekend. It won't take long." Zeb bounced a bony fist against Rick's shoulder in a quarter-strength version of one of Jethro's punches. "Give me a heads-up before I come over if you've got company."

"That's not likely."

"Isn't Elizabeth coming back?"

He gulped a mouthful of his coffee. "I never know when she'll show up."

"What's she like?"

"She's a dream."

"Cool."

"Can you do me a favor?"

"Sure," he said, ramming in more chips.

"Don't say anything to your dad about Elizabeth."

"Why not? We all think it's great you're seeing someone again."

"I'm not."

Zeb twisted his mouth to the side, appearing to be digesting more than the Doritos. He tapped his index finger alongside his nose. "Okay then, whatever you say. Guess you don't like the family inquisitions any more than I do."

"Everyone means well, but I wouldn't know what to tell them about Elizabeth, anyway."

"She's nice though, right?"

"Yeah, once you get past the armor plating."

"Is she from around here?"

"Nope."

"Then how'd you meet her?"

He finished his coffee, rinsed the cup, and turned it upside down on the edge of the sink. "You wouldn't believe me if I told you. Go ahead and polish off the rest of that bag. I'll be ready to go in ten."

By the time he'd showered and dressed, Rick was feeling almost back to normal. Not that it was an improvement. He liked the way he felt when he was with Elizabeth, a little on edge, his senses heightened, his heart pumping that extra few beats a minute. Her absence left an emptiness inside him. Which was nuts, considering she existed solely in his head, so in fact she *was* inside him.

He paused on the edge of his bed, one boot dangling from his hand. Was he nuts? Aside from the confusion with his dream woman, he thought he had a good handle on things these days. Sure, construction work was scarce, and his singing career wasn't progressing all that fast, and every now and then he got ambushed by the old sorrow, but he was doing okay. The music got him through.

If the sorrow sometimes found its way into his songs, it was because he wrote from the heart. That didn't mean he was going to check out, or go out back and eat his Winchester. Facing the void between life and death once had been enough. It had shown him what real loneliness was, and he never wanted to be trapped in that loop again.

Was that why he'd dreamed of being held prisoner? Was it possible that by helping Elizabeth escape death, he was working through his own decision to keep living?

Rick snorted. He should stick with music. He would never make a living as a shrink any more than he could pass himself off as a rescuer of fair damsels.

NINE

ELIZABETH WOKE UP SCREAMING. HER THROAT WAS RAW from it, yet she could barely hear herself over the grinding roar of the engines. She was momentarily weightless, only held to her seat by the belt that stretched across her lap. Then she slammed down and her face bumped hard against her knees.

The impact was cushioned by the thick pants that covered her legs. A matching down-filled jacket swaddled her upper half. She was wearing what appeared to be a ski suit. She braced her palms on the slippery nylon and pushed herself upright.

She could see nothing but the back of the seat in front of her. She turned her head to the right. Snow blurred horizontally past a round-cornered window. Through it she watched streamers of black smoke whip across a white wing . . .

Wing?

She was on a plane, a small one. The side of the fuselage curved low over her head. And the engine appeared to be on fire.

"Liesel!"

She looked to her left. A flight attendant stood in the aisle, speaking to her rapidly in a language that could have been German. She shook her head to indicate she didn't understand but he'd already turned to work his way toward the front where the rest of the passengers were seated. The ones who weren't crying or screaming were praying. Elizabeth battled her rising terror and glanced behind her.

The seats at the back of the plane were empty, except for a tall man who sat in the very last row. He was folded double, his head wedged against the back of the seat in front of him and one arm hanging limply beside his legs. Though a bulky sheepskin coat concealed the upper half of his body and his face was turned away, she recognized the color of his hair and the unruly curls that poked against the edge of his collar. Then again, she'd never had any trouble recognizing this man. "Rick!" she shouted.

The plane dipped and rose. His head lolled on his knees. He showed no signs of life . . .

No! He was alive. He had to be. She could feel his energy. She unbuckled her belt and staggered down the aisle to drop into the seat beside his. She touched his face. "Rick!"

His skin was warm. Her palm tingled from the contact for an instant before she was thrown into the air by another bump. She quickly belted herself in and stretched her arm over Rick's back.

She felt his groan more than heard it above the din of the engines and the panicked passengers. She nudged her leg against his. "Rick?"

He lifted his head. He blinked a few times. She could sense him going through the same process she had as he took in his surroundings. He turned to look at her. Confusion clouded his eyes. "Elizabeth?"

She caught his hand. She understood what he was thinking. How had they gotten here? Where were they going? What had happened to the forest and Chester and the fog?

Other questions, larger ones, jostled for her attention. Something about the fog, something important, niggled at the edges of her mind, hovering beyond her grasp . . .

She decided to ignore it. There was no time for questions. The why and the how of the situation didn't matter anyway. All that mattered was survival. She held Rick's fingers to her lips. She wasn't going to lose him. She couldn't. That was the only thought that was perfectly clear.

He touched her cheek. "Are you okay?"

She had a wild desire to laugh. Okay? How many times had he asked her that in their short acquaintance? "Ask me again after we land."

The noise of the engines sputtered out. A man's voice crackled over the cabin speakers, all but drowned out by the desperate sounds from the passengers. She couldn't understand his words, but the gist of them was obvious. They were going to crash.

Rick's gaze sharpened. He looked out the window. Through the haze of smoke and snow, the jagged silhouettes of mountains came into view.

The plane suddenly nosed downward.

"Cover your head with your arms!" Rick yelled as he guided her head to her knees. "And brace yourself."

The next few seconds seemed to last an eternity. Though the engines were silent, the body of the plane itself hummed like a missile as it plummeted through the blizzard. Elizabeth pushed her feet against the floor to keep from sliding forward. The plane leveled off briefly. Rick flipped his coat collar over his ears and curled his arms around her an instant before they struck the ground.

Elizabeth's jaw cracked hard against her knees. The seatbelt cut across her hips. Rick grunted and tightened his hold.

The plane had come down atop a small plateau in the midst of the peaks. It slid on its belly across the snow, its momentum carrying it forward unchecked until a wing tip caught an outcrop of bare rock. Metal screeched and twisted as the fuselage ripped clean apart directly in front of their seats. The leading edge of the tail section rammed into the snowpack and came to a shuddering halt. The rest of the plane kept going, skidding across the plateau and over the edge.

For a heartbeat all was silent. Then there was a distant crunch, followed by an explosion that shook the ground and echoed from the mountainside.

Elizabeth lifted her head from her knees. The storm whipped a mix of snow and ice pellets into her face. She shielded her eyes with her hand as cauliflower billows of fire rose above the edge of the plateau to tint the sky orange.

She squeezed her eyes shut. *Oh God, oh God, oh God.*

"Elizabeth?" Rick eased his weight off her and ran his hands down her arms and legs. "Are you hurt?"

She gave herself a mental shake. She couldn't afford to fall apart. "No, I'm fine." She glanced at Rick's face, and her stomach rolled as if they'd crashed again. A line of red curled above his left eyebrow. She touched the edge. "You're bleeding!"

He pressed his palm across the wound. "It's just a scratch. The cold'll dry it up."

She didn't breathe freely until she saw he was right—the blood was beading, not flowing. She pushed herself upright. Or as upright as she could. The floor had buckled, tilting their seats at a thirty degree angle. She unfastened her safety belt and tumbled to the snow outside.

They spoke little as they followed the trough that had been carved into the snow by the rest of the plane. By the time they reached the spot where it had gone over, the wind had shifted to blow the smoke aside, allowing a view of the scene below. Flames shot into the storm from a tangled black smudge of debris at the bottom of a sheer-sided ravine. There was nothing recognizable in the wreckage. The plane—and everything it had carried—had completely disintegrated.

The image belonged in a nightmare.

A nightmare.

A dream.

The words jogged a memory, not of something she had seen but of sounds and smells and a feeling of hopelessness . . .

"I can't see any way to get down there." Rick had to raise his voice to be heard above the wind. "Not without equipment."

Elizabeth choked on a rush of tears. He wanted to help, but he saw the same thing she had. He realized as well as she did that no one could have survived both the crash and the fire.

Except for the two of them.

It defied belief. If the plane hadn't broken apart, if the tail section hadn't dug into the snow and stopped, they would be dead, too. More than that, if she hadn't left her seat and gone to the back row to join Rick, she would have been in the section that had crashed and burned. He had saved her life yet again, and all he'd had to do was be there.

He wiped her cheeks.

She tipped her face against his hand, feeling the moisture of her tears on his fingers. His touch was as gentle as the real one had been.

The real one?

Another memory stirred. She had felt someone wipe a tear from the corner of her eye. She had been crying about something important, something about Rick and dreams. When? Where?

Rick looped his arm around her back and turned her away from the drop-off. "No one will come searching for us until the storm lets up. It's getting dark. We need to rig a shelter while we can still see."

The trench the front of the plane had left was already beginning to drift over as they retraced their steps. Rick pulled the cuffs of the sweater he wore beneath his coat over his hands to protect them from the cold, then gathered pieces of metal that had torn loose from the fuselage to fashion a low, boxlike shelter within what was left of the tail. Though Elizabeth tried to help him, she had trouble concentrating. Every action seemed to trigger a thought from another time, as if her mind was attempting to drag her away from what was happening here. Away from the nightmare and death. Away from the swirling white snowstorm that looked so much like the fog where she'd lost Rick . . .

Her heart stuttered. For a second—or a minute or an hour, she couldn't tell—time suspended. Clarity returned. The bed, the electronic noises from the machines, the sterile smells . . .

The truth burst through her brain. No, she hadn't lost Rick. She'd never had him. He wasn't real. None of this was real. It was her mind's way of dealing with its imprisonment in her body.

"Duck your head," Rick said, tugging her into the shelter.

She went with him numbly. There wasn't enough room to stand up so she crawled to one of the two seats he'd salvaged. "Rick," she said. "We don't need to do this."

"If we don't, we'll be icicles by morning." He slid a piece of ceiling panel across the opening behind him. The air stilled. "I know it's not exactly the Ritz, but the space is small enough to hold in our body heat, and the padding on these seats should keep our butts from freezing. It's the same principle as a doghouse."

"Rick . . ."

"It wasn't a livestock analogy, I said dog."

"This isn't happening."

He sat beside her and pulled her into his arms. "We'll be all right, Elizabeth. We already beat some long odds."

"No, you don't understand. This isn't happening. The plane didn't crash. The people didn't die. It's a dream."

"Don't think about it. Concentrate on the fact we're still alive. Can you wiggle your toes?"

"What? Yes."

"Good. Wouldn't want you to get frostbite. Those boots look warm."

She pushed herself off his chest and leaned back. The light outside was fading, but enough filtered through the cracks in their shelter for her to study him. His large nose, his lean cheeks, his hard jaw were all so familiar to her, she didn't want to lose him, even if it meant never waking up . . .

What was she thinking? Rick. Wasn't. Real.

She moved her hands to his face. "Rick, I'm not here," she said. "I'm imagining all this."

He turned his head to kiss her thumb, then took her hands in his and rubbed them briskly to warm them up. "Did you check your pockets for mittens?"

"Rick, please listen. You have to help me."

"That's what I've been doing."

"I mean you have to help me wake up."

He pressed a swift kiss to her mouth.

Warmth spread through her cold lips. A knot of emotions—worry, grief, hope—spilled from his mind to hers. Strength flowed through her limbs even after she broke the contact and pulled back.

She touched the tip of her tongue to her lower lip. How could a figment of her imagination have left his taste on her mouth? She regarded the scratch on his forehead. The blood had clotted into a ridged scab that appeared exactly like the real thing. For a moment, she had doubts . . .

But then her gaze fell to his sheepskin coat. "Rick, if this isn't a dream, then where did you get the coat? And why am I wearing a ski outfit?" She shoved her hands into her pockets. It didn't surprise her when she found a pair of balled-up gloves. She held them up. "Isn't this too much of a coincidence? And how did we get from a medieval castle to an airplane in the first place? Did the guards recapture us? Did they suddenly discover modern technology?"

"I don't know. Maybe whoever's been doing this drugged us and dumped us on a plane."

"How could they have timed the dose to wear off immediately before the plane crashed? Why did they bother dressing us for cold weather unless they knew we *would* crash?" She tossed the gloves aside. "And why were they speaking German?"

"Were they?"

"It sounded like it."

"Guess we're in the Alps."

"That doesn't explain why the flight attendant called me Liesel."

"Liesel?"

"That's a German form of Elizabeth. How could he know who I was?"

Rick frowned.

"It's completely illogical, and I don't understand why my subconscious chose to make up this particular scenario, but it's following the same pattern as the other times. I woke up in the middle of a dangerous situation. I was supposed to die. Because of you, I didn't. You keep saving me. I asked you to help me live, and you do."

"When you put it like that, I agree there are similarities, but—"

"Don't you see? It's useless trying to figure out how or why because it isn't supposed to make sense. It never has. No one's powerful enough to manipulate our lives this way. The power is in our minds. We're doing it to ourselves because this is a dream."

"It can't be." He cupped her shoulders. "I can feel you. You're right here."

"No, I'm not. I'm actually lying in a hospital bed. I don't know where, but after you left me last time, I surfaced enough to hear what was going on around me and—"

"Stop. This is crazy."

"Rick, the truth is, I'm in a coma."

He shook his head. "You're saying that because you're stressed. You've been through a lot in the past few days. Weeks. Whatever."

"That's another thing, my sense of time. It's all mixed up because they said I've got . . ." She swallowed hard before she could say the words aloud. Only, she wasn't saying them at all, was she? She was imagining that she was speaking. As she was imagining the man she was speaking to. "I heard the doctor say I have possible brain damage," she finished.

"No way. There's nothing wrong with your brain. You're the sharpest person I know. You can think circles around me."

"Of course you'd say that. I created you."

"You what?"

"You're a product of my dreams. I made you up. My subconscious put together a man I never would have met in real life. A man who's kind, sensitive, funny, and strong. A man whose music touched my soul. A man who actually believes in love. That alone should have tipped me off that you couldn't be real." She wiped her eyes on her sleeve. It was slick nylon and no more real than the purple wool had been. For someone who never cried, she was imagining a lot of tears lately.

He stroked her cheek to wipe away the tears she'd missed. "You're tired, that's all. You'll feel better once you rest."

"No, I won't. If I fall asleep now, I'll wake up in another dream where you need to save me. It happens every time, don't you see? Whenever I black out, the pattern starts all over."

"Elizabeth . . ."

"I'll prove it." She pushed out of his embrace, slid aside the fragment of ceiling panel that served as the door, and crawled out of the shelter.

"Elizabeth, wait! Where are you going?"

She straightened. The ice pellets hit her face like a hundred tiny needles. She pivoted away from the wind and found she could see no more than a foot in front of her. The storm was as featureless as the fog in the forest had been, only it was propelling her forward. She stretched her arms and walked blindly where the wind led her, listening for voices, for the beep of the heart monitor. She spread her fingers wide, feeling for the phantom touch of Monica or the doctor or the woman named Norma, anyone to guide her back to reality.

She felt only the cold and emptiness. The further she walked, the more she regretted not putting on the gloves that had been in her pockets.

But the gloves and the snow were as unreal as the wind that pushed at her back and the ice that was starting to coat her hair. It shouldn't matter if she froze her fingers or her toes. It would make no difference if she walked off the edge of the plateau and dropped into the ravine. Her injuries would heal like the scratch on her neck and the black eye and the stab wound in her side. Her mind would make her whole in time for the next dream, and the one after that, and the one after that.

How many times would she need to face her own death before she could take back her life?

A heavy weight hit her from behind, tackling her to the snow.

She fought back instinctively, using her elbows and her feet, trying to dislodge her attacker.

"Whoa, settle down. I won't hurt you."

At Rick's voice, she went still.

Yet inside, within her memories, she continued to fight. She hadn't seen him coming. He'd hit her from behind. She'd turned to defend herself. Pain unlike anything she had known before had sliced through her skull.

Rick rolled her to her back, grabbed her hands, and tugged her into a sitting position.

She barely felt the ice pellets on her face as the memory continued to unfold. It had been a warm night. Summer. She had parked at the curb instead of turning up the drive. She had wanted time to mull over the olive branch Delaney had offered.

Delaney. Willowbank. That's what she was remembering. She'd gone to the house where her stepmother had been staying. She remembered how quiet the street had been, with only the rustle of leaves from the trees that arched overhead. The air had smelled of freshly cut grass and the acrid bite of cedar from the hedge. She had lingered beside one of the gateposts, her hand tracing the edge of a stone. It had felt timeless. Peaceful. So unlike the steel security gates at the entrance to the Graye estate.

And then someone had attacked her. She had fallen. She had hit her head.

"Elizabeth!" Rick shook her to get her attention. "We have to go back inside."

The storm had masked the onset of dusk. Darkness was rapidly falling. Rick was little more than a blurry shape in front of her. She couldn't see his face.

But she'd seen her attacker beneath the streetlight. The image flashed from her memories. A pale, sickly looking man with thinning hair and drooping jowls. His black eyes had glittered with rage and madness. And he'd been a total stranger.

It was her last memory, that stranger's face. Her final

sight before the void had opened and she'd been lost. Drifting. Unable to think or feel. Completely helpless . . .

"Elizabeth!"

. . . until her mind had latched on to Rick. And he'd helped her build a different reality. One where she was somebody else.

Was her life that bad? Did she have a deep-seated wish to be an Elspeth or an Isabella or a Liesel instead of who she was? She wiped her face. Her hands were shaking. So was her body. She was going numb.

Rick bent forward. Before she realized his intention, he hauled her over his shoulder and straightened.

Blood rushed to her head. She dangled upside down against his back. She wriggled, trying to break his grip. "Put me down!"

"Sure. In a minute." He clamped one arm around her legs and started back the way they'd come.

"Rick! I can walk on my own."

He didn't respond. Or if he did, the wind stole his words. He slogged through the deepening snow. When they reached the shelter he'd made, he set her on her feet and brushed the crusted ice off their clothes before guiding her inside.

"Whatever you were trying to prove," he said, yanking off his coat, "I hope you're done."

"Prove?"

"I'm not going to lose you, Elizabeth." He unzipped her jacket and pulled her arms free of the sleeves. "I'm getting awful accustomed to having you around."

There was a tremor in his voice. She didn't think it was only from the cold. "I'm sorry I worried you, but—"

"Worry? No, that wasn't worry. Worry is wondering if you remembered to turn off your headlights. What you did scared the crap out of me." He cupped her hands in his and blew on them, then swung her legs over his lap and draped both their coats around their shoulders. "Tuck your head under my chin. That'll help your hair dry faster."

The tears returned. "You're acting as if you care about me," she murmured.

"You picked up on that, huh?" He eased her cheek against his sweater. "Like I said before, you're smart."

"But you don't care. Not really. I'm only imagining that you do."

He slid his arms around her back beneath their coats. "Let's talk about this tomorrow."

"Tomorrow we'll be somewhere else. It might not even be tomorrow. It could be days or weeks from now. They said I've been in the coma for a long time."

"It's okay. I know things don't look good now, but we'll get out of this. Don't give up."

"I'm not giving up!"

"That's my girl."

"You don't believe anything I said, do you?"

"You mean about this being a dream?"

"It is, Rick. It has to be. Nothing else makes sense."

"Not everything has to make sense. Trust me; I understand how it feels to want to escape. You think you're doing fine, your life ticking along like you wanted when boom, fate hits you like a freight train you never saw coming. You lose it all. Trying to figure out the how and why of things can make you crazy."

"I'm not crazy. I have a brain injury. There's a difference."

"All right."

"It's true. I even remember how it happened."

"Okay, how?"

"I was mugged and fell against a stone gatepost."

He rested his chin on the top of her head. "I'm sorry."

"That must be why I've been having those headaches."

"Do you have one now?"

"No, they disappeared once we got out of the dungeon. But I'm still trapped. I need to wake up."

A gust of wind rattled their shelter. Fine snow sifted through a crack to settle on her face. Rick blew it away. "What happens when you wake up?" he asked.

"I'll do my damnedest to get my life back."

"In Manhattan."

"That's where I live."

"It's a long way from Oklahoma."

Why was he doing this? He was an intelligent man. That is, she imagined him to be an intelligent man. He must realize there was little chance of the two of them surviving long enough to be rescued if they actually were huddling in the wreckage of a plane that had crashed into a mountainside during a blizzard. What was the use of pointing out how far apart they lived? Once she did wake up, they would be separated by far more than geography.

Yet for the time being this was her only reality. And regardless of the circumstances, it felt good to be in Rick's arms. She treasured the feel of his breath on her skin. She loved the rumble of his voice against her ear. He made her feel safe. Cherished. It was a rare luxury, not to be alone.

Idiot. She *was* alone.

She rubbed her cheek against his sweater. The light had faded completely. She couldn't see him anymore, but she knew he was there. She felt him, both inside and out, the same way she'd felt his music. "I do want my life back," she said. "But I lost everything long before I ended up in this coma."

"How's that?"

"I told you. When my father died before he could change his will, my stepmother inherited the entire estate."

"But you're rich anyway."

"Yes, I have money of my own, but my father was worth billions. The house alone was valued at close to twenty million."

"Is wealth that important to you?"

"It's not the money, it's the principle. It's about claiming what should have been mine. What I'd been promised. It's about . . ." She trailed off, uncomfortable with the word that had come to her mind.

He filled it in anyway. "Winning," he said.

"It's what my father would have done. It's why he cut me out of his will in the first place. I injured his pride when I refused to fall into line and pretend I was pleased with his second marriage, because it was obvious that Delaney was nothing but a trophy wife."

"You never know. Maybe they loved each other."

"Please. He was sixty-eight when they got married and she's only two years older than me. She was a possession to him. He liked pretty things and she bolstered his ego."

"What about your mother? Did he divorce her so he could marry Delaney?"

"No, she died when I was thirteen."

"I'm sorry."

"It was a heart attack. There were no warning signs, it was very sudden."

He combed his fingers through her hair, separating the damp strands to spread them out. "What was she like?"

"Beautiful. Busy. I didn't see her very often."

"Why not?"

"I went to boarding schools so I was away most of the year. When I was home for holidays, she was usually too immersed in entertaining to spare much time for me. We didn't have much in common until I started to play the piano. Sometimes, she would invite me to play for her guests. There was a Steinway concert grand in the front sitting room."

"Sounds classy."

"It was a wonderful instrument. It had a rich tone that was full-bodied and perfectly balanced. At school I practiced on the uprights that were in the music rooms, but they were institutional grade and built sturdy to tolerate abuse. There's no comparison between the responsiveness of those workhorses and our old Steinway."

"It sounds as if you were serious about your music."

She nodded against his shoulder. "When I was young, I used to dream of being a concert pianist."

"What happened?"

"Short answer, I grew up."

"We've got all night. Give me the long answer."

Even though the shelter was pitch-black, she closed her eyes. She could feel the pressure of tears behind her eyelids again. She hadn't spoken of this to anyone. Ever. Part of her continued to be conscious of the fact she wasn't really talking to anyone now, either. The awareness didn't change her urge to confide in Rick.

Maybe it wasn't only her death she had to keep facing before she could wake up. Maybe she had to face the truth about her life. That could be one of the reasons her subconscious had created a man who was such a sympathetic listener.

"Lizzie?"

He uttered the nickname so naturally, she couldn't take exception to it. It seemed right that he would call her something no one else did. "I wasn't close to my mother," she said finally. "We didn't have displays of affection in our house. I started taking piano lessons as a way to please her, but then I discovered I liked music. It was different from anything I'd known because it was honest, with no expectations or hidden price attached. The pleasure was free for the taking. There was a world of emotion in the pieces I played. It was the only true intimacy I had ever experienced. I could connect with total strangers who had been dead for centuries by fitting my fingers to the same notes they had written, and that was amazing. Once I became skilled enough, my mother enjoyed listening to me play. She said I made her proud. Our passion for the classics was the one bond we shared. She encouraged me to pursue it as a career. I set my sights on someday winning a spot at Julliard."

"You must have been good. Why didn't you?"

"Things changed when she died."

"How?"

She hadn't touched on the memory for years. Now it rose full-blown in her mind. The lines of cars. The streams of people she didn't recognize who talked about her mother as if she were a stranger, and later the utter silence in the house. "The day after her funeral, the chauffeur was supposed to take me back to school but I refused to get in the car. Instead, I sat at the piano and channeled my feelings into Chopin, because I didn't know how else to handle my grief. It was self-indulgent and irresponsible. My father was furious when he came home from the office and found I had overruled his instructions."

"What did he expect? You were only thirteen. You'd just lost your mother. He shouldn't have left you alone in the first place."

"I was old enough to understand that what had pleased my mother had the opposite effect on my father. He valued self-discipline and control, and he despised emotional weakness. He had little respect for the arts in general, unless it was to buy a painting or a first edition as an investment. But with my mother gone, he was all I had left, so I was desperate to find a way to please him."

"What did you do?"

"The next time I had a break from school, I accompanied him to Grayecorp. He fitted an extra chair at the side of his desk and showed me how to balance a ledger. I caught on fast because I was good at math. It turned out I had an aptitude for business, too. I forgot about Julliard and eventually majored in business at Harvard. I was on my way to making my first million before I graduated."

"What about your music?"

"I thought my father needed me, Rick. That was more important to me than a childish dream. I changed the direction of my life to earn his . . . approval."

"You were going to say love, weren't you?"

It hadn't really been a question, so she didn't give a reply.

"That was the carrot-on-a-stick love you once mentioned," he said.

"Whatever faults Stanford Graye had as a parent, he was a brilliant businessman. I was fortunate to have him for a mentor. He taught me invaluable lessons, including how to win. He named me his heir and groomed me to be his successor at Grayecorp in recognition of my loyalty. I knew I would never earn his love, and that was fine, because I would have what he considered most important."

"His money."

"Exactly. Money and power, that's what counted. When he changed his will, it was to punish me. He publicly rejected me. He not only humiliated me personally, he undermined my position at the company. It was as if giving up my dream and spending fifteen years molding myself into a person he could love meant nothing. I was angry."

"You were hurt."

"And I was angry that I still had the capacity to be hurt. I had been raised to be tougher than that. I knew the kind of man he was, and it was my own fault for trusting him. So I decided to use what he'd taught me about manipulating emotions and I turned his ego and his vanity against him."

"How?"

"He didn't love Delaney—he'd started cheating on her within weeks of returning from their honeymoon—but it would have been a blow to his pride if she left him. I told him I would expose his unfaithfulness to her unless he reinstated me in his will and signed a contract that would eventually put me in control of Grayecorp."

"You blackmailed him?"

"It would have worked. He'd agreed to my terms, but he died before he could get to his lawyer." She was grateful for the darkness. It made it easier for her to ignore the tears that were now streaming down her cheeks. Her father would have mocked her for crying, even over him. "One minute he was there, bigger than life, the next there was a huge hole where he'd been. The wealth I'd helped my father earn, the house I grew up in, and the Steinway that I had poured my heart into were gone, too. Everything went to the brainless twit whose only skill was being able to ornament an old man's arm."

"Yeah," he said softly. "That must have hurt."

There was no condemnation in his voice, only sympathy. God, Rick was too good to be true. Literally. She swallowed hard, but was unable to get rid of the lump in her throat. "Doesn't it bother you that I blackmailed my own father? Most people would consider that despicable."

"I've got no right to judge anyone. We all do things when we're in pain that we wish we hadn't. We don't stop to think about what it'll do to other people, all we want is to find a way out."

A way out, she thought. Like dreaming up a storybook hero to save her from the wreckage of her life.

He rearranged their coats to tuck them more firmly around her, then settled her against his chest. "Are you warmer now?"

"Yes. Thanks. Rick . . ."

"It's all right, Lizzie. We'll get through this."

He'd said that before. How she wanted to believe him. And how she wanted to believe *in* him.

He pressed a kiss to the top of her forehead. "On second thought, Oklahoma isn't all that far from New York."

Her sob startled her. Even with the hum of the wind and the constant swish of the snow and ice against the shelter, it echoed loudly through her head. She bit her lip. *Rick, I want to wake up, but if I do, I'll lose you.*

His voice floated through her mind. *You won't.*

But I'm not here. I'm in a coma. You're not really here, either.

Uh-huh, sure. He stroked her hair. *Whatever you say.*

I need *to wake up.*

Okay then, I'll hold you until you do.

TEN

So we clung to each other, adrift in the night,
One kiss, one touch, one soul.
My blue-eyed angel, my dream come to life,
My sweet Liz, I won't ever let go.

Rick accompanied the final line with a minor chord, then bent the G string until it lifted into a major. He bowed his head to listen as the last note faded to silence. He'd written "Angel Liz" last week. He usually preferred to polish an arrangement longer than that before he performed it in public, but this ballad had felt right. Ending with a major chord was also a departure from his usual pattern, but that had seemed right, too, so he'd trusted his instincts. Not all love songs had to be sad.

For a moment no one stirred. The audience seemed to be holding their breath. Either that, or he'd finally managed to put them to sleep. He swung his guitar to his side as he slid off the stool. "That's all for tonight, folks. Thanks for—"

The sudden applause made him jerk. He shielded his eyes from his brother's low-wattage version of stage lights and peered into the barroom.

People were on their feet. It took him a beat to realize they weren't heading for the exit. They were giving him a standing O.

At least, he assumed the response was for him. He

glanced over his shoulder to make sure Garth Brooks hadn't magically appeared on the stage behind him. The only guys there were the trio who were playing backup. Eddie, the bass guitarist, was blowing kisses to the audience while Hank used his fiddle to make a sweeping bow. Dwayne spun his drumsticks and gave the cymbals a few celebratory smacks, then motioned wildly for Rick to take a bow.

He did. Man, it felt good. Beer bottles clinked as some of the people who were still in their seats slapped their palms on the tables. Boot heels stomped the floor. The women nearest to the stage appeared to be wiping their eyes. Jethro whistled from his post behind the bar and gave him a thumbs-up.

Rick grinned and returned the gesture. He wished Elizabeth could see this. She understood the power music could have. Here was proof of how his emotions could connect with strangers, exactly as she'd said. Fans of the classical stuff she liked probably wouldn't express their appreciation with beer bottles and boots, though . . .

His grin slipped. Hell, he was doing it again. When he was awake, he understood that what happened while he was with Elizabeth wasn't real, yet she seemed more alive every time he encountered her. The line between what he dreamed and what he knew to be true was getting blurrier, because the feelings his dreams left him with were genuine. In fact, the memory of holding Elizabeth while she slept had been strong enough to inspire this song.

The applause tapered off as the audience got back to what they'd come for, namely drinking and hooking up. He took a final bow with the guys, reminded everyone his CD was for sale at the bar and through his website, then propped his guitar on its stand and left the stage.

Zeb slapped him on the back as he reached the bar. "That was terrific, Uncle Rick! They loved it!"

"Yeah, I gotta admit you didn't totally suck for a change," Jethro said. "Was that new?"

Rick nodded. "I thought I'd try something different."

"We've got to record that," Zeb said. "It's going to make us a mint."

"It's still got a few rough spots."

"No way. It's perfect. Can you round up the guys for Sunday morning?"

"If they're not too hungover. Why?"

"My friend at the studio said the whole place is getting painted this weekend. No one's using it, so as long you keep clear of the walls and ignore the smell, we're in."

"Sure, why not?"

"Great." Zeb rubbed his hands together, as if he was already envisioning dollar bills, or maybe cyber money. "Do you have any more songs like that one?"

Before Rick could reply, a hand settled on his arm. A cloud of flowery perfume enveloped him.

A petite redhead stood at his elbow. He searched for a name. Ginger Lensky. She worked the cash register at the lumber yard. She'd been a few years ahead of him in high school. "Hello, cowboy," she said. "Great show. Especially the last song."

"Thanks."

"You made me cry."

"Sorry."

She laughed, shaking back her hair and launching an explosion of perfume. "Not in a bad way, Rick. It was beautiful."

"Glad you liked it."

"I never knew you were such a sensitive man. It's real sexy."

"Uh, thanks."

"So, who is she?"

"Hmm?"

"Liz. Your angel. Anyone I know?"

He noticed Zeb and Jethro were following the conversation with interest. He shrugged. "Just someone I dreamed up."

"I liked what I heard. Maybe you could sing it again for me sometime."

"I'm on again at ten tomorrow."

She leaned closer, her fingers sliding around his biceps.

She stroked his sleeve. "But you're through for the night now, aren't you?"

"That's right."

"Can I buy you a drink?"

"Sorry, I'm heading home."

"Then can I give you a ride?"

"Thanks, but I've got my truck."

"You sure? It's no trouble."

He tried not to flinch as she pressed her breast against his forearm. She probably wanted to be sure he understood her invitation, but a man would have to be blind, deaf, and gelded not to have figured it out already. "I appreciate the offer, Ginger, but I wouldn't be good company. I'm really beat. Sorry."

"Don't be." She ran a crimson fingernail down the center of his chin. "We'll do it some other time."

He blew out his breath as she walked away. She likely knew he wasn't the only man watching her, since she gave her hips an extra swing. The jeans she wore could have been painted on, and she did have a shapely rear view, but the display left him cold. He'd never gotten a good look at Elizabeth's lower half. It had been draped in yards of wool or baggy pants or padded nylon. Odd that he was so certain he would enjoy watching her from the back. Not that he'd want to see her walk away from him. The memory of her going off on her own in the blizzard was enough to curl his gut with panic . . .

Ginger was real. Elizabeth wasn't. As she herself had pointed out before she'd walked into that blizzard.

Yeah, the line was getting blurred all right. There was little wonder why. The plane crash dream had been more vivid than any of the others. Surviving that disaster had brought their relationship to a new level. Elizabeth had opened up to him, painting a picture of her life that had been all too believable. She'd shared details he knew couldn't have been easy to confess. She'd let down her guard, she'd trusted him. They had never been closer.

Yet she regarded *him* as a figment of *her* imagination.

He must have one convoluted subconscious for his dream woman to insist *she* was the one who was dreaming.

But where the heck had he come up with the idea that she was in a coma? She'd managed to make a pretty convincing case for it, too. He wouldn't have thought he had that much imagination.

It made sense, though. The fact she was only a dream hadn't proven enough of a deterrent to stop his feelings for her from growing. Might as well throw in an added complication, namely that she was comatose, to help point him back to reality.

"Hello?" Jethro reached across the bar to rap his knuckles against Rick's forehead.

Rick was a second too late knocking his arm aside. He rubbed his head. "Cut it out."

"Are you that thick? Couldn't you see Ginger was hitting on you?"

"Wow. Really?"

"She's a good-looking woman. You could do worse."

"She's not my type, old man."

"You don't have a type, little brother."

"Sure he does," Zeb said. "He likes blondes."

Jethro snorted. "With a face like his, he can't be that picky."

"Elizabeth's—" Zeb realized his mistake before he finished saying the name. He compounded it by grimacing. "Sorry, Uncle Rick."

"Elizabeth," Jethro repeated. He snapped his fingers. "That's the woman you mentioned last month. The one you claimed you're not seeing. Elizabeth is Angel Liz."

"Leave it alone, Jethro, it's just a name. I thought about using Brunhilda but it wouldn't fit into the lyrics."

"What's wrong with this woman? How come you don't want us to meet her?"

"That would be kind of difficult."

"Why? She in jail?"

"Does a dungeon count?"

"I'm being serious. Why all the secrecy?"

"Sometimes a man likes his privacy," Zeb put in. "That's why I don't bring my dates home. The way you and Ma interrogate them scares them off. It cramps my style."

"Wait a minute, what dates?" Jethro asked. "Who are you seeing? Does your mother know her?"

"See? I rest my case."

One of the waitresses set a tray of empties on the bar. "I need five Millers and a Bud, Jethro," she said. "Hey, good going, Rick."

"Thanks."

"Everyone loved that last song, but I didn't see it on your CD."

"I'm working on material for a new one."

"I'd say it won you some new fans." She hefted the refilled tray. "Hope you remember all us little people when you hit the big time."

He laughed. His grip on reality might be iffy when it came to a certain woman, but he had no illusions about becoming an overnight success. The music business didn't work that way. He had to pay his dues, build up a fan base, get some name recognition working for him before he could consider approaching a record company.

Yet he never thought about success or money when he wrote his songs. He did it because he had to. It wasn't so much creating the tunes as letting them out. Elizabeth would understand. Music fulfilled a need for him as it once had for her . . .

Damn, he had to get a better grip. How many times did he have to tell himself that Elizabeth wasn't—

Rick.

He froze. He hadn't heard her voice, he'd felt it in his head. It was no louder than a whisper, softer than a breath, yet it came through like a shout.

He glanced around. He tried to keep the motion casual, even though every muscle in his body was suddenly throbbing with tension. Zeb had joined his father behind the bar and they both were busy filling orders. Neither of them appeared to have heard what he had. They were acting perfectly normal. He scanned the Cantina. There were a few blondes, but none with Elizabeth's wild, wheat gold hair . . .

He stopped when he realized what he was doing. What was wrong with him? He was awake. He was sure of it.

Rick?

Her voice wasn't only in his head, it spread along his nerves, warming him like sunshine breaking through clouds. It was sensation, not sound. He replied the same way. *Elizabeth?*

You can hear me?

To describe it as *hearing* didn't come close to what he was experiencing. This was like the mental bond they'd shared in those dreams when their minds had joined. Only he wasn't dreaming. *Where are you?*

She didn't answer the question with words, she answered with feelings. A wave of loneliness swept over him. It reached deep inside, straight to the place he kept his own.

Instinct overruled logic. He stopped trying to analyze what was happening. His only thought was to find her. He grabbed his jacket from behind the bar and headed outside.

Jethro didn't skimp on the lighting for the parking lot. A floodlight near the eaves of the building revealed two lines of vehicles, mostly pickups, along with a handful of departing customers. Rick scrutinized the people but none of them was Elizabeth. He closed his eyes, reaching for her with his other senses.

The ground beneath his feet suddenly tilted. He put his hand against the side of the building for balance. Instead of rough stucco, he felt something smooth and soft. Like a flannel sheet or a blanket. The air smelled crisp. Clean. With the after bite of plastic and alcohol. Not booze alcohol but disinfectant. He recognized that smell. It was a hospital. His eyes snapped open.

The floodlight was gone. So was the parking lot. In its place was a dense, colorless . . . nothingness. It was like the blizzard on the mountainside, without the wind and cold. Or the fog he'd dreamed of riding through during the dream about escaping the castle, only even more featureless. It was as if he'd stepped into a pocket of a separate reality, here, yet not here.

He should be afraid. In fact, he didn't understand why he wasn't freaking out, but he felt no threat from the fog. Instead, he felt a sense of . . . anticipation.

"Rick?"

A figure slowly took shape in front of him. His pulse kicked with an extra beat, as it always did when he imagined her. "Elizabeth."

Her face gradually appeared out of the emptiness. She clutched a knitted shawl around her shoulders. Beneath it, she wore what seemed like a hospital gown. She stared at him for a few seconds—or a few minutes, he couldn't tell—before she extended her fingertips to the back of his hand. She pressed lightly, as if testing whether he was there. "Can you feel that?"

Her touch was strange, like her voice. It was more substantial than what he felt in his dreams, yet less direct. He sensed it from the inside out. "Yeah, but I don't know how I could. I'm awake."

"So am I. Or as close to awake as I can manage." She touched his forehead. Her chin trembled. "Your scratch healed. How long has it been?"

"Since the plane crash?"

She nodded. A lock of hair slid over her cheek.

"That was six nights ago."

"It was only a dream, like the other times."

"I know that." He brushed her hair behind her ear. That felt strange, too, sparking through his fingers from the inside, as if the sensations started in his brain before they spread to his body instead of the other way around. "At least I understand they were only dreams whenever I'm awake. How come—" He broke off and dropped his hand. "Hell, I must be cracking up," he muttered. "You can't be here. I'm talking to myself."

Tears welled in her eyes. "I'm the crazy one. If I ever do wake up fully, I'll probably need counseling. I felt you . . ."

She pointed at her temple. "In here. As if you were thinking about me."

He had been thinking about her. He couldn't seem to stop. She was as impossible to ignore as a melody that got stuck in his head.

"That's why I tried calling to you," she said. "I realize I shouldn't, because I need to ground myself in reality but I . . . missed you, Rick."

Her need was as tangible as her touches had been. He responded reflexively. He opened his arms and pulled her to his chest.

They fit together perfectly, as if they were exactly where they both belonged. Nutty or not, it felt right. He sighed. "I missed you, too."

She slid her hands beneath his jacket and pressed them to his back. "I hate being like this."

"You want me to let go?"

"No! I meant I hate being so helpless. This isn't me."

"It's okay. We all need help sometimes."

"The staff here are trying their best. Sometimes I can hear people reading aloud to me. They often leave the television on or play music. They're trying to stimulate my brain. I can feel when they touch me, but I can't respond. Not like I can with you."

"You still believe you're in a coma."

"What else could it be? Look around us."

He still couldn't see anything besides Elizabeth, but he became aware of faint electronic noises. Muted beeps penetrated the fog. They could be monitors, as would be expected next to someone in a coma. The sound of an orchestra floated in the background. It was playing something classical.

Yet he couldn't be in a hospital. He was in the Cantina parking lot.

At the thought, the ground shifted again. The sounds of the machines and the orchestra dimmed.

He dipped his cheek against Elizabeth's ear. Her hair tickled his chin. Her familiar scent, like warmed spices, mixed with the hospital smells. The heat of her body spread through his. Right now, he didn't care if he was in loony-tunes land, all he knew was that he didn't want to let her go. He tightened his embrace, trying to hang on.

Light flashed from his right. A horn honked. "Hey, cow-boy!" a woman called. "Did you change your mind?"

The voice wasn't Elizabeth's. It was too sharp. He blinked and lifted his head.

The fog disappeared. His arms were empty. Elizabeth was gone.

A red hatchback idled in front of him. Ginger Lensky regarded him through the open driver's-side window. "It's not that late," she said. "We can go for coffee somewhere if you're in the mood to talk."

Rick rubbed his face. His hands were shaking. He shoved them into his coat pockets, feeling for his keys as if grabbing a life ring.

What the hell was going on in his head? Sure, he didn't want to go out with a real woman, but fantasizing about Elizabeth wasn't going to help him overcome that.

Somehow he must have managed to dredge up enough words for a polite refusal, because Ginger smiled and drove off as if everything was completely normal, as if the park-ing lot hadn't been a foggy void a second ago, as if he hadn't been holding his fantasy woman while he was wide awake.

He made it as far as his truck. He didn't trust himself to start it up. He folded his arms on the steering wheel and concentrated on his breathing. The air was cold. It bore whiffs of his dog and the Big Mac he'd grabbed on his way to work tonight. There was a star-shaped ding in the wind-shield where a piece of gravel had hit it last spring. A few cars to his right, a door slammed and an engine revved. In the distance a siren whooped briefly.

This was reality. He understood that. He hadn't been trying to escape it.

So what the *hell* had just happened?

ELEVEN

"SHE'S CRYING AGAIN, BERYL."

"I see that, Norma. Dr. Shouldice believes it's an involuntary response. Her eyes are producing excess moisture. It's a reflection of the general rise in the level of her autonomic functions."

"Or maybe she's sad. Did he think of that?"

"As there's no way anyone could tell the difference, probably not." Crepe soles squeaked beside the bed. A motor hummed briefly as the head was raised. "Either way, it's a good sign."

Elizabeth felt something soft wipe the moisture from her cheek. *I'm here!* she cried. *I can hear you!*

But as she already knew, the nurses couldn't hear her. They couldn't span the void that separated her from them. These were flesh-and-blood women and they couldn't see her attempts to blink back her tears, either, or understand that it was frustration more than sadness that made them flow faster.

"Have you observed any difficulty with the monitors since the overhaul?"

"No, they're ticking along great."

"Mrs. Harrison has been calling for daily updates." The cloth dabbed around her lips. "She was adamant about ensuring those alarms were functioning properly."

"I can't blame her, with creeps like Lidstone hanging around."

"Be careful, Norma. If one of the doctors hears you talking about him like that—"

"Lay off, Beryl. You know as well as I do that they didn't want him coming in here, putting his nose into their case."

"That may be, but it's been my experience that doctors stick together. We're supposed to follow their orders, not question them."

"I don't have any problem following orders that I agree with."

There was a quiet chuckle. "Cheeky girl. When you've been at this as long as I have, you'll know better. Your opinions don't carry any weight unless you've got medical diplomas on your wall."

"Or you've got pockets as deep as Mrs. Harrison's."

Beryl grunted under her breath as she picked up Elizabeth's wrist and fitted her fingertips over the pulse point. "You're lucky that she does have deep pockets. A job like yours wouldn't be that easy to come by. Getting paid for reading. In my day we did real nursing."

"Say what you want, but I'm sure the strategy has been helping." Chair legs scraped against the floor. When Norma spoke again, her voice was closer, as if she had sat beside the bed. "And I don't care what the machines show, I can tell she's starting to hear us."

Yes, I hear you! Elizabeth strained to move her hand, but it continued to hang limply in the nurse's grasp. She wondered who Mrs. Harrison was. The director of the hospital? Possibly. She must be someone in authority. If she'd had anything to do with the nurses' program of mental stimulation, then Elizabeth owed her a debt of gratitude. This was the first time she'd heard anyone mention Dr. Lidstone. Judging from the tone they'd used, he wasn't highly regarded. She wished she had remembered to tell Rick more about her surroundings the last time she'd seen him. She had meant to, but she'd been sidetracked by the pleasure of touching him, and hearing his deep voice strum through her mind, and feeling his arms around her . . .

No, she reminded herself. She'd imagined him, that was

all. She'd been so desperate not to be alone that she had deliberately conjured up her fantasy man to keep her company, and she'd done it while she'd been awake. She couldn't fall back on the excuse of claiming it was only a dream. He was an adult version of an imaginary playmate. She'd never had one as a child. She hadn't felt the need to escape then. She'd had her music instead.

God, she was pathetic.

Beryl squeezed her hand before she laid it back on the bed. The cloth dabbed her cheeks again. "Her eyes do seem to be watering more than I would have expected," she said. "I'll make a note of it in her chart before I leave."

"Okay, have a good weekend."

"You, too."

Footsteps retreated from the room. The chair scraped briefly again. There was the whisper of flicking pages. "Where was I," Norma muttered. "Oh, right. Here we are." She cleared her throat and began to read:

They followed the stream to a clearing. It seemed empty until the mist parted to reveal the outline of a small cottage. A layer of velvet moss softened the slate roof while lush, glossy-leaved swaths of ivy blanketed the walls, giving the illusion that it had grown from the earth like the trees that surrounded it.

Raoul, Lord of Hawksreach, leaned forward to stroke the neck of his destrier before he turned to Heloise. His long hair had come loose from its queue, draping his shoulders in a cape as black as a raven's wing. "Behold, my lady, we have found sanctuary."

"'Tis but a hovel."

"Nay. Magic imbues it, for upon the instant a beautiful woman crosses its humble threshold, it will seem a palace." He swung down from the enormous horse in one graceful motion, then stepped up to the dainty palfrey she rode and held out his arms to her. "Let us begin the transformation."

"You tease me, sir."

"Come, Heloise, we must not tarry. Darkness approaches."

Though many a nobleman had paid court to Heloise dur-

ing the years she had dwelt with her father, never had one
affected her as deeply as Raoul. His features were so handsome, his body so tall and well formed, her heart fluttered
like a captive butterfly in her chest. She pressed her hand
over her heaving bosom, unfamiliar with the longings he
stirred. "We have no chaperone."

"We have passed this whole day with no company other
than each other."

"Aye, we have been together for the day, but what of the
night?"

"Do you fear I plan to ravish you?"

"Nay, that is not what I fear."

Raoul's pale blue eyes sparkled as he slid his hand
beneath her skirt to ease her foot from the stirrup. His long,
callused fingers caressed her ankle. "Then why do you
hesitate, my lady?"

She moistened her lips.

His gaze heated as he watched her tongue. "Neither your
cousin, the king, nor his captain will find you here," he said
hoarsely. "If the gods are just, the baroness will already be
upon your evil cousin's throne and he will end this day in
the very chains he dared command Ganulf to put upon you."

"I do not fear the king or his minions, my lord. You have
well and truly rescued me."

Raoul curled his fingers around her calf. His index finger
teased the sensitive skin behind her knee. "Then tell me
what is amiss so that I may banish that which troubles you.
I am yours to command."

Would that it were so, she thought, then blushed at her
own audaciousness. "We have traveled long and far in our
flight from the castle."

"Do not worry. You will be safe here."

"You misunderstand, Raoul. I worry only that you may
not wish to ravish me."

Laughing, he pulled her off the horse and into his arms . . .

Elizabeth listened, intrigued, as Norma continued to
read. The prose was florid but oddly captivating. The dia-

logue between Raoul and Heloise progressed from flirtatious banter to a sensuous, verbal mating dance. Obviously, this was a romance novel. She had never read a romance before, but what else could it be? This must be the book Monica and the nurse had been talking about the first time Elizabeth had become aware of where she was, when she had heard their voices in the fog.

Good God, was this why she had repeatedly dreamed about being in the Middle Ages? It made sense. From the sound of it, the story was well underway, so Norma must have read it to her before. Though the names of the hero and heroine were different, the other names were the same, as were the setting and the time period. Her mind must have processed what she'd heard subliminally. Her subconscious had used the idea as the framework for her dream.

But she was no blushing virgin, and Rick wasn't anything like Raoul, aside from the fact he knew how to handle a horse. He was no smarmy, black-haired chunk of beefcake from a book cover. His eyes were amber, not blue. His features were a long way from what people would call classically handsome, but he was smart and talented and sensitive and . . .

And no more real than Heloise's Raoul.

Pathetic.

Norma had her attention on the book, so she didn't see the fresh round of tears that trickled over Elizabeth's cheekbones and dripped past her jaw to fall into her hair. Elizabeth felt the track of each one. In her mind, she scrubbed them aside with her fists, while in reality her arms remained at her sides. This was more than frustrating, it was maddening. She tried to block out Norma's voice. She didn't want to hear how two totally fictitious characters were going to find love and a happy ending. She needed to concentrate on getting back to the real world if she was ever going to reclaim her life.

Yet for now she had no choice other than to lie here and listen as the story unfolded. The author's words wove among her thoughts, painting the featureless void around her with fingers of sunset gold. Dusk sifted through the branches of an ancient forest. The joyous babbling of a stream drowned out the monotonous beep of her heart monitor. It took several pages for the protagonists to work their way into the picturesque, fairy-tale cottage. Half a chapter more to get a blaze going in the cozy stone fireplace with the fortuitously placed stack of tinder and firewood. Though Elizabeth fought to remain anchored in her surroundings, the effort was exhausting. Her consciousness faded. Gradually, inexorably, she drifted to sleep.

She wasn't sure how long she dozed. When she awoke again, it was to the smell of smoke. It clawed at the back of her throat, triggering a spurt of panic. Norma's voice was gone. She could hear nothing except the crackle of a fire.

Fire! No, not that! She couldn't move. She was completely helpless, trapped in the bed to be burned alive. Her eyes flew open.

Orange light flickered across the walls. Swaths of white smoke hung in the air above her. She rolled to her side. Bed ropes creaked. Across the room a man was kneeling in front of a fireplace of rounded stones, his lean body silhouetted by the flames. He wore a loose shirt of worn-thin cotton and leggings that molded his butt and every flexed muscle in his legs. What on earth . . .

The moment of disorientation didn't last. She recognized the scene. She wasn't in the hospital room, she was in the cottage from Norma's book. She ground her teeth, willing herself to wake up—to really wake up—but the scene in front of her didn't waver. She flipped aside the blanket that covered her and pushed herself up on one arm. Her elbow sank into a mattress that felt as if it were stuffed with feathers.

The man at the fireplace coughed as he turned. "Sorry about that, Lizzie. Doesn't look as if anyone's cleaned this chimney for years."

Elizabeth raked her hair off her face. "Rick?"

"You sound surprised." He cocked his head. "You expecting someone else?"

Her pulse leapt at the sight of his lopsided smile. Her heart fluttered in her chest like . . . like a captive butterfly.

Damn, she was worse than Heloise. She dropped back on the bed. "I don't believe this."

"We got lucky. There's a well out back, and I saw what looks like a game trail. I'll set a few snares once the fire's going." There was a dull thunk, as if he'd knocked two pieces of firewood together. Light flared on the rafters overhead. "With any luck, we'll have roast rabbit for breakfast."

She flung her arm across her eyes. This was all a trick of her mind. More fantasies wouldn't help her. She had to snap out of this delusion.

"What's wrong?" The bed dipped as he sat beside her, sending her sliding against his hip. He rubbed her shoulder. "Elizabeth?"

Her skin warmed beneath his touch. Pleasure spread through her body. She fought the urge to arch like a cat. "I'm not here," she muttered. "This isn't happening. It's a construct of my subconscious based on the framework of a romance novel."

"A romance novel, huh? I'm flattered."

She heard the laughter in his voice and swatted his leg. "It's not funny."

"It won't be if Ganulf's boys catch up with us, but we should be safe enough here. I think we can finally relax." He slid his fingers down her arm to caress the inside of her elbow. Long, callused fingers, like Raoul's, except Rick's calluses were from playing the guitar, not wielding swords and battle-axes. "How are you feeling?"

"You tell me."

"I might be slow on the uptake when it comes to women—that's what my brother says anyway—but I'm going to go out on a limb here and guess you could be a bit cranky."

She sat up. It wasn't easy, because the mattress was essentially an oversized pillow. All the better for Raoul to seduce Heloise on. She bumped into Rick's side. He put one arm around her shoulders to steady her. She allowed herself no more than a moment to enjoy the contact before she leaned aside. "I'm beyond cranky, Rick. I'm frustrated and fed up with bouncing between one insane scenario and another.

You can quit pretending you don't know what I'm talking about because you're a product of my subconscious so you must know everything that I do."

"Whoa there. I'm a what?"

"Product of my subconscious. A figment of my imagination. A fantasy of my damaged mind. This is all a dream. I explained it to you after the plane crashed. You do remember that, don't you?"

He took her hand and pressed it against his cheek. "We were in a plane crash?"

"Snowstorm? Mountainside? You used the debris to build a shelter in what was left of the tail. Any of that ring a bell?"

He went still and appeared to mull it over for a while. "Yeah," he muttered finally. "I remember it now. How the hell did we get here?"

"Easy." She tapped her forehead. "I'm dreaming. Anything's possible in a dream."

"Sure, I remember now that's what you said before, but you were stressed. This can't be a dream. The plane crash wasn't, either. You can't make up the kind of things you told me." He kissed the underside of her wrist. "Did I ever tell you I like the way your skin smells? It's sort of like Christmas cookies but sexier."

"No. I'm imagining this."

"Just because a lot of the stuff going on around us is weird doesn't mean none of it's happening."

"That statement doesn't make sense."

"Not everything does." He enclosed both her hands in his. "But I am sure what I feel when I touch you is genuine."

"Why are you being so stubborn? Don't you see that only makes it harder?"

"Makes what harder?"

"Leaving you. Doing without you. Waking up on my own. That's what I need to do if I ever want to get my life back." She withdrew her hands from his grasp. She missed the contact immediately, but the loss wasn't followed by weakness as it had been when she'd first begun to imagine him. She was regaining her strength in these dreams the same way she was healing in actuality. "It was a mistake to call you last time. It's pathetic enough to imagine you in my dreams. I shouldn't let the line blur when I do manage to stay awake."

"The line blurred," he said. "I remember thinking the same thing, but I don't know when."

"It was probably the last time I saw you. You understood none of this was real then. You said you were awake, too."

His forehead furrowed. He pressed his fingertips to the puckers and rubbed hard. "That's right. I heard you call to me," he said. "Was that tonight?"

"Maybe. I can never be certain of the time or the day in this limbo."

"I dreamt I was at the Cantina. I played the new song I wrote for you. I went to the parking lot to look for you and there was this weird fog . . ."

"That wasn't a dream, Rick, that was my reality. I can't see anything because I'm in a coma. *This* is the dream," she said, sweeping her arm toward the room. "Surely you can grasp how impossible . . ." Her words trailed off when she saw his gaze drop to her chest. She glanced down.

The familiar purple gown she expected to see was gone. She wore nothing but a white cotton camisole over a pair of long, baggy bloomers. Or whatever they called lingerie in the Middle Ages. She grabbed the blanket she'd tossed off earlier and tried to cover herself, but couldn't pull it past her waist because Rick was sitting on one side. "Where's my dress?" she asked.

"I suppose you took it off."

She tugged up the neckline of her camisole. It was edged with a row of tiny pleats that flared softly over her breasts. The fabric was so fine it outlined her nipples. Which were obviously hardening. "I didn't take my dress off," she said. "The character in the story that the nurse was reading did."

"What nurse?"

"Try and keep up, Rick. I'm in a coma. I'm in a hospital. People read to me to stimulate my brain."

His lips twitched. "Seems to me that's not all that's getting stimulated."

She slapped his chest and shoved him off the bed.

"Hey!" He staggered backward a few steps before he regained his balance. "What are you mad at me for?"

"You're not taking this seriously. This is my life. I realize what I left behind might not have been ideal, but I don't want to stay here. I want to get out of this limbo and live." She slid off the other side of the bed, dragged the blanket from the mattress, and draped it around her shoulders. She clutched it closed at her throat. "And I am not Lady Elspeth or Heloise or any of those other characters my feeble mind has decided to dress me up as."

"Lizzie . . ."

"And I'm not Lizzie, either. I am Elizabeth Baylor Graye, managing director of Grayecorp. I live in Manhattan. I drive a black Mercedes. I wear pearls and power suits. I would have to be starving before I'd eat roast rabbit."

"Okay."

"And I have never had a secret desire for a romantic tryst on a feather bed with a cowboy or wandering minstrel or knight in shining armor, so if my nipples are puckering it's because of the cold."

"Glad to see you're feeling better."

"I'm not better! I'm still in the coma."

"I meant your head. Your headache must be gone for good if you can yell like that."

"I am not yelling. I do not yell. I speak assertively."

"Not that I want to give you something else to speak assertively at me about, but I did notice more than your nipples. There's no blood on your underwear. The stab wound must be gone, too."

She gripped the blanket in one hand and slipped her other hand beneath the lower edge of her camisole before she realized how ridiculous it was to check on something that hadn't been there in the first place. "Of course, it's gone. It was imaginary. The headache and the stab wound and the black eye and all the other injuries were symbolic manifestations of my condition. They're gone from my dreams because I'm healing in real life, but I'm still not awake."

"Uh-huh, whatever you say."

"Stop patronizing me."

"I'm not patronizing you, I'm . . . humoring you."

"Dammit, Rick, sometimes that easygoing cowboy thing you do can really get on my nerves."

"If you want to pick a fight, you're wasting your time because I won't bite. We're warm, we're dry, we've got shelter for the night, and we're together, so we're better off than we've ever been before."

"What is this? More live-in-the-moment philosophy?"

"Works for me. Most of the time, anyway." He held out his palms. "I didn't create this situation, Elizabeth. I'm only trying to make the best of it. Don't be mad at me. I'm on your side."

Yes, he was. She had trusted Rick from the instant she'd heard his voice. Or imagined she'd heard his voice. God, everything was so tangled, it was a wonder her headache hadn't come back. "I'm not really angry with you. This is how I handle being scared."

"By fighting?"

"It's better than crying. I've been doing far too much of that lately."

He moved closer. "What are you scared of?"

"Haven't you been listening to anything I've said? I'm trapped. I'm helpless. I want to live."

"That's what we're doing."

"It's more complicated than that."

"It's not. Deciding to live is the simple part. It's not easy, but it's a yes-or-no choice so that's what I mean when I say it's simple. Once you've got that straight, everything else follows."

She clenched her jaw. Pressure built in her throat. She couldn't tell whether it was a sob or a scream. She lifted the lower edges of the blanket clear of her feet and walked past him to the fireplace.

"I know the real reason you want to pick a fight, Elizabeth."

She focused on the log that sat on top of the fire. Flames

darted from the underside, racing tentatively from end to end until they joined to engulf it. "Fine. I can't wait to hear your diagnosis, Dr. Rick."

"It's because of what you told me the night on the mountain. You let me see what's inside you, and you're afraid we got too close."

His guess was precisely on target. Then again, who would know her better than someone who lived in her mind?

"You're not used to trusting anyone," he continued. "And you hate needing to. You're afraid I'm going to hurt you unless you come out swinging."

"What do you know about it? You're not even real."

He moved behind her. Though he didn't touch her, he stood close enough for his breath to stir her hair. "I know about being afraid to get close. And I admit there was a time I didn't have that good a grip on reality. That's what happens when the world hits you upside the head."

"Boom," she said. "You lose it all. That's what you told me."

"That's right."

He hadn't really told her anything, she reminded herself. He wasn't here. He didn't have feelings or a past because he was a figment of her imagination. And she hated being so lonely and weak-minded that she wished he wasn't. This was so confusing. "Tell me about it, Rick. What did you lose?"

"Everything."

The change in his tone made her shiver. His voice had roughened. The easygoing lilt was gone. She fisted her hands in the blanket, waiting for him to go on.

"Remember how I told you I used to own a farm?"

"Yes, I remember. You said it was near Enid. You left it a few years ago."

"It'll be four years ago next April. It wasn't much of a farm, that's why I could afford it. The bank owned most of it, but in another forty years or so it would have been mine."

This was about more than real estate, much more. She could sense it. "What happened?"

"It all changed over the space of one day. When I got up that morning I thought I was the luckiest guy in the world. I had everything I wanted. By nightfall I had lost the farm, my house, my wife, and our unborn child."

The air froze in her lungs, as if someone had punched her. She spun to face him.

Firelight couldn't soften the tension in his features. His jaw was hard, his cheekbones stark ridges. Echoes of old pain swirled in his gaze. It was the same pain she had seen when he'd first spoken about love.

Wife. Child. The words zinged around her brain. She'd never consciously considered the possibility that he might have been married, but her subconscious must have. Character as sensitive and compassionate as his couldn't have developed in a vacuum. She laid her hand on his arm. "How?"

"I was in town, framing a house for a custom-build outfit I used to sign on with from time to time. Sue was due in July, and I'd wanted the extra money so I could build an addition for the baby's room. That's why I wasn't there when the alert went out. First thing I knew about it was when the warning siren started wailing."

"Warning?"

"Tornado. There was a whole string of them that day. The feds said later ours was an EF4. It missed the town but hit the farm dead center."

She knew what was coming—she'd seen enough pictures of the aftermath of storms like that to have an idea of the devastation—yet she didn't attempt to stop him from going on. How many times had he listened to her? Now that he'd started, he had to finish.

"By the time I got home, there was nothing left of the house except the front steps and the chimney. There was nothing left of the barn at all. The wind was so strong it had stripped the bark off the trees. It skinned the cows. It blew the doors right off the storm cellar but Sue hadn't gone down there. I didn't find her until after midnight. Close as I can figure, she'd gone to the barn to set Chester loose because she knew how I loved that horse. He outran the storm.

She—" His voice broke. He pressed his lips together before he went on. "She didn't."

Elizabeth spread her arms to wrap the blanket around both of them. She remained silent as she held him, simply held him, while the fire crackled in the hearth behind her. She wished she could think of the right phrases to express her sympathy. How could she have whined about losing her father's money? How could Rick have had the patience to comfort her? The loss he'd suffered defied comprehension. The strength it must have taken to get past his grief was humbling.

He slid his arms around her waist. "I need to tell you something else, Elizabeth."

She steeled herself. How could there be more?

"You're the first woman I've held since I buried my wife."

A feeling too fierce to name shot through her heart. She tightened her embrace. "Oh, Rick. I'm so sorry."

"I had promised to keep her safe."

"It wasn't your fault."

"In my head I know that now, but it took a while for the rest of me to get the message."

If I took credit for the good luck, I'd have to take the blame for the bad. That was what he'd once told her. She'd never guessed there could have been such a tragedy behind the comment. "You're an exceptional man, Rick, to have survived a loss like that."

"For a while it was touch and go. There was a time I didn't believe that choosing to live was simple. My landmarks were gone. All I saw was the emptiness so I . . . drifted. It was like trying to find my way through fog."

"Or a blizzard."

"Yeah, you know what I mean. My family helped bring me back. My friends did, too. My old jamming partner's widow rented me her attic so I stopped living in my truck. My parents took in Chester and kept him safe until I didn't want to kill him anymore. I had blamed him, too. Dumb, huh?"

"No, it wasn't dumb. You were in pain." Something else

he'd once said came back to her. *We all do things when we're in pain that we wish we hadn't.*

"The nights were the worst. That's why my brother got me started singing in bars, to give me a way to fill those hours. Even my great aunt Betsy got in on things. She gave me a puppy so I wouldn't need to talk to myself. It was getting to be a nasty habit."

"That was Daisy?"

He nodded. "The only female I was willing to get close to. I've steered clear of women. When you first asked me to help you, I thought for sure you had the wrong guy."

"I didn't. You . . ." *You were made for me.* Literally. "You've been a rock. I can't begin to imagine how painful losing your wife that way must have been."

"Sure you can. You've heard my music."

She pressed her face to his neck. He was right. It was his music that had first sparked her consciousness back to life. She'd heard his emotions. She'd felt them all the way to her soul. "Love hurts."

"No, it's losing love that hurts. Love itself is the most powerful force in the universe. It's what makes life worth living." He laughed softly. "Damn, I can't believe I said that. It's even too corny for a country song."

"You don't need to crack a joke, Rick."

"Mmm?"

"You try to lighten the mood with humor, but you don't need to. Not for me. I want to see you as you are."

"This is me, Lizzie. It's like the way you get mad."

"Because it's better than crying?"

"You got it." He rubbed his cheek against her hair. "But I don't see why you're so dead set against shedding tears. They make your eyes even more blue. Your voice gets a special rasp to it, and you get this little hitch in your breathing that's as sweet as a nuzzling kitten. Me, I just get a runny nose."

"Rick . . ."

"And considering how ugly my nose is to start with—"

"Rick!"

"Yeah?"

There was so much she needed to express but not aloud. She stretched up on her toes and kissed him.

How could every time their mouths touched be different? It didn't seem possible the sensations could get better, yet they did. This was intimacy in its purest form, a sharing that went beyond the limits of the physical. She absorbed his pain and sent him comfort, giving him what he'd given her countless times before. She didn't consider resisting when the comfort changed to passion. His pain mixed with pleasure, both reflecting back to her in ripples of pure thought.

Here?

Yes, oh yes, like that.

How does it come off? There's no hooks.

There's a ribbon at the front.

Is this too fast?

It's perfect, Rick. I must be insane.

Why?

Because what we're doing isn't even real.

Our feelings are real, Liz.

Feelings had no substance, they couldn't be weighed or measured or proven scientifically to exist. Neither could thoughts.

But at this moment, thoughts and feelings were all Elizabeth had.

The world beyond the storybook cottage faded from her mind. Reality became the taste of Rick's mouth, the warm slide of his skin, the soft thud of the blanket as it dropped to the floor, and the weight of his body pressing over hers.

Make-believe or not, Rick was a tender, considerate lover. And Elizabeth had never felt more gloriously alive.

TWELVE

RICK SCANNED HIS SCRIBBLED NOTES ONE LAST TIME, THEN wiped his palms on his jeans and eyed the blinking cursor. Zeb had given him a crash course in computers last weekend when he'd delivered this one. He'd set up arrowy things he called shortcuts to start up programs and connect with the Internet, and had made the entire process look like a piece of cake. Even though the hookup was through the phone line and according to Zeb was dead slow, it was more than enough technology for Rick. The amount of information available through this gizmo was mind-boggling. All a person needed to do was type the subject into the blank space and click a button. Simple. Private, too. No one else needed to witness what he was searching for, which was good. Otherwise, someone was liable to call out the men in white coats with big nets.

The thought didn't trigger a smile. He could no longer shrug this off. For weeks he'd tried to convince himself that Elizabeth was only a dream, but if she was only a dream, how could she have talked to him at the Cantina while he'd been awake and stone-cold sober? How could he have seen her and touched her? How could he have woken up this morning with his body still humming from the memory of their lovemaking?

The questions kept piling up. The more he thought about them, the less the dream explanation made sense, especially after what he and Elizabeth had shared last night. Either he'd gone clear 'round the bend and had lost what little mind he had left . . .

. . . or Elizabeth wasn't a dream.

The idea was a radical leap in perspective. So was allowing himself to consider it. Once he had, though, he couldn't stop. It explained a lot of her reactions. If she was real, then she would be as baffled by what was happening as he was. Naturally, she would assume he was a product of her imagination, and she would do her best to deny her feelings for him. She wouldn't have believed two minds could merge in real life any more than he would. That was too . . . *Twilight Zone*. They both would be working hard at convincing themselves the other didn't exist.

It was a radical idea, all right. It was convoluted enough to make his brain spin. Still, it could be the reason his feelings for Elizabeth seemed so genuine, and making love with her had been so good. The sex had been the clincher, because he couldn't have done that on his own. Okay, technically, he could have accomplished a physical release solo, but the pleasure he'd shared with her had been on a different level altogether. And 100 percent mutual. From the start, he'd suspected that his encounters with Elizabeth had been too vivid to be ordinary dreams. Therefore she must be real.

"That's not a leap," he muttered. "That's a goddamn sky-dive."

Daisy's nails clattered across the floor as she came over to nudge his leg.

He scratched behind her ear. "What do you think, girl? Have I finally flipped out?"

She woofed and rested her chin on his thigh.

"Maybe I have, since I'm asking you." He gave her another scratch. Satisfied, she went back to the patch of sunshine in front of the fridge and curled up to resume her nap. Rick returned his attention to the computer. The plan had seemed reasonable when he had gotten up this morning, but deciding to pursue it could be the first step down a slippery slope. By wanting to find an alternate explanation for his dreams, he could undo all the progress he'd made toward accepting reality in the last three years, seven months, and . . . what? He grasped for a number that wasn't there. Had it been three years and seven months or three years and eight since Sue had died? Probably eight and a few days, but he couldn't say exactly. He'd lost track. The calendar in his head was no longer as clear as it used to be. That was a surprise. Since when had he stopped counting?

Around the time he'd dreamed up Elizabeth.

Had he replaced one impossible situation for another?

He pulled his chair closer to the kitchen table and regarded the keyboard. Why was he hesitating? If nothing else, this could prove once and for all that Elizabeth wasn't real. He could move on, as he had before. He could survive without her. Live the life he had instead of acting like a lonely, pathetic moron longing for the impossible.

"Oh, what the hell," he muttered, poking the *e* with his index finger. He hunted for the *l* next. Once he finished the first name, he stopped to consider. She had said her last name was Gray, but he hadn't thought to ask her to spell it. He decided to start with the most obvious.

It took a while for the results of the search to appear on the screen. The information next to the links didn't appear promising, but he doggedly followed every one of them. None of them led to the Elizabeth he knew. He tried Elizabeth Grey next, with no better luck. That changed when he tried Elizabeth Graye. The first link took him straight to the Grayecorp website.

It was a property development company. In Manhattan. Founded by the late Stanford Graye. The photo that materialized in one corner of the page showed a ritzy-looking office building. Above the glass entrance doors, "Grayecorp" was spelled out in brass letters next to a company logo.

Grayecorp was real.

Stanford Graye was real.

And Elizabeth Graye was on the list of company executives.

This was too easy. The truth had been here all along,

waiting for him to look for it. Waiting for him to trust his heart.

There was a link beside Elizabeth's name. Rick clicked it so hard he sent the mouse skidding across the table. He hauled it back by its cord as the page loaded.

The text appeared first. The information was sparse but it all fit. Elizabeth Baylor Graye. Graduate of Harvard University. Managing director of Grayecorp. Currently on a leave of absence.

A leave of absence. That was all it said. It could mean she was on a vacation in Bora-Bora, sipping a martini under a coconut tree.

Or it could mean she had been mugged while she was visiting her stepmother in Willowbank, hit her head on a stone gatepost, and was lying comatose in a hospital.

Rick shoved back his chair, went to the sink and splashed cold water on his face. Then to make certain he was completely awake, he leaned over and dunked his head under the faucet.

There might still be a logical explanation for what he'd found. The rebel camp in the jungle he'd dreamed about had been based on reality. His subconscious had picked up the story he'd heard on the news. He could have gotten the idea for the plane crash dream the same way. Elizabeth had maintained the whole Middle Ages thing was from a romance novel. His mother and sister-in-law devoured romances like candy, so he could have heard them talk about one of the plots, or gotten the idea from a book cover that he'd glimpsed. Could the same thing have happened with Elizabeth and Grayecorp?

He turned off the tap and braced his fists on the edge of the counter. Water droplets fell from his hair to ping against the stainless steel sink. He concentrated on each one as he fought to catch his breath.

He didn't recall hearing about Stanford Graye's company before Elizabeth had mentioned it. The construction projects Rick worked on were small-time and run by local firms, not a Manhattan developer. As far as he knew, Grayecorp hadn't been in the news. He would have no reason to have heard Elizabeth's name, either, or to know details like where she'd gone to school or who her father was. A rich, classy woman like her was way out of his league. Their paths never would have crossed. His subconscious could have created the backgrounds of his dreams from snippets he'd heard or seen, but that theory didn't extend to Elizabeth. She was no background. She had been central to every dream. She herself had to be the key.

Then how had this happened? Why had he randomly connected in his sleep with a total stranger? Where had this sudden psychic ability come from? That's what it must be, because *Twilight Zone* or not, how else could she be in his head?

Oh, man, maybe he had gone off the deep end. Psychic power? Telepathy? His family had cut him a lot of slack over the past three years and whatever, but they would never put up with this. Jethro would laugh himself silly if he found out what his brother was thinking.

Yet Elizabeth did exist. The Grayecorp website proved it.

Rick raked his wet hair off his forehead, dried his hands on his jeans, and returned to the computer. A picture had scrolled into place on the page.

It was a studio portrait that showed only Elizabeth Graye's head and shoulders. She was wearing a beige business suit with a string of pearls at her throat. Her hair was the unique golden blonde that he'd sifted through his fingers countless times, but rather than being loose around her shoulders it was twisted up behind her head. Her expression was as distant and cool as a January sunset. There was no warmth in her firmly compressed lips or sparkle in her blue eyes. Her angled-up chin bore no compromise. Every aspect of her body language screamed "hands off."

This wasn't the lover who had sighed her pleasure in his arms a few hours ago. She was hard. Elegant. Aloof. The kind of woman who would blackmail her father, who would regard emotions as signs of weakness, and would care only about winning. The kind of woman who wouldn't normally give him the time of day in the waking world. He could see no hint of Lady Elspeth or Isabella. Or of Angel Liz.

But they shared a face and a name. Those facts couldn't be coincidences. She *must* be his Elizabeth.

He pictured how she had appeared in the firelight. Her hair was messy and half covering one eye. Her cheeks were flushed. Her lips were moist from his kiss and angled into the sweetest smile. Only she would probably deny it was sweet.

The image from his memory replaced the one on the screen. Other memories followed to cascade across his vision: Elizabeth in the snow, her teeth chattering and her gaze defiant; Elizabeth smiling her gratitude as he freed her wrists from the plastic tie; Elizabeth in front of the gallows as she fought against the grip of Ganulf's guards to touch him in his mind . . .

Something stirred in his head, like a breeze except that it didn't move. It was his thoughts that seemed to move, following his memories, drawing him toward Elizabeth. He was still awake. He knew that because he could feel water from his hair drizzling inside his shirt collar. He heard the hum of the computer, but he also heard a faint, electronic beeping.

All right, this was weird. He was still in his kitchen. Daisy was sleeping in the sunshine on the kitchen floor. Everything was as normal as it could get. Yet as he watched, the scene retreated. A dense, colorless nothingness rose in its place.

Rick's pulse began to pound. He was having trouble catching his breath again. This looked familiar. He'd seen the same thing in the Cantina parking lot when he'd imagined Elizabeth.

Only he hadn't imagined her. She wasn't a dream, and he didn't have to be asleep to see her. "Elizabeth?"

His voice sounded hollow, as if it came down a tunnel. He extended his other senses, trying to duplicate what he'd done before. *Elizabeth?*

There was no reply.

Probably because he was stark, raving mad . . .

Rick slammed a lid on his doubts. If he was wrong, he would get over it. He wouldn't be any worse off than he'd been before. But if he was right . . . damn, wouldn't that be worth another try? He closed his eyes and opened his arms, concentrating on the way he felt when he held her. *Hey, Lizzie! Wake up!*

ELIZABETH DREAMED THAT RICK WAS SINGING TO HER. It was one of his songs about lost love that she'd heard before, yet she detected more than sadness in his voice. This time, she heard the strength that got him through the pain and kept him going. She smiled.

"She must know I'm here." Rick's music ended suddenly, as if someone had switched off a radio. "There, that's better. Hello, Elizabeth."

Her smile faded as she surfaced to wakefulness. The familiar smells and textures of the hospital room surrounded her. The man who had spoken to her wasn't Rick. Of course, he wasn't Rick. Rick was make-believe. This was reality.

"How are you today?" the man continued. He picked up her hand. "You're looking as lovely as always."

Elizabeth opened her eyes to the ever-present nothingness.

"Can you smile for me again, Elizabeth?"

She glanced at her hand. She couldn't see anyone touching her, but she felt it. The man's skin was damp. His grasp wasn't clinical like a doctor's, it was cloying. She tried to tug her hand free. She failed.

"Come on, darling. I'm sure you can if you put your mind to it."

"I'm not certain the smile was voluntary, Mr. Rashotte."

"Of course, it was, Beryl. She recognizes her fiancé."

Alan! He was here. She hadn't placed the voice, but she should have. It was the same smooth, precise tone she remembered. It was little wonder she hadn't recognized his touch, because she'd felt it so seldom, aside from during their brief romance a few years ago. And aside from that interlude on her desk last June. She cringed at the memory. How could she have gained any physical satisfaction from him? She must have been deluding herself. The thought of his skin against hers made her flesh crawl. Now that she'd experienced what true pleasure could be like . . .

But she hadn't, had she? There had been nothing true about that fantasy with Rick. It had been as much a fairy tale as the romance novel that had inspired the dream. In real life, she never would have dropped her inhibitions and opened her heart. She wouldn't have dared. The only reason she'd been so free to indulge herself with her make-believe man was *because* he was make-believe.

Tears heated her eyes but she would not cry. No indeed, she was beyond that. No more feeling sorry for herself. She was alive. As imperfect as the real world was, and as unpleasant as her life had been, she did want to keep living. Rick's story had helped put her own problems in perspective. That must have been why her subconscious had come up with it.

Alan squeezed her fingers. His fingertips were smooth— he wouldn't tolerate any activity that would cause calluses. Manicures had been a regular part of his grooming regimen. He cultivated his appearance as assiduously as he cultivated his charm.

"I was sorry to hear Dr. Shouldice already left for the day," Alan said. "I understand he has run more tests?"

"Yes, Miss Graye continues to make progress. Her brain activity has increased significantly since you were here last."

"You have no idea how happy that makes me. I've missed her so much."

"Of course."

"Some of the other staff mentioned she might hear us. Do you believe that's true?"

"There's no way to know for sure."

"But she does seem to be responding, correct?"

"Not directly. Dr. Shouldice could answer your questions better than I could."

"Yes, but as we established, he isn't here. I wish to know whether it's possible for her to understand what we say."

"Yes, it's possible."

"That's wonderful."

"As I said, she's making progress. The technicians checked the monitors since your last visit, so there shouldn't be a problem, but please let us know if you notice anything unusual."

"I certainly will, Beryl."

"All right then, have a good visit." A set of light footsteps moved away from the bed. A moment later, the door hissed shut.

Alan dropped Elizabeth's hand to turn on the television and tune it to CNN. He'd been a news junkie. To some extent, she'd been one as well, but not any longer. Some of the items she'd heard during previous waking periods had reminded her far too closely of the scenarios she'd experienced in her dreams. A Swiss Air flight had crashed in the Alps with no survivors. Hostages had been killed during a raid on the hidden base of Colombian drug smugglers. She couldn't regard the stories with the same detachment that she used to. The victims were more than statistics. Those had been real people, with their own hopes and fears and dreams.

Alan didn't speak again until the news anchor's voice had been replaced by a commercial. "Perhaps we can have a spring wedding, darling." He patted her hand. "Would you like that?"

She wrenched her mind back to Alan. Wedding? What was he playing at? She'd had good reasons to go along with the engagement, yet she'd never intended to let it progress further. Surely he realized that.

Alan rubbed his thumb across her knuckles. "Whatever you want, sweetheart. I'm here for you."

His caress made her stomach roll. She renewed her efforts to free her hand.

"You can count on me to stand by you, as I have been from the beginning, regardless of what the future brings.

We'll employ the best specialists in the world. No matter how long it takes, all that matters is that you get better."

She gritted her teeth. He sounded sincere. If Alan did believe their engagement was genuine, then she only had herself to blame. She had been the one to make the first move because she'd needed an ally at the company. Alan's transparent ambitiousness had made him easy to manipulate, or so she'd thought. She'd planned to use him as a pawn in her ongoing battle with Delaney even before he'd provided her with the phony alibi.

If she'd had it to do over, she would have taken her chances with telling the police the truth. Contemplating marriage to a man like Alan Rashotte was revolting. Prison would be preferable to tying herself to an emotionless relationship, now that she'd tasted real passion . . .

Real passion? *Real?* She had to stop dwelling on her fantasy lovemaking. Of course, no flesh-and-blood man could compare to an imaginary one. That was why romance novels were so popular.

"I do want so much for you to get better, Elizabeth."

Alan's voice seemed suddenly closer. She caught a whiff of Aramis aftershave and stale coffee.

"It's hard for me to wait, but of course I will." His breath warmed one side of her mouth. "You've come such a long way already."

Oh, *God*, he was going to kiss her. Every fiber in her body recoiled at the thought, yet she was powerless to move away. Whatever he believed, he had no right to take this intimacy. She fisted her hands.

Alan's lips touched hers.

Her lungs seized. She couldn't draw in enough oxygen. She was unable to turn her head. She strained to shove him away but her hands lay at her sides. The full scope of her helplessness had never been clearer. Panic swelled. *No! Get off me!*

The pressure on her mouth disappeared. A second later, the door opened. "Excuse me, Mr. Rashotte?"

"What is it, Beryl?"

"Dr. Shouldice hasn't gone home after all. He's in the solarium, if you still want to speak with him."

"Fine, tell him I'll be right there." He stroked Elizabeth's hand. "I'll be back soon, darling."

Elizabeth gulped in air as she listened to his retreating footsteps. Her body trembled with relief. In her mind, she scrubbed her hand against the blanket and used the sheet to wipe her mouth. She felt sick. And violated.

This couldn't go on. She had to wake up. She had to resume control of her life or someone else would.

Alan never did anything that didn't benefit him, and not for an instant did she think he could have enjoyed that kiss. Was he demonstrating his power? Staking a claim? He must want something, but what?

That was a stupid question. He wanted more money and more power, and he would use whoever would get him there. From what she'd heard, Alan had visited here regularly and was in the habit of discussing her condition with the doctor. He would be aware of the possibility that she might have brain damage. Could he be hoping to take advantage of her reduced mental capacity when she did regain consciousness? She wouldn't put it past him to have already prepared a power of attorney and a prenup weighted heavily in his favor. It would be consistent with his character. She wiped her mouth again. She had the urge to spit, which was *not* consistent with her character. She never spat, unless she was at her bathroom sink or her dentist's office. Crude gestures like that were completely foreign to her. Then again, she wouldn't have thought she would be the type of woman to enjoy dressing up in a period costume and making love by firelight . . .

She jerked her mind away from the memory. Enough. She couldn't afford to take refuge in a fantasy. That wasn't the way out.

Lizzie?

She blinked. The voice seemed to have come both from her memory and from her mind.

The void beside her shifted. A large figure moved toward her.

She rubbed her eyes. "Rick?"

He grinned. "Well, I'll be damned. It worked."

She started to smile back. He seemed so happy, the response was automatic. So was the impulse to rush into his arms. She shook her head fast. "No. This has to stop. You're not really here."

"Yeah, I know. I'm in my apartment."

"What?"

His grin widened, creasing the dimple into his cheek. His eyes sparkled, not with humor but with what appeared to be excitement. He took her hands. His fingers were unsteady. And his hair was wet. Why on earth would she imagine him with wet hair?

She retreated. "Go away. You're not real."

"It's okay. I understand why you're saying that. It still hasn't sunk in with me yet, either. It's sort of a leap." He laughed. "A damn big leap."

She turned her back to him. She was the one generating his image, so she should be able to control it. "I'm not talking to you."

"Don't be scared. I know it's freaky, but—"

"I told you to go away."

He stroked her hair. "Why?"

"Why? Because I don't want you here. I already have enough problems I'll need to deal with when I wake up. I can't afford to depend on a make-believe crutch."

"Hey, I understand why you think you dreamed me up. I thought the same thing until I goggled you."

"You what?"

"Looked you up on the Internet. I found the Grayecorp website and—"

"You *Googled* me?" In spite of her resolve to ignore him, she turned.

He was still smiling. She loved the way his features lightened when he smiled. It gave her a glimpse of how he must have looked when he was younger.

No. He was a product of her subconscious. He had no age. No substance. No more past or future than a mental hiccup.

"Right, Google, that was it," he said. "My nephew showed me. Not that he saw me look for you. Wouldn't want to worry the family more than usual. Like I said, I can understand why you don't want to believe this. Before I met you, I never went in for all that woo-woo stuff. I don't even know what to call this thing we've got going but—"

"What are you talking about?"

His smile softened. He leaned down and spoke against her lips. "I'm talking about this," he said.

He kissed her. And she was unable to stop him. Not powerless in the way she couldn't stop Alan from kissing her. Her lack of resistance was in her mind, not her body. Though she endeavored to remain unaffected, pleasure flooded her senses. This was exactly what she needed to erase the memory of Alan's kiss. It was open give-and-take. Sharing. Trusting. Rick didn't need the romantic backdrop of a cozy cottage, a crackling fire, and a feather bed. Even in the nothingness that comprised her coma world, his touch could arouse her . . .

No! she thought desperately. *This isn't real!*

He drew back. "I'm sorry, Lizzie. I shouldn't rush you. I guess I'm too eager." He kissed her temple. "Last night was incredible."

"It was a dream, Rick."

"Sort of." He kissed her nose. "The background was, but we weren't."

"Stop that."

He tunneled his hand into her hair and brought a lock to his mouth. He kissed that, too. "Did I do something you didn't like?"

How could he? He knew what she enjoyed because he was in her head. "You know you didn't."

He wrapped his arms around her, the way she liked. Though she could feel tension humming through his frame, he kept his embrace gentle, coaxing her until she relaxed and melted against him. The next kiss found her mouth again. She gave in and enjoyed it, because there was no point pretending she didn't. He would know that, too. It was different from the intimacy she'd experienced in her dream.

Not better or worse, more like a connection on a deeper level. Or perhaps on multiple levels.

He nuzzled her neck. "I've been wanting you back in my arms since I woke up. I need to find you."

"You did."

"No, I mean truly find you." He lifted his head to glance around. "Where are we? Do you know what hospital this is?"

"What difference does that make?"

"I want to see you." He laid his palm against her cheek. "Genuinely see you and touch you, not join you through your mind."

"I don't understand."

"Neither do I. Not completely. All I'm sure of is there has to be a reason we found each other in our dreams."

"Then you finally admit you're a product of my imagination."

"No, Lizzie. That's only where we first met."

She shook her head. "Please, stop this, Rick. You're making things worse. I need to wake up."

"That's another reason I have to find you. I can help." His smile returned. "That's what you've been asking me all along, but I hadn't put it together."

She moved her hands over her ears. It wouldn't shut out his voice, because she wasn't actually hearing his words, she was feeling them.

"I know what you're worried about because I was, too, but you're not cracking up," he said.

A figment of her imagination was telling her she wasn't crazy. As an endorsement of her sanity, it didn't carry much weight.

He eased her hands away from her ears and kissed her palms. "It's probably because you're so smart that we're able to meet like this. You must have some power in that gorgeous head of yours. Tell me where you are. Is it New York? Or maybe Willowbank? That's where you were when you got hurt, right?"

"I don't know where I am. You see as much of this place as I do."

"Then I'll ask someone. Who would know? Your step-mother?"

"You're serious."

"Elizabeth, no matter how nutty this must seem, there's nothing more important to me than finding you."

She considered what he'd said. Her imaginary lover wanted to help her wake up. Was this a new phase of her climb back to full consciousness? Or was it her pathetic attempt to justify prolonging her fantasy?

"The Grayecorp website says you're on a leave of absence," he went on. "Someone at the company must know where you are."

Perhaps this was her mind's way of focusing on what she had left behind. Fantasizing about escaping this hospital room might be more constructive than the other escapes she had dreamed about . . .

Lord, she was being ridiculous. How could she possibly consider continuing this delusion? She would need all her mental faculties working properly if she was ever going to reclaim her life. Alan's visit had reinforced that fact. Who knew what he'd been doing at Grayecorp in her absence?

And what about Delaney? She had spread rumors that had questioned Elizabeth's emotional stability in retaliation for the lawsuit. She and her lawyer would have a field day if they learned how tenuous her grip on sanity had become. If she kept indulging herself with Rick, she might as well abdicate all control of Grayecorp and stay in this coma.

She snatched her hands from Rick's grasp. Curling her nails into her palms, she looked through him to the void. "Go. Away. Now."

His image wavered. Alarm tightened his face. "No. Wait!"

"I started this, so I can stop it. The power's in my mind. I want you to go away and not come back. We're through. Finished."

The nothingness crept up his legs until it engulfed the lower half of his body. He reached for her, but his hands felt no more substantial than a puff of air. "It can't be over." His voice was fading. "Give me a chance."

"Do you care about me, Rick?"

"You have to know I do."

"Then for my sake, stop touching me. Don't look for me. This isn't what I need."

"But—"

"Leave me alone. Please!"

Lizzie!

She covered her ears again. Then she imagined barricading her mind the same way. She tightened her thoughts into walls as thick and high as the ones in her imaginary castle. She drew back her emotions.

And before the next beat of her heart, Rick was gone.

Elizabeth knew she'd done the right thing, the only sane thing. This proved she was on her way back to reality. This was how reality felt.

Because she had never felt more utterly alone.

THIRTEEN

RICK ZIPPED THE DUFFEL BAG AND SLUNG THE STRAP OVER his shoulder. He eyed his guitar for a beat, then grabbed it, too. He whistled to Daisy. "Come on, girl. Time to go see Stella."

She jumped off the bed. She whined as she followed him out of the apartment.

He ruffled the fur around her neck. "You'll be fine. Think of all the cheese you can con her out of."

The dog's ears pricked up at the mention of cheese, but the woeful expression in her eyes didn't change.

"You'll be better off with her," he said. "The heater in the truck's been acting up again, and it's going to be a long drive."

She plodded behind him as he went down the stairs. She perked up the instant she stepped into Stella's kitchen. His landlady was in the midst of baking what smelled like raisin bread. Daisy scampered across the floor, vacuuming crumbs of dough as if she hadn't eaten in days.

Stella wiped her hands on her apron, then knelt to give Daisy a hug. "There's my sweetums. You're such a hungry girl."

"I already fed her," Rick said, "so don't fall for that starving pooch act."

"A woman needs meat on her bones." Stella directed Daisy to a stray raisin. "A few extra pounds won't hurt anyone. Makes for added insulation at this time of year."

"I really appreciate you watching the dog for me."

"She's good company. The grandkids love her, too."

"Then your daughter and her family are still coming?"

"As long as the weather holds, they'll be here by Christmas Eve." She tipped her head for a canine kiss, then grasped the edge of the counter to pull herself back to her feet. "I plan to close the shop for the week anyway. Got to rest up for the New Year's rush. For some reason, a lot of people want to kick off the year with tattoos."

He pointed his chin to the snowflake on the back of her left hand. "Is that a new one?"

She preened, tilting her hand toward the window. "I was getting in the spirit. I thought it would look festive."

"It does."

"You sure you have to leave today? I thought you were doing Christmas at your brother's place."

"With all his kids running around, plus our parents and Josie's relatives, they won't even notice I'm not there."

"They'll notice, Rick."

"They'll get over it."

She pulled a round tin from a cupboard and pried off the lid. It was packed to the rim with gingerbread men whose bellies were adorned with icing versions of her snowflake tattoo. She offered it to him. When he shook his head, she took one herself, broke off an arm and fed it to Daisy. "Is it seeing Jethro and Josie's kids that bothers you?"

"No."

"They won't be kids forever, so it'll get better."

"They don't bother me. Not as much as they used to."

"Then why the sudden trip?"

"It's something I need to do."

"This woman you're meeting. You even sure she's a woman? I heard people can say anything on those Internet sites."

"I realize it's been a while, but I think I can still spot the difference."

"What happened to that other one? The blonde you thought you were chasing a few weeks ago?"

"There hasn't been anyone else, only her."

"Ah. So that's why you didn't want to talk about her."

"Yeah. I don't want people to get funny about how we met."

She shook her head. "Not that it's any of my business, but I don't see why you need to go that far to find a date."

"She's more than a date. She's . . . special."

"How do you know if you've never met face-to-face?"

It was a good question, one he couldn't yet answer.

He was saved from having to try when the buzzer on the stove went off. He left Stella to her baking, gave Daisy one last ear scratch and carried his things to his truck. It started grudgingly. He put it into gear and backed out of the driveway before it could reconsider and go into one of its sulks. He wasn't sure how fast it would get him to New York, but it would be quicker than taking a bus and he couldn't afford the cost of a last-minute plane ticket. Besides, he didn't know how long he would be gone. This way, if he ran out of money to pay for a motel, he could stay in his truck. Another reason it was better not to bring Daisy.

He hadn't liked lying to Stella any more than to his family, but in this case he'd had little choice. Claiming that he was driving across the country to visit a woman he'd met over the Internet would worry them a lot less than confessing he'd met her in his dreams.

Only, he hadn't exactly dreamt her. He didn't know what to call it. A mind link? A psychic bond? It wasn't easy to find a term that didn't sound a bit wacko so he'd given up trying to label it. He'd also given up trying to figure out the why of it. That would be as pointless as trying to understand why a tornado had hit his farm and left his neighbor's place untouched. Some things didn't have an explanation. Attempting to find one was what could truly drive a person crazy.

Once he'd accepted the fact that Elizabeth was real, it had been a simple matter to find her. He'd phoned Grayecorp. Although the people he'd spoken with initially had been reluctant to give him any personal information about her, probably because she was rich, he'd struck pay dirt when he'd asked for the mailroom the next time he'd called. The guy he'd reached there had had no problem telling him where the daughter of the company's late president was being treated. Pretending that he was a delivery man verifying an address had helped. The mailroom people had needed to forward hundreds of cards and gifts from well-wishers when Elizabeth had first been hospitalized.

She was no longer in a hospital, though. Her stepmother had had her transferred to a private clinic near Bedford. It was in Westchester County. Not that either name had meant anything to him—he'd had to look them up on a map. He had no idea what he would find once he got there, or how he was going to get in the door. The truth would likely get him locked up in a rubber room.

There were moments he had trouble believing the truth himself. Getting a woman as smart as Elizabeth to believe it was going to be a challenge. After all, she hadn't reacted all that well the first time he'd tried.

"Smooth, Denning," Rick muttered. "Real smooth."

He shouldn't have sprung it on her the way he had. Yeah, he'd mucked up big time. For one thing, he'd seen that Elizabeth had been upset, but he'd been too excited over what he'd discovered. For another, he hadn't known what he was going to say until the words had been out of his mouth. Or wherever the words came from when they communicated in their heads. Instead of breaking it to her gently, he'd come off like a raving lunatic. No wonder she hadn't bought it. She hadn't wanted to see him anymore. She'd made good on that, too, because in two days he hadn't been able to find his way back to that weird void where he'd left her. She hadn't shown up in his dreams since then, either.

Which was why he had to see her face-to-face. He needed to show her what they had was real. While he was at it, he could prove it to himself, too. He did have strong feelings for her. Their lovemaking wouldn't have felt as good if he didn't.

Yet if the real woman was anything like the Elizabeth in

the photo on the Grayecorp website, he might not even like her.

"HIS NAME IS RICK DENNING." NORMA OFFERED THE jewel case to Monica as they moved into the corridor. "He's a country singer."

Monica regarded the photo on the front. It appeared to be a candid snapshot rather than a professional portrait. The man was sitting on a wooden stool, his head angled downward as he strummed the battered guitar he held balanced on his bent leg. His shirt was red plaid cut in a Western style. His jeans were faded and well broken in, as were the scuffed cowboy boots he'd hooked on the rungs of the stool. He certainly fit the image of an authentic country singer. "I'm not familiar with that genre of music, so I have to confess I've never heard of him."

"Not many people have. He's a complete unknown. The only reason I've got this is my brother was passing through Tulsa a few months ago and stopped at the bar where Denning was playing. That's where he bought the CD."

Monica turned the case over to read the back. There was a list of songs, but there was no line identifying the record company. "I don't see a label. This must be homemade."

"That's how a lot of people start out. Once the tracks are recorded, anyone with access to a half-decent computer can burn the CDs."

She resumed her study of the singer's photo. He wasn't a handsome man by any stretch of the imagination, yet there was something compelling about him. It could be from the set of his shoulders and the intense way he bent over his instrument. "I wonder how he found out you were playing his music to Elizabeth."

"Actually, I'm not sure he did know. He seemed surprised that I recognized his name. Do you want me to phone Mrs. Harrison?"

Monica returned the CD to Norma. "No, we agreed

I would be here Christmas Eve. It's her turn tomorrow, so there's no reason to disturb her. I'll go talk to him."

A twelve-foot-high pine tree had been set up in one corner of the clinic's atrium. Tiny fairy lights twinkled among the boughs and threw pinpoint reflections in the windows. No snow remained from the storms of the previous month. Instead, a bleak drizzle pattered against the glass. The parking lot beyond had been busier than usual today with arriving and departing vehicles. Patients' families and friends hurried through the entrance, many of them carrying brightly wrapped gifts. Some were pushing wheelchairs. The patients who were able to be moved would be spending the holiday at home.

A lone man stood near the tree, his hands stuffed in the pockets of a sheepskin coat. His rustic clothing immediately set him apart from the well-dressed visitors who frequented the clinic. Monica recognized his face from his photograph—there was no mistaking that prominent nose and the unusual amber shade of his eyes. She moved past the reception desk and walked toward him. "Mr. Denning? I'm Monica Chamberlain."

He shook her hand. "Are you a doctor?"

"No, I'm a friend of Miss Graye's."

"Is she okay? Did something go wrong? I don't understand why they told me I can't see her."

She studied him before she replied. Beard stubble shadowed his cheeks and fatigue darkened the skin beneath his eyes. His hair bore furrows from a recent finger combing. Under his coat he wore a crumpled chambray shirt, jeans, and cowboy boots. He was tall and lean like a cowboy, too. Overall, he gave the impression of strength. Not in an overpowering, aggressive way, though. He had an aura of quiet masculinity, like a throwback to the age of old-fashioned, Gary Cooper-type heroes.

"There are standard security procedures here," she replied. "You're not on the list of approved visitors, and the clinic doesn't allow anyone in without the proper authorization."

He dug inside his coat. "If they need ID, I can show them my driver's license."

"It's not so much a question of verifying your identity, it's to ensure you have a valid reason to visit."

"Valid reason? Like what?"

"Why don't you tell me, Mr. Denning. Why are you here?"

"To see Elizabeth."

"Are you acquainted with her?"

"Absolutely."

"Really. I don't recall her mentioning your name. When did you meet?"

"A while back. Look, I realize I probably don't seem like the kind of guy she would hang around with, but I do know her. We both . . ." His jaw worked, as if he were chewing over what he would say. "We share an interest in music."

"I understand you're a country singer."

"My day job's construction. When I can get the work," he added. "But yeah, I sing country music."

"I see."

One side of his mouth quirked. "It's about as far from the classical stuff Elizabeth likes as you can get, but she once told me good music's universal. Not that I'm saying mine's good. I never studied it like she did, so she knows way more about it than I do."

"Elizabeth studied music?"

"That's what she told me. She played piano."

Monica hid her surprise. She was one of the few people who were aware of Elizabeth's musical ability. Her friend had deliberately distanced herself from that facet of her life, something that had saddened Monica. "Is that right?"

"I know she runs her father's company now, or at least used to run it before she ended up in here, but she's a smart woman. She could do whatever she put her mind to."

"Yes, she's been very successful."

"I'm not after anything, ma'am."

"Excuse me?"

"You probably figure a guy like me has to have some

ulterior motive for showing up out of the blue and wanting to see a wealthy woman like Elizabeth, but I don't."

This man was telling the truth about one thing at least. He didn't seem like the type of man Elizabeth would befriend. "You mentioned Elizabeth's wealth, so obviously you're aware of it."

"Wouldn't do much good to ignore it. That's why you're so worried about security, isn't it?"

"Many people have arrived here claiming she owed them money, or promised them a reward for a service rendered. Others wanted to view her like an exhibit. We've learned to screen her visitors."

"I get that, and I can't blame you. I'm glad she has friends looking out for her. She hates being helpless. I mean, I'm guessing she would hate it."

"Yes, she would. Mr. Denning, Elizabeth has been here for several months. Why would you choose Christmas Eve to visit her?"

"It's the soonest I could get here. I only found out about her coma a few days ago. I came because I want to help."

"How do you think you could help?"

"By talking to her. Being there. She said she likes my music, so I'm willing to sing to her if you figure that would do any good. She wants to wake up more than anything. I'm no doctor, but I've got to believe something's bound to reach her."

"It's what we all hope."

"If tonight's a problem, I'll come back tomorrow or whenever else visitors are allowed. Say the word and I'll be here."

Monica's initial impression of him hadn't changed. He seemed to be a strong, secure man. Furthermore, it did sound as if he knew Elizabeth. A friendship between them might be unlikely, but it wasn't impossible. Since he was in the building trade, they could have met during one of her visits to a Grayecorp work site. Simply because Monica hadn't heard Elizabeth mention him didn't mean much, since plenty of things had happened during their estrangement that she wouldn't have known about. Besides, what could be the harm? The more mental stimulation they could provide, the better. And unless she had lost all capability of reading body language, Rick Denning's concern for her friend was genuine. Much more so than Elizabeth's fiancé.

Alan professed to love her, yet as far as she knew, he wasn't planning to visit her over the holidays. He would probably be livid when he learned Monica had allowed an ordinary construction worker access to his intended.

The thought tipped the balance in Rick's favor. She gestured toward the reception desk. "Let's get you signed in."

He smiled. "Thanks!"

The smile lifted his face from plain to intriguing—he wore his emotions with as little pretension as he wore his clothes. How completely dissimilar he was from Elizabeth, and from the people with whom she normally socialized. And how refreshing. She waited while his name was entered in the visitors' log, then guided him down the corridor that led to Elizabeth's room. "Before you see her, I should prepare you for what to expect."

"Damn, she did get worse, didn't she."

"No, in fact her condition has been steadily improving over the past few weeks. I meant she appears much different from how you would be accustomed to seeing her."

"I know she'll look different, but I've got to believe that inside, she's still Lizzie."

"Lizzie?"

"That's what I call her sometimes."

"I'm amazed she lets you get away with it."

"She didn't at first. It doesn't go with the way she sees herself. Not tough enough."

Surprise kept her from responding immediately. Not only from what he said, but in how he'd said it. There was tenderness in his voice. He did indeed know Elizabeth, almost as well as she did. "How was it that you two met?" she asked.

"She heard my music and, uh, she called me."

Norma's voice reached them as they neared Elizabeth's room. She was deep into the exploits of Raoul and Heloise again. An odd expression crossed Rick's face. Recognition? Amusement?

"We often read to her," Monica explained. "We think it helps stimulate her brain."

"Yeah, it does that, all right. She's . . ." His words trailed off as he followed her across the threshold. He stopped dead, his gaze riveted on Elizabeth.

Norma closed the book and set it on the bedside table. "Hi, Mr. Denning. I'm glad they let you in."

If he heard her, he gave no indication. He rubbed his face hard. Beard stubble rasped beneath his palms. He had the look of a man who'd had the breath knocked out of him.

"I think she likes your music, you know," Norma continued. "I'm sure she listens."

"Apparently, Elizabeth was already familiar with it," Monica said. "Rick, I did warn you she's—"

"Here," he said. His voice had roughened. He jerked forward. "She's really here. Elizabeth!"

His shout, and his eagerness, took her off guard. Had she made a mistake allowing him in? She moved to intercept him. "Rick, she's not strong. We need to be careful not to stress her heart."

He went around her, his gaze never leaving the bed. The smile she'd seen earlier was nothing compared to the grin that split his face now. Honest joy shone from his eyes. He touched his fingertips to the gold hair that spilled over Elizabeth's pillow, then took her hand. "Hey, Lizzie. It's me."

Monica saw immediately that her caution had been unnecessary. He held Elizabeth's slender fingers in his reverently, as if they were the most precious things on earth. As if he had every right to touch her. As if they had once been much more than friends.

The light dawned. She should have realized it before. Rick must be one of Elizabeth's old lovers.

Oh, yes, Alan was going to be livid.

ELIZABETH SURFACED TO THE SOUND OF RICK'S VOICE. THE song was sad, as they all were. The words were about lost love and hopeless yearning, sorrow too deep for pain. For a while she drifted where the melody led her, riding the emotions his music carried, imagining she was back in his embrace.

But then she remembered. This wasn't the way out. She'd told him to leave. She wasn't going to let him into her dreams anymore. She knew better than to get emotionally attached to anyone, especially a make-believe man. She was better off without him.

The song ended. She was sliding back into sleep when she heard the scrape of chair legs on the floor.

"That was wonderful," Monica said.

There was a dramatic sigh. "Wish I was loved like that," Norma said. "It's sad, but it's so romantic."

A guitar chord floated through the room. "Thanks."

Elizabeth yanked herself back to awareness. She was in the hospital room. She could tell by the smells and the sounds. Monica was here again. So was the nurse named Norma. But the third voice had been a man's. And he had sounded exactly like Rick.

No, she must have imagined it. Of course, she had imagined it. She understood the difference between her dreams and this semi-awake state she was able to achieve.

"To tell the truth, the song's not that popular with the regulars at the Cantina. They tend to throw peanuts. Makes it hard to get off the stage, 'cause walking on those things is like walking on ball bearings."

It *was* Rick. She glanced around her, but could see no one else in the void. She was alone, as she'd been for days. Or was it weeks? How long had it been since she'd sent him away?

"Where did you learn to play the guitar, Rick?" Monica asked.

"I sort of picked it up here and there." He strummed a slow arpeggio. "I started out by listening to the radio and trying to imitate what I'd heard. I had some friends who shared what they knew, too. They were great."

"My brother plays guitar," Norma put in. "Only his is electric."

"I've used electric guitars, but for tone, nothing can beat this old acoustic. I guess I'm old-school." His fingers slid across the strings. "Elizabeth called me a Luddite."

Monica laughed. "That sounds exactly like something she would say."

"Remember that, Lizzie?" he asked.

Yes, I remember. How can you be here? I sent you away.

"You can't call me one anymore. I did learn how to work a computer. I might get used to it, too, now that I see how handy they are."

He couldn't have heard her thoughts because they hadn't left her mind. Her words echoed inside her skull as if . . . as if they had bounced back from a stone wall.

"Still don't want a cell phone, though. Those things are a plague."

"Well, my brother thought some of your riffs were awesome. He's going to kill me when he finds out he missed this. Have you got a second CD?"

"Not yet, but I'm working on it. My nephew's helping me record some new tracks. He's the tech wizard in the family. He's also volunteering as my manager."

The door hissed open. "Norma, who's . . . oh, hello Miss Chamberlain. I didn't realize you were still here."

"Hi, Beryl. I hope we're not disturbing anyone."

"Not tonight. Many of the patients are spending the holidays at home. I wanted to open the door so we could hear the music better. Young man, you have an exceptional voice."

"Uh, thanks."

"Beryl, this is Rick Denning. He's a friend of Miss Graye's."

Elizabeth rubbed her eyes and looked around again. There was no change in the nothingness, no tall form coalescing, no familiar face smiling at her. Where was he?

"I'd love to hear one of your new songs," Monica said. "As long as it's not too much of an imposition."

"Sure, I'm not going anywhere." He picked out a melody on the bass strings. "This is one I wrote for you, Lizzie."

No, he couldn't have. He couldn't be talking to her. She couldn't have heard him talking to Norma and Monica, either, or heard him introduced to Beryl as if he were a real person. He was a dream. He was in *her* head, not theirs.

"I call it 'Angel Liz.'"

No, *no*! This couldn't be happening.

He began to play. She quit trying to make him hear her, because he wasn't able to any more than Monica or the nurses could. He wasn't in her coma world, he was in the real one.

But that was impossible.

She must be insane. The idea panicked her. She was trapped in her head. If she lost her grip on reason, she would have nothing left.

Yet the music was the most beautiful she'd ever heard. She recognized the story the ballad told. He was singing about her dreams. It was different from his other work. It drew her out of herself and into a new melody of hope. Possibilities. Survival. Each verse added another layer to the one before, building the pleasure like one of Rick's kisses.

> *So we clung to each other, adrift in the night,*
> *One kiss, one touch, one soul.*
> *My blue-eyed angel, my dream come to life,*
> *My sweet Liz, I won't ever let go.*

The final chord quavered to silence. She'd been wrong. The song hadn't been about her dreams, it had been what she'd never dared to dream. It was another song about love.

But love didn't exist any more than Rick did.

Elizabeth fought to hold back her tears. How many times now had she vowed not to weep? It was humiliating, having no control over her body.

There was a scattering of applause from the direction of the doorway. She heard Beryl's voice, as well as several others as they exclaimed about the song. Someone sniffed and laughingly asked for Kleenex. Another woman requested an encore. Rick started to thank them when his words cut off. There was a hollow, twanging thud, as if he'd dropped the guitar. "Elizabeth?"

Damn these tears. This wasn't her.

Rick stroked her cheek. "I didn't mean to make you cry."

She choked back a sob.

"But it's okay. Like I told you, there's nothing wrong with tears. They make your eyes more gorgeous."

She groped along the blanket for his hand.

"Oh, my God," Norma murmured.

"Elizabeth!" Monica exclaimed.

Rick laced his fingers with hers. "Lizzie?"

She swallowed. Her throat felt clogged, as if she hadn't used it in months. The side of her tongue slid against a thick tube. She tried to speak, to tell him this wasn't real, but it came out as a garbled croak.

Someone gasped. Footsteps shuffled near the door.

Rick pressed their joined hands to his lips. "Feel that?"

She jerked.

"I'm as real as you are." He curled their hands to his chest. "Let me show you. Open your eyes for me, Angel Liz."

He made it sound easy, as if what she'd endured since July had been nothing but a nap.

"Come on, you know how. Think of all the other times you woke up with me."

Yes, but those were dreams, she thought. They were different. She had been someone else in those dreams.

"Lizzie?" There was a catch in his voice. His hands tightened around hers. He trembled with an urgency that she felt outside as well as in.

She gritted her teeth, summoned every shred of energy she could gather, and concentrated on lifting her eyelids. They felt sealed shut, as if her lashes were glued together.

"Please," he whispered. "I don't want to be alone."

Neither did she. *Rick, help me!*

His lips touched hers.

The kiss was brief, no more than a fleeting contact at the side of her mouth, but the force of it continued to rumble through her mind after he pulled back. She grabbed his energy to add to her own. A crack appeared in the void.

The first thing she saw was Rick's face. He was leaning over her, and he was a mess. Dark circles shadowed the skin beneath his eyes. He looked as if he hadn't slept or shaved since she'd ordered him out of her head. Why was he smiling? And why was everything so bright? She blinked.

"That's my Lizzie."

Monica crowded against Rick's side. She was smiling, too. "Elizabeth?"

"I'm getting the doctor," Beryl said. "Excuse me, ladies. Move back from the door."

She glimpsed movement past Rick's shoulder. The fog was gone. A group of women were crowded outside the doorway. They were all in blue dresses. Or maybe uniforms. There was a television on the wall, right where she'd heard it. A wooden coat-tree. A rain-streaked window with topaz curtains. Two armchairs. Machines. Metal rails on her bed. The details whirred through her brain between one heartbeat and the next. A heartbeat she heard echoed from the monitor. It sounded impossibly loud and fast and *God*, the light hurt. She squeezed her eyes shut.

"Elizabeth, no!" Monica cried. "Hang on!"

An alarm shrieked. People were running. Pain spread from her eyes to her chest.

Rick slid his arm beneath her shoulders. "Stay with me!"

No, she couldn't stay with him. He was only an illusion.

"Elizabeth!"

Wasn't he?

FOURTEEN

DELANEY HELD TIGHTLY TO MAX'S HAND AS THEY NEARED Elizabeth's room. He returned the squeeze and sent her an image of the rabbit that lived beneath their back deck. He'd coaxed it out last week with a handful of carrot tops. The sweet picture and the memory it evoked soothed her, as he'd intended, but it couldn't eliminate her anxiousness entirely.

For months, she'd concentrated only on helping Elizabeth wake up. Now that the end of the coma was imminent, so was the day when she would need to deal with the issues between them. Her life had moved forward, thanks to Max. Elizabeth's hadn't. All the coma had done was put their problems on hold.

The rabbit faded. Max tucked her hand into the crook of his elbow as they crossed the threshold. *One step at a time, Deedee.*

Right.

Elizabeth's feeding tube had been removed. Other than that, she appeared the same as the last time Delaney had seen her. She lay motionless on the bed, her eyes closed, her face lax. The room was darker than usual—only one lamp was on and the curtains were closed to shut out the daylight. From what Delaney understood, it was to help minimize the shock to Elizabeth's eyes the next time she opened them. A brown-haired man sat in the chair beside her. His arms were folded on the edge of the mattress and his cheek was pillowed on his forearms. He appeared to be as deeply asleep as Elizabeth.

Penny was the nurse on duty today. She placed her book on the table beneath the window and came over to meet them. "Did you speak with Dr. Shouldice?" she asked softly.

"Yes, he called before we left Willowbank to give us an update. He told us she stabilized. How is she now?"

"Her vitals are good and she's still resting easily."

"Has she regained consciousness again?" Max asked.

"Not yet, but the doctor told us it's only a matter of time. Now that she's done it once, she'll do it again." Penny smiled. "Oh, and merry Christmas."

"Same to you."

"This is quite the Christmas present, isn't it?"

"Better than we could have hoped for." There was a grating snore. Delaney glanced at the sleeping man. "I take it he's the musician?"

"That's him. Rick Denning. He didn't fall asleep until an hour ago. I hope you don't mind that we let him stay, but he was really insistent, and Miss Chamberlain said it was okay. From what everyone said, he was the reason she woke up in the first place."

Monica had described in detail Rick's role in Elizabeth's brief awakening. If Delaney had heard it from anyone else, she would have assumed they were exaggerating, but Monica was too practical and levelheaded a woman to embellish the truth. "It must have been some song," she said.

"And some kiss. It's all anyone could talk about when I came on shift this morning. The way she responded to it was so romantic."

Romantic? Elizabeth? She would not only deny the possibility, she would sneer at the term. Delaney moved her gaze from her stepdaughter to the man at her side. They were an unlikely pair. Elizabeth might have had a fling with this man, as Monica suspected, but she wouldn't have taken it seriously. Even without meeting him, Delaney could tell that he and Elizabeth were from two different worlds.

We were, too, Deedee.

Maybe at first, Max, but we were never as far apart as them. She looked at Rick's hair. It was as rumpled as his clothes. The ends curled over his collar, which was frayed at the edges. The guitar that was propped against the shelf was in almost as rough a shape. *Monica said he knew about her wealth.*

It wasn't a secret.

What if he's doing all this in the hopes he'll get money from her?

Then she can pay him off. She can afford it. Wouldn't you say waking up was worth it?

For all we know, the timing could have been coincidence. I don't want to see him take advantage of her.

You're still trying to protect her. Once she's back on her feet, she'll be able to do that herself.

Sure, but—

Deedee, relax. Any way you look at this, it's good news.

The nurse moved to the door, then paused and cleared her throat. "We still haven't been able to contact Mr. Rashotte. Would you know if he planned a trip for the holidays?"

Delaney raised her eyebrows. "Have you tried his cell phone number?"

"Yes, and his home, but there's been no response."

"He'll turn up," Max said.

"I hope it won't be awkward," Penny said, glancing back at the bed one last time before she left.

The reason for her comment was readily apparent. Although Rick was still snoring, his hand had found Elizabeth's. He was clasping it against his chin.

Too bad we can't stay until they track Alan down. Might be interesting to see how he reacts to having some competition.

It won't be pretty, Max.

Depends on your point of view. I'd put my money on this guy in a fight. From the look of those hands, he's done more with them than thumb a BlackBerry like the Ken doll.

Can you really see Alan getting physical?

Max snickered. *Good point. He might break a nail.*

If he cares about her at all, it shouldn't matter how she woke up, only that she did.

I thought you didn't like Alan.

I don't, but for all we know, Rick Denning could be as bad as he is.

The man's snoring cut off. He lifted his head. He rubbed his cheek against Elizabeth's knuckles, then reached out to smooth her hair with his free hand. His motions were unexpectedly gentle for someone of his size.

Seems sincere to me, Max commented.

He might realize he has an audience.

And here I thought I was the cynical one.

Rick turned his head. His gaze went to Max first, then to Delaney.

Even in the dim light, she noticed the distinctive color of his eyes. They were a rich shade partway between gold and brown. There was nothing notable about the rest of his features, except for the weariness that was clear in every one of them. His nostrils flared as he suppressed a yawn. Several days' worth of beard stubble bristled from his jaw. "Hi there," he said quietly. His voice was a mellow baritone, resonating with power held in check. "Are you friends of Elizabeth's?"

"I'm John Harrison," Max said, giving his professional name. "This is my wife, Delaney."

"Rick Denning," he responded, rising to his feet to shake hands with Max. His forehead furrowed as he transferred his attention to her. "*You're* Delaney?" he asked.

"Yes, Delaney Graye Harrison. I'm Elizabeth's stepmother."

The change in his demeanor was immediate. His weariness disappeared as his shoulders squared and his body tensed. He gripped the bed rail, bracing his arm as if to block her from getting closer. "You shouldn't be here."

"Excuse me?"

"Elizabeth's heart rate spiked when she woke up. The doctor said it might be dangerous if it happened again, and from what I've seen, she got pretty worked up whenever she talked about you. I think it would be better if she didn't see you."

"My wife has more right to be here than you, Denning."

"Yeah, I heard she's footing the bills." He kept his gaze on Delaney. "I know I can't make you leave, but please, ma'am, give her a chance to get her strength back."

"That's what we all want."

"Good. Then you wouldn't mind holding off with the legal stuff?"

"Legal stuff?"

"What's between the two of you isn't any of my business. Making sure Elizabeth is up for it, well, that is my business."

"There have been developments that she isn't aware of. She'll want to know."

"But they'll keep, won't they?"

"Of course, they'll keep. I care only about my stepdaughter's welfare." She stopped herself before she could explain further. She didn't need to defend herself to this man. It should be the other way around. "We may not be related by blood, but we are family. How was it that you met her?"

"We met through my music."

"How?"

"She heard me play and called me."

That was what Monica had related, but it still didn't explain much. "Where were you performing?"

His gaze flickered aside. "I meant she heard the music." *Deedee . . .*

"Do you mean she heard a CD, like the one the nurses have been playing?"

"That's right. That's what happened."

"In that case, it's quite a coincidence that your music was played here, isn't it? I understand you're not well-known."

Deedee!

Max, look at his eyes. He's not telling the whole truth.

Never mind his eyes, look at Elizabeth's.

She glanced past Rick. Elizabeth's eyelids were fluttering. *Get the doctor, Max.*

He was already out the door when he replied. *On my way.*

Delaney moved to the opposite side of the bed from Rick. "Elizabeth?"

Rick thrust his hand across the mattress as if to stop her from getting closer. "Please, ma'am. Don't—" His words cut off as he followed her gaze. "Hot damn," he muttered. He retrieved Elizabeth's hand. "Lizzie?"

The steady tones from Elizabeth's heart monitor accelerated. Her eyes opened slowly, as if the movement were a tremendous effort.

Rick grinned. "Hi there, gorgeous."

Elizabeth blinked. Her lips moved, but no sound emerged.

"Welcome back." He rubbed her knuckles against his cheek, then grimaced. "Sorry, I know I need a shave. You want some water?"

Delaney stepped closer. "Better wait until the doctor gets here before you give her a drink. She wouldn't be used to swallowing yet and might choke."

Elizabeth startled at her voice. She shifted her gaze to meet Delaney's.

Flat on her back or not, Elizabeth's gaze had lost none of its impact. Delaney smiled. "Merry Christmas, Elizabeth."

Her eyes widened. She looked from Delaney to Rick.

"Yeah, it's Christmas morning. How's that for timing?" he said. "Hope they spring for turkey in this place. Don't know about you, but I'm going to try bumming a drumstick or two. Better than Doritos for breakfast any day."

Elizabeth made a rasping noise.

Delaney found a washcloth and dipped it in the water pitcher. She reached toward Elizabeth, then stopped when she saw her flinch. She passed the cloth to Rick. "To moisten her lips," she said. "That should be safe enough."

He touched the cloth to Elizabeth's mouth. "It's okay, Lizzie. We're here to help. We want you to get better."

"That's right," Delaney said. "Oh, it's good to see you again."

Elizabeth tipped her head away from the cloth. She stared at Rick. "Awake?" she whispered.

"Uh-huh. Want me to pinch you?"

Her chin trembled. "You . . . here."

"Yeah." A dimple folded into his cheek. "How about that?"

"Impossible."

"Nope. On second thought, maybe you better pinch me." She splayed her fingers in his grasp.

He angled his head so that she could touch his face. Her fingertips trembled. He slid her hand to his nose, then along his jaw to his chin, helping her trace his features. "Feels different, doesn't it, Lizzie?"

Tears pooled at the corners of her eyes. "How?"

"Beats me."

"Rick . . ." Her voice cracked. The sounds from the heart monitor accelerated again.

He returned her hand to her side. "It's okay," he said. He squeezed her shoulder. "Relax. We'll have plenty of time to figure out the details later. All that matters now is getting better."

Although Delaney hadn't moved away, she felt as if they no longer realized she was in the room. Monica's guess was right, they must have been lovers. Their conversation had the shorthand intimacy of two people who were very familiar with each other. There was no mistaking the electricity in the air between them, either. Rick was acting like a man in love, and Elizabeth looked like a stranger. In fact, if Delaney wasn't witnessing it herself, she wouldn't have believed her stepdaughter could behave this way.

Could this be a consequence of the head trauma she'd suffered? Dr. Shouldice had repeatedly warned them there could be aftereffects from a brain injury. Regardless of her physical condition, the Elizabeth she knew would never display her emotions as openly as this woman did. Stanford had seen to that.

FIFTEEN

ELIZABETH WOKE TO MUSIC AND THE SMELL OF FLOWERS. She inhaled slowly, savoring the distinctive scents. She could identify carnations. Roses. Perhaps a few gardenias. More arrangements seemed to appear in her room each time she opened her eyes. And doing that, opening her eyes, was getting easier by the hour.

The first thing she saw this time was Rick's face. He was sitting in the chair beside her bed, idly picking out a melody on his scratched guitar. No daylight showed around the edges of the curtains behind him, so it must already be night again. She had been dropping off to sleep at irritatingly frequent intervals during the past week, but it had been healing, healthy sleep, not unconsciousness. Her periods of wakefulness were lengthening.

He smiled. "Hey there."

Her brain did an odd skip at the sound of his voice. After hearing it only in her imagination so often, she wasn't completely accustomed to hearing it aloud. She no longer had any doubts he existed, since she had witnessed other people seeing him and speaking with him. She hadn't made him up. Though the initial shock of that realization had worn off, she was still grappling with the ramifications.

Rick Denning was a real, living, breathing man. Everything he'd told her about himself appeared to be true. He had the same characteristics, mannerisms and, well, *pres-*

ence as she remembered. He'd taken the time to shave and clean up, yet he managed to bear an endearing resemblance to an unmade bed. Warm and rumpled. And . . . inviting. His hair had dried in uneven lumps, one edge of his collar was flipped up, and there was a drop of blood on the side of his chin where he'd nicked himself with the razor. Yes, he was the same person who had been her lifeline in the void, only the flesh-and-blood version.

"How're you feeling?"

The answer was complicated. The flood of emotions that had accompanied her awakening had ebbed. What was left bore a tinge of awkwardness, like the morning after a night of overindulgence. She continued to be kiss-the-ground grateful that she was no longer a helpless mannequin. Drawing breath, opening her eyes at will, and exerting even a modicum of control over her environment seemed like wondrous abilities. Nevertheless, she fatigued easily and remained physically weak. The weakness frustrated her. Patience had never been her strong suit. It was hard not to be overwhelmed by how far she yet had to go.

The battery of tests she'd been put through confirmed what was already obvious to her. The mind-to-nerve connections had lain dormant for a long time and would take a while longer before they were firing at full capacity again. She would need weeks, perhaps even months, of rehabilitation therapy to regain her muscle tone and coordination. According to the doctors, she already had made remarkable progress since returning to consciousness. They attributed her success to their prescribed program of regularly exercising her limbs, and to the excellent physical condition she'd been in before the attack that had put her in the coma.

Not one of the medical professionals who had poked and prodded and scanned could explain the astonishing speed of her mental recovery, though. How could they? They weren't aware she'd begun waking up weeks ago in her dreams. She had no intention of enlightening them. If she did, they might transfer her to a different kind of clinic altogether.

Regardless, those dreams had been a form of therapy for her mind. Unconventional, yet very effective therapy. Because of them, she had already fought through the fuzziness and memory gaps that many brain-injury patients experienced upon awakening. The problems she'd encountered in each of the imaginary scenarios had forced her to exercise her thought processes and her verbal skills. Her brain had established fresh neural pathways to circumvent the damaged ones. The doctors had called it an example of neuroplasticity, the brain's ability to heal by rewiring itself. As a result, her speech was unimpaired, as was her reasoning. In essence, her connection to Rick had helped guide her back to life.

Just as she'd asked him the first time they had met.

Gratitude. That was what she felt for him. Gratitude and . . . fondness. Both were understandable and completely justifiable emotions. Real world emotions.

But the power of these feelings was overwhelming. Unfamiliar. Sometimes they made her heart clench and her eyes burn with tears when she looked at him or heard his voice or felt his touch.

"Lizzie?"

"I'm feeling better," she said finally. "Thanks."

"Can I get you anything?" He set his guitar aside and stood. He raised the angle of the bed to a more upright position and adjusted the pillow to help steady her head. "The doc said it's okay for you to have as many fluids as you want."

"Perhaps later. What time is it?"

"Around six."

"What day is it?"

"New Year's Eve."

In the past, she had made sure to spend New Year's Eve at whatever event was most socially advantageous, whether it was a black-tie gala in the city or a private party hosted by one of her clients. Rather than being a celebration, it had been a chance for strengthening business contacts. "You look tired. Have you eaten?"

"I'll grab a hamburger on the way back to the motel."

Rick was staying in a motel. The idea set off another brain skip.

"What?"

His question disturbed her, but then she realized he hadn't read her mind. He was reading her expression. "I never thought of you having to live anywhere before," she said. "It seems . . . odd."

"Yeah. I know what you mean. Talking about what I'll have for dinner seems too ordinary, too."

"It does."

"Sort of tame after worrying about getting shot or frozen to death."

"Or chased by a medieval army."

"Speaking of that . . ." He reached past a potted violet on the bedside table to pick up a paperback book. "I asked Norma to leave it here so I could show you. Look familiar?"

The couple on the cover were half dressed and locked in a passionate embrace. A fire glowed in a fieldstone fireplace behind them. "It's the cottage from my dream," she said.

"Our dream."

The title of the book was embossed in flowing gold letters: *Love in a Mist*. The author's name was Ingrid Weaver. Elizabeth had never heard of her. "Do you think that's what they were? Dreams?"

"I guess."

"It still doesn't seem possible. How on earth would we be able to . . . do whatever it is we did?"

"I've been wondering about that, too." He replaced the book on the table and picked up a CD. "This might have had something to do with it."

The front of the CD bore a photograph of Rick. "That's yours," she said.

"Uh-huh. Zeb and Jethro helped me put this together a few months ago so I could sell them in the bars where I played. Norma's brother happened to buy one and she brought it in to play for you."

"Are you saying that's how we connected?"

"Maybe. It makes as much sense as snagging dreams from books or stories on the news. Your imagination used the other things you heard. You heard me singing."

"And my mind followed the song back to the singer?"

He shrugged. "You once told me that you felt as if you connected to the composers of the old classical stuff when you played their work. You might have done the same kind of thing when you heard me. Only difference is, I wasn't dead, I was just asleep."

"That's a rather creative theory."

"I've had a few more days than you have to come up with one. Takes a while to get used to all this."

"And are you?"

"Hell, no."

"Have you considered the possibility we're sharing an even more complex delusion?"

"Don't think so." He rolled his shoulders. "I'm still working out the kinks from three days in my truck."

"Truck . . . you *drove* here? All the way from Tulsa?"

"Yep. Seemed to have misplaced the keys for my private jet."

She touched her index finger to his dimple. "Thank you for coming."

"No problem. Turned out Oklahoma really isn't all that far from New York."

"And thank you for helping me. For not giving up. If you hadn't been willing to believe the impossible . . ." She couldn't finish the thought. If not for Rick, she would still be trapped in nothingness.

He brushed a kiss over her fingertips. "It's not every day a guy like me gets to wake up his own Sleeping Beauty."

Though he'd made the comment with a smile, it unsettled her. She let her hand fall back to the bed. "This isn't a fairy tale, Rick."

"Don't have to tell me that. With a face like mine, I would never be cast as Prince Charming."

"Please, don't joke."

"All right. What do you want me to do?"

It was difficult to answer the question honestly. The weak, not-fully-recovered part of her wanted him to hold her the way he used to, to slip into her head and her dreams. That was something else that had changed since she'd awakened. The bond they'd forged in their make-believe world had broken. They were two separate people. Asleep or awake, she no longer felt him *inside*.

That was good. The distance between them was normal. Sane. Safe. Being alone was a fact of life in the real world. So was speaking aloud. "You can't tell anyone the truth about how we met."

His smile dimmed. "Even if I wanted to, who would believe me?"

"Whether or not they believe you isn't the issue. I haven't told the doctors what I experienced in my coma, because it would be sure to raise psychiatric concerns, and I don't want to spend one more minute under medical supervision than necessary. I also can't afford to let any rumors about my mental competence get started. There are people who would use them to their advantage."

"You mean Delaney?"

"For starters. She didn't come back again, did she?"

"No. I heard she's been calling a few times a day to get updates on how you are. She and John sent those white flowers on the shelf," he added nodding toward the gardenias. "He's got a show opening at a gallery in Manhattan next week where he needs to put in an appearance, and Delaney told me she'll be staying in the city with him."

Delaney had remarried. That was another adjustment Elizabeth needed to make in her thinking. Her stepmother had apparently wed the artist she'd been amusing herself with last summer. Elizabeth had encountered John Harrison only once, so she hadn't made the connection to his name when she'd heard the nurses refer to Mrs. Harrison. "I don't want to see Delaney. Not until I'm back on my feet."

"She wasn't what I expected. She seemed . . ."

"Nice? Sweet?"

"I was going to say *concerned*. She was okay about giving

you space, too. She was up front about not being your favorite person, and she seemed really sorry you got hurt because you were on your way to meet her."

"Don't let the innocent act fool you. My stepmother might be paying for my upkeep, and she and her current boy toy might have sent me gardenias, but she's using money that should have been mine to do it."

He appeared as if he wanted to comment, then shook his head, pulled his chair closer, and resumed his seat, folding his arms on the bed rail. "I'll make sure she doesn't bother you until you're ready."

"Thank you, Rick, but you won't be here all the time. I'll speak to the administrator of the clinic myself about restricting my visitors."

"What about Alan?"

She tensed. "Alan Rashotte? He's not here, is he?"

"No, he probably doesn't know you're awake. No one's been able to reach him, which is kind of surprising, since Beryl told me he's been visiting pretty regular. They all believe you two are really engaged."

"That's another matter I'll need to address, but not while I'm in this condition."

"Don't worry about that. When he does show up, I'll be happy to tell him to get lost."

"Alan has to be handled carefully. I can't risk alienating him before I learn the status of the case against me." She ignored Rick's frown and spoke before he could argue. "I would prefer not to see Monica Chamberlain yet, either."

"Monica's still in Florida. She's been phoning, too. She told me she had promised to spend the holidays there with her mother, but she's coming back tomorrow. She seems eager to talk to you."

The mention of Monica's mother set off a wave of guilt. "Tell her not to change her plans on my account."

"I thought she was your friend."

"We had a falling-out."

"She's sure been acting like you made up."

"Perhaps what was said has faded for her, but I haven't forgotten. Her mother needs her more than I do."

"Is she sick? Monica didn't tell me."

"Her parents separated last winter. Jenna didn't take it well. It promised to be a nasty divorce."

"Jenna's her mother?"

She nodded. The problems she would need to deal with kept mounting. She really had made a mess of the life she'd left behind. "Until I'm back on my feet, the only person I would like to see is my lawyer."

"Okay, if that's what you want, but—"

"Rick, I'm not asking your permission." She endeavored to sit up straighter. The shawl that covered her shoulders slipped to her elbows. When Rick reached out to hitch it up, she waved him away. "I was fully capable of making decisions and taking care of myself before my coma, and I plan to resume doing so as soon as possible."

His smile disappeared altogether. "Well, sure. I didn't mean to step on your toes, I just want to help."

"You can help by not saying anything about that . . . connection we had."

"No problem. Never cared much for rubber rooms."

"Then it's agreed we forget about it."

"Forget? I didn't agree to that."

"I'm grateful for your help during my coma, and I always will be, but what happened between us was a fluke. It's over. There's no point dwelling on it."

"Over?"

"Our mind link is gone, Rick. It broke before you came to find me."

"It didn't break by itself. You kicked me out of your head."

"I believed I had to do that in order to wake up. As it turns out, it was the right thing to do. It forced me to stop relying on my imaginary world."

"Yeah, I guess."

"And now that I am awake, I need to concentrate on coping

with the real world. Getting my life back is my number one priority, so I need to deal with the issues I left behind. For the sake of our mental health, we should move on."

"I'm getting a bad feeling about this 'move on' part."

"I'm not denying we shared some dramatic experiences but—"

"We made love, Lizzie."

Love. The word hovered between them. Awkward. Uncomfortable. Like another reminder of a night of over-indulgence.

It hadn't been love. Love didn't exist outside the bounds of sentimental music and fairy tales. She'd understood that in her coma, and she was even more aware of it now. The problems with Delaney, Alan, and Monica were good reminders of the damage that could be done in the name of love. She tugged her shawl together at her throat to cover her hospital gown. She would have to arrange to have someone send her own clothes at the earliest opportunity. "What you're referring to could more accurately be described as a sexual fantasy. We never actually touched each other."

"Whatever you want to call it, it's not over for me, and I'm not liable to forget it. I'm an old-fashioned kind of guy. I don't go for one-night stands."

"It was less than that. It was a temporary aberration based on a few paragraphs out of *Love in a Mist.* It was only possible because I was comatose."

"Didn't you enjoy it?"

She had more than enjoyed it, she had reveled in it. But it wouldn't have happened if she'd known then that Rick was real.

"I'm sorry," he said. "We shouldn't get into this now. You need your rest."

She shook her head. The motion was sluggish, a telltale sign this particular period of wakefulness was nearing its end, but she wouldn't give in to it yet. "No, this discussion was inevitable, and this is one issue we can settle now. I don't want either of us to have any illusions. You're a good man, Rick. I admire your inner strength, and I appreciate the compassion you showed me. I can't thank you enough for driving halfway across the country to help me. The last thing I want to do is hurt you, but you must admit the circumstances that brought us together were wholly imaginary. We can't expect to repeat the feelings those circumstances produced."

"I don't have to repeat them, I still feel them."

"You can't. The dreams are finished. We're not living a fairy tale. Everything has changed."

"Not everything. We're still the same people."

"No, we're not. *I'm* not. You knew me when I was desperate. I was helpless and vulnerable. I will never be that woman again."

He searched her gaze. "I agreed not to tell anyone about the weird stuff. That's nobody's business but ours."

"All right. Good."

"But that's not what you're really afraid of."

"I'm not afraid."

"Sure, you are. You're working yourself up to getting rid of me again. I can tell. This is the same thing we ran into before."

"Rick . . ."

"You're afraid of getting close to me. I saw you when you didn't have your armor on, and that scares you. That's why you're pushing me away."

There wasn't much she could say to that. They both knew he was right.

"Weird or not, something special happened between us while we were in that never-never land, Lizzie." He laid the back of his hand against her cheek. "Can you honestly tell me you believe nothing's left?"

His touch, like his voice, was something else she'd experienced countless times in the make-believe world. It couldn't compare to the immediacy of the real thing. In spite of her increasing exhaustion, a whisper of sexual awareness tingled through her body. She waited, half fearful—half hoping?— but there was no corresponding echo in her mind.

He hooked a strand of hair with his finger and tucked it behind her ear. "Lizzie?"

"I'll admit our physical compatibility might not have been temporary."

He kissed her earlobe. "Physical compatibility, huh?" he murmured. "And that's it?"

"You asked me to be honest."

He pressed a kiss above her cheekbone. "I guess I can live with that."

More tingles slid through her body. This was nothing to be alarmed about. There was strong chemistry between them. Her being conscious of that fact was a symptom her nervous system was returning to health and beginning to function as it should. It wasn't much different than her ability to enjoy the scents of the flowers in the room. It was as understandable—and normal—as the gratitude she felt for him. "And I . . . like you, Rick."

"Well, that's good, because I've grown mighty partial to you, myself."

"But you have to understand that getting my life back remains my priority."

"All the more reason to have someone in your corner. We made a good team before, didn't we?"

"You have a life back in Tulsa."

"Some life. Playing for peanuts in bars, and talking to my dog. You weren't the only one who needed to wake up, Lizzie." He pulled back to meet her gaze. "I've been drifting in my own fog for almost four years. Coming here to find you was the first time anything's really mattered to me in too long. Please, for both our sakes, don't send me away again until we see where this can go."

The sensible thing to do would be to say good-bye cleanly before either one of them got hurt. Their beliefs about love were too far apart. The differences in their lifestyles that had meant nothing in the dream world couldn't realistically be ignored anymore. He wouldn't fit in to the life she intended to reclaim. Beginning any kind of relationship with him would be a distraction she didn't need. Practicality should trump emotion. Eye on the prize, as her father had lectured.

But she couldn't bring herself to let Rick go yet, because

her gratitude was threatening to overwhelm her again. It made her heart clench and her eyes burn, and now it was causing a lump to grow in her throat that was too painful to swallow. She touched his jaw, repeating his words in her head like a promise. *Until we see where this can go.*

Something seemed to spark in his eyes, almost as if . . .

As if he had heard her.

She held her breath. Waiting. Reaching. *Rick?*

His expression didn't change. There was no answering whisper through her thoughts.

That was a relief, wasn't it? She looked away.

Footsteps hurried down the corridor. A woman spoke from the doorway. "Excuse me?"

"Hi, Norma," Rick said. "What's up?"

"We had the TV on in the lounge to catch the weather and you've got to see this." Norma took the remote from the shelf and switched on the television as she spoke. She punched channels. "Great! It's still on."

"Hey, is that me?"

The image on the TV screen was unsteady and of poor quality, but it was clear enough to show a dark-haired man who was sitting on the arm of a chair, a scratched guitar propped on his leg.

Norma turned up the volume. "This is a local cable channel. They do a news roundup every evening, mostly stories that viewers send in."

Rick's deep voice flowed from the TV speakers, along with the sound of his guitar. Although Elizabeth had heard the song only once, she recognized it instantly. He was singing the final line of "Angel Liz." There was a scattering of applause. The camera wobbled briefly, then followed Rick as he dropped his guitar and moved past a bank of machines to a bed with metal rails where a blonde woman lay.

The sight of her own face shocked her. Until now, she'd given no thought to her appearance. She hadn't even asked for a mirror. She touched her hair self-consciously. How could she have thought Rick resembled an unmade bed? She looked like a waif. "How . . . ?"

"I don't know who shot the video," Norma said. "I think it was one of the part-timers who was filling in on Christmas Eve. She must have used her cell phone."

The scene continued to unfold on the screen, supplying images to what Elizabeth had experienced only through her other senses. She saw how tenderly Rick wiped her tears and took her hand. She saw him smile as he urged her to open her eyes. Then she watched as he leaned over and kissed her . . . and her eyelids slowly lifted . . .

Good God, that couldn't possibly be her. She looked lonely. Needy. Like a thirteen-year-old girl yearning for love and pouring her heart into her music.

A pair of news anchors came on. They were smiling, calling her Angel Liz, talking about the moment when she had broken free from her coma as if it had been a sideshow. It was entertainment to them. They bandied terms like "Christmas miracle" and "real-life fairy tale."

She gripped the bed rail in an attempt to get up. To her disgust, she couldn't lift her shoulders from the pillow. "Turn it off!"

Rick took the remote from Norma. The screen went black. "Don't get upset, Lizzie. No one meant any harm."

"It's a wonderful story," Norma said. "Everyone's happy for you. It still chokes me up."

"It's an egregious invasion of my privacy. It's humiliating. My life is not a feel-good fluff piece to round out a newscast. And I am most definitely not the pathetic, teary-eyed weakling that video makes me appear. I'm the managing director of Grayecorp and—" Her voice gave out. She fell back and gasped for air, her mind whirling. It was bad enough that Rick and the clinic staff had seen her like that. Now she was exposed to complete strangers. "Get me a phone," she said through her teeth.

"Lizzie . . ."

"I need to call the station. That story has to be killed. Now. Before it goes any further."

SIXTEEN

THE THAW THAT HAD LASTED THROUGH CHRISTMAS WAS over. A cold front had rolled in with the New Year, bringing a week of clouds that never seemed sure whether or not they should snow. Some mornings they thinned enough to give teasing glimpses of blue sky, then by evening had bunched into steel fists. The few flakes that managed to drift down never amounted to more than a dusting, like a taunt from the hovering storm. To Rick, the weather seemed to be marking time, caught in a holding pattern the same way he was.

It was midafternoon and beginning to sprinkle snow again as he pulled his pickup into the clinic's parking lot, coasted to a stop in an empty parking space, and shut off the ignition. Elizabeth had been scheduled to undergo a comprehensive physical assessment this morning and then step up her rehab program. He'd promised her he would be here by lunch, but the truck had been getting ornery about starting lately. Now it didn't want to stop. The engine continued to sputter, coughing puffs of blue smoke with the exhaust. He gave the steering column a thump. It didn't stop the dieseling, but it did help dislodge the key.

Someone rapped on his window. "Hello?"

A bald man in a navy blue overcoat stood beside the truck. A white silk scarf puffed under his chin. He appeared annoyed.

Rick rolled down the glass. "Hi. What can I do for you?"

"This parking lot is reserved for visitors to the clinic."

"Thanks. I know." He rolled up the window and got out.

The man stepped back. "You'll have to move."

The engine finally chugged to silence. Rick shook his head. "She probably won't start again for at least an hour, but it seems to me I'm not in anyone's way."

"The service entrance is around the back," he said, moving away. "I'll send one of the security staff to direct you."

Rick glanced around the parking lot. He couldn't blame the guy for assuming he was in the wrong place. His old F150 stuck out like a sore thumb in this collection of shiny sedans. There were a few SUVs, but they were the high-end luxury kind and had likely never gone near a dirt road, much less gone off-road. Elizabeth had once told him she drove a Mercedes. She probably wouldn't want to set one toe in this rust bucket.

Sure, but she'd never complained about riding Chester. She'd even seemed grateful. He pictured how she'd looked on his horse, her legs sticking out from her purple dress, her hair streaming loose behind her. *Remember that, Lizzie?*

The question bounced around his mind like a pebble tossed into a well. It didn't go anywhere. The only reply was its own echo.

He scowled and shoved his hands into his coat pockets. He didn't know why he kept searching for their old link. They didn't need to talk in their minds anymore, they could talk in person. That was terrific. It was what he'd made this trip for, wasn't it? To help her recover? To be with a real woman instead of a dream?

Things had been a lot simpler in the dream world. The issue of what he drove or how he dressed hadn't mattered. There had been no gulf between them. They'd only had each other. And she'd needed him. She made it clear she didn't need him now. The experts at the clinic were providing medical care and physical therapy, and everyone said her progress was astonishing. She'd begun getting out of bed on her own days ago, and yesterday she'd gone as far as the solarium with the aid of a walker. She was attacking the issue of her recovery with the same determination she had displayed during her coma, even though her efforts often left her shaking from exhaustion. He couldn't do much to help her, except to offer her a sympathetic ear and maybe a shoulder to cry on. She resisted accepting either one. Sure, she'd conceded they had good chemistry, and she'd let him kiss her, sort of, but each time he saw her, he had to fight to keep her from slipping back into the prickly, I'll-take-care-of-myself mode that he'd gotten to know when he'd first encountered her.

Well, what had he expected? That a smart, classy, rich woman like her would throw herself into his arms and declare her undying love the instant she opened her eyes?

Yeah, right. He'd been so caught up in finding her, he hadn't thought past the opening-her-eyes part.

"Excuse me, sir?"

He pushed away from his truck and started walking. "I'm a visitor."

"Wait! You're Rick Denning, aren't you? The singer."

He halted. "Singer?"

A man was fumbling with a nylon backpack as he hurried toward him. " 'Angel Liz.' That was your song, right?"

"Sure, it's my song. Where'd you hear it?"

"Are you kidding? It's on the Christmas Eve kiss video. You're the one who woke up Elizabeth Graye."

Rick grimaced. He'd thought that story had died. Evidently more than only the nurses on afternoon shift had been watching that cable channel last week. This man must have recognized Elizabeth. It wouldn't have been difficult to track her here—after all, Rick had done it himself with a phone call. "Do me a favor and forget about it, okay?"

"Sorry, no can do." The man pulled a camera from his pack. "I'd like to ask you a few questions, Mr. Denning."

Rick blinked at the flash. He hadn't had a chance to duck his head. He blocked the camera with his palm. "What's with the picture? Are you a reporter or something?"

"That's right. Sam Genessee with the *Toronto Sun*."

"How'd you hear about this in Canada?"

"Your video's on YouTube."

He'd never taken a look at YouTube, but he would have to be living under a rock not to have heard of it. "And you happened to see it, huh? Well, I'm sorry you came all this way, but no one's going to want to read about this."

"You're wrong. The Christmas Eve kiss had more than five million hits last time I checked."

Hits? That probably meant viewers. Oh, hell. "How'd you find out my name?"

"Everyone knows it. Just search 'Angel Liz.' It's on your website."

"It is?"

"Sounds like you missed your coffee this morning," the reporter muttered. He produced a business card from his pack and thrust it into Rick's hand. He clicked on a palm-sized recorder. "According to your website, you live in Oklahoma. How did you meet Miss Graye?"

"Look, Sam, I know you're just doing your job, but I'd sure appreciate it if you could give the lady some privacy."

"It's too late for that. This is a great human interest piece."

"Must be an awful slow news day."

"It's what everyone needs at this time of year. Besides, anyone in Elizabeth Graye's tax bracket *is* news. Could you tell me her current condition?"

"No comment."

"What inspired you to write 'Angel Liz'?"

"No comment," he repeated.

"I understand Miss Graye is already engaged. How would you describe your relationship with her?"

Rick shook his head, returned the man's business card, and resumed walking.

"Have you two made any plans for the future?"

He lengthened his stride. The reporter broke into a jog to catch up with him but was cut off when a van swerved between them to pull up at the clinic's main entrance. It had a satellite dish on the roof and the call letters of a TV station, along with the NBC peacock, painted on the side. Several men got out, one carrying a portable floodlight, another hauling coils of electric cable. They moved toward a group of people who were milling around beneath the portico that sheltered the front doors. A woman in a red suit jabbed a microphone at two security guards who blocked the way inside.

Oh, *hell*. Didn't these people have real stories to cover? Rick flipped up his coat collar to shield his face and decided to take the bald guy's advice. He used the service entrance.

Rick had gotten to know most of the staff during the time he'd been visiting here. The security guard positioned inside the door smiled and waved him through. "Well, if it isn't the celebrity."

"Afternoon, Jason. Guess you heard about the video."

"My wife sent the link to my phone a few minutes ago. Our girls put her on to it. They've been playing your song since yesterday. They love it."

"Uh, thanks."

"No, thank *you*. They've been into metal lately. I can't hear myself think when their stuff's blasting."

"I'm surprised they like it. They do realize it's country, right?"

He laughed. "I don't know how you did it, but I like it, too. Too bad, because all hell's breaking loose down at personnel."

"How come?"

"Whoever posted that video violated a good dozen of our privacy rules, and now the thing's gone viral."

He didn't know what viral meant, but it couldn't be good. "What happened to phones that only let you talk?"

He gave Rick a look, then turned his attention to the door. The reporter from the *Toronto Sun* was trying to get in. Rick left Jason to deal with him and headed further into the building. It was obvious from the reactions of the other staff members he encountered along the way that everyone was aware of the video. Beryl appeared worried. She returned his greeting curtly as he passed the nurses' station. She was in the process of contacting the part-timers, and confessed she was afraid someone would lose their job. The prospect bothered him. The clinic employees had seemed like good, hardworking people, and jobs in a place like this probably didn't crop up all that often.

Elizabeth's door was closed when he reached her room. He was about to push it open when he reconsidered. He wouldn't have hesitated walking in on the Lizzie of his dreams. They'd had more urgent things to worry about than manners or privacy. But he shouldn't take his welcome for granted with the flesh-and-blood version. He brushed the stray snowflakes off his coat, did his best to smooth his hair, and rapped lightly on the door.

The woman who pulled it open was a stranger to him. She was tall and dark, with a sharp face a few ounces this side of gaunt. Her black hair was styled into short spikes, showing off a pair of diamond ear studs that were big enough to adorn the lobes of an NFL wide receiver. Her black suit was cut as sharply as her face. Her upper lip curled subtly as she regarded him. Other than that, she displayed no expression, which could explain the lack of wrinkles. "Yes?"

He tried to peer past her but she was almost as tall as he was, and the way she stood on the threshold blocked his view of the bed. "I'm looking for Lizzie," he said.

Her eyebrows went up. It was an impressive sight, since they had been plucked and penciled into perfect arches.

"It's all right, Cynthia. Let him in."

At Elizabeth's instruction, the woman gave him a once-over and stepped back, allowing Rick enough space to enter. She closed the door behind him. "Ah, yes. I recognize him now. He's Richard Denning. The singer."

Rick scanned the room. The bed was empty. Another strange woman was sitting in one of the armchairs beside the window . . .

That was no stranger, it was Elizabeth. She'd done something to her hair. It was twisted up into a bun and clipped to the back of her head. It was the same style he remembered from her picture on the Grayecorp website, and the difference it made to her appearance was startling. Her expression was as smoothly under control as her hair. She'd traded in the hospital gowns for her own clothes a week ago. Today she wore a zippered jogging jacket and matching warm-up pants in a deep green, velour fabric. It covered her body from her neck to her toes while still managing to reveal her most interesting curves. He smiled, remembering how the purple dress used to do the same thing. *You're gorgeous, Lizzie, whatever you look like.*

She tugged her cuffs over her wrists.

Guess that didn't make sense, but you know what I mean.

The silence stretched. Damn, he had to stop trying to talk to her in his head. It could become as bad a habit as talking to himself had been. "Hi. Sorry I'm late," he said aloud. "Truck trouble."

She waved one hand without meeting his gaze. "I've been rather busy."

"How did the rehab go?"

"Fine, except it's too slow." She nodded toward her companion. "This is Cynthia Wetherall, my lawyer."

"Mr. Denning."

He should have guessed she was a lawyer. She looked like one. She shook hands like one, too, firm and brisk, as if she was getting paid by the minute. "Most people call me Rick," he said.

"Indeed. Elizabeth, perhaps we should continue our discussion later."

"No, I would like to know my options now."

"Very well." Cynthia crossed the floor to sit in the armchair that matched Elizabeth's. She motioned Rick to the chair beside the bed. "We were discussing the video that was shot here on Christmas Eve, Rick. What do you know about it?"

He shucked his coat and tossed it over the coat-tree. "I heard it's gone out on the Internet. I suppose there's no stopping it now, huh?"

"It was too late to stop it the moment it was posted. However, we certainly can take steps to see that those responsible are held accountable."

He glanced from Cynthia to Elizabeth. "Did someone fess up?"

"No individual has admitted shooting the video or publishing it," Cynthia said. "Since there is little doubt a member of the Seven Pines staff was involved, we have sufficient grounds to bring a suit against the clinic. Patients have an expectation of privacy. There's no question it was violated." She scrutinized Rick again. "Once we initiate our action, I'm confident the guilty parties and their motives will be exposed."

It seemed as if she wanted to be sure he understood her point. He nodded to show he had. "I don't think whoever did it meant any harm. It's those darn phones."

"What about my stepmother?" Elizabeth asked. "It was her decision to have me moved here."

"Do you wish to name her as a codefendant?"

"She's the only one who will benefit from the video."

Rick paused beside Elizabeth's chair. He wanted to bend down and kiss her hello, not talk about suing people. She didn't appear as if she would welcome any gesture of affection at the moment, though. She might be wearing an outfit that practically made his palms itch with the urge to run his hands over her, but she was angling her chin away from her collar as if the garment was cut as sharply as her lawyer's suit. He limited himself to giving her shoulder a light squeeze, then grabbed the straight-backed chair from beside the bed, reversed it, and straddled the seat. "I don't understand how the video would do Delaney any good. Does she own a TV station?"

"No. She would benefit from anything that would undermine my credibility. She and her lawyer have already used rumor and innuendo to question my competence. When I first filed my wrongful death lawsuit against her, they countered with outrageous accusations."

"They suspected you of trying to run her down," Rick said.

"Among other things. They had no grounds whatsoever, but Delaney was determined to destroy my reputation."

Cynthia cleared her throat. "Elizabeth, there have been several developments with respect to the incidents last summer. I thought we should deal with our immediate concerns first, but perhaps it would be better if I touched on a few of those to bring you up to date. You might wish to reconsider having your, ah, friend sit in on our discussion."

Elizabeth met Rick's gaze for the first time since he'd entered the room. Though her expression was carefully neutral, she couldn't hide the spark of longing in her eyes.

The desire to kiss her became overwhelming. He didn't want to give her a gentle peck hello, but a genuine, lip-melding, tongue-tangling, kiss. The kind they'd shared in their imaginations, only real. *You don't need to hide anything from me, Lizzie. I'm feeling it, too.*

She touched her fingertips to her coiled hair. She gave no sign that she'd heard him. "You already know most of this, Rick," she said. "If you want to stay, I won't object. It's up to you."

Maybe he'd only imagined the longing. It could have been fatigue. He folded his arms across the back of his chair. "I'd like to stay."

"Very well." Cynthia addressed Elizabeth. "I gather you remember the attack that resulted in your coma?"

She fisted her hands in her lap. "I remember it vividly. I was mugged."

Rick pictured covering her hands with his. She seemed to start, or was that his imagination, too? He didn't like all this second-guessing. Things had been a lot simpler in their dreams. How many times today had he thought that?

"The individual who attacked you was actually targeting your stepmother."

"Is that what Delaney said?"

"No, the culprit later confessed to the mugging. He also confessed to attempted murder regarding the hit-and-run of which you were suspected. He was mentally unstable and terminally ill. He died before reaching trial, so there will be no need for you to testify. I have copies of the police reports if you wish to see them."

"He confessed?" Elizabeth repeated.

"Yes. There is no question of his guilt. You are no longer under suspicion for any crime."

"That's terrific," Rick said.

"It is welcome news," Elizabeth said.

"I have more. Your stepmother withdrew her harassment suit, and given the circumstances, the restraining order she had filed against you became superfluous. In addition, her lawyer drew up a formal letter of apology to you for his overzealous actions. Personally, I don't believe it was sufficient in light of his deliberate attempt to damage your reputation. You may wish to seek punitive damages."

"Her lawyer, Leo Throop?"

"I'm sorry, am I going too fast?"

"My body may still be weak, Cynthia, but there's nothing wrong with my mind. I'm attempting to clarify the facts. You're making it sound as if Throop was behind the smear campaign, not Delaney."

"That's correct. Throop orchestrated what he intended as preemptive strikes against you in order to acquire leverage to protect his client from your wrongful death suit. It was quite without her knowledge."

"Or so she says."

Rick swallowed a protest. Yet again, he had to suppress his first response. He'd spent a lot of time waiting with the Harrisons on Christmas Day while the doctors had been busy with Elizabeth. He'd also spoken on the phone with Delaney, and he didn't agree with Elizabeth's harsh view of her stepmother. Delaney's concern for her stepdaughter struck him as sincere. It was difficult to see her as the scheming fortune hunter he'd been told about. John had seemed like a decent guy, too. Rick had gotten the impression there had been a lot more going on between the two of them than met the eye, though. "I might have missed something here," he said, "but this is good news, too, isn't it?"

"Indeed," Cynthia said. "Regardless of who was actually

behind them, Elizabeth, the attacks on your professional reputation and your mental competence have stopped. Your stepmother has switched tactics. Apparently she has decided she would benefit more from reconciliation than from continued antagonism."

"She must have a guilty conscience."

"Be that as it may, there has been no new evidence concerning your father's accident. I should advise you that if you choose to proceed with the suit, I don't believe we could win."

"Has she withdrawn her offer to settle?"

"We suspended negotiations when you were hospitalized." Cynthia reached into the briefcase that leaned against the side of her chair and withdrew a long, flat envelope. "However, she has informed me that the offer she originally intended to propose is still open."

"What are the terms?"

"They remain the same."

"I would like specifics, Cynthia."

The lawyer balanced the envelope across her knees and laid her palm on top of it. "Elizabeth, I must ask you once again whether you want your friend present for this discussion. It may not be prudent."

"And why is that?"

"You're recovering from a serious medical condition. Please forgive me for being blunt, but you must be aware that your judgment could be impaired as a consequence."

"As I told you before, there's nothing wrong with my brain."

"I would be negligent in my duties as your attorney if I allowed someone to take advantage of your situation."

"*Someone*, huh?" Rick asked. "Seeing as how there's only the three of us here, I'll take a wild guess. You're talking about me."

Cynthia continued as if he hadn't spoken. "He's aware that you're wealthy, Elizabeth."

"He's also aware I have blue eyes. Neither fact has any bearing on our relationship."

"The fact that you're refusing to acknowledge the obvious proves my concern is valid." She placed the envelope on the table between them. "I'll leave this copy of Delaney's offer with you so you can go over it in private, but it would be rash and irresponsible of me to discuss the financial specifics in this man's presence."

Rick swung the chair aside as he got to his feet. "I came here to see Elizabeth, that's all. I don't give a damn about her money."

It was as if he hadn't spoken. Cynthia steepled her fingers on the envelope, pressing it to the table. She kept her gaze on Elizabeth. "In all the years of our association, I have never known you to be naïve about people. This isn't like you. I can understand you feel a certain amount of gratitude toward this person for the role you perceive he played in your awakening, but please, try to view the situation objectively. It should have raised several red flags by now."

"Cynthia, my relationship with Rick is not open to discussion."

"Very well, then let's return to our original topic. We were discussing the video. You mentioned the only person who might benefit from its release is Delaney."

"Yes, and you explained she has changed tactics, so it might not be true."

"Correct. However, there does remain someone who stands to profit from the airing of this video: an amateur musician whose song is currently receiving international publicity."

"Wait a minute," Rick said. "I had nothing to do with that video."

"He's right. What you're implying is absurd, Cynthia."

"Think, Elizabeth. An unknown singer learns his music is being played for a wealthy young woman in a coma. Is it absurd to suppose he might write a romantic song for that woman and then perform it for her as a publicity stunt? It wouldn't be difficult to find an impressionable young nurse to record the event for him, since musicians have been known to hold a certain kind of appeal."

"That's ridiculous."

"Is it? Why would he choose to arrive on Christmas Eve, when security is relaxed and temporary help would be employed? Furthermore, news media outlets have a history of airing sentimental stories during the holiday season. Their interest in this one was quite predictable."

"Stop. The video couldn't have been a premeditated stunt. Rick couldn't have known I would wake up when I did."

"Of course, that couldn't have been anticipated. He no doubt intended to gain publicity by associating Elizabeth Graye with 'Angel Liz.' Having you regain consciousness was a fortuitous coincidence."

And he'd thought that *he* had an active imagination? "I'll be as blunt as you, ma'am. I haven't needed to wade through that much bullshit since I left the farm."

"Cynthia, what you're implying is insulting. You owe Rick an apology."

Rather than complying, Cynthia took a rectangular, zippered pouch from her briefcase. Inside was a small laptop computer. She opened it, hit a few keys, and set it on top of the envelope that she'd left on the table. "I checked his website before I arrived." She rotated the laptop so that the screen faced Elizabeth. "Would you like to take a look at it?"

Elizabeth curled her hands around the ends of her chair arms. Her fingers whitened.

Rick squatted beside her chair so he could view the screen himself.

The website had changed since he'd last seen it. The picture from the cover of his CD was still there. So was the short blurb about him and his music that Zeb had helped him write. Both elements were dwarfed by the banner across the center of the page that flashed "Angel Liz" in Day-Glo pink letters. An image of a musical note twirled beneath it, inviting viewers to order the track. No wonder the reporters hadn't had any trouble connecting him with the song.

"You're selling 'Angel Liz' on your website," Elizabeth said.

"Yeah, I only found out about that when I got here today."

"Please," Cynthia said. "Now who needs to wade through manure?"

"It's the truth. My nephew has a pal who works at a studio. The recording equipment they've got there isn't the greatest, but he lets us use it for free. We recorded 'Angel Liz' because it went over real well at the Cantina. We did that the day before I left to drive to New York. I hadn't thought about it again. He must have put this stuff on the website himself while I was gone."

"Why would he do that?"

"He's my manager."

"And how fortunate that he updated your site in time to cash in on what is undoubtedly an upsurge in sales."

"Come on. Things don't happen that fast."

"On the contrary. With the current state of global communications, information can be spread at the speed of light. There have been several recent phenomena concerning complete unknowns propelled to sudden fame through YouTube in a matter of days." She pulled a cell phone from her briefcase and held it out to him. "Aren't you curious to learn how your sales are going? I know I am."

"What's that for?"

"Call your manager. Unless you're afraid to let Elizabeth know what he'll say?"

Leave it to a lawyer to give him no way out. He took the phone and entered Zeb's number. Nothing happened until Cynthia pointed out another button he needed to press. He lifted the phone to his ear.

His nephew answered on the first ring. "Rick Denning's office."

Rick's stomach went hollow. Since when had Zeb started answering his phone like that? For more than a year, it had been "Denning's Web Design and Computer Repairs." "Uh, hey, Zeb. How's—"

That was all he was able to get out before Zeb started shouting. "Uncle Rick! Where've you been? I've been calling your motel all day."

"I spent most of the day wrangling with the truck. What—"

"You're all over the Internet! That clip with 'Angel Liz' went viral and everyone's been asking about you. There's reporters at the Cantina. Dad ran out of your CDs. Why didn't you tell us your girlfriend was Elizabeth Graye? Is she really a millionaire?"

The spate of questions went on. Rick promised he would phone back later and ended the call. He passed the phone to Cynthia as he looked at Elizabeth. "She's right about the publicity. I've made some sales."

"Congratulations."

"This isn't what I wanted. I mean, I did want people to like my music, but not like this. This is a flash in the pan. It's bound to blow over as fast as it came up."

Cynthia closed her laptop and returned both it and the phone to her briefcase. "We shall see, won't we?"

"This is crazy," Rick said. "You're twisting everything around. You're *trying* to find reasons not to trust me."

"I'm doing what's best for my client," Cynthia said. "A very valued, highly esteemed client who happens to be recovering from a brain injury and needs to be shielded from unscrupulous individuals who might wish to profit from her circumstances."

Elizabeth slapped the arm of her chair. Her body vibrated from the impact, knocking loose a lock of hair from her bun. "Now you're insulting me as well as Rick. Regardless of how I appeared during those few seconds on the video, I am fully in control of my faculties. I'm the same woman I was before my coma."

Cynthia looked pointedly at the chair arm. "The woman I knew never indulged in displays of temper."

"You never provoked me to this extent before."

"I'm doing what you employ me to do, Elizabeth. I'm protecting your interests. When you calm down and are feeling more like yourself, I hope you'll remember that." She picked up her briefcase, aligned her feet together precisely and stood. "Shall we proceed with the action against the clinic? As I mentioned before, the ensuing investigation should reveal the identity of all the guilty parties."

"I'll call you tomorrow to let you know what I decide."

She took the black coat that had been draped over the back of her chair and slipped it on, then indicated the envelope she had left on the table. "I trust you'll think about what I said and wait until you're alone before you review Delaney's offer."

"Good-bye, Cynthia."

Her heels clicked toward the door. Rick beat her to it and pulled it open. He braced for another volley, but she left without saying more. She hadn't needed to. What she'd already said hung in the air like the stink of a stable floor in July.

He closed the door and leaned his back against it. He raked one hand through his hair as he searched for something to say. "I don't think she likes me much."

The comment didn't get even a glimmer of a smile out of Elizabeth.

He tried again. "Maybe her shoes are too tight. Or she could be hungry. She looked like she might make a habit of skipping lunch."

"Cynthia has been my lawyer for more than ten years. She has an extremely analytical mind and I appreciate her frankness."

"You're not starting to buy into what she said, are you?"

She rubbed her eyes. She didn't reply.

Her silence hurt. He didn't want to blame her. Her lawyer had pushed some major buttons. He shoved away from the door, caught the armchair Cynthia had vacated and dragged it around to face Elizabeth. When he sat, his knees were close enough to press against hers. He felt they both needed the contact. He leaned forward and took her hands. "You can trust me, Lizzie. I'm not like the people who hurt you in the past. I'm not out to use you or take anything from you. You know the truth. You've seen it in my head."

"I've decided I'm not going to sue anyone over that video."

That wasn't the response he wanted to hear. "Why?"

"First of all, it's too late to stop it. More importantly, any damage it might do to my professional credibility is outweighed by the benefits to you."

"This isn't about me."

"It is now. After everything you've done for me, it's only fitting that you receive some compensation. I should have considered it before."

"What exactly do you mean by compensation?"

"As long as you remain here, you're missing your work at the Cantina. You had traveling expenses, and you're continuing to pay for a motel. This has to be a strain on your budget, and I know you have limited funds."

"When I run out of cash, I'll earn more. I've got my guitar, and if I can't find any bars around here that'll hire me, I've still got two good hands and a strong back."

"Yes, but—"

"Lizzie, I sure hope you're not thinking of offering me money."

"It would be fair, considering how much I have, and how much help you've given me."

"It would be a kick in the teeth. How many times do I have to tell you I'm not interested in your money? I'm getting tired of saying it. Maybe I should get it tattooed across my forehead. That won't break my so-called budget. Stella would probably give me a discount."

"Stella?"

"My landlady. She's a tattoo artist."

"You need to be realistic, Rick. Since the idea of taking money from me offends you, then consider what you can earn from 'Angel Liz.' If Cynthia is right, the publicity the video could generate might prove to be the opportunity of a lifetime for you. Managed properly, it could kick-start your career."

"I let Zeb do the managing. I came to New York to see you, not worry about my career."

"That doesn't mean you shouldn't make the most of the situation. You're a talented musician. Don't you want to be successful?"

"Well, sure I do. I just didn't know you were real when I wrote the song."

"It doesn't matter. Neither do my feelings. Emotions have no place in business decisions."

"The hell they don't. I never wanted to hurt you or humiliate you or embarrass you or whatever the hell it is I've ended up doing here."

"You haven't embarrassed me."

"Why else were you so worried about that video? I've seen the looks I get from people like Cynthia. I know you're not the kind of woman who would normally hang out with a guy like me."

"No, Rick. You've got it wrong. It's my own appearance on the video that embarrasses me, not yours."

"Geez, don't be so hard on yourself. I thought you looked damn good for someone who was in a coma for almost half a year. I get bed head from a ten-minute nap."

"It also distresses me that I hadn't already considered what Cynthia said."

"You mean about not trusting me?"

"In part, yes. Normally I'm far more cautious. Before my coma, I wouldn't have needed my lawyer to point out how you could profit from this publicity. I would have thought of it on my own."

He kissed her knuckles. "Then I'm glad you didn't think of it. It must have been hard to be so suspicious about everyone twenty-four seven. You must have been miserable. Heck, I bet you skipped lunch and wore uncomfortable shoes, too."

"I did what I had to do. Maintaining my position required constant vigilance. No matter how I felt, I had to appear in control. I couldn't afford to trust anyone."

"But you were the boss, weren't you? It's your choice who works for you."

"All the more reason to be cautious. If someone received wages from me, it wouldn't necessarily buy their loyalty. A year ago I learned one of the drivers employed by Grayecorp had been recording every conversation and telephone call I had made in the car and had sold the information to a competitor. A similar issue arose with the woman I hired while my personal assistant was on maternity leave. Sometimes the damage was more overt. Last spring I discovered a foreman on my condominium project had been sabotaging progress on the site in order to obtain overtime for his crew. There's also the theft of building materials, the misuse of company equipment, the private deals certain sales reps make in order to inflate their figures, the occasional creative accounting by suppliers . . . The list is endless."

He chafed her hands between his. "I guess being the boss isn't all it's cracked up to be."

"It got worse after my father died. It was as if people were testing me, trying to see how much they could get away with and whether I was really in charge. Then there was all the additional trouble with my stepmother."

"But that's changed, right? Cynthia said that guy who attacked you confessed to the hit-and-run, so you're not in trouble with the cops anymore. And your stepmother wants to settle your lawsuit. You're already better off now than you were before your coma."

She regarded the envelope that her lawyer had left on the table. "Don't be so sure," she said, tugging free from his grasp to pick it up. "I didn't trust Delaney then, and I have no reason to trust her now."

He stifled a sigh.

"What?" she asked.

"Like I said, it must be hard to be so suspicious all the time."

She flicked one corner of the envelope with her thumb. "I can't afford to lose my edge."

"Do you want me to leave?" Rick asked.

"Why?"

"So you can take a look at Delaney's offer in private, like Cynthia said."

"Don't be an ass," she muttered, sliding a finger beneath the flap to rip open the envelope.

He grinned and pictured giving her a hug. *That's my Lizzie.*

She inhaled sharply. Another chunk of hair sprang free from her bun. But there was no response, either aloud or in his mind.

Rick settled back in his chair. He wished he could stop reaching for her that way, but he couldn't seem to help doing it. It was as useless and as hard to control as probing at a sore tooth with his tongue.

Elizabeth withdrew a thick sheaf of stapled papers. She leafed through them quickly, then went back to the beginning. Her eyes tracked across the words with businesslike efficiency as she took her time reading each page.

Several minutes passed in silence while Rick tried in vain to gauge her expression. She was keeping her thoughts hidden, but she was unable to keep her hands steady. The papers rattled in her grip. When she finally lowered them to her lap, her fingers were shaking.

"What's wrong?" he asked.

"When Delaney first broached the possibility of settling, I assumed her offer would be a token gesture and would involve only a few million at most."

Only a few million? "It's not?"

"She's offering me half."

"Half a million?"

"Half the estate."

He had to let that sink in. "You said your father was worth billions. If she's willing to give you half of everything, that would be . . . damn, that would still be billions. That's a lot of money."

She shook her head.

"It's not a lot of money?"

"There's more. She's giving me the property in Bedford."

"What property?"

"The house where I grew up, the surrounding grounds, the entire contents . . . she doesn't want any of it. She's willing to sign it all over to me." She looked around the room, her gaze touching on the hospital bed, the bank of medical equipment that hadn't yet been removed, and the floral arrangements that crowded the shelves. "You told me earlier that you had truck trouble."

The change of topic startled him. "That's right. Why?"

"Were you able to drive it here?"

"Yeah, I got it running. I know you're going to be even more filthy rich now than you were before you read those legal papers, but I hope you're not about to volunteer to pay to have my truck fixed, because then I'm gonna have to think about that tattoo for my forehead again."

"Don't be paranoid."

"Whoa. You're calling *me* paranoid?"

She tossed the sheaf of papers to the table, grasped her chair arms and struggled to stand.

Rick leapt to his feet to catch her around the waist. "Take it easy. You sure you should be doing that?"

Her knees buckled. She clutched his shirt to keep herself upright. She panted a few times before she was able to steady herself. "I asked about your truck because I want you to give me a ride."

"I don't think the docs are going to let you out of here."

"Unlike when we first met, I'm not a prisoner." She tipped back her head. "They can't stop me from leaving."

Whatever had been keeping her bun in place dropped to the floor, sending the rest of her curls tumbling past her shoulders. The sight made him feel like cheering. The sensation of her body pressed to his made him feel like doing a lot more. The velour was every bit as soft as he'd guessed. Her curves molded into his angles as perfectly as he remembered. So what if she was only hanging onto him because she was unable to stand on her own? Whether the embrace was passionate or not, she belonged here, in his arms.

And for the first time since he'd watched her wake up, reality felt . . . right. He rubbed his cheek against her hair. "I'll do whatever you want, Lizzie. You know that. I'm on your side."

"Good, because I intend to ensure that Delaney keeps her word."

"How?"

"I'm going home, Rick."

SEVENTEEN

ALAN TORE OFF A PIECE OF CROISSANT AND DABBED IT WITH strawberry jam. The French chef was the only redeeming feature of this hotel. The offerings in the dining room had been spectacular, but this suite was far smaller than he was accustomed to, and the decor was too fussy for his taste. Room service had set up breakfast on a wobbly table in front of the drafty balcony doors. The view consisted of nothing but snow, which had been blowing around since dawn. It was a welcome change from the bleakness of the so-called historic buildings on the other side of the street. History was overrated, and was far too often thrown up as a roadblock in the way of development. Three-hundred-year-old buildings weren't quaint, they were money-losing, inefficient uses of space. He used the remote to switch on the news, grateful they had CNN in this backwater.

Montreal wouldn't have been his first choice for a holiday destination. It did have one significant advantage over Manhattan, though. Jamal didn't know he was here. For two marvelous weeks he'd been spared the phone calls and the not-so-veiled threats. For the sake of peace, he could put up with a few inconveniences.

"Good morning, Alan."

He smiled. This was another advantage of taking a holiday in Canada. Or did Quebec still count as Canada? "Good morning to you, too, darling."

Sherri Stock draped herself over his shoulder to give him a kiss. "I'm starving." She took the morsel of croissant he held and popped it into her mouth. "I hope you ordered enough for me."

Sherri had proven to be a woman of large appetites. Like him, she was wearing one of the white velour robes that had been provided by the hotel. And like him, she had left the belt loose. "Have all you want," he said, enjoying the view beside him much more than the one outside the window. "Ensuring your satisfaction is one of my greatest pleasures."

She sat in the chair across from his. "Not as great a pleasure as mine, *Alain*."

He passed her a plate with a second croissant, as well as the jam pot, then muted the TV. "I like the way my name sounds when you say it in French."

"Then I'll have to do it more often, *n'est-ce pas*? I can add that to my resolutions for the New Year. Oh, that reminds me. I need to go shopping."

"Again?"

She laughed. "Spoken like a typical male. I have nothing to wear."

"I don't find that a problem. The less you have on, the better I like it."

"Mmm. I noticed. But I can't very well show up at Daddy's party like this."

His mind jumped ahead. Jack Stock's birthday party was going to give him the perfect opportunity to cultivate some fresh connections and possibly some new investors. The people in the mining community didn't move in the same circles as the people he'd met through his Grayecorp connections, so there would be little risk of anyone comparing notes. He gave her a genuine smile. "I'm looking forward to meeting your family. If they're anything like you, I know I'm going to love them. Thank you again for inviting me."

"Daddy insisted. I've told him so much about you."

"Then he's aware of my, ah, situation?"

"You mean with Elizabeth?"

He glanced away. "Sorry, I shouldn't have brought it up."

"No, don't apologize. Your life hasn't been easy. My father understands that, and he appreciates your honesty, as I do."

He sighed. "I should forget about my promise to her and break the engagement now. This isn't fair to you."

"No, *Alain*. You're a man of your word. I admire your determination to honor it to the end."

"The doctors say she can't hang on much longer. Her condition is deteriorating."

"I'm so sorry."

"It will mean an end to her suffering, so really, it will be a mercy."

"Let me be there for you. Anything you need, please, don't hesitate to ask."

He sighed. "You're one in a million, Sherri. I don't believe I've ever known a woman as generous as you."

"You deserve it, *Alain*."

"I can't remember when I've felt this good. It's as if a giant weight has been lifted from my shoulders. After so many months of worrying about her needs, this past week with you has been wonderful. You've brought me back to life."

"You have needs, too." She stretched her arm across the table to take his hand. "It takes strength to admit it."

"I'm not strong where you're concerned. I don't know how I managed to resist you for so long."

"Don't blame yourself, the responsibility is entirely mine." She leaned closer. "I am impressed by your capacity to love so selflessly. It's rare in a man."

Now wouldn't be a good time to ogle Sherri's breasts, so he kept his gaze on her face. "Would you think less of me if I told you I don't want to talk about her anymore?"

"Of course, I wouldn't."

"I would prefer to talk about us."

"*Moi, aussi.* You must stop feeling guilty. Let me sign the contract."

He shifted, feigning discomfort. "No, it wouldn't be right. I can't do business with my lover."

"That's ridiculous. Why should I leave my money in the bank when you could put it to much better use?"

"I shouldn't take advantage of our relationship."

"Take advantage? *Alain*, it's the other way around."

"I don't understand."

"I believe my lover is going to make me very rich." She tickled his palm with her thumb. "And the bonus you gave me last night isn't taxable."

He laughed. "You make a convincing case."

"That's because you drive a hard bargain."

Not yet, but it was getting there. The prospect of watching Sherri's agile fingers sliding around a pen as she signed their partnership contract and wrote out a check was already exciting him. The timing couldn't have been better. This infusion of cash would cover his immediate expenses. He could use any additional money he talked her father's mining cronies into investing to keep Jamal off his back. With enough new cash, he wouldn't even need to build a shopping mall. As long as he regularly added fresh funds to the pot, he could prolong the project indefinitely.

Sherri withdrew her hand and dipped her fingertip into the jam pot. "Then we're agreed?"

"Only if you're certain."

"Absolument." She made a show out of tonguing the jam from her finger, then toyed with the edge of her robe. "Now that's settled, perhaps we could find some way to celebrate our new partnership?"

Happy to oblige, Alan rounded the table and pulled Sherri out of her chair. He was angling his head to taste the jam she'd left at the corner of her mouth when his attention was caught by a figure on the edge of his vision. He glanced past her to the television. They were showing video footage of a man leaning over to kiss a blonde woman in what appeared to be a hospital bed . . .

He froze. No. It couldn't be. What the hell was she doing on CNN? And who the hell was the man who was kissing her? Kissing Alan's fiancée. He looked like a bum.

"Alain?"

He jerked away from Sherri and fumbled for the remote

". . . tremendous interest in this real-life fairy tale since the video first appeared on YouTube. Our sources have found that 'Angel Liz' is in fact Elizabeth Graye, a prominent New York City real estate developer who awakened on Christmas Eve after spending five months in a coma."

Sherri turned toward the TV as a photo of Elizabeth was flashed on the screen. It appeared to be the one from the Grayecorp website. *"Mon Dieu,"* she murmured. "Did they say . . ."

"Elizabeth."

"She's awake?"

"Apparently."

"But how is that possible? You told me the doctors said she was dying."

"They must have been wrong."

"Why didn't anyone call you?"

"I switched off my phone. I needed a holiday."

"But . . ." She pulled her robe closed and knotted the belt. She smiled tightly. "It's a miracle. A Christmas miracle, that's what they're saying."

"It's . . . unbelievable."

"You have to go back. It's the right thing to do. She'll be expecting you."

He hesitated. "Your father is expecting us, too."

"I'll explain it to Daddy. Given the circumstances, he wouldn't expect you to make the party. Your place is with her."

"You'll come with me, won't you?" *And sign the damn check?*

"No, *Alain.* I think it would be best if I went home. I'll have Daddy send a car to pick me up."

"But, darling, I still need you."

"Your fiancée needs you more." Snow hissed against the window. She hugged her arms to her chest. "I do hope the weather won't get any worse. They might have to close down the airport."

Damn. *Damn!* This was exactly like Elizabeth. The

woman thrived on finding ways to screw people over. She couldn't have chosen a more inconvenient moment possible to wake up if she'd tried. To add insult to injury, after Alan had danced attendance on her for five months, playing the devoted boyfriend, some stranger had horned in at the last minute to steal his thunder.

Whoever the bastard was, and whatever scam he was trying to run, Alan wasn't about to let him steal anything else.

EIGHTEEN

THE GRAYE HOUSE GLOWED THROUGH THE STORM IN A halo of snow that swirled out of the darkness. It stood at the top of a small rise, illuminated by buff-tinted floodlights along the foundation. It was built of rose granite and accented by pale limestone. Two wings extended backward at right angles from the rounded corners of a central, flat-roofed structure. Rows of long, narrow windows reflected the headlights of Rick's pickup like a blank stare. The overall effect was one of cold implacability. Elizabeth thought it appeared more like a fortress than a home. Oddly, she had never noticed the similarity before. From this angle, it bore a resemblance to the castle where she'd been imprisoned in her dreams.

She pulled her chin deeper into her coat, suppressing a shiver as the steel security gates hummed shut behind them. "What do you think of the place?"

Rick started up the driveway. The windshield wipers had difficulty keeping up with the snow. "It sure is big."

"It was built to my father's specifications. He had wanted to make a visual impact."

"It does that, all right." The back end of the truck slid sideways. He geared down and corrected the skid. "Must cost a mint to heat."

"Economizing wasn't a consideration when I was growing up."

"Yeah, I bet."

She was grateful it wasn't a consideration now, either. It had taken little more than forty-eight hours to organize her departure from the clinic. As Rick had predicted, the medical staff had opposed her decision. Her wealth had provided her the means, while her experience at Grayecorp had provided her the skills, to counter every one of the doctors' objections. She had arranged for a live-in nurse to be on hand in case an emergency arose, although she no longer required assistance with her most personal needs. Dr. Shouldice would be visiting regularly to check on her condition and monitor her progress. She had hired a rehabilitation specialist who would be coming to the house daily, and the exercise room and the indoor pool in the east wing would provide more than adequate facilities to continue her therapy.

Having the house itself prepared for her arrival had been relatively easy. Elizabeth hadn't contacted Delaney directly—she'd had Cynthia do that. They would be meeting in two weeks to settle the legal matters between them, but apparently her stepmother had had no objections to granting Elizabeth immediate access to her family home as a show of good faith. Although Delaney hadn't resided in the house since Stanford's death, she had continued to have it maintained. Hilda Foster, the Graye family's longtime housekeeper, and her husband Harold, who had been in charge of Stanford's stable of cars, had been serving as live-in caretakers for the property. The Fosters had already engaged a cook and a cleaning staff. The transition promised to be a smooth one.

The only remaining rough spot could be the reporters. The number at the clinic had thinned down considerably over the past day, since media requests for interviews were being referred to Rick's nephew. It appeared as if Zebadiah Denning was handling the situation like a seasoned professional, doling out enough information to maintain public interest while whetting their appetite for more. At Rick's insistence, he had put a spin on the story that emphasized

Rick and his music rather than his relationship to Elizabeth. She was relieved about that. In spite of how beneficial the video could prove to be for Rick, her part in it still bothered her. At least now that she was home, any reporters who attempted to reach her wouldn't be able to get past the gates. The house had a state-of-the-art security system as well. There were advantages to living in a fortress.

"Did you need a map and compass to find the can?" Rick asked.

She realized he was trying to make her smile, and she tried, but it turned out to be more of a grimace. "There are ten bathrooms, give or take a few, so I can't remember it being a problem."

He whistled. "What did you do with all that space?"

"I used only a small portion of it. When I still lived at home, that is. You can pull up beside the portico," she said, pointing toward the pillared archway that extended over the front entrance.

Rick slowed the truck to a halt and turned off the key. The wipers stopped, but the engine kept going. "Don't worry," he said. "She won't keep it up for long."

"With this storm, I'm grateful you were still willing to give me a ride. I suspect this truck managed better in the snow than a car would have."

He shut off the lights. The dashboard went dark, leaving only the light from the house filtering through the windshield. He thumped the steering column with the side of his hand, then pulled out the key. He turned it over in his fingers a few times. "I said I would help you, and I meant it, but are you sure you want to do this?"

"Do what?"

"Move back here."

"Why wouldn't I? This house is rightfully mine."

"Sure, but I can see you've been getting tenser the closer we got, and I don't think it was because of the storm or my driving."

"The place has a lot of memories."

"They make you sad, right?"

"Some of them, but I am very pleased to claim possession of this property."

"Because it's item number one in your plan to get your life back."

"Precisely." She unfastened her seat belt. "This is where I want to be, Rick."

The truck's engine coughed and sputtered to silence. Rick nodded once, then got out and rounded the hood to open her door. He held up his arms.

They had brought a wheelchair with them from the clinic. It was beneath a tarp in the back, along with the belongings she had accumulated during her stay there. She hated the idea of using it, but for now it was a necessary evil. She couldn't walk far on her own, even with the aid of her walker. "Shouldn't you get the wheelchair first?"

"I'll come back for it later. Let me carry you."

"There's a ramp to the right of the stairs that should be clear of snow. I can manage on my own with the chair."

"Yeah, I know you can. That's not the point. I want to carry you, okay?"

"Why?"

"Because I want you in my arms."

She hesitated.

"Hey, whether you're firing on all cylinders or not, you're a gorgeous woman, and I'm twisted enough to use any excuse to cop a feel."

Her lips twitched. "That would be rather difficult to accomplish through this wool coat."

"Dang, I never thought of that. Guess I'm out of practice. You'll have to give me pointers about this, too."

This time he did succeed in making her smile. "Seriously, Rick. I'm walking farther every day. Exercise is good for me. I don't need to be coddled."

"I might as well. The rate you're going, you'll be running laps around the driveway by the time I get this bucket of bolts started again, and I'll be kicking myself that I missed my chance to hang on to you." He put his hands on her waist. "Come on, it'll be easier than getting off Chester."

She grasped his shoulders. He lifted her off the seat and let her slide down his body until her feet touched the ground, just as he had when he'd helped her off the horse. In spite of the heavy wool coat she wore, and his own sheepskin jacket, she was jolted by the contact. It felt as if her bare breasts had brushed his chest.

She shuddered. Her legs gave out.

He scooped her into his arms. "It's cold out here. We better get you inside."

She put her arms around Rick's neck. As soon as he started moving, an image of the first time he'd carried her flashed through her mind. She saw herself pressing hard against his chest while he pushed his way through the melee in the castle courtyard, his head bent over hers as he tried to shelter her from the rain of arrows.

This was a fragment from her dream, and yet it wasn't how she remembered it. It was as if she was experiencing the scene from Rick's point of view.

He tightened his hold on her as he climbed the steps to the front door. It swung open before he reached it. Light blazed from the crystal chandelier that hung over the foyer. A pale, middle-aged woman stood to one side of the threshold, her hands clasped over her midriff. "Welcome home, Miss Graye."

The image from her dream dissolved as quickly as it had arisen. It was as if a switch had been thrown, or a leak had been plugged. Layers of winter clothing once more blocked any hint of Rick's body.

Elizabeth took a moment to catch her breath. It had been her imagination, that was all. The stress of coming home must have affected her more than she'd thought. "Hello, Mrs. Foster. It's been a long time."

The housekeeper pursed her lips in a tight smile as Rick stamped the snow from his boots and carried Elizabeth inside. Her black hair was parted in the center and hung poker straight to her jaw. Apart from a tasteful, gold chain around her neck, her cardigan set and pleated skirt were unrelieved brown. She greeted Rick politely and inquired after Elizabeth's health, but expressed no surprise at her sudden homecoming. She didn't act pleased or displeased; she was as neutral as the brass door knocker and about as warm. Stanford had trained her well. "We've prepared the guest suite in the west wing for you, Miss Graye, as a temporary arrangement. We'll move you to the master suite as soon as you can manage the stairs. Do you have luggage?"

"My things are in the truck. There's a wheelchair and a walker as well."

"Harold will fetch everything. The nurse has been installed in the room adjacent to your suite. Shall I send for her now?"

"That won't be necessary."

"Cook won't be here until tomorrow. If there's anything you would like from the kitchen in the meantime, please, let me know."

"Thank you, Mrs. Foster. I will."

Another tight smile, a nod to Rick, and she glided away silently on her sensible, brown, crepe-soled shoes.

Rick ducked his head to bring his face to Elizabeth's. "Great Morticia impersonation. Was she always like that?"

"For as long as I can remember. She's a very efficient housekeeper."

"There's a lot of house to keep." He surveyed the foyer, then nodded to the hallway to the right of the staircase. "If my sense of direction's still working, I'd say that's west. Is your bedroom through there?"

"Yes, but I don't want to go there yet. I'd like to sit up for a while. Are you in a hurry to leave?"

"I'll stay as long as you'll have me, Lizzie."

Before she could direct him, Rick turned and started toward the doorway on his left. His footsteps resonated on the foyer's marble floor, then thudded on cherry wood as he carried her into the front sitting room. Only one lamp on a table near the doorway had been left burning, softening the contrast of the dark wood with the cream-toned walls and area carpets. It appeared as if Delaney hadn't changed a thing. A pair of low-backed, white couches flanked the fireplace. Wing chairs covered in cream and white brocade were arranged near the windows. Thick, burgundy drapes muffled the sound of the storm to give a hushed, cozy feel to the space. Two large ferns marked the place where the room widened into a semicircle at the far corner, forming a dramatic showcase for the Steinway concert grand.

Elizabeth's gaze sought it immediately. The instrument was still there, gleaming gracefully from the shadows. The ledge where she used to lean her music books was empty, and a huge floral arrangement was in the center of the closed lid, but otherwise, it was the same as the last time she'd seen it. And it was what she'd pictured even before she'd realized she was thinking of it. "How did you know?" she asked.

"Mmm?"

"That I wanted to come in here?"

"From what you've told me, you liked that piano." He tightened his hold into a brief hug, then leaned over to place her on her feet. He kept one arm clamped firmly around her waist to steady her. "I figured this would be a good place to hang out."

"You figured right. It's my favorite room in the house. But how did you know where it was?"

He shrugged. "Beats me. Must have been a lucky guess. I think you mentioned that the piano was at the front, too. Where to now? You feel like playing?"

She flexed her fingers. They felt as uncoordinated as the rest of her. "I'm not up to that tonight. Just seeing it is enough for now. I'm relieved Delaney didn't get rid of it."

"Why would she? She knows how important it is to you, doesn't she?"

"I hope not. I was careful not to let her know."

"Why?"

"It would have given her a reason to get rid of it."

His cheek jumped, as if he were chewing the inside of it. He swallowed whatever he'd been about to say, extended his free arm in front of her so she could hang on to his wrist, and guided her toward the nearest couch. When he moved to help her take off her coat, she gently waved him away, determined to manage that much on her own. He waited until she was safely seated before discarding his own coat, then went to light the logs that had been readied on the hearth.

Elizabeth finally felt herself begin to relax. The scene before her was familiar, and not only because of the amount of time she'd spent in this room. The fireplace was surrounded by white marble instead of fieldstones, yet it reminded her of the one in her final dream. The entire make-believe cottage in the woods would have fitted into this sitting room with space to spare. It was Rick who bridged the gap between the two scenes. He was crouched in front of this fire in the same easy pose he'd assumed at the other one. His jeans tightened over his legs and buttocks, while his shirt stretched tautly across his shoulders. His modern clothes displayed his body as enticingly as the medieval leggings and tunic. It was a pleasure to watch him, wherever he was, or whatever he was wearing or doing.

A different picture superimposed itself on her vision. She saw herself, dressed in nothing but a white camisole and drawers, her cheeks flushed and her lips moist. Her hair tumbled wildly over her bare shoulders. Then she felt the heat of her skin beneath Rick's fingers as he fumbled to untie the ribbon at her neckline . . .

He wiped his hands on his knees and stood. "That should do it."

As before, the image seemed to have been from Rick's point of view instead of hers. It dissolved as suddenly as it had appeared, but the sensation of his touch on her skin persisted so vividly that Elizabeth darted a glance at her chest.

Her body was still covered by the sapphire blue sweater and loose wool pants she'd put on before she'd left the clinic.

The couch cushion dipped as Rick sat beside her. "Are you okay?"

Feeling twinges of sexual arousal was a sign her nervous system was returning to normal, she reminded herself. It was pointless to think about actually having sex in her condition, though. Regardless of how appealing Rick looked, and the teasing comment he'd made earlier, plus the chemistry she had acknowledged was between them, these feelings couldn't go anywhere. She didn't even have the energy to sit at the piano. "Yes, I'm fine. I was just . . . reminiscing. I haven't told anyone this before, but I was here last summer."

"When?"

"The day of the hit-and-run attempt on Delaney's life. I had known the Fosters visited their daughter on weekends and I would have the house to myself. I had been coming here every weekend for months."

"Why would you do that?"

"To play the piano. I still had my keys, and my stepmother hadn't bothered to change the locks. The combination to the gates and the alarm codes were the same, too. Technically, I was trespassing. That's why I couldn't admit where I was and needed an alibi."

"Why didn't you come clean? Trespassing is a lot less serious than attempted murder."

The reasons for her silence had seemed valid at the time. Coming here had been a sentimental, self-indulgent thing to do, and quite out of character. It would have given Delaney more fodder for her campaign to paint her as incompetent. Most of all, she hadn't wanted to admit her need for familiar surroundings, or for the emotional outlet her music had given her. It would have made her appear weak. "Once Alan spoke up, it was a moot point. What was the house where you grew up like, Rick?"

"It couldn't compare to this place, that's for sure."

"Tell me about it."

"It was white clapboard and more than a hundred years old. My mother liked to say it was two stories but it was really only a story and a half. It was the kind with the gable window in the front."

"I'm familiar with the design. It was common in the late nineteenth century."

"There were only two bedrooms upstairs. Jethro and I shared one, my parents had the other. There were plenty of fights over the bathroom, because we only had one of those. Most of the time, everyone hung out in the kitchen." He leaned over to pull off her shoes, then grasped her legs and swung them over his lap. "Here. You'll be more comfortable if you stretch out."

She snuggled her back into the corner of the couch. "I've seen pictures of farm kitchens. They looked . . . warm. Was it?"

"Uh-huh, especially in the summer, but that was okay because there were windows on both ends and the front veranda kept out the sun. It was full of good cooking smells, too. They soaked into the walls like the smell of wood smoke. I liked that. I could have walked in there blindfolded and still known I was home."

"Was that your favorite room?"

"I guess it was. You could say I left my mark on it. There were grooves carved into the doorframe where my father measured me and Jethro on our birthdays to see how much we'd grown. His dad had done the same for him and his sisters, so it was pretty scratched up. The posts on the veranda were scarred up, too, but that was from target practice." A dimple creased into his cheek. "I used to be real handy with a pocket knife. I got one for my seventh birthday."

"When I turned seven, I received seven hundred shares of AT&T."

"Huh. Couldn't have had much fun with that present. Not unless you scrunched them up and played garbage can basketball."

She smiled and touched his dimple. "Where does your brother live?"

"He and Josie have a bungalow not too far from the Cantina. Don't ask me how they fit all their kids into it. The routine probably involves crowbars and shoehorns."

"How many children do they have?"

"Eight. Five boys and three girls. Zeb's the oldest. He's twenty-two. Eli's the youngest. He'll turn one next week."

"Eight children! That's quite a full house."

"I keep offering to help Jethro build an addition, but they seem happy with the crowbars and shoehorns."

"You sound as if you're very close to your brother. Is he much older than you?"

"There's a nine year gap between us. He just turned forty, so I'm halfway between Zeb's age and Jethro's. My brother was eighteen when he and Josie got that particular surprise."

"So young, and yet they're still together."

"They were made for each other. She's the only woman on earth who would be able to put up with him."

"Why?"

"He nags. At least, he nags me."

"About what?"

"You name it. My music, my eating habits, my love life. I know he means well, though. He's got my back, and I'd do anything for him." He rested his hand on her knee. "Just like I'd do anything for the people I love."

The word hovered between them for a moment. She tensed.

"Did you ever wish you had a brother or sister?"

The moment passed. "Perhaps when I was very young. I grew out of it."

"Like your wish for a dog?"

"That's right."

"Must have been lonely for you, rattling around in this big place with no one to play with."

"It wasn't that bad. I had nannies and, later, governesses. They had a full schedule of activities to keep me busy. I also had a friend."

"That was Monica, right?"

"Yes. Her family owns the property adjoining this one. The Chamberlains used to be good friends of my parents, so they didn't object if we were constantly back and forth visiting each other's houses. Monica and I attended the same boarding school and were roommates for several semesters."

"It sounds as if you two were close."

"We were when we were young. We took different paths when we went to college. Reading was her passion, so she majored in English literature. She's currently teaching at the same boarding school we used to attend."

"Now that you mention it, she does look like a teacher."

"How so?"

"Smart. Sharp. She's like you, only not as intense. What happened between you two?"

"We had a falling-out."

"Yeah, I remember that's what you said before. What triggered it?"

"Short answer, I did."

He slid his hand down her leg to her ankle. "I've got no where else I have to be. Even if I did, I probably wouldn't get there until it stops snowing. Give me the long answer."

He'd said almost exactly the same thing to her once before, after the plane crash. It had been snowing then, too. It was strange, how tonight seemed to be mirroring her dreams. "Why don't you stay here tonight, Rick?"

He slipped his fingers beneath the hem of her pants to tickle her calf. "Is it going to be that long an answer?"

"Very funny. The drive to your motel could be treacherous in this storm. It would be more sensible to stay here."

A log in the fireplace snapped. Sparks flared, reflecting in his gaze. "You want me to spend the night with you?"

His deep voice gave the question a different meaning. Though he was no longer moving his hand, her leg tingled as if he was. She shifted her feet on the cushion. "Given my current condition, I didn't mean in my bed."

He smiled crookedly. "Who says we need a bed? Seems comfy here."

"Rick . . ."

"I could help you take off your clothes. These ones don't look that complicated." He skimmed his fingertip from the base of her turtleneck to the dip between her breasts. "Unless you've got hidden bows someplace. I'm not much good with bows."

"I don't think—"

"You won't need to think. All you'll need to do is lie back and enjoy. I'll do all the work."

"You're teasing again, aren't you?"

His smile disappeared. He unfastened the clasp that held

her French twist in place and dropped it beside her. Her hair uncoiled. He tunneled his fingers through the strands to spread them out, then brought a handful to his face. He inhaled slowly, his nostrils flaring. "Yeah, I'm teasing," he muttered. He guided her head to rest against his shoulder. "Thanks, I'd like to stay."

God, she wished her recovery wasn't so slow. Pointless or not, the sexual twinges she'd been feeling were turning into pangs. She slid her hand over his chest. Warmth spread into her palm and up her arm. She was keenly aware of how familiar this position was—she had nestled into Rick like this countless times in her dreams. He was a physically powerful man. Even through his shirt she could easily trace the contours of his muscles. Though he'd made the offer in jest, she had no doubt he was fully capable of doing all the work, as he'd put it. At the risk of scandalizing Mrs. Foster, what would be the harm . . .

He flattened his hand over hers. "I'm not in a hurry to do the deed, Lizzie. It's enough for me to hold you."

Warmth suffused her cheeks. She wasn't sure why. She was accustomed to speaking frankly about sex, but the kind of intimacy she shared with Rick was new to her. Technically, they had never even had sex, they'd only imagined it.

"You were going to tell me about the trouble with Monica."

She sighed. This was one topic guaranteed to douse thoughts of Rick's body. It was just as well. When—or if—they took their relationship to the next level, they would both enjoy themselves more if she had the stamina to participate. "Do you remember how I told you I blackmailed my father to force him to change his will?"

"You said he cheated on Delaney."

"That's right. He had been unfaithful to her for years. I could have chosen any of his past lovers as an example, but I felt it was more effective to name the woman he was having an affair with at that particular time. She happened to be Jenna Chamberlain."

"Uh-oh. Monica's mother?"

"Yes. When I exposed their affair, I was focusing on the leverage I would gain with my father. I didn't consider what it would do to Jenna. I never thought it might lead to the breakup of their marriage. She was what you could call collateral damage."

"So Monica got mad at you."

"She was furious. She's very protective of her mother, which was understandable. Jenna doesn't have much business sense, and under the terms of the prenup she signed before she married, she would get no alimony and next to nothing in the way of a settlement if adultery could be proven."

"From what I've come to know about your friend, I'm guessing it wasn't just her mother's finances she was upset about."

"Monica is a romantic, like her mother. It's why she's better suited to working in the academic field rather than in business. She believed Jenna's claims that she was actually in love with my father."

"Don't you think that was possible?"

"Jenna was infatuated with Stanford's wealth and power, the same way Delaney was. I did feel some responsibility for the events that led to her reduced circumstances, because until then she had been discreet in concealing her affair from her husband, but she turned down my offer of financial assistance. The fact that I offered made Monica even angrier with me. She said money couldn't buy love."

"She didn't have to tell you that. You already knew it better than anyone."

"It was one of my first lessons in life. *This* is what money buys," she said, waving her arm at the room. "A showpiece of a fortress full of polite servants and polished furniture and doorframes that no one would dare carve grooves into."

"And now you've got it back."

"Yes, I do."

"You won."

"In the end, that's all that counts."

He stroked her hair. He didn't respond.

She spoke to fill the silence. "Monica said I was obsessed with revenge, but that was wrong. I only wanted what should have been mine."

"You were trying to be tough."

"I *am* tough. I could never have achieved what I have if I'd been weak. If Monica took her nose out of her books she would see the real world bears little resemblance to the school where she hides herself. She would wake up and see me for who I am now, not the idealistic child I used to be, but Elizabeth Baylor Graye, my father's daughter."

"That's what the fight was really about, wasn't it?"

"That's right. She's hanging onto an illusion. She doesn't want to be friends with the real me."

"How can you be sure if you won't talk to her?"

She drew back to better look at him. "Why are you taking her side?"

"I'm on your side. Always. But other people would be, too, if you give them a chance. You don't have to come out swinging."

"I do, Rick. It's the only thing that works for me."

"It's not working for you anymore, is it?" He touched his hand to her cheek, then held it in front of her. Moisture glistened on his fingertips. "It's making you miserable."

She swiped her sleeve across her eyes. "I don't believe this."

"Believe what?"

"All these tears. Before my coma, I never cried."

"Maybe Elizabeth Baylor Graye never cried, but Lizzie does all the time."

Her chin trembled. She threw up her hands. "You're as bad as Monica. Why can't you call me Elizabeth, like everyone else?"

Because you'll always be Lizzie to me. My Lizzie.

The words drifted on the fringes of her mind, like a snatch of conversation overheard through a door. The voice was faint, but there was no mistaking Rick's velvety baritone.

Yet his lips hadn't moved.

Rick stroked her arm.

She felt the softness of her sweater on her own palm. An image of her own face filled her vision. Firelight flickered on her skin, but this was no fragment from her memory. She was wearing her blue sweater. She could see the shape of a wing chair behind her, and beyond that a set of closed drapes. This was here and now.

Lizzie?

Rick's voice seemed nearer, as if the door were inching open, spilling his eagerness like sunshine. Power crackled across the gap between them. It aroused her emotions as effortlessly as his touch aroused her body. She swayed closer.

Rick's face came back into focus. Concern furrowed his brow. "Lizzie, what's wrong?"

He had spoken aloud.

Of course, he had spoken aloud. Just as those images had been from her own overactive imagination. Anything else was impossible. She was home, and she was resuming control of her life, just as she wanted. She no longer needed to take refuge in fantasy. Now, more than ever, she couldn't afford to let her attention lapse.

He eased her backward to lean against the arm of the couch and slid her legs off his lap so he could stand. "I'm going to find the nurse."

She caught his hand to stop him from moving away. "No, don't."

"You didn't look so good a second ago. It's like you faded out."

"Yes, that's what must have happened," she said, grasping the explanation as quickly as she'd caught his hand. "I nodded off. I'm more tired than I had realized."

"Miss Graye?"

The voice made her start. She craned her neck to look past Rick. "What is it Mrs. Foster?"

The housekeeper switched on a second lamp as she moved into the room. "I'm sorry to disturb you. I had assumed you had retired for the evening."

"Yes, I was about to. Is there a problem?"

"You have a visitor."

She tried to drag her thoughts back on track. A visitor? Surely it couldn't be a reporter. The Fosters knew better than to allow one into the house. Had Delaney hoped to catch her off guard? Her cooperation could have been a ruse.

A man entered the room behind Mrs. Foster. He paused, as if getting his bearings, then smiled and strode past the housekeeper. "Elizabeth! Darling!"

She had a mad impulse to crawl back into Rick's arms and ask him to take her away again, to escape, to keep her safe.

But that was something Lizzie would have done. Instead, Elizabeth withdrew her hand from Rick's, squared her shoulders, and did her best to summon a smile. The respite was over. Whether she was ready or not, it was time to contend with her real life. "Hello, Alan."

NINETEEN

RICK STARED IN DISBELIEF. *THIS* WAS ALAN RASHOTTE? From the way Elizabeth had described the man's character, Rick had been expecting some oily-looking sleazebag with a bad case of prison pallor. Or at least, that's what he'd been hoping the guy looked like.

"Darling, you never cease to astound me. You look wonderful!"

"This is a surprise. What are you doing here, Alan?"

"I came to welcome you home." He stopped with a flourish and leaned over, as if he meant to kiss her.

Rick shifted sideways to block him. "Elizabeth's told me about you, Alan. I'm Rick Denning."

Alan redirected his smile toward him without missing a beat. His teeth were perfectly straight and dazzling white. His jaw was as smooth and squarely chiseled as a model's in an ad for aftershave. His nose was on the small side, so it didn't detract from the impact of his manly cheekbones. His eyes were the same pale blue as his tie. His shirt was as white as his teeth. His suit was charcoal gray without so much as a speck of dandruff on his broad shoulders. A few flakes of melting snow darkened his blond hair, but not a strand was out of place.

Damn.

"I've heard all about you as well, Rick," Alan said. He had a slender build and appeared to be less than an inch or

two shorter than Rick. Their gazes were nearly level. "Th
clinic staff seem very fond of you. I must express my sincer
thanks for all you've done for my fiancée. Your help ha
been invaluable. I'm in your debt."

How the hell was he supposed to respond to that?

Before he could, Alan stepped around him to take Eliz
abeth's hand. "Forgive me for not getting here sooner. M
flight was delayed, and you wouldn't believe how terribl
the roads are."

"Where have you been?" she asked.

"Canada. I came as soon as I heard. I apologize for being
out of touch, but it couldn't be helped." He pressed her hand
to his mouth. "I've prayed for this moment for five months
I can't begin to tell you how overjoyed I am to have yo
back."

Rick's knuckles stung, as if he could feel Alan's lip:
against his own skin. He recoiled.

Elizabeth pulled her hand free at the same instant
"Thank you, Alan. It's good to be back."

"You're an amazing woman." He swallowed, as if over
come by emotion. "Your recovery is nothing short of miraculous."

"I couldn't have done it alone."

"Then you realized I was there? The doctors weren't sure
I, for one, was certain you could hear me."

"Toward the end, I had some awareness of what was
going on around me, but I'd rather not talk about it."

"I understand completely. It was a nightmare for all
of us."

"I hope to put this episode behind me as soon as possible."

"From you, I wouldn't expect any less. Did I mention
you're amazing?"

She tightened the corners of her mouth in a brief smile.
"While I appreciate your flattery, I do have considerable
work to do before I can resume my former routine."

"Now that I'm here, you can leave everything to me.
Rick," Alan said, gesturing toward the doorway. "I noticed

wheelchair in the foyer. Would you mind fetching it for lizabeth before you leave?"

"I'm not going anywhere, Alan."

"Excuse me?"

"Elizabeth invited me to stay here tonight."

"Rick was good enough to drive me home, Alan," Elizaeth said. "The weather has since deteriorated."

"I see," Alan said. "I had noticed that, ah, pickup truck hen I arrived. I assume that's yours, Rick?"

"That's right."

"Then I can understand Elizabeth's concern. Driving in is weather could be foolhardy in such an old vehicle."

"It's not what you've got, it's how you use it."

"I'm sure," Alan said dismissively. He edged between ick and the couch to sit beside Elizabeth. "Thank goodness ou arrived home safely, in spite of your choice of transporation. Why ever didn't you use an ambulance?"

"Are you questioning my judgment, Alan?"

"It's your condition that worries me. I went straight to e clinic from the airport. They told me you had checked ourself out against medical advice."

"I've made arrangements to continue my rehab here. here was no reason to remain."

"It's true, you're looking much better. I can understand our desire to move in here, since this was your family ome, and it would be a fabulous place to recuperate, but our stepmother's generosity surprises me. Doesn't it strike ou as suspicious?"

"Why?"

"Given the situation between you two, I have to wonder vhat she hopes to gain by opening her home." He paused. She does know you're here, doesn't she?"

"I couldn't very well have moved in otherwise. That vould have been trespassing."

Alan patted her thigh. "I'm glad you're still on your uard. I'll notify her tomorrow that she has another guest. Irs. Foster?" he called.

The housekeeper had been hovering near the doorway

throughout the conversation. She stepped forward soundlessly. "Yes, Mr. Rashotte?"

"Have Harold put my suitcase in Miss Graye's room."

Rick tightened his hands into fists. "That's not going to happen."

Elizabeth spoke at the same time. "You can use the blue bedroom, Alan."

Alan ignored Rick and kept his gaze on Elizabeth. "There's no reason to feel uncomfortable about your physical condition, darling. I've been at your side throughout your ordeal, and I've been fully involved in your treatment. I understand your limitations."

"Then you understand that I need rest."

"Of course, but you also need your fiancé. For better or worse, remember?"

"We're not married yet, Alan."

"That's a situation we need to remedy as soon as possible, sweetheart."

Why wasn't she telling him to get lost? Rick wondered. She wasn't facing criminal charges any longer, which meant she didn't need Alan to give her an alibi. There was no reason to keep up the pretense of the engagement or to let him touch her. There sure wasn't any reason to let him think he had the right to move in. Alan would have to realize that, as well. *Lizzie?*

Elizabeth wouldn't look at him. She wasn't making the denial he'd hoped for, either. She groped along the cushion beside her and retrieved her hair clasp. She gathered her hair at her nape with one hand and stabbed the clasp toward it with the other. Her movements were clumsy, but she managed to click it into place. "We'll talk more tomorrow, Alan."

"I look forward to it." He stroked a stray hair from her cheek. "I've missed you, Elizabeth."

Tell him now! Rick thought.

"I've missed you, too, Alan." She raised her voice. "Mrs. Foster? After you get Mr. Rashotte settled in the blue bedroom, you can show Mr. Denning to the west corner room. First, though, I would like you to bring me my wheelchair. I believe I'll retire now."

Rick lifted his arms. "I can carry you to your bedroom."

"No, thank you. Mrs. Foster knows the way."

She was retreating before his eyes, reining in her emo-
ons the same way she had corralled her hair. When the
ousekeeper returned, Elizabeth again refused Rick's help
d tottered into the wheelchair herself.

He wanted to take her in his arms anyway. He was sure
at if he could only hold her, or touch her, he could get his
zzie back, but that would have to wait. Her cheeks had
led, and her movements were becoming jerkier. Both were
re signs of fatigue. This must be why she had postponed
e confrontation with Alan. The events of the day had
ught up with her. She should have gone straight to bed in
e first place.

Rick buried his frustration and forced himself to remain
here he was as she bade both him and Alan a polite good
ght and disappeared with Mrs. Foster. He was losing count
the number of times he'd had to restrain himself from
uching her lately. Much more of this and he was going to
an expert at self-control.

"She's quite a woman, isn't she?"

Rick turned.

Alan had opened the button on the front of his suit coat
d was lounging back, one ankle resting on the opposite
ee. His arms were spread across the top of the couch as
he owned it. The smile that he'd kept on his face for
izabeth was gone. There was no friendliness in his expres-
on now. He studied Rick coolly. "Sit down. We need to
lk."

Rick crossed his arms and remained standing. "What
out?"

"You seemed confused earlier about the sleeping arrange-
ents. Elizabeth did tell you we were engaged, didn't she?"

"Yeah. She explained why you would say that."

"I don't much care for your tone, Rick. Perhaps you
ould elaborate?"

"You're not really engaged. You forced her into it."

Alan laughed. "You certainly don't know Elizabeth if

you think anyone can force her to do something she does want."

"You gave her an alibi."

"Of course I did. She's my fiancée."

"She's not in trouble with the police anymore, so you ca drop the charade."

"Charade?"

"Like I said, you're not really engaged."

"Oh, but we are. Elizabeth is mine, Rick."

"You're the one who doesn't know her if you think tha

"We've had an understanding for years. We decided make it public when the trouble with the police cropped last summer, but we've always intended to marry."

"I don't believe you."

"Why not? Because she let you sleep with her?"

Every muscle in his body clenched. Somehow he resist the temptation to smash his fist into Alan's nose. He wa glad that Elizabeth had left. He wouldn't want her to he how Alan was talking about her. "That's none of your busness."

"I beg to differ. According to the clinic staff, you hav made no effort to conceal your interest in Elizabeth, a your current behavior bears out what I heard. Since am her fiancé, that makes it my business, hence this litt chat."

"Okay, cards on the table. I do care about Elizabeth. Sh deserves to be happy, and she deserves way better than you

"And you're naïve enough to assume you could be t man in her life? That's absurd. You could never fit in."

"I'm already in her life."

"Don't delude yourself. You're nothing special. Yo weren't the first of her diversions, and you likely won't the last."

"Where I come from, a man wouldn't talk that way abo a woman he respects."

"Ah, yes. Where you come from. Arkansas, isn't it?"

"Oklahoma."

"A veritable hotbed of sophistication."

"Uh-huh. At least out there, you're more likely to find a horse's ass in a barn instead of dressed up in a suit." He sniffed. "Smells the same, though."

Alan sneered. "How droll. Elizabeth does have a taste for the primitive now and then. Slumming titillates her. She's very much like her father in that regard. Stanford had a prodigious appetite as well."

"You're full of crap."

"I'm trying to save time. How much do you want?"

"How much?"

"Ten thousand? Twenty? What did she promise you? I can give you a check right now and save her the trouble. Consider it a parting gift."

"I don't want money."

"Then what's your price? Are you after contacts?"

"What?"

"If that's your angle, I know people who could open doors for you in the entertainment industry."

"Forget it."

Alan drummed his fingers on the back of the couch. "Although it's difficult to believe, it seems you actually might be as stupid as you look."

"Not half as thick as you, if you think you can buy me off."

"Rick, wake up. Elizabeth played you. You're not the first one to be taken in by her." He laughed again. It was openmouthed and mocking. "When I saw the YouTube video, I had assumed you were putting on a performance, but you weren't, were you?"

"What's your point?"

"You're a fool. Not only a fool, but delusional. It appears as if you've convinced yourself you're in love with her."

"Well, you sure as hell aren't."

"On the contrary. I adore her. We're a perfect match. We understand each other because we're two of a kind. Ask anyone."

"You don't want her, you only want money and a job."

"I already have money and a job, as you so quaintly put

it." His lips twitched as he regarded Rick's clothes. "Which is more than one could say about you. It must have been horribly awkward for Elizabeth to have you show up as you did. She usually is careful to end her affairs cleanly. She likely would have already done so if not for her coma."

"You don't know what you're talking about."

"I've known Elizabeth since she joined her father's firm. What about you, Rick? When did you meet her?"

His hands cramped. He uncrossed his arms and flexed his fingers.

"You couldn't have known her for long," Alan continued. "Not if you're still harboring romantic illusions."

They weren't illusions. Or were they? "She needs me."

"You couldn't possibly give her what she needs."

"You don't want to give her anything. You only want to take."

"Wrong. I can give her Grayecorp. Granted, she enjoys the way I satisfy her other needs as well, but apparently you already are familiar with her talents in bed."

"That's enough." Rick grabbed Alan by his lapels and hauled him to his feet. "Our talk is over."

"Take your hands off me!"

"Well, now, that could be a problem," he drawled. He lifted Alan on his toes and shook him hard enough to make his head snap back on his neck. "If my hands aren't busy hanging on to your fancy suit, one of my fists might just end up in your face. Seeing as it's so pretty and all, it would be a shame to mess it up."

"I'm warning you—"

"No, I'm warning you. Next time you try spreading filth like that about Elizabeth, I'm liable to forget my manners and not be so gentle."

"I've prepared the blue bedroom for you, Mr. Rashotte. Would you like Harold to show you there, or do you remember the way?"

Rick jerked his gaze from Alan.

Mrs. Foster stood less than two yards away. Her mouth was pinched like a prune. A stocky man with a bulldog face stood behind her. He laid a protective hand on her shoulder as he leveled a disapproving stare at Rick.

Great. So much for his self-control. Rick released his grip on Alan and wiped his hands on his jeans.

"Don't trouble yourself, Harold," Alan said, addressing the man behind Mrs. Foster. He straightened his lapels. "I can find my way around this house quite well. It's like a second home to me." He knocked hard into Rick's shoulder as he stepped past him.

"That the best you can do?" Rick asked.

Alan waited until he had reached the doorway before he responded. "You couldn't begin to imagine what I can do, Denning. I advise you to leave now before you find out."

"DID YOU THINK TO HIDE FROM ME, MY FRIEND?"

The phone slipped. Alan switched it to his other hand so he could dry his palm on his pants. "Hide? Jamal, I was away on business."

"I do hope it was profitable, because your debt has grown."

"I told you I would get you the money, but it will take more time."

"Then you don't have it. That's very disappointing."

Alan moved away from the door. The walls were thick, but he wouldn't trust the servants not to eavesdrop. "No, no, I can get it, I promise. Things have changed."

"I take it you're referring to your fiancée's recovery."

"She hasn't recovered, she's a veritable invalid."

"Do you expect sympathy?"

"All I'm asking for is time. She's clearly unable to manage on her own. Once I'm in control of her finances, you will get the entire three hundred thousand."

"And why should I believe that? You did not show good faith when you took your little vacation to Montreal."

Jamal had known where he was? Now not only his palms were moist. He blotted his forehead on his sleeve. "It wasn't a vacation. I was trying to get your money."

Jamal's laugh grated like static. "You should be thankful you did not succeed."

"I don't understand."

"I have heard of the Stock family. Did you think their mining empire was acquired through the lottery?"

"What's your point?"

"Jack Stock is not as forgiving as I am, particularly when his little girl is involved. It is rumored more than gold has turned up at the bottom of one of his mine shafts."

Alan crossed the bedroom and pulled back the drapes. He stepped close to the window, welcoming the cold draft as he began to sweat in earnest. He should have realized it himself. No wonder Sherri had seemed like such easy pickings. Her father had probably done her thinking for her. At least there was no protective daddy in the wings where Elizabeth was concerned. In addition, she had cut herself off from her friends and her family, which is precisely how Alan wanted it. She would be completely dependent on him . . . as long as he could get her pet cowboy out of the picture. "I need more time. I'm a ring and a couple of 'I do's' from having access to a fortune."

"In one week, your debt doubles."

"Half a million is pocket change to a woman like Elizabeth. We're both businessmen, Jamal. There's no reason we should be on opposite sides of this deal."

"Your arithmetic is faulty. Three hundred thousand doubled is more than half a million."

"Let's not quibble. If we work together, you'll have a piece of billions."

There was a pause. "Explain."

"I know how to handle Elizabeth Graye. I've been playing her for years. You've got a different skill set, as you keep reminding me. Your expertise could come in useful."

"I am hoping there will be a point to this?"

"There's a man who might be an impediment to our plans. If you get rid of him, it will clear my path to the Graye fortune."

The silence was longer this time. Alan hoped it was a good sign. "Jamal?"

"Tell me about this man."

"He's a nobody. A complete simpleton. A man of your experience shouldn't have any trouble making him, ah, disappear."

"And if your fiancée doesn't cooperate?"

"Oh, she'll cooperate. One way or another. Are you going to help me?"

"If the man does become a problem, I will consider it. In the meantime, you have two weeks."

"That's not enough time!"

"I'll be in touch. Pleasant dreams, Alan."

"Jamal—"

"And do move back from the window. You could catch your death in that cold."

He dropped the phone and cupped his hands around his eyes to peer through the glass. Snow swirled in front of him, lit from below by the floodlights at the base of the wall. Beyond that, the grounds were dark until they reached the road that bordered the property. There a set of headlights came on and slowly pulled away.

TWENTY

A PATTERN TOOK SHAPE IN RICK'S MIND, BREAKING APART and re-forming with each breath he drew. A curve of silver became a flash of white around two pools as hard and dark as stone. Were those eyes? A face? He strained to grasp the image, but the more he tried, the further away it got until it dwindled to nothing.

He opened his eyes to an unfamiliar room. He was lying on a big four-poster bed, his legs tangled in the sheet and his clothes on the floor where he'd dropped them the night before. It took a few seconds to orient himself. This was Elizabeth's home. Weak, predawn light slanted through a series of tall windows set into a curved wall. He rolled out of bed and went to look outside. A handful of stars glinted in the brightening sky. Snow covered the lawn and laced the branches of the trees near the road with lines of white. Not a breath of wind stirred, yet the back of Rick's neck tingled as if another storm was building.

Lizzie?

Her name bounced back from his thoughts, just like the other times he'd tried calling to her, and yet . . .

There was a twinge on the edge of his consciousness, a whisper of sound that was felt more than heard, like sharp, shallow breathing in a darkened room.

Lizzie!

The twinge winked out.

Rick gathered his clothes and pulled them on, filled with an uneasiness he didn't stop to analyze. He stepped into the hall. The door to the room Alan had been given was closed, so Rick guessed he was still asleep. His guess was confirmed a moment later by a muffled snore. He headed downstairs. When he reached the foyer, he heard the faint sound of piano music, but it wasn't coming from the front room. It led him in the opposite direction, toward an open doorway near the back of the house.

He found Elizabeth seated behind a large, rolltop desk in a room filled with dark wood and green leather. Despite the early hour, she was already dressed in a sweater and slacks, and she had used a scarf to tie her hair into a ponytail. She hadn't noticed his arrival. Her elbows were propped on the desk and her face was in her hands.

"Lizzie? What's wrong?"

She looked up quickly. "Rick! What are you doing here?"

"I was going to ask you the same thing. Are you okay?"

"Yes, I'm fine."

"Where's the nurse?"

"I came here on my own," she said, indicating her wheelchair. It stood beside a glass-fronted bookcase.

He moved into the room. It was obviously meant to serve as a home office. There was a fancy telephone with an array of buttons on the desk, as well as a notebook computer and a green-shaded banker's lamp. A small, flat-screen TV hung on the wall nearby. A compact Bose system that sat on a filing cabinet was the source of the music. "You're not already working, are you? Wasn't the doctor supposed to check you out this morning?"

"I wanted to review some files before he got here." She tapped a few keys on the computer. "Fortunately, the passwords haven't been changed, so I was able to access the Grayecorp server."

"But it's only your first day home."

"I don't want to waste any more time. I've wasted almost half a year."

"You sure you're okay? You seemed kind of tired a few seconds ago."

"This is something I have to do, and I've told you before, I don't want to be coddled, not·if I'm going to get better."

"I'm just concerned."

"There's no need to be." She paused. "How did you know where I was?"

"I followed the music. It's nice."

"It's Glenn Gould's version of Bach's *Goldberg Variations*." She took a remote from one of the cubbyholes at the front of the desk and shut the music off. "I didn't think it was loud enough to disturb anyone."

"It wasn't. I didn't hear it until I was downstairs. You didn't need to turn it off."

"It's better if I do. It was self-indulgent and nonproductive. I should be concentrating on my work."

He rounded the desk and hitched one hip on the edge. The light from the lamp was centered on the desktop, leaving most of Elizabeth's face in shadow. Still, he could see tension in the line of her jaw. This was how she had appeared after Alan had arrived, as if she had closed herself off. "I got up in the first place because I felt like something was wrong."

"Well, everything's fine."

It wasn't fine. She was strung as tight as a drum. He stroked her cheek. She started at the contact, knocking her elbow against a silver-framed photograph that had been placed beside the phone. It was of a smiling, young woman standing arm in arm with a white-haired man. He recognized Elizabeth immediately. The man seemed familiar, too.

Rick tilted the picture frame toward the light. "Is that your father with you?"

She nodded. "That picture was taken when I began working at Grayecorp. I found it in the bottom drawer. He likely tossed it in there when he disinherited me. I'm surprised he didn't throw it out, since he did his best to eradicate me from all the other aspects of his life."

"I'm sorry."

"There's no need to be. As soon as the property transfer is finalized, I will have regained half the estate."

"I know it wasn't only about the money, Lizzie."

"Yes, well, that's what mattered to him, so I still consider this a victory. He would have, too."

He studied the photograph. Aside from their chins, there was little resemblance between Elizabeth and Stanford Graye. His face was much broader than hers, and his eyes were dark brown. Although his lips were curved upward, his expression couldn't be called a smile. "You don't look much like him."

"I take after my mother."

"He looks like a hard man."

"He was a brilliant man. He was also very adept at manipulating people into doing what he wanted. He was like a modern-day Tom Sawyer, talking everyone else into painting his fence for him. He taught me everything I know."

Rick could easily picture Stanford manipulating people. In fact, the man in the photograph fit perfectly with what Rick had learned about his character. He had the puffed-chest body language of a bully, and the calculating gaze of someone who thought they were smarter than everyone else. He was only a few inches taller than Elizabeth, and he appeared to be drawing himself up to exaggerate his height. He didn't seem like a man who would give away anything for free, especially his love.

"It's ironic," she said. "For fifteen years, I tried to make him proud of me, but the only time I saw any respect in his eyes was when I blackmailed him, and he realized that I wasn't backing down. He hadn't expected me to follow through, so he admired the way I did."

He could picture that, too. Stanford likely would have enjoyed seeing proof of how well he'd influenced his daughter. There would have been no regret in those flat brown eyes. His gaze would have been as hard and dark as stone . . .

Stone? That niggled something in his memory. Rick frowned, his mind going back to what he'd seen when he'd awakened. The picture frame was silver. Stanford's hair was white and his eyes were dark. Was this why the face had seemed familiar? "You're not going to believe this," he muttered.

"What?"

"Were you looking at this photograph a few minutes ago?"

"Yes. Why?"

He slid off the desk and went to close the door, then came back and stabbed his finger at Stanford's image. "I think I saw this in a dream."

"When?"

"This morning when I woke up. It was all garbled inside these weird shapes, but I remember those eyes." He grinned. "You must have put the image in my head."

"What? No."

"Lizzie, I saw the same thing you did."

"No!" There was a thread of panic in her voice. She rolled her chair back from the desk, putting a good yard of space between them. "That's impossible."

"Not really. We've done it before."

"Our mental connection ended with my coma."

"Maybe the connection wasn't because of the coma, maybe it was because of us."

"There has to be a reasonable explanation. If you really did dream of my father's face, you probably saw his picture somewhere else and only remembered it. There are snapshots of him all over the house. Stanford Graye was not what anyone would call a modest man."

Rick's grin faded. He set the picture back on the desk. Was that what had happened? Possibly. Or he could have misinterpreted what he'd seen. The image hadn't been clear. He hadn't been sure that it had even been a face. "Okay, maybe that's too big of a leap, but there must be something left between us because how else would I know you were upset?"

"I wasn't upset. That's overstating it."

"I don't think so. You had your head in your hands when I got here."

"You guessed when we were on our way here yesterday that this place holds some unpleasant memories for me. That's logic. It has nothing to do with a mental link. The link was a fluke. It's gone. We've already settled this."

"I know that's what we said, but we could have been wrong. I've been getting these . . . flashes."

She chewed her lip for a while, rubbing her palms over her sleeves as if she were cold. "What kind of flashes?"

He wondered how to put this so he didn't sound like a lunatic. The last time he'd tried to convince Elizabeth of anything, she had thrown up her mental walls and banished him from her head. "They've been happening a lot over the past few days. I feel you, even when I'm not touching you. Sometimes, it seems as if you can hear my thoughts. It's as if we're still joined in our minds."

"It could be stress. Fatigue can also play tricks with the mind."

"Uh-huh, but what if it isn't?"

"Rick, we've established the fact there's a sexual attraction between us, and I had thought we were getting along well. We're building a real-life relationship. Why isn't that enough for you?"

"I never said it's not enough."

"But it's true, isn't it? Why else would you want to look for something that isn't there?"

She was right, that's what he'd been doing. In spite of what he knew to be reasonable, he kept trying to reach her. He couldn't quite believe that a connection as special as theirs could have died.

Don't delude yourself. You're nothing special. You weren't the first of her diversions, and you likely won't be the last.

Alan's words from the night before rose to taunt him. Rick shoved them aside. "So what if I am? How come you're so dead set against considering the possibility?"

"I'm starting to get my life back," she said. "I'm not going to jeopardize my progress by escaping into a fantasy with you. I have enough credibility issues to deal with, as I've told you on more than one occasion."

He held up his palms. "Don't get mad. I'm just saying—'

"I've made clear from the beginning what my priorities are, and they haven't changed."

"Right. I realize that."

"Do you?"

"Sure."

"Good, because playing make-believe with you won't help me regain control of my company." She pulled her chair back into place in front of the computer. She picked up the picture of herself and her father, regarded it briefly, then inserted it facedown into one of the desk's cubbyholes. "Neither will talking about my feelings over the way my father rejected and humiliated me. While I appreciate your sympathy, I can't afford to get emotional. I need facts and financial data. I need to focus on my goals the way I used to."

A strand of hair swung loose from her ponytail. He reached out to brush it from her cheek, then moved to stand behind her. His fingers itched to free her hair from the scarf that bound it. He dropped his hands to her shoulders instead. "Okay, I'm sorry if I got carried away. Whatever brought me here this morning doesn't matter. I just don't want you to push yourself too hard with this work stuff. You need more time to recover."

"I don't have time. Or have you forgotten my other house-guest?"

"Alan?"

"He's the main reason I can't delay. I'm certain you grasped how awkward our current situation has become, and it didn't take any mind reading to sense that. Yesterday when he arrived, you looked as if you wanted to hit something."

He grimaced. "I guess Mrs. Foster told you."

"No, told me what?"

"Alan and I had a discussion last night after you went to bed. He's a sleazebag, Lizzie. I don't understand why you put up with him for even a minute."

"It's temporary."

"He's claiming your engagement is real."

She jerked open a drawer and pulled out a pad of paper. "He's mistaken."

"I don't understand why you didn't straighten him out right away. Was it because you were tired?"

"No. I needed to find out how matters stand at Grayecorp first."

"What does one thing have to do with the other?"

"It's complicated."

"You told me that before. You said you got engaged in exchange for an alibi, but there's more to it than that, isn't there?"

She fumbled for a pen. She held it clumsily, her fingers shaking, then dropped it on the paper without writing anything. "You're right. There's more."

He kneaded her shoulders. "What's going on, Lizzie?"

"Before my coma, Delaney had been trying to squeeze me out of the company. Whether her lawyer or she herself had been behind the attacks on my mental competence is immaterial. I had needed an ally. I used Alan."

"How?"

"I exploited his ego. I gave him more responsibility and implied I would let him share control of Grayecorp with me. Given our previous relationship, he made assumptions about my intentions on a personal level. In retrospect, I realize it was my own actions that gave him cause to believe there were feelings involved."

Her muscles tensed under his palms. His fingers were stiffening, too. He forced himself to relax his grip.

She'll say anything that serves her purpose. You're not the first one to be taken in by her.

No. Alan was full of crap. He was the one who would say anything. "How?"

"What else did he tell you, Rick?"

"A bunch of crap."

"Did he tell you we had an affair?"

"You told me yourself that you two were involved. You said it ended years ago."

"Yes, that's what I implied. I neglected to tell you that I

lured him into my office at Grayecorp one evening last June and seduced him on my desk."

There was no humor in her voice. He was the one who cracked jokes to ease tension, not Elizabeth. He knew she was telling him the truth.

"Although, to be accurate, it was my father's desk," she said. "It's a lovely piece, and much larger than this one. My mother bought it at an auction when I was a child. I took it over after Stanford died. It wasn't the most convenient location for a tryst, but I had a tight schedule and needed to conclude the encounter as quickly as possible. I deduced from my previous experiences with Alan that he wouldn't be inclined to linger if he wasn't comfortable. My plan was successful. The sex bought his support. Our engagement cemented it, which was the main reason I allowed it to stand. I realize that probably disgusts you, but I'm not going to lie in order to pretend I'm someone I'm not."

Anger, jealousy, everything ugly he never thought he could feel about Elizabeth, slammed into his gut and spread a red haze across his vision. He was an idiot. He'd been celibate for nearly four years, because he'd believed making love involved more than just joining two bodies. He must be as delusional as Alan had said. He'd been treating Elizabeth like a piece of spun glass. He'd left his family behind and had driven across the country for her based on nothing but his faith in a dream.

She'd warned him, though, hadn't she? She'd told him time and again that she didn't believe in love. She didn't make decisions based on emotions. Even so, he'd never imagined that the woman he had come to know could have viewed having sex like it was a business transaction.

Yet that's what she'd done. She had bartered her body to Alan. Deliberately. Cold-bloodedly. The same way she'd said Alan had tried to use her to advance his career. Maybe Alan had been right and they were two of a kind. Rick could see her lying back on the desk, her skirt hiked to her hips, Alan smiling that smug, perfect smile while he unzipped his pants and moved between her thighs—

Rick snatched his hands from Elizabeth and stepped back. The image of her with Alan faded. Instead, he saw her sitting alone at the desk afterward, her spine rigid and her fingers curled like claws over the wooden arms of a massive chair. Her clothes were smoothed into place, her hair was neatly twisted behind her head, a string of pearls adorned her throat and tears flowed unchecked down her face.

She returned her hands to the computer keyboard.

Another image crept into Rick's vision. A girl in a black dress sat in front of a grand piano. A black ribbon trailed down either side of her blonde ponytail. She bent over the keyboard, her fingers blurring across the keys as her shoulders shook with her sobs. She had needed love. Instead, she got Grayecorp.

And so she had grown up to become the kind of woman who trusted nobody, who would sleep with a sleazebag and would blackmail her own father. All because she'd been taught by a master manipulator to value money and power and winning above all else.

Sure, Rick understood why she'd done what she'd done. When life smacked you upside the head, sometimes you did crazy things to stop the pain. But he still wanted to hit something. He went to the window and braced a fist against the frame. The sun was rising. The snow sparkled in pure, untouched drifts. It wasn't only the light that made his eyes water.

"I didn't tell you this to hurt you, Rick. I thought you deserved to know the truth."

"Hey, it happened before we met, so I've got no reason to be hurt," he said, as much for her benefit as for his own. "I've got no right to be jealous, either. It's not as if you cheated on me or anything. I didn't know you then. I had no claim on you."

"I'm glad you realize that."

"Yeah, but that doesn't mean I'm okay with him hanging around you now. He acts like he owns you."

"As I said, that's partly my fault. You need to trust me to handle Alan in my own way, all right?"

"In other words, you want me to butt out."

"I need to extricate myself from this situation carefully. He has a tremendous amount of influence with the board of directors, and keeping Grayecorp is important to me."

"Right. Those priorities of yours. The next item in your to-do list, like getting this house back."

"Yes."

You couldn't possibly give her what she needs. Rick used his knuckles to shove off the window and turned to look at her. "How far would you take it?"

"I'm not sure what you mean."

Would she sleep with Alan again? Would she pull him down on her desk and open her legs . . . Rick inhaled hard through his nose. He couldn't voice those questions aloud. They would hurt her almost as much as they would hurt him. "To keep Grayecorp. Would you marry him?"

"No."

"Do you love him?"

"What? No."

"He says he loves you."

"There is no emotional attachment between us. Alan and I are both realists."

"He ridiculed me. He said I had convinced myself that I was in love with you."

Elizabeth swiveled the chair to face him. Her body tensed, as if she were bracing herself for a blow.

"He called me a fool."

"You're not a fool, Rick. You're a good man."

He didn't know about being good, but Alan had been wrong about one thing. Rick hadn't needed to convince himself he was in love. He had started falling in love with Elizabeth the first time he had felt her tears on his fingers. He had tried not to love her, because it was pathetic to be in love with a figment of his imagination.

He might still be. Maybe the woman he loved didn't exist, and he was only imagining he could see his Lizzie underneath all her armor. After all, she was prepared to make nice with a trash-talking slimeball who might help her make another few million, but she knotted herself into a self-protective fist every time Rick mentioned love. He could be doing the same thing with love that he kept trying with their mental link, looking for something that wasn't there. From the start, she had been up front about her priorities. Fool that he was, he'd thought he could change her mind.

Yeah, things had been a lot simpler in their imaginary world. It was little wonder why he wanted to go back.

"So where does this leave us?" he asked. "This real-life relationship you said we're working on. How's that fit into your engagement to Alan?"

"Until the situation is resolved, we'll have to be discreet."

Discreet. Like the way her father had been having an affair with Monica's mother. Would Stanford be proud of Elizabeth over this, too? "Don't expect me to sneak around, Lizzie. I won't do that. I respect us both too much."

"The only alternative is not to see each other at all."

"For how long?"

"Only until the next board meeting."

"And then what? Are you going to introduce me to the rest of your snooty friends like Cynthia? You didn't want anyone to see a three-minute video of the two of us together."

"I explained that to you. It was my appearance on the video that bothered me, not yours."

"You're worried that other people might see Lizzie instead of Elizabeth."

"We had that conversation. Let's not get started on it again."

"We never really finished it. You said Delaney's lawyer spread rumors about your mental competence. You're concerned about showing people how tough and in charge you are. Since we're into honesty, I better come clean, too."

"About what?"

"Hanging around with me isn't going to do your reputation any good. It sure won't help you fulfill this agenda you're so determined to follow."

"We've gone over this before, too. No one else needs to know what we experienced during my coma."

"I'm not talking about your coma. The dreams I shared with you weren't my first trip to never-never land."

"I don't understand."

"After my wife died, I wanted to kill Chester."

She was silent for a while. "I remember you told me you blamed him," she said finally. "Sue died because she'd gone to set him loose."

"Right. What I didn't tell you is that I nearly succeeded. I had already jammed the gun in his ear when I realized killing him wouldn't end the pain, so I turned the thing around and shot myself instead."

Her eyes filled. She lifted her hand. Though she was still at the desk, warmth spread over his cheek, as if she had cupped it in her palm.

Damn, he was pathetic. Even now, he was still imagining their link. "Lucky thing I was too drunk to shoot straight. The bullet only left a groove in my scalp and knocked me out. I woke up two days later in the psych ward. They kept me there for three months. My family wouldn't let them release me until I could convince them I wouldn't try it again. I didn't, either. Deciding to live wasn't easy, but once I did, everything else followed."

"Oh, Rick. I'm so sorry. I should have realized."

"I hadn't wanted you to know, because it was a stupid thing to do. Trouble is, it's not a secret, and with all those reporters poking around for a story, this is bound to come out sooner or later. You've already got credibility issues. Being associated with a genuine nutbar isn't going to help."

"Don't call yourself that. Your mental condition was nothing to be ashamed of. I can only admire your strength even more. You're—"

"A good man. Yeah, you said that already, but I'm not good for your to-do list, am I? Not like Alan."

She wouldn't meet his gaze. "It's only temporary, until I can be sure of my position."

"Or until the next time you decide I'm not convenient."

"I truly didn't want to hurt you."

"One minute you said you want to build a real-life relationship, and the next you want me to pretend we don't have one."

"I'm doing what I need to do to get my life back. I thought you understood."

"Sure, I understand. I can even understand why you slept with Alan. You've got a void inside where love should have been, and you think getting the money and the house and Grayecorp will fill it up."

She flinched, as if he had struck her.

He kept going anyway. "You were given a second chance when you woke up from your coma, and I know all about second chances, because that's what I had. You asked me to help you live, and that's what I've been trying to do, but you've been so damn obsessed with getting your old life back, you never stopped to wonder whether or not you should."

"I think it would be best to end this conversation before we say something we regret."

"I only regret that I held it inside for this long. Every day since Christmas, I've watched you trying to turn yourself into the woman I had only heard about, not the one I had known. It's like you're walling yourself back up in your own dungeon. You refused to see your best friend, and you've concocted paranoid reasons to hate your stepmother. The real reason you push both of them away is because they're trying to love you, and that scares you shitless. That's the real reason you've been trying to push me away, too."

She hung on to the edge of the desk and pulled herself to her feet. Leaning heavily on the desk for balance, she worked her way toward the bookshelf where she'd left her wheelchair.

He shoved away from the window, prepared to steady her.

She guessed his intent and shook her head. "Please, don't touch me."

"You know what I'm going to say next, don't you?"

"You've said more than enough."

"I shouldn't even have to tell you this. You're smart enough to see it yourself by now. Everyone else has."

"Stop."

"I love you, Lizzie."

She half fell into the chair. Her hands shook as she propelled it toward the door.

He got there before her and blocked her path. "I love you, and the hell of it is, saying it aloud doesn't change anything, except to make you want to get away from me faster."

"I'm sorry, Rick, but I can't give you what you want. I already told you, I won't lie and pretend I'm someone I'm not."

"I know, but I love you anyway. I love you whether you're being Elizabeth, Lady Elspeth, Isabella, or just my Lizzie." He leaned over to grasp the wheels, bringing his face to hers. "That's the real connection between us. It's not a make-believe, fantasy love, either, because if this was the dream world, I would fantasize a love that didn't hurt."

TWENTY-ONE

THE DINING TABLE WAS A GLEAMING EXPANSE OF MAHOG-
any, edged with an inlay of walnut, that had been designed
to seat forty people. The dinner parties Elizabeth's mother
had given had been lavish affairs. Every detail from the menu
to the table decorations to the seating order had been planned
in minute detail. There had been no room for a child at the
events, so Elizabeth had never attended one, but she had
watched the guests arrive from her bedroom window. Later,
she would read about them in the society pages. After her
mother's death, when she'd become mistress of the house,
she'd been too occupied by her duties at Grayecorp to turn
her energy toward playing hostess. Once Stanford remarried,
his new wife hadn't entertained on the same scale as her
predecessor, so the room had gone largely unused. Elizabeth
had found its regal furniture and cavernous ceiling somewhat
intimidating, yet it was the most formal room in the house,
so it was the perfect location for this meeting. She had wanted
a backdrop as impressive as the occasion. She had anticipated
this day for more than a year.

She had selected her wardrobe as carefully as the room.
During the two weeks since she'd come home, she'd had the
bulk of her belongings transferred from her Manhattan
apartment, so she had chosen to wear one of her favorite
power suits. The conservatively cut taupe wool paired with
an ivory silk blouse and her trademark string of pearls pro-

jected exactly the right image. Although it felt more cor
stricting than the sweaters and pants she'd grown accustome
to wearing, and the pins from her French twist were begin
ning to dig into her scalp, she wouldn't have considere
appearing any other way.

Cynthia slid the final document in front of her. "We'
need your signature here," she said, flipping to the last page

Elizabeth had reviewed the entire agreement earlier, s
it wasn't necessary to go over it again line by line. Sh
skimmed through it anyway, just to savor the moment, the
uncapped her pen and scrawled her name. Her real name
Elizabeth Baylor Graye. After all, that was who she was.

Cynthia reversed the document and pushed it across th
table.

Leo Throop, Delaney's lawyer, directed his client wher
to sign. She did so immediately, passed both the paper an
the pen to Leo, then clasped her hands on the table an
smiled at Elizabeth.

She had been a beautiful woman when she had marrie
Stanford. He wouldn't have looked twice at her if she hadn'
been. Though she wore her hair short now, and the scars sh
bore from the accident that had killed him weren't com
pletely concealed by her collar, she appeared even mor
striking than the last time Elizabeth had seen her. She ha
a glow in her eyes and a stillness in her body. It was peace
She didn't look like a woman who had just given away
multimillion dollar house as well as a three billion dolla
fortune. There was no hint of discomfort on her face. There
wasn't any regret, either. Instead, there was relief. "Than
you, Elizabeth."

She could detect no sarcasm in her stepmother's tone
She responded warily. "I appreciate your willingness to
allow me to move in before the title was transferred."

Delaney glanced around the room. "I never felt at home
here. It was Stanford's house, not mine."

Leo cleared his throat. "I would also like to express my
appreciation, Miss Graye. It was very generous of you to

ccept my apology for my actions last spring, some of which ould be interpreted as overzealousness on my part."

"It was more than overzealousness, Mr. Throop," Cynhia said. "It was vindictiveness. Your conduct was outraeously unprofessional. You're very fortunate that my client as decided not to press charges."

The lawyers embarked on an edgy exchange. Elizabeth uned it out. She had gone against Cynthia's advice with espect to Leo, since she saw no advantage to reminding veryone of the mental competency rumors that the passage f time would have buried. She also was reluctant to initiate nother lawsuit. She would prefer to enjoy her triumph with his one. True, she wasn't getting everything that her father ad promised, but it hadn't been only about the money, it ad been about winning. Controlling half of Stanford's esate was going to boost her status at Grayecorp. Taking oossession of the Graye house also sent a clear signal to the ooard of directors that she was ready to follow in her father's ootsteps. The timing couldn't have been better, as the board vas due to meet in two weeks. Yes, it was working out as he'd planned. The next item on her to-do list, as Rick had out it.

His presence whispered across her mind as gently as mist ising from a stream. Elizabeth gritted her teeth, attempting o keep her thoughts on track, but they turned to Rick, anyvay. It had been thirteen days since he'd left. His effect on er should have faded by now, yet merely thinking about iim seemed to set off a reaction in her brain, like a door opening, or a light switching on. They were memories of he way he used to make her feel, though, not evidence of a mental link. She was firmly rooted in reality now.

Rick should be, too, now that his career was taking off. 'Angel Liz" was becoming a phenomenon. Its sudden popularity because of the video hadn't disappeared the way he had expected. Though she hadn't spoken with him, it had been easy to keep track of his progress. During the past weeks, he'd given countless interviews, and tomorrow he

was scheduled to sing on a network TV morning show. Sh
was thrilled for him. He deserved to be successful, and no
he had the chance. It was just as well that he'd gone hom
She'd been selfish to let him stay as long as he had. He'
put his own life on hold while he'd been keeping her con
pany. It was far better for him to spend his days pursuing hi
own goals. This way, they both would be getting what the
wanted.

Yes, it was better that he had left. He'd been a distraction
He likely would have had another confrontation with Ala
if he'd stayed. Alan's smugness over the departure of hi
rival had made it difficult for Elizabeth not to have a con
frontation with him herself. He'd been pressuring her to se
a wedding date. So far, she had been able to put him off b
steering their conversations to business. Nothing please
Alan quite as much as talking about money. He had mad
an impressive amount of it while he'd been managin
Grayecorp. The company was showing a healthy profit. Sh
wanted to dig deeper before she trusted the numbers, bu
his apparent success had been enough to impress his croni
on the board. Alan was currently their golden boy. Alignin
herself with him was more crucial than ever.

It truly had been the right decision to let Rick go. Th
logical, reasonable choice. She had known their relationshi
couldn't have lasted. She would have spared them both need
less pain if she hadn't allowed him to talk her into lettin
him stay the first time she'd tried to send him away.

Nevertheless, against all logic, she missed him. She misse
the way his smile crinkled the corners of his eyes, and th
way that deep, velvety voice of his sometimes gave her goos
bumps, especially when he said her name. No one else calle
her Lizzie. Oddly, she missed that, too.

Her father wouldn't have approved of Rick Denning. H
would have mocked his appearance, his drawl, and his easy
going manner. If he had abided him long enough to see pas
the unsophisticated packaging, then he would have dislike
him even more. Rick had a strong sense of right and wrong
and he wasn't afraid to stand up for his principles. He cer

tainly hadn't balked at telling the truth, regardless of how painful it had been for her to hear. He'd been right, there was a void inside her. She wasn't capable of returning the feelings that he wanted, and he deserved someone who would. In his own way, he was as perceptive about people as Stanford had been, but that was where the resemblance ended. Apart from his intelligence, Rick was nothing like Stanford Graye. He didn't use his perceptiveness to manipulate people. He was honest and open and generous. Kind. Funny. Strong. Loving . . .

Rick had said he loved her. She wished he hadn't. All her life, hoping for love had led to pain. So, yes, it was good their relationship had ended. Excellent. Marvelous. Splendid.

"Elizabeth, could we speak privately?"

She blinked, annoyed at the moisture in her eyes. This should have been a moment to celebrate. Instead, the meeting had already broken up while she'd been woolgathering. The lawyers sorted through and stored the copies of the various documents. Delaney moved around the table to stand beside her.

"Is there a problem?" Elizabeth asked.

"I've been hoping to get the chance to talk since you woke up, but you've continued to refuse."

"There hasn't been a convenient time."

"I'll try to keep it brief. John's visiting a gallery in town and will be picking me up shortly."

As of five minutes ago, the house was Elizabeth's, and she could have Delaney arrested for trespassing if she chose. She was no longer a helpless invalid, either, so she might as well get this over with. She nodded to Delaney and twisted toward the chair on her other side where she'd leaned her cane. She propped it against her own chair and motioned for her stepmother to sit.

Delaney waited until Cynthia and Leo had left the room before she spoke. "It's good to see you've regained your mobility," she said, nodding at the cane. "Your progress is astounding."

"Thank you. I have a good therapist."

"It's more than that. I remember how painful my own rehab was after the accident, and I know how much willpower it takes to keep going."

It did take willpower. Elizabeth had thrown herself into her rehabilitation program, exercising to the limits of her endurance. She was proud of the results. In fact, with the aid of a cane, she was now able to walk under her own power from one end of the house to the other. The experience had given her a sense of accomplishment that surpassed anything she'd experienced during her years at Grayecorp.

She glanced at Delaney's scars. She hadn't liked to think they had something in common, or to sympathize with her stepmother. She couldn't help doing so now, though. "What you went through was much more extensive because of your injuries. My body doesn't need to heal, it just needs to . . . wake up."

"I knew you would, Elizabeth. I never gave up hope."

"I appreciate the way you oversaw my care, given the situation between us."

"That's one of the things I wanted to talk about."

"I have dropped my lawsuit, you withdrew the harassment charges, and my father's estate has been divided. I had assumed the situation was resolved."

"It's far from resolved. I can't leave things like this. I would like the chance to apologize."

"Your lawyer already apologized for the slander."

"That's not what I mean. I feel responsible for not standing up for you in the first place. I knew in my heart that you couldn't have done the horrible things we suspected you of doing. If I had trusted my instincts sooner, the real criminal would have been behind bars and you wouldn't have been attacked."

It would be easy to agree. If Delaney wanted to take the blame, why not let her? Somehow, though, Elizabeth couldn't. "I couldn't have expected you to take my side. I probably wouldn't have trusted you if you had."

"I feel responsible for that, too."

"I don't understand."

Delaney clenched her hands in her lap and leaned forward. "I've had a lot of time to think while you were in your coma. I've realized the truth about many things, including the root of the problems between us."

"There's never been any mystery about that. You killed my father."

Her gaze wavered. Pain? Guilt? She shook her head quickly. "I went through hell to come to terms with that accident, Elizabeth. I finally have, and I hope someday you will, too. I will forever regret that I was unable to save your father, but I won't let that keep me from living my life. I survived and was given a second chance. I mean to make the most of it."

"I heard you remarried. Congratulations."

"It's all right. I know you don't mean that right now, but I'm hoping with time you'll be sincerely happy for me."

She was uncomfortable with her reflexive urge to continue sniping. This was how most encounters between the two of them had played out in the past. She used to find it satisfying. Now it seemed petty. She softened her tone. "Your new marriage seems to agree with you. You're looking well."

"I feel like a new person. I wish I had listened to you in the first place. You were right about everything. I never should have married Stanford."

Surprise momentarily stole her breath. Of all the things her stepmother might have said, this was the last one she would have expected.

Delaney chuckled. "I can see I've shocked you, but I mean every word. From the day of our wedding, you maintained your father didn't love me. You called me a brainless twit of a trophy wife, among other things."

"That was cruel."

"It was the truth, and often the truth hurts, particularly when a person doesn't want to hear it. I had been in denial about everything, including Stanford's unfaithfulness, because I was too eager to be loved."

"And his money had nothing to do with it?"

"That's right. It was never about the money. I realize it's difficult for you to believe I wasn't a fortune hunter. It's what anyone thinks when there's a fortune involved. The more I protested, the more suspicious you got."

She was reminded of Cynthia's suspicions about Rick. But that was different, because he truly hadn't been concerned with her money. He'd wanted no part of it. He probably would have been happier if *she'd* had no part of it. "You claim you didn't want the money, and yet you kept half," she said.

"Actually, I plan to give what's left of Stanford's estate to charity."

Once again, she was caught by surprise. "That's . . . unexpected. Why?"

"Keeping it would be a burden. I already have everything I need."

"My father would have been livid about this, Delaney."

"I'm aware of that. Stanford viewed his wealth as an extension of himself. It was his way of keeping score. He measured his success by what he had, not what he was. Wealth gave him power. I want it to do some good for a change, instead of being wielded as a weapon."

Those were insightful comments. Her stepmother had indeed been doing a lot of thinking.

"He used his power against you, by cutting you out of his will," Delaney continued. "I knew the way he treated you was abominable, but I was too afraid of displeasing him to protest. I wanted him to love me, and so I did nothing as he went on to banish you from his life. It was wrong, and I'm more than guilty, I'm ashamed."

"It was his decision, not yours."

"That doesn't absolve me of blame. I was too weak to fight what was happening, and I played right into his hands. He pitted us against each other as a way to control us both, and I hadn't seen it. So I understand why you would hate me. I kept saying I wanted to be your friend, but I failed to stand up for you then, too."

"I didn't need you to defend me. I managed on my own."

"That's because you're the strongest woman I know, Elizabeth, but being strong all the time can be exhausting." Delaney reached across the space between them to grasp her hand. "Although I realize we can't undo the past, I do hope we can leave it behind."

Before her coma, Elizabeth would have shaken off Delaney's hand. She didn't like to be touched, and she certainly wouldn't have accepted such a gesture from the woman she'd viewed as Stanford's brainless twit of a trophy wife. She wouldn't have needed to contend with this lump in her throat, either. There was no practical reason to make peace with Delaney, now that the estate had been split and the property transferred. Given their past antagonism, she shouldn't trust this olive branch. It would be smarter to stay on her guard. That's what her father would have advised.

And after all, he'd taught her everything she knew . . .

She surveyed the room, noting the stiff furniture, the cold walls, and the empty chair at the head of the table. She had chosen not to take it for this meeting, because sitting on opposite sides of the table sent a better message, but there was more to it than that. The chair had been designed for her father, not her. Her instincts had told her not to take his place.

"That's all I wanted to say. If you still want nothing to do with me, I'll understand."

Elizabeth let her instincts guide her now, too. She *didn't* always need to come out swinging. She reversed her hand to clasp Delaney's before she could withdraw it. "I accept your apology."

Delaney smiled. "Thank you."

"And I would like to offer one of my own."

"You don't need—"

"Please, let me finish. I should have spoken with you sooner, out of courtesy if nothing else. I should have thanked you immediately for seeing that I received the best medical care, but I have a habit of searching for ulterior motives, and I didn't want to accept your concern at face value."

"Believe me, I know how hard it is to break a behavior pattern once it's established."

"I can't guarantee I'll be able to break this one completely, but I would like to try."

"So would I. More than anything."

She returned Delaney's smile. "What made you change your mind?"

"I've always wanted to be friends with you, Elizabeth."

"No, I meant you had been so adamant about being in love with my father. What finally made you stop believing in it?"

Delaney's gaze grew distant. She tipped her head to the side, as if she were listening to something Elizabeth couldn't hear. "Oh, I never stopped believing in love," she murmured. "I just got better at recognizing the real thing."

Footsteps sounded in the hallway. A moment later, a tall, dark-haired man stepped into the room.

The skin on the back of Elizabeth's hand tingled, as if she were too close to an electric field. At first glance, she thought the man might be Rick, but then she recognized John Harrison, Delaney's new husband.

He was dressed all in black, and he was as ruggedly handsome as she remembered. He kept his gaze riveted on his wife as he approached. Though they didn't speak to each other, they seemed to share a silent communication.

More tingles slid up her arm. They stopped as soon as she pulled her hand from Delaney's. "Hello, John."

"Elizabeth."

Apart from his height, John didn't look anything like Rick. His eyes were piercing blue instead of warm amber. His hair was combed ruthlessly back from his face and his clothes were high quality and tailored to fit his large frame. No one would describe his manner as easygoing. There was a dangerous restlessness about him—slap on an eye patch and a bandana and he would have made a good pirate. Yet for some reason, he reminded her of Rick.

She and Rick had been able to communicate with a look, too.

"Hello, darling. Am I interrupting?"

Elizabeth started at Alan's voice. She had been concentrating on John and hadn't noticed that he'd arrived as well. She gripped her cane and rose to her feet. "No, Alan. Our meeting is over."

"I PROPOSE A TOAST," ALAN SAID. HE EXPERTLY WORKED the cork from the champagne bottle with his thumbs, filled two crystal flutes and handed one to Elizabeth. "To getting what we deserve."

"That's an odd way to put it."

"I would have expected you to be in more of a celebratory mood."

She turned away from the dining table, leaning heavily on her cane as she carried the glass toward the window. Dusk had turned the patches of snow that were left on the lawn blue. Beyond the trees at the edge of the property, lights twinkled in the Chamberlains' house. Monica didn't live there anymore—she rented a modest bungalow closer to the school where she taught. The thought made Elizabeth feel strangely alone. This should be one of the most memorable days of her life, but she wouldn't be sharing her triumph with her best friend. The only person who wanted to celebrate was a man she neither liked nor trusted. She would have preferred withholding the terms of the settlement from him altogether, but since she planned to use it to enhance her position at Grayecorp, she couldn't keep her sudden change in status a secret. "It's been a long day."

He laughed. "Yes, I can imagine it would have been, considering the company. Well, after today, you won't need to put up with Delaney and that Neanderthal she married."

"Why don't you like John?"

"He's a thug masquerading as an artist."

"I understand his paintings are in high demand. He's very successful."

"What's this? Don't tell me you approve of your stepmother's new husband?"

"They appear happy. I would like to keep an open mind."

"I would say that receiving half the estate has gone a long

way to improving your attitude toward Delaney. She should consider firing her lawyer. How could he have allowed her to give away that much wealth?"

"It was legally hers. She had the right to do whatever she wanted with it."

"I suspect she was trying to ease her conscience more than she was trying to settle your lawsuit."

"Regardless of her motives, I'm pleased with the outcome."

"Needless to say, so am I." He returned the bottle to the ice bucket on the sideboard and came back to clink his glass against hers. "Congratulations, Elizabeth. Stanford would have been proud."

"I would rather not talk about my father."

"All right. Let's talk about us." He emptied his glass in three swallows. "Now that you have legal title to the house, there's no reason why we can't hold the ceremony here."

"Ceremony?"

"Our wedding."

"I would prefer to postpone that discussion for the time being."

Alan caught her elbow. "We need to set a date soon."

His grasp tipped her off balance. She yanked free and took a quick sideways step, using her cane to steady herself. A few drops of champagne sloshed on her chest.

"I'm sorry, darling." He brushed his free hand down the front of her blouse. "I keep forgetting about that cane."

She moved away before he could make contact with her breasts. Bile rose in her throat at the thought that he might have. She set the glass on the table. "Excuse me, Alan. As I said, it's been a long day."

"You've been postponing this discussion since I got here, and I would rather not delay it again. The events of this past year have taught me how fleeting life can be."

"Although several months passed for you, for me it's only been a matter of weeks. I feel no need for haste."

"But I do. I can't take the chance I might lose you again."

"Then we're at an impasse, because I will not be rushed."

"That was never my intention. I'm simply eager to get on with our lives." He placed his glass on the table beside hers and took a cell phone from his pocket. "I know. We'll compromise."

"How so?"

"We'll have a civil ceremony first and have the formal wedding later. You remember Judge Oliver? He earned back double his investment in our condominium project last fall. I'm positive he would be delighted to marry us immediately." He scrolled through his directory. "I'll give him a call."

"No, Alan."

"An elopement is the perfect solution. I've already taken the liberty of drawing up a prenuptial agreement. Getting the legal issues out of the way will ensure plenty of time for us to arrange the public ceremony. It will be the social event of the season, particularly if we hold it here. These grounds could easily accommodate a thousand guests."

"Alan, put the phone away. I told you, I will not be rushed."

"I understand what you're worried about, but I'm sure you'll be rid of that cane soon. Your progress has been remarkable. If we schedule the formal ceremony for June, I have no doubt you will not only be able to walk down the aisle without any impediment, you'll be able to dance with me afterward. You'll be a beautiful bride, Elizabeth." He touched her arm. "And you'll be an even more beautiful wife."

"June is out of the question. It's far too soon."

"Don't underestimate yourself. You're looking remarkably fit now."

"Alan, stop."

He returned the phone to his pocket as he studied her face. "Why does discussing this upset you?"

"Perhaps the more pertinent question would be why are you so anxious to get married?"

"If you want an answer to that, all you need to do is look in a mirror."

"I suspect the true answer has more to do with the documents I just signed."

He smiled. "We're two of a kind, Elizabeth. Think of everything we can do now that we have access to Stanford's fortune. Grayecorp is only the beginning. Together, we'll build a business empire beyond our wildest dreams."

"Then perhaps it would be better to limit our partnership to business."

"Why would we want to do that?"

"It's worth considering, Alan. It's really only Grayecorp that we have in common."

"We have far more than that." He snaked his arm behind her waist and pulled her against him. "Let me refresh your memory."

Her stomach rolled at his scent. She shoved him away and stumbled backward into one of the dining chairs. "Not now, Alan."

"Why not? You enjoyed my attentions before your coma."

"I'm not fully recovered."

"Yes, so you've maintained, and I've been the soul of patience for almost two weeks, but you're my fiancée, Elizabeth. Surely you're not so infirm that you can't at least kiss me." He reached for her again.

She deflected his hand. "Don't."

He scowled, retrieved the champagne from the ice bucket, and poured himself another glass. He gulped half as he studied her. "Has that cowboy come back?"

"If you're referring to Rick, no, he hasn't contacted me since he left."

"You didn't mind him touching you. The clinic staff told me he could hardly keep his hands off you."

"He helped me wake up. I'm grateful to him."

"His infatuation with you was embarrassing. He took blatant advantage of your fragile mental state."

"There was nothing wrong with my mental state."

"You're still not entirely yourself. Otherwise we would be having our champagne in bed."

She pushed the chair aside and backed up so she could

perch on the edge of the table. She didn't want him to notice that her legs were unsteady. She fingered the pearls at her throat, striving for calm. "My current limitations are only physical, Alan. I'm in full grasp of my mental faculties."

"I'm not so sure of that. I believe you're still suffering the aftereffects of the head trauma you received."

"Simply because a woman doesn't wish to be intimate with you isn't a sign of diminished mental capacity."

"No, you've changed, Elizabeth. I'm not the only one who's noticed."

"What does that mean?"

"I hadn't wanted to say anything, because it's a delicate topic, but Cynthia's been concerned. So have Tirza and Floyd."

"You've talked to my staff about me?"

"Even the servants are beginning to talk. You've lost the ability to make decisions. Your avoidance of setting our wedding date is a perfect example. I've covered for you as much as I could, but I don't see how I can continue supporting you without some sign of your commitment to me."

"And in this instance, you would consider sleeping together a sign of commitment."

He took her hand. "It won't take much to start the whispers again, and I'm sure you would prefer not to contend with a competency hearing at this point. You must see how vital it is that we present a united front, particularly if you expect me to take your side when the board meets next."

She was no stranger to the game he was playing. She had initiated it herself when it had served her purpose. God, how could she have ever believed it was a viable option? She tugged against his grip. "Let go of me, Alan."

He didn't. Instead, he caught her other hand as well, clamping his fingers around both her wrists. "You need me."

"Let go!"

"Don't you want to marry me, Elizabeth?"

Bile rose in her throat again. This time, it made her gag. She couldn't do this for another two weeks, not even for Grayecorp. She couldn't do this for another day or another second. Her flesh shrank from Alan's touch. Instead of his fingers, she saw bands of iron that weighed down her arms. Then she saw a plastic bundling tie that cut into her skin. She remembered how it felt to be helpless. Trapped. Shackled . . .

No! Not again! She pulled her legs up fast and flung herself backward. Her sudden move took Alan off guard. She broke free from his grasp, sliding across the table on her back. She twisted as she reached the other side and fell off the edge, knocking over two chairs before she crashed to the floor.

"Elizabeth!"

She rolled to her knees. Pain throbbed in her shoulder, but it was refreshing. It cleared her head, like a bucket of cold water. She rubbed her wrists.

Alan hurried around the table. He went to the door first, as if checking to see whether anyone had been alerted by the noise, then came to where she had fallen. His expression was pinched. "Are you all right?"

She nodded. A large chunk of hair slid loose from her French twist and straggled over her eyes. She pushed it aside, got her feet beneath her, and grabbed the seat of one of the toppled chairs.

He seized her elbow. "I don't understand what came over you. What was that display about?"

She jerked her arm from his grasp. "Instinct."

"Instinct? It appeared more like insanity. I believe I have good reason to be concerned about your mental stability."

"Perhaps before, but I assure you, I'm thinking more clearly now than I have in weeks." She used the chair to pull herself upright. The rest of her hair uncoiled to fall over her shoulders. She shook out the pins, happy to be rid of them. "And to answer your other question, no Alan, I don't want to marry you."

"What?"

"I'm breaking our engagement."

His face reddened. "You don't know what you're saying. You're not yourself. This proves it."

"You're right, I've changed since my coma. I finally realized I don't *have* to be the woman I used to be."

"This is about Denning, isn't it? I knew that man was trouble. He's filled your head with romantic illusions."

"No, this is about me. All Rick did was help me see the truth. I'm sorry it took this long, but—"

"You're *sorry*? That's all you have to say?"

"I realize it's inadequate. I should have ended this engagement as soon as I saw you. It was inexcusable to prolong it."

"It isn't over."

"I don't love you, Alan."

"So? You never did."

She paused. "You knew?"

"What do you take me for? Of course, I knew. We both went into this engagement with our eyes open."

She took a steadying breath. It was what she had assumed, but it was a relief to hear him admit it. "I am sorry. If it's a matter of saving face, you can tell people that you were the one to call it off."

"I'm not calling it off. I've invested half a year in this. I've made commitments. I've counted on you."

"Alan, we're done."

"We'll discuss this tomorrow. You're obviously overwrought."

"Please, don't make this situation more difficult than it has to be."

"Do you need more time before you come back to my bed? Fine. Take all you want. But we're going ahead with the wedding, sweetheart, or you can kiss your daddy's company good-bye."

"Don't threaten me."

"Threaten you? I was stating a fact, but evidently your reduced mental capacity is preventing you from grasping it. Don't worry, though. I've taken the liberty of having a power of attorney prepared, as well as that prenup I mentioned earlier."

"You can't seriously believe I would sign control of my assets to you."

"Why not? As every staff member at the Seven Pines Clinic can testify, I'm your loyal fiancé. My devotion knows no bounds, despite your disturbingly irrational behavior."

The skin on her arms prickled. It wasn't the sensation of standing too close to an electric field. No, the prickling was from a sense of danger. She eased backward, placing a chair between them. "I want you to leave this house immediately. Don't bother to pack. I'll have your belongings sent to you."

"One way or another, you'll give me what I want."

She pointed at the door. "Get out, Alan."

"This isn't over."

Elizabeth chose not to respond to his parting comment. She had a sinking feeling that he was right.

TWENTY-TWO

"LET'S DO THE SOUND CHECK AGAIN, MR. DENNING. THIS time, bring in the band."

Rick nodded to the production assistant. Chandra wore a Bluetooth in her right ear and carried a tablet computer in her left hand. It was a good thing she had used his name, because half the time, he couldn't be sure whether she was talking to him or to the Borg gizmos. He twisted on his stool. "Okay, guys. You ready?"

Dwayne sipped yet another cup of coffee as he took his place behind the drum set. He yawned. "Man, this is way too early."

"Told you to go easy on the minibar last night." Eddie looped the strap of his guitar around his neck. "You should've known better."

"I needed something to help me sleep. That plane ride got me all wound up. I hate flying."

Hank snorted as he tucked his fiddle beneath his chin. "Aw, forgot your teddy bear again, Dwayne?"

Chandra tapped her computer screen. "Gentlemen, if you please? You're due in makeup at six-o-five."

Dwayne chugged the coffee and picked up his drumsticks. He gave the cymbals an experimental tap. "Makeup," he muttered. "I don't want that gunk on my face. No one's gonna be looking at us."

"Speak for yourself," Eddie said. He thrust out one hip,

his fingers blurring as he plucked a lightning riff. "That chick beside the camera can't take her eyes off me."

"She's taking a light reading."

"That's just an excuse. What do you think, Rick?"

His mouth quirked. "I'm thinking I can dress you guys up, but I can't take you anyplace."

"Holy smokes, was that a smile?" Hank used his bow as a pointer. "Quick, someone take a picture."

Rick rolled his eyes and turned back to the microphone. "We'll pick it up at the last bridge." He strummed through a key change and started to sing. The guys came in on the next beat. His friends were trying hard to act cool, but he knew they were as impressed as he was with the opportunity to perform on network TV. The producer had originally wanted to use studio musicians for backup, but Rick had held firm. This was fair. The guys had helped him get here, so he wasn't going to leave them behind. Besides, he could use all the friends he could get.

The change in his life still hadn't completely sunk in. He half expected to wake up back in the Cantina, dodging peanuts, but things continued to go better than he could have imagined. The interviews he'd done had paid off. "Angel Liz" was getting airtime on every country radio station and a lot of the pop ones. Yesterday, the taxi driver who had brought him from La Guardia had recognized him. So had a teenager who had asked him for his autograph in the hotel elevator. Zeb had been contacted by not one but two bona fide record companies who were sniffing around about an album deal.

Uh-huh, things were going great. Just humming along. Absolutely terrific. Super-duper. He should be the happiest guy in the world. He should be wearing an ear-to-ear grin. If he was riding to success on any other song, he would be. But he'd written "Angel Liz" from the heart, and each time he sang the words, his heart bled some more.

Not a day went by that he didn't replay his final conversation with Elizabeth, and every time he did, he wished he'd kept his mouth shut. He'd managed to hang on to his self-control with Alan, but it had deserted him where she had been concerned. It had been nearly four years since he'd lost his temper that badly. That wasn't because he was getting mellow with age, it was because he hadn't cared about anything or anyone enough to get so mad. He'd lost it with her because she was a damn frustrating woman to love.

Hank dragged his bow slowly across the fiddle strings, signaling the end of the song. Though Rick tried to keep his tone steady, his voice roughened on the final words. "My sweet Liz, I won't ever let go."

But he had let her go. He'd allowed his pride to get in the way. Why couldn't he have just done what she'd asked and given her space to square things with Alan? She'd said she would. If he hadn't shot off his mouth, they could have picked up where they'd left off afterward, and maybe with more time and a truckload of patience, he would have been able to convince her . . .

That's where his thoughts hit the proverbial brick wall. Elizabeth had made herself clear. She didn't want his love. He didn't know what he could try next that he hadn't tried before. Coming to New York meant that he was only a few hours from her house, but he couldn't be sure of his welcome if he showed up there. He had to face reality. His Lizzie was gone. She was as gone as Sue, and only an idiot kept longing for the impossible.

"Uncle Rick, are you okay?"

"Sure, Zeb." He unhooked his boot heel from the rung of the stool and stood. Chandra was herding the guys off the stage toward the dreaded makeup room. He wasn't in the mood to put up with their banter, so instead he picked his way across the cable-strewn floor to the coffee urn where Dwayne had been filling up. He shoved a cup under the spout.

Zeb followed. "You seem sort of down."

"I just need a hit of caffeine."

"Is the idea of singing on TV making you nervous?"

"Don't think so. It might if I could see the million or so faces on the other side of the camera. The ones in the studio seem pretty decent."

"Okay, but if something's bothering you, I hope you sort it out before you go on."

"Nothing's bothering me."

" 'Angel Liz' is supposed to be a happy song."

"You don't need to tell me what the song is supposed to be," he snapped. "I wrote it."

"Geez, Uncle Rick. I'm only trying to help."

"Damn, I'm sorry. It's the low caffeine level talking."

"The guys are worried, too. Maybe you should call her."

He dumped two packets of sugar into his cup, picked up a plastic stick, and stirred hard. "Call who?"

"You know who. Elizabeth."

"Yeah, maybe I will."

Zeb offered him his cell phone. "I programmed her number, just in case."

Rick took a slug of coffee to keep himself from reaching for the phone. "It's six in the morning, Zeb."

He put it away. "Sorry. I wish there was something I could do."

"Hey, you're doing a great job. You got me this gig, didn't you?"

"Sure, but—"

"Relax, I won't let you down." He glued on a smile. "But I can't give any guarantees about the makeup people. Do you think they'll be able to do anything with this face?"

Zeb gave him the laugh he'd expected and moved off to speak with one of the sound guys. Rick turned to catch up with Chandra and the others. He'd gone three steps when he was stopped by a light tap on his arm.

A slender, dark man stood in front of him. Unlike the casually dressed crew on the set, he wore a suit and tie beneath a black overcoat. His mouth was framed by a neatly trimmed goatee. "Mr. Denning?"

"That's right."

"This is a matter of great urgency," he said, starting for the exit. His words bore a trace of a foreign accent. "You must come with me."

Rick hesitated. "Wasn't I supposed to go to makeup?"

The man returned quickly and spoke under his breath. "Please, we do not want the news to be made public yet. Dr. Shouldice has asked me to bring you directly to the hospital."

Dr. Shouldice? He was Lizzie's doctor. "Has something happened to Elizabeth?"

"I am afraid Miss Graye has suffered a serious relapse. She doesn't have much time."

Rick didn't think about the TV show or the song or his career. He didn't think at all, he acted on pure instinct. He tossed his half-finished coffee toward the nearest garbage can and ran for the door.

ELIZABETH WOKE TO A PUSH OF ADRENALINE. THE BEDroom was still dark, but a face swirled across her vision. Dark eyes, a black beard. It blurred into the gleam of a black car and a shadowed alley. Her heart raced and her body trembled as fear flooded her mind. It tangled with regret and hope and warmth and . . . Rick's voice. She didn't hear it, she felt it, just as she felt her name. *Lizzie!*

Pain shot through her skull. She clapped her hands to her temples. Her vision blanked.

When she awoke again, pink-tinged sunlight slanted through a crack in the bedroom drapes. The pain was gone. So were the images. She didn't feel Rick's voice or his presence. What had happened? A dream?

She rubbed her eyes and sat up. Her hands were shaking and her pulse was still elevated. Shivering, she drew on her robe. She was fastening the belt when she heard the buzz of her cell phone from the bedside table. She snatched it fast and pressed it to her ear.

"Miss Graye?"

The voice was deep and rich and close enough to Rick's to make her breathless. But it didn't set off the echoes inside, so she knew it wasn't him. "Yes?"

"It's Zebadiah Denning. I'm sorry to be calling you so early."

"It's all right. I was awake."

"Uh, have you heard from Rick?"

"No, I haven't. Why?"

"I can't find him. Do you know where he is?"

"No, I don't know . . ." She suddenly remembered what day it was. She checked the clock. "It's almost seven. Wasn't he scheduled to appear on the *Today* show this morning?"

"That's right. I didn't know whether you knew that."

"Isn't he in New York?"

"We got here last night. He was at the studio an hour ago, but no one's seen him since."

"He must be there someplace."

"That's what we figured, but there's no sign of him anywhere. He's supposed to be on in twenty minutes. I thought he might have called you before he left."

"Why?"

"You probably think this is none of my business, but I know you two broke up, and he's been really bummed about it. I was kind of hoping he would settle down if he talked to you."

"As I said, I haven't heard from him."

"If you do, or if he shows up there, could you let me know?"

"Certainly."

"Thanks." The connection terminated.

An ache sprang up behind her eyes. She rubbed her forehead. Rick must have lost his way backstage. He was bound to turn up soon. He wouldn't have walked out without telling anyone. He was too responsible to do that.

As much as she tried to find a reasonable explanation, she wasn't buying it. Something was very wrong. She threw on a sweater and slacks, slipped her phone into her pocket, and went to her father's old office. She flicked on the TV. Twenty minutes went by, then an hour, and Rick still hadn't appeared. By the time the show ended, the ache in her head had stretched to every joint in her body. She jumped when her phone buzzed.

It was Zeb again. "Is he there?" he asked.

"No. Have you called the police?"

"I tried. They said they can't do anything because he hasn't been gone long enough to be a missing person."

"What about the television studio? Don't they have security cameras? He couldn't simply have disappeared."

Zeb promised to look into it. His attempt to sound reassuring fell flat.

Elizabeth fought down her rising panic. Rick had to be all right. Even if she never saw him again, she couldn't imagine him not being *somewhere*. She left the television on and moved to the office window. It was turning into a beautiful day. There wasn't a cloud in the sky. Yet once again, she saw the dark alley from her dream.

A footstep sounded in the office doorway.

She whirled to face it.

"Good morning, darling."

"Alan! How did you get in here?"

He wore an overcoat and leather gloves. In one hand he carried a leather briefcase, in the other, he dangled a set of keys. "I took the liberty of having duplicates made. I also learned your alarm codes. I suspected both would be useful."

"Get out, or I'll have you thrown out."

"Really, Elizabeth. No need to trouble the servants." He closed the door and moved to the desk. "We wouldn't want them to gossip."

She kept a firm grip on her cane with one hand and lifted her cell phone with the other.

"If you're planning on calling the police, I would advise against it."

"I don't have the time or the patience for your games this morning, Alan."

"I'm through playing games, Elizabeth." He opened the briefcase. "I've brought some papers for you to sign."

"You're out of your mind," she muttered. She thumbed nine-one-one.

"Put the phone down. I have Denning."

It took a moment for his words to register. She paused with her thumb above the *send* button. "What does that mean?"

"It means that you will do exactly as I say." He smile
"I told you this wasn't over, didn't I?"

The phone dropped from her fingers.

He waved one hand at the television. "I can see you'
been watching, so you know by now that your cowbo
missed his debut. What a shame. It could have been his b
break, and it's entirely your fault. This unpleasantness cou
have been avoided if you had married me as you had agreed

"You said you had him."

"Actually, my associate has him. He's much more expe
rienced in these matters than I am. From what he describe
it was ridiculously easy to accomplish. Denning truly is
simpleton."

Her knees shook. She put both hands on her cane. "Wh
have you done?"

"I took a page from your playbook, my dear. After al
you were the only person I know who ever managed to be
Stanford Graye, or you would have if you'd had the for
thought to get his promises in writing. But your basic stra
egy was sound, so I did what you did. I obtained leverage

"Leverage. You mean you kidnapped Rick."

"Kidnapping is rather a harsh term, but you left me n
choice. As I mentioned yesterday, I've made commitment
To be blunt, I owe money. This seemed the most expedie
way to get it." He placed a pile of papers on the desk, spu
the desk chair toward her, and patted the seat. "Sit dow
Elizabeth. This won't take long."

A scream pushed at her throat. Her arms ached wit
the urge to lunge across the room and rake his eyes out. Sh
tamped it down. She couldn't show weakness. It was th
number one rule in any negotiation. She couldn't give in t
emotion now or she would fall apart completely. "I'm no
signing anything until I can be sure Rick is unharmed. Le
me speak with him."

"That's not possible at the moment."

"Then how do I know this isn't a bluff? You could hav
concocted this scheme after you saw that Rick missed th
show. For all I know, you have no idea where he is."

Alan pulled his cell phone from his coat. He spoke into briefly, then turned the screen toward Elizabeth.

At first, she wasn't sure what she was seeing. The shapes dn't make sense. Then she picked out the curve of a shoul-r and the pale oval of a face. A man was crammed into the unk of a black car, his knees bent to his chest and his head ngled against the wheel well. She grabbed Alan's wrist and rought her face closer to the phone. The man was Rick. His yes were closed, and his forehead was covered with blood. here was no way to tell whether or not he was breathing.

Her legs gave out. She stumbled against the desk. Oh God, h God, oh God. No. He had to be alive. Rick. *Rick!* "He's urt!"

"A minor bump on the head. You would know how that els, wouldn't you?"

"It's not minor. He's bleeding. He needs a doctor."

"My associate will drop him at the nearest hospital as oon as I give the word."

"I have no reason to trust you'll do as you say."

"You really have no choice, Elizabeth." He patted the hair seat again. "Because if you don't cooperate, we'll ump him in the river."

She sat.

There were three documents. The first was a power of ttorney that authorized Alan to exert complete control over er finances, effective immediately. The second gave him ontrol over her personal and medical care in the event that he was physically or mentally incapacitated. The third was n outrageously generous prenup. "You're insane," she whis-ered when she saw it. "You can't believe I would marry ou now."

"I'm a thorough man, Elizabeth. Even if you don't marry ne, this provides the basis for a palimony suit. And if you're oping to later prove you signed under duress, the witnesses vill testify otherwise."

The lines that had been provided for the signatures of vitnesses were already filled in. One of the names was Judge)liver, the man Alan had said would marry them. The fact

someone of that stature was in collusion and willing to pe
jure himself proved how thorough Alan was. But then, sh
was already aware of his attention to detail. It was why he
been so good for the company, and why he'd been such
valuable ally.

"Ticktock, darling."

If she signed these papers, she would be handing h
entire fortune to Alan. The house, her investments, her ban
accounts, everything. She would lose her bid to gain contr
of Grayecorp as well. She would lose it all.

But those things would never fill the void inside her.

Rick had been right.

Alan was right, too. She really had no choice. Withou
further thought, she picked up the pen and signed her nam
on every line he pointed to.

"Very good, darling." He returned the papers to his brie
case. "I will also be requiring some cash." He regarded th
office. "I remember Stanford liked to keep a healthy su
on hand, and you are your father's daughter. Where is h
safe?"

There was no point holding this back now that she'd give
him everything else. She pushed herself out of the chair an
went to the television. She switched it off, swung it awa
from the wall, and opened the safe that was behind it. Sh
watched helplessly as Alan transferred more than a hundre
thousand in cash to his briefcase.

Was this how her father had felt when she'd bested him
How Delaney had felt when Elizabeth had sued her for Stan
ford's death, how Monica's mother had felt when Elizabet
had destroyed her marriage? She could tell herself the situ
ation was different, that she'd only wanted what should hav
been hers, yet Alan believed he was owed this, too. The en
justified the means.

She'd been a monster. She deserved to pay for what she'
done, but not Rick. Never Rick. He was a good man. He wa
wonderful and kind and loving and dear God, he had to b
all right. "Let him go, Alan," she said. "Please."

He closed his briefcase and moved to the door.

"Alan!" She followed him as quickly as she was able. "You ave what you came for. Tell your accomplice to let him go!"

"I'm afraid that's impossible. It was never part of our lan."

She lurched forward to grab his sleeve. "I won't call the olice. I won't tell anyone what you did. I swear. You're elcome to the money. All I care about is Rick."

"Unlike you, Denning has no reason not to go to the uthorities the moment we release him. You, on the other and, won't be believed even if you do." He shook his head n mock sympathy. "It's such a shame. He was terribly depressed by your breakup. He tried to commit suicide before, nd it will be assumed he succeeded this time. The strain f hearing about his disappearance caused your fragile mind o snap. You have a history of paranoia and instability. How ortunate you had a loyal fiancé to ensure you receive the roper psychiatric care, in spite of the bizarre accusations ou might make against him."

She shook his arm. "For the love of God, Alan. We're alking about a man's life! You've got your revenge on me, ut he's innocent in all this. I'm begging you, don't hurt him!"

He peeled her fingers from his coat. "No need for hystercs, darling. Even though I happen to detest the man, it's othing personal, it's only business. Surely you, of all peoole, can understand that."

She did understand. She didn't know who she hated more ight now, Alan or herself. With a scream that tore from her hroat, she gripped her cane in both hands and swung it at Alan's head.

He deflected the blow with his briefcase, backhanded her across the face and strode out the door.

Already off balance, she fell backward. Her head struck he corner of a bookcase and her legs crumpled.

An all-too-familiar darkness spread over her vision. She truggled against it. No! She was not going back to that void. Never again.

She had to help Rick.

She had to find him . . .

TWENTY-THREE

RICK SURFACED TO THE SOUND OF MUSIC. IT WAS DISTANT
and poignant, like pleasure wrapped in pain, tugging him
toward consciousness. He didn't recognize the tune. He recognized the instrument, though. It was a piano. He struggled
to open his eyes. The effort left him panting. Damn, he must
have really been out of it. Where was he? The bedroom
wasn't his, but it seemed familiar. He was lying on a big
four-poster. Moonlight sifted through a series of tall windows set into a curved wall . . .

This was the Graye house. What the hell was he doing
back here? He'd left her, hadn't he?

Or had that been a dream?

Pain rolled through his skull. He pushed at his temples
with the heels of his hands until the pain receded enough
that he could sit up. The music drew him downstairs.

There were no lights on in the sitting room, but someone
had built up the fire. The blaze filled the fireplace, illuminat-
ing the space around it in flickering orange. Elizabeth sat
on the bench in front of the piano. No, that was too simple
a word. She wasn't merely sitting, she was leaning over the
keyboard, her fingers blurring back and forth across the keys
while her body rocked in time with the rhythm she was
creating. Passion crackled around her. She seemed too
absorbed in the music to hear him approach.

He stopped behind the piano bench. Warmth radiated

from her body, bringing the delicate scent of spices tinged with the feminine, earthy scent of her skin. Her hair was loose. She wore the sapphire blue sweater, just as she had the night he'd brought her home. It was the only other time he'd been in this room. Firelight danced across the rich wool, accentuating the graceful curve of her spine and the flare of her hips with strokes of gold. She had discarded her shoes—he glimpsed the tips of her toes as she depressed the pedals.

Chords crashed through the air. The vibrations traveled through the soles of his boots and down to his fingertips. At least he had clothes on. The last time this had happened, he'd been nearly naked and halfway down the stairs to Stella's before he'd realized he'd been dreaming.

Dreaming?

His head throbbed. The floor tilted. The air was suddenly stale and cold. He couldn't hold his train of thought. He couldn't breathe.

He focused on Lizzie and his lungs filled again. He felt the slide of warm keys beneath his fingertips, and the cool arch of brass pedals beneath his toes. The music soared. Chords were followed by a dizzying run down the keyboard. There was a lull as the melody hovered, waiting, building. It swelled to one final, climactic burst and it was done.

It left him breathless. Better than sex.

"Rick?"

He blinked.

Elizabeth had twisted on the bench to look at him. Her cheeks were flushed. Strands of hair clung to her damp forehead. She brushed them aside and grasped his hand. "Rick! You're here!"

"I followed the music."

"Thank God." She smiled. It was dazzling. Pure joy shone from her gaze. "It worked. It really worked."

"You're beautiful."

"Rick—"

"I mean, you're always beautiful but you look different." He touched her face. His fingers hummed, as if he felt her from the inside out. "The music was awesome. I figured you were good, but you're more than that. You're incredible."

She pressed her cheek into his palm. "I'm not, Rick. I'm stiff and out of practice. I couldn't have played the *Sonata Pathétique* like that."

"What are you talking about? I just heard you."

"You heard what's in my head. This is a dream."

Her image wavered. The floor shifted again. Darkness gathered on the edges of his vision. Stale air. He couldn't move. *Pain.*

"Rick, wait! Don't go yet!" She stood and hurried around the bench. She laced her fingers with his. "Feel me. You have to hold on."

Her image strengthened. The room solidified once more. It was hard to think past the pain in his head, but he tried. She was right, this had to be a dream. He couldn't be here, because he'd left her. She didn't want his love. She didn't want their mind link, either. She'd said it was gone, but it couldn't be, or he wouldn't be here . . .

His thoughts looped around on themselves. Other images flickered through his head. "I was at the TV studio," he said. "A guy told me you . . ." His lungs constricted with remembered fear. He pulled their joined hands to his chest. It helped him breathe. "Damn, you had a relapse. You're back in the coma! That's what's going on."

"No, Rick. I'm not the one in trouble, you are. You were hit on the head. You're unconscious."

"Me?"

"They showed me a picture. I saw blood on your face and you weren't moving, but you're alive. You have to be alive or this wouldn't be happening."

"What picture?"

"On Alan's cell phone. He got someone to abduct you. They—" Her voice broke. She swallowed. "They knocked you out."

"Alan? Why?"

"He wanted money from me. They promised to let you go but they didn't. I need to find you."

He fought to concentrate. "So this is really a dream."

"More or less. I don't know what to call it. All I could think of is that I had to find you, and my imagination brought me here."

"And you were only imagining playing the piano."

"It was the best way to reach you. Music was how you reached me. I hoped you would hear my emotions the same way I heard yours. I didn't know what else to do. People are looking for you. I need to tell them where you are. What do you remember?"

It was hard to grasp her words, but her feelings were coming through loud and clear. Her joy had given way to anxiety. Her fear mixed with the memory of his own. Disjointed pictures rose in his mind. A coffee cup. A man with a beard. He remembered running from the studio. There had been a black car parked in an alley. The man had said he would drive him to the hospital, but Rick had stopped listening because all he could think of was that Lizzie was in trouble and then pain had exploded in his skull and then . . . nothing.

He began to shiver. His teeth chattered.

Elizabeth wedged one shoulder under his arm and locked her arms around his waist. She helped him walk as far as the fireplace when his knees buckled. He collapsed to the floor. When he tried to get up, he found he didn't have the strength. He rolled to his back.

She knelt beside him. "Please, Rick. I don't know how long we'll be able to keep our connection going. You need to think."

"I would, but it makes my head hurt."

"I'm sorry. This is my fault. I thought I could handle Alan but I was wrong. I was wrong about everything."

He raised his hand to wipe her cheek. "Don't cry. It'll be okay."

She made a noise that was half sob, half laugh. "You're still trying to help me, even after what I did."

"I shouldn't have left you."

"I deserved it. I thought I was being strong, but I was

being a coward. I knew our link wasn't dead, because I had been feeling you inside me since I woke up, the same way you said you felt me. I hadn't wanted to believe it so I lied to myself and to you." She kissed his knuckles. "I knew you were hurt, too. I felt your pain when it happened, but I hadn't wanted to believe that, either. I'm sorry. If I had told someone right away, things might not have gone this far."

He was still having a hard time processing what she was saying. The one fact that he did grasp was that they were together. For a few precious instants, the pain ebbed from his head and from his heart. "I'm sorry I lost my temper. The things I said . . . I wish I hadn't."

"You told the truth, Rick. I had a second chance at life and I was on the verge of throwing it away. I don't know how many more chances I'll get, so please, come back to me."

He smiled. How could she keep getting more beautiful? The passion he'd heard in her music glowed like an aura around her head. He touched her hair. It seemed to spark.

"Concentrate," she said. "Tell me where you are."

"There's a fireplace behind me, and the most incredible woman in the world beside me."

Her chin crumpled. She blinked back her tears, then stretched out on the floor and wrapped herself around him. "Damn it, Rick. I won't be any good to you if I fall apart. Work with me. We need to figure this out. When I was in the coma, I could still sense things around me, and I'm hoping you can, too. In the picture Alan showed me, you were in a car trunk. Could you still be there?"

Stale air. Cramped muscles. Total darkness. The smell of blood and metal and oil . . .

She pounded his chest. "Breathe!"

He gasped. Her face came back into focus. She was leaning over him. "Yeah," he said. "I think you're right. It's a car trunk."

"Do you remember the car? The one in the picture was black."

"A black Caddie. I remember now I figured it had to be a doctor's because it was so fancy."

"Can you feel anything around you? Are you moving?"

His mind drifted back to the darkness. He was motionless. "No."

"Hear anything?"

He could hear her breathing. It was harsh and rapid. He meant to tell her not to be scared, but he drifted further. There was an odd clopping noise. He heard a whinny. A dog barked, children laughed . . .

"Rick!" Elizabeth crawled on top of him and caught his face in her hands. "Stay with me."

He tried. It was what he wanted more than anything. But he couldn't feel his hands or feet, and his back was going numb. "Horse," he whispered.

She brought her ear to his mouth. "I didn't hear you."

"Horse," he repeated. "Dog. Kids."

She sobbed. "Chester's fine. So are Daisy and all your nieces and nephews. Don't worry about them. Help me help you."

Even though she was still on top of him, he could no longer feel her weight. *Don't cry because of me, Lizzie. I don't want you to be sad.*

"Don't you dare leave me again, Rick."

He brought his arms around her back, but he held only air. His awareness faded. *I love you, Lizzie. Be happy.*

Rick, wait!

The agony in his skull turned blinding white. Piano chords slammed through his head. He clung to them as long as he was able, but inevitably they faded, too, and he sank into the beckoning silence.

THE GATES CRAWLED OPEN. THE INSTANT THE GAP WAS wide enough for a car to pass through, Elizabeth pounded her fist on the back of the front seat. "Go!"

Harold guided the Mercedes through the gates. This wasn't the first time his employer had demanded speed, even though in the past, the reason for haste had been a flight to catch or a meeting to attend. He needed no more prompting. He burned rubber when he hit the road.

Elizabeth didn't look back. If Alan's scheme succeeded, she could be leaving the house for the final time. She didn't care. It was Stanford's house, not hers. It was a cold, barren shell of a fortress, not a home. She could live without it. She waited until Harold reached the highway and opened up the car's powerful engine before she called Zeb for another update. "How is he?"

"He's still unconscious. They said he lost a lot of blood."

"But he'll be all right, won't he?"

"The paramedics are working on him. He's en route to the hospital. I'm meeting them there."

She closed her eyes. He had to be all right. *Rick?*

Nothing.

She bit her lip and tried again. *Rick, please! Answer me!*

No presence whispered through her mind. No warmth, no pleasure. No Rick.

She'd been alone before. It had been a fact of life for her. But nothing in her past compared to the terror of this . . . emptiness.

"He was heading into hypothermia, too," Zeb continued. "He was found just in time."

"Thank God."

"Yeah, and thank whoever gave the cops that tip."

She was a long way from smiling or from feeling any satisfaction whatsoever. She had put together the clues the moment she'd regained consciousness. She'd wasted precious seconds trying to steady her hands enough to dial the phone. Even in her panic, she'd realized she couldn't tell the police the whole truth, not if she wanted to be believed, so she'd refused to give her name, claiming she was an eyewitness to an assault.

They'd found the black Cadillac near the south end of Central Park where the bridle path looped near a playground. The odds against finding the right car and the right path within more than eight hundred acres of park land had been astronomical. So was finding the right park. The information Rick had given her didn't begin to explain how she'd known where he was, or the vivid picture she'd had of the location, or her ability to describe it in exact detail. Far more than logic had led her mind to him. She had followed his love, and as he'd once told her, love was the most powerful force in the universe.

Please, be all right. Please, Rick. It can't end like this.

The trip to the city seemed endless, despite Harold breaking every speed limit between Bedford and Manhattan. When she reached the hospital, her path was blocked by a crowd of reporters. After his very public disappearance and dramatic rescue, Rick was once again at the center of a media frenzy. The uproar escalated as soon as Elizabeth was spotted. She gave no thought to her appearance, other than to acknowledge that she likely looked like a crazy woman. The bruise Alan had left on her cheek was swollen, and her hair was a tangled mess. She didn't attempt to hide the worry on her face or her impatience with the questions that were shouted at her. Cameras flashed as she made liberal use of her cane to push her way inside.

She spotted Zeb as soon as she stepped off the elevator outside Intensive Care. He looked so much like Rick, he was easy to recognize. He was in the waiting area with three men in blue jeans and plaid shirts, probably Rick's band. They were speaking with a pair of what appeared to be plainclothes detectives. A small, dark-haired wren of a woman sat in one of the chairs, and uniformed police stood near a set of swinging doors. Elizabeth was heading for Zeb when her gaze went back to the woman. She stopped in shock. "Monica?"

Monica Chamberlain rose to her feet. "I'm sorry, Elizabeth. I know you don't want to see me, but when I heard the news, I guessed you would be here so I had to come."

"Why?"

"I thought you might need a friend."

She had heard Monica's voice many times during her coma, but it had been more than a year since they had spoken to each other. Their final words had been shouted in anger. The longer the rift had gone on, the more unbridge-able it had felt. Making peace with Delaney had been easier, because they had never been close in the first place.

Yet as she looked into those familiar, soft brown eyes, she didn't see the angry woman who had told her things she didn't want to hear, she saw the girl who had been her best friend, her only friend.

She took a tentative step forward. Could it really be that simple?

Monica held out her arms.

God, yes, it could! Elizabeth moved into her embrace. The time and distance between them collapsed. "I'm sorry, Monica."

"I'm sorry, too."

"I was a bitch. A blind, selfish, destructive bitch."

"Yes, you were, but I was a self-righteous prig."

"No, you weren't. You were worried about your mother. I never meant to hurt her, I really didn't."

"I blamed you because I hadn't wanted to blame her."

"I should have thanked you for standing by me these past months, just like you've always stood by me, but I didn't know how to start."

"Don't feel guilty. I didn't get past my snit overnight. It was August before I started visiting you at the clinic."

"You prig."

"You bitch."

They both smiled. The words continued to pour out, like a wound being lanced. When the embrace ended, Elizabeth wasn't willing to lose the contact. She kept her free hand clasped around Monica's. "It *was* all my fault. This is, too," she added. "It shouldn't be Rick in there, it should be me."

Monica shook her head. "No way, kiddo. Stop blaming yourself. Rick would hate that."

"He has to be all right."

"He's got a lot of people pulling for him."

"You sound as if you know him."

"You might not have wanted to talk to me these past few

weeks, but he did. We have a lot in common. You do realize he loves you, don't you?"

She tried to laugh, but it came out as a sob. "He said everyone else had figured it out."

"It wasn't hard. I was there when he woke you up, remember?"

"I don't deserve it. After the things I've done . . ."

"Will you stop that?" Monica said fiercely. "What's past is past. You control what happens now."

"Control? I've never felt less control over anything in my life."

"I meant with yourself. No one's pulling your strings anymore."

The doors at the edge of the waiting area swung open. A doctor in green scrubs walked through. He wasn't smiling.

Elizabeth was hampered by her cane, so Zeb was the first to reach him. "Dr. Tice!" he said. "How is he?"

"Mr. Denning is stable, but we need to monitor him closely. He hasn't regained consciousness."

"When do you think he will?" one of the detectives asked. "We need to ask him some questions."

"I'm afraid we don't know. He suffered a serious concussion, and we don't yet know the extent of any possible brain injury."

"Brain injury?" Elizabeth repeated. "No! Not Rick."

Monica squeezed her hand. "They don't know anything yet. It's too soon."

The doctor returned his attention to Zeb. "Are you his next of kin?"

"I'm his nephew. His parents are in Oklahoma."

"Has he spoken to you about his views on organ donation?"

Elizabeth let go of Monica and pushed her way forward. "Rick is not going to die."

"In cases like these," Dr. Tice began.

She stabbed her finger at his chest before he could continue. "He is not going to die! He's going to wake up and be fine."

"I didn't mean to alarm you. It's standard procedure to inquire—"

"To hell with your standard procedure." She grasped the sleeve of one of the men who were with Zeb. "Are you Rick's friend?"

"I'm Dwayne. His drummer."

"I'm Elizabeth Graye."

"Yeah, we know who you are," one of his companions said.

She heard a thread of antagonism in his voice, but didn't let it stop her. "I hope you're as protective of Rick as you sound. Until I can arrange private security guards, I'm relying on you to keep him safe. Don't let any vultures masquerading as surgeons lay one hand on him. I'll sue the first person who tries. I will not give up on Rick. Ever."

"No, ma'am."

"And he's going to get another chance to sing."

"We aim to see he does."

"He deserves to be happy. He's a good man. The best. He's . . ."

Lizzie?

She whirled. *Rick?*

What's the matter? I can hear you yelling.

Elizabeth didn't stop to wonder how she knew where to go. Without another word, she slipped around the doctor, pushed past the doors he'd come through, and went directly to a room halfway down the corridor.

A nurse looked up in surprise as she entered. "Excuse me, you shouldn't be here. We're not allowing any visitors yet."

Rick was lying on a bed with metal rails. A bandage was wrapped around his head, an IV dripped into one arm and oxygen was being fed into his nose. Machines beside him monitored his vital functions. The sounds were horribly familiar. So were the smells. She walked to the bed. "I'm here, Rick." She took his hand. "Right here."

I can feel your fingers, Lizzie.

Open your eyes.

They're stuck.

She rubbed her cheek against his knuckles. *I know it's hard, but you have to try.*

"Miss?" The nurse tapped her shoulder.

"There's no need to worry," she said. "I've been through this before. I know what I'm doing."

"I'm sorry, but you'll have to wait outside."

Elizabeth traced the edge of Rick's bandage, slipped the oxygen tube from his nose, then leaned over and kissed him.

The contact rumbled through her mind, like the roll of distant thunder. Her skin tingled. She smiled against his lips. *I love you, Rick.*

His mouth twitched beneath hers. *Hot damn. That's worth getting conked on the head for.*

The comment was so typically Rick, it shattered what was left of her restraint. She threw her arms around him and pressed her face to his neck. *I'm sorry I didn't realize it sooner. I'm sorry for all the things I said and did.*

Don't be. You saved my life.

And you keep saving mine, in so many ways.

Lizzie . . .

The nurse grasped her arm. "Miss! I can't let you tamper with the equipment."

The door to the room swung open. "Miss Graye!" Dr. Tice said. "I must ask you to leave."

She wiped her eyes and fitted the tube back in place. "It's all right. I wouldn't hurt him. I love him."

Don't go!

I'm not going anywhere, Rick. I'll be here when you wake up. No matter how long it takes, I'll be waiting.

You shouldn't have to wait.

Until I can share your life, I'll be happy sharing your dreams.

"I'd rather do both."

So would I, but— She stopped. She lifted her gaze to his.

She found herself looking into eyes of clear amber, as deep as his voice, as sweet as the melody he'd put in her heart. "Rick?"

"Hello, Lizzie."

The beeps from the monitors accelerated. More people crowded into the room. Zeb swore happily and took out his phone. Monica squeezed past the men and came over to put her arm around Elizabeth's back. Someone cheered. Everyone seemed to be talking at once.

Rick's gaze never wavered from hers.

There was so much to say, so much time to make up for, that words could never be enough. She was already leaning closer when he curled his hand around the back of her head and pulled her down for another kiss.

Tell me this is real.

It's real, Rick. We're both wide awake.

Finally.

Yes, finally!

EPILOGUE

Two weeks later

THE SOUND OF RICK'S GUITAR REACHED HER THE MOMENT Elizabeth stepped into her apartment. She closed the door softly and toed off her shoes. He was strumming one of the tunes from the new album he was putting together. Though she had always known he was a gifted musician, in her opinion, the songs she'd heard recently were even better than "Angel Liz." Since he'd been released from the hospital, he'd thrown himself into his music with renewed purpose. His talent was blossoming to another level. It was as if his brush with death—his second brush with death—had inspired him to make the most of each minute of every day.

They hadn't wasted a minute of their nights, either. Their relationship was blossoming, too. She'd once thought that fantasy could never compare to reality, and she'd been right. Making love with Rick in the flesh was better than any fantasy. He was still a tender, considerate lover. He could also be funny or passionate or playful or so over-the-top sexy that he could actually make her mouth water. It wasn't just good chemistry. That was obvious to her now. It wasn't only their mental bond, either. It was good, old-fashioned love.

There had been no question whether he would move in with her. The only issue to be settled had been where they would live. They had decided to reopen her apartment, since its location was more convenient for both of them, and it provided the luxury of privacy. She couldn't have guessed how much she would love seeing him here. She paused at the living room doorway, simply to enjoy the picture he made. He was slouched against the corner of her couch, with his guitar resting on his chest. His feet were propped on the coffee table next to a stack of scribbled staff paper, a Coke can, and an open bag of Doritos. He looked big and male and rumpled and . . . perfect. "Hi," she said.

"Lizzie!" He yanked his feet off the table and stood. "You're back already! Is the board meeting over?"

"No, I left early."

Daisy lifted her head at their voices. She scrabbled up from her spot in the sunshine and came over to bump her nose against Elizabeth's hand.

"The mutt still hasn't figured out she needs to get in line," Rick said, easing the dog aside. He smiled and drew Elizabeth into his arms.

She lifted her head for his kiss. *Hi again.*

Hey, yourself.

She slid her fingers into his hair, taking care to avoid the healing gash on his scalp. *Are you all right?*

Fine. Better now that you're home. He broke the kiss. "How come you left early? They better not have kicked you out."

"Not exactly."

"Everyone knows those papers Alan made you sign were bogus. You had the right to be at that meeting."

It was true, Alan's scheme to steal her fortune had been a spectacular failure. Thanks to Rick, the police had been able to arrest Jamal Hassan, a loan shark posing as a financier, and he had been quick to name Alan as the plan's mastermind. The full extent of Alan's crimes wouldn't be known until the forensic auditors got through with Grayecorp. The criminal investigation had already spread to include Judge Oliver as well as several members of the Grayecorp board.

"We'll sic Cynthia on them," Rick went on. "She's darn scary when she skips lunch. She'll straighten them out."

"Rick, relax. I left willingly."

"Why?" He clasped his hands behind her waist and

leaned back to study her face. "You've been preparing for this fight all week."

"I hadn't needed to. Now that Alan and his cronies are in disgrace, the board decided they need someone who's above reproach to restore confidence in the company. Since I happened to be comatose while Alan was using Grayecorp as his personal piggy bank, and I also happen to share the name of the company's founder, they made me their unanimous choice. They offered me the directorship."

"That's terrific!"

She shook her head.

"That's not terrific?"

"I turned them down."

"Why?"

"Because while I was listening to their offer, I thought about how I had spent my entire adult life wearing pins in my hair and uncomfortable shoes, and being suspicious about everyone twenty-four seven. I thought about how miserable I feel when I have to come out swinging all the time. Then I pictured having to do that for the next thirty or forty years. I had been good at my job, because I had wanted to win, but it hadn't been my first career choice." She flattened her hands on his chest. "I also thought how close Alan had come to succeeding. If I hadn't reached your mind, and if the police hadn't found you in time . . ."

"Shh. It didn't happen."

"But it could have, Rick. Life is precious. Because of you, I have a second chance, and I'm not going to waste it following someone else's dream. Grayecorp was my father's dream. It's high time I lived my own."

He regarded her carefully. "Going to give me a hint?"

"I would like to turn the Graye house into a music school."

"What?"

"It's not as crazy as it sounds. That place is huge, and it's solidly constructed. The rooms could easily be converted to studios and practice halls, and there's enough empty land on the grounds to construct a dormitory. Cynthia will handle the zoning regulations, and I intend to offer Monica the position of principal. I'll use my inheritance to establish a scholarship program, so any child who has the talent will get the chance to develop it in a supportive environment. I want them to be able to pursue their passion, regardless of their musical genre."

"Wow," he murmured. "You've really thought this through."

She moved her hands to his shirt buttons and started to unfasten them. "It was a boring meeting. My mind wandered. Do you want to know what else I was thinking about?"

He laughed. Turning her around, he backed her toward the bedroom. "Your plan sounds awesome, Lizzie. It's a perfect fit."

"It should keep me busy while you're on tour."

"Uh, speaking of that, Zeb called while you were out."

She put out one arm to hook the bedroom doorway. "Did you make the deal?"

"Well, I have to get input from the guys first." He picked her up and carried her to the bed. "Dwayne doesn't like to fly, so he's negotiating for a bus."

"You don't have to make the tour part of the recording contract." She knelt in the center of the mattress and skimmed her dress over her head. "Why don't you let me ask Cynthia to take a look at it?"

"Okay, whatever you say."

"Really? I thought you didn't like Cynthia."

"Uh-huh. Sure."

"Rick, are you listening to me at all?"

You're naked. Is that a trick question?

She smiled and pulled him into her arms. *I love you, Rick. I love you, Lizzie.*

They were already joined in their minds when they completed the link with their bodies. The power of what they felt for each other filled her with wonder, as it always did. It would never change, except to grow stronger. This was real. This was right. Fate had given them both a second chance.

And even if she looked for it, Elizabeth would never again find the void she used to carry in her soul. It had long since begun overflowing with love.